# DOC SAVAGE

The Wild Adventures of Doc Savage

Please visit www.adventuresinbronze.com for
more information on titles you may have missed.

PYTHON ISLE
WHITE EYES
THE FRIGHTENED FISH
THE JADE OGRE
FLIGHT INTO FEAR
THE WHISTLING WRAITH
THE FORGOTTEN REALM
THE DESERT DEMONS
HORROR IN GOLD
THE INFERNAL BUDDHA
DEATH'S DARK DOMAIN
SKULL ISLAND
PHANTOM LAGOON
THE MIRACLE MENACE
THE ICE GENIUS
THE WAR MAKERS
THE SINISTER SHADOW


Also from Altus Press

The Wild Adventures of Tarzan

RETURN TO PAL-UL-DON

# THE SECRET OF SATAN'S SPINE

## A DOC SAVAGE ADVENTURE

### BY WILL MURRAY & LESTER DENT

#### WRITING AS KENNETH ROBESON

### COVER BY JOE DeVITO

ALTUS PRESS • 2015

*First Edition — November 2015*

DESIGNED BY
*Matthew Moring/Altus Press*

SPECIAL THANKS TO
*James Bama, Jerry Birenz, Gary A. Buckingham, Condé Nast, Jeff Deischer,
Norma Dent, Dafydd Neal Dyar, Elizabeth Engel, Steve Holland, Dave McDonnell,
Matthew Moring, Ray Riethmeier, Richard Weyland, Christopher Wood,
Howard Wright, The State Historical Society of Missouri, and last but not least,
the Heirs of Norma Dent—James Valbracht, John Valbracht, Wayne
Valbracht, Shirley Dungan and Doris Leimkuehler.*

COVER ILLUSTRATION COMMISSIONED BY
*Victor De Long*

Like us on Facebook: "The Wild Adventures of Doc Savage"

Printed in the United States of America

Set in Caslon.

For Charles Moran, the *Doc Savage* editor who killed this idea back in 1943....

# The Secret of Satan's Spine

# Chapter I
# CHANCE ENCOUNTER

TWO MEN WERE walking down a noisy New York City street, enjoying an argument in the sweltering summer heat.

There was nothing unusual about two men sharing a disagreement in Manhattan. Men—not to mention women—frequently have outdoor arguments in Manhattan. As for the noisiness of the street, during the day the city's streets are perpetually bustling.

This particular street was, to be candid about it, exceptionally noisy. It was so loud that it was difficult to overhear the argument between the two men strolling along.

The street in question was a side street, rather short as New York blocks are measured. Virtually every storefront on either side, with only a few exceptions, sold commercial radio receivers.

Radios being the modern and indispensable device that they have become, each proprietor filled his window displays with the most recent models. Since a mute radio draws little attention by itself, affixed to the façades of the storefronts were loudspeaker horns, all of which were reproducing a broadcast program of one sort or the other.

One establishment, which sold elegant console radios, was playing classical music. Across the street, a more down-to-earth shop boasted a loudspeaker that was blaring swing music. It peddled so-called "midget" radios.

Further up the block, war news bulletins were competing for attention, detailing the latest on the invasion of Europe. From still another radio store came a creepy laugh signifying one of the popular mystery horror programs that have come to dominate the airwaves.

It might have been an omen, that weird laugh.

Into this cacophony, strolled the two arguers.

They insulted, hectored and upbraided one another with the familiarity of brothers. These two men were not brothers. It was not even conceivable that they could be cousins. For they were as unalike as a bear and a squirrel.

The shorter of the two was homely, while the taller individual was rather handsome in a snooty way. The homely man was extraordinarily homely, being short, wide, snub-nosed, and furred with reddish bristles that almost resembled rusty finishing nails. A mouth so big it seemed to hook over his ears gave him the rather pleasant aspect of one of Snow White's pals.

His handsome companion was dressed to the nines. Were he still living, Beau Brummell could conceivably have matched him. The latter was as impeccably dressed as his homely companion was sloppily attired.

They could hardly be related; in fact, they appeared to be the most unlikely of friends. As they strolled along, it could be heard above the raucous squawking of many loudspeakers that they were arguing about lunch.

"There is a fine restaurant around the corner," remarked the dapper man, flourishing an elegant cane, which concealed a thin sword blade.

The homely man brightened. Fishing into his trouser pockets, he removed a quarter, giving it a spin. It flashed in the noonday sunlight.

"Match you for the check," suggested the homely one.

The dapper individual appeared to take offense at that. For he said sharply, "The last three times I matched you for a restaurant check, I ended up paying each time."

"In that case," grinned the other, "your luck is bound to turn. Tell you what. Let's order the most expensive dishes on the menu, and if you end up winning, the bill will probably equal those last three checks."

The handsome man frowned darkly, but it could be seen by the shadows in his dark eyes that he was extremely tempted to take up the homely one's offer.

"I have a better idea," he countered. "Why don't we match for the check now, and if I win, you will do exactly as you say. But if you call the turn correctly, we will eat more modestly."

The homely man hesitated. "That don't seem exactly fair," he muttered.

"What is not fair about it?" returned the other. "Did you not suggest that we match in order to give me a chance to square up accounts against your previous winnings?"

"Yeah. But I'm hungry enough to eat a tree, like a beaver."

The other scowled. "In other words, you intend to fill that rain barrel you call a belly to overcapacity."

The other grimaced. "I got to keep my strength up, to get through this war."

The handsome man's scowl grew darker. "If they don't let us get back into uniform," he grumbled, "we may never see the end of this conflict."

That brought a pause to the argument. Neither man was young enough to be of draft age, yet both appeared healthy and hardy enough to enlist, if they were of such a mind.

At the present progress of the World War, able-bodied men were becoming scarce in the streets of New York City. Most were in uniform. Those who had been classified as 4-F, looked their classification.

These fellows most assuredly did not. They had the demeanor of men who had knocked about the world some. In fact, they had been in U.S. Army uniforms when they first became friends, long ago.

The handsome individual, who was thin-waisted and fastidiously dapper, continued his argument.

"Either we match here and now," he declared, "or we go Dutch."

The homely one, who resembled nothing less than a bull gorilla crammed into a loud checkered sport coat, narrowed his tiny eyes as he thought speedily.

In his squeaky little-boy voice, he remarked, "I'm for matching now. Call it. Heads or tails?"

"Tails," snapped the dapper one, pulling a silver dollar from his vest pocket and sending it spinning upward.

The homely one's jaw dropped and his little pig eyes popped. He had been about to flip his own quarter, but the dapper one beat him to it.

"Wait a dang minute!" he growled. "I was going to use this here quarter."

"But you were too slow," returned the other as the coin struck the pavement with a ringing clatter.

Both men stared down as the heavy coin finished its jittering dance, revealing the tail feathers of the eagle.

The homely one's face fell, while the dapper man's handsome features lit up with unconcealed joy.

"I win," the handsome individual said superciliously.

Stooping, the homely man snatched up the silver dollar in one hairy paw and examined both sides twice, beetling brows furrowing.

"What are you doing?" the handsome one snapped.

"Checking for the head side. There is such a thing as trick coins, you know."

"While we are checking one another's coins," the other said skeptically, "kindly hand over that quarter, so that I may perform the identical inspection."

The apish individual suddenly looked guilty. He hesitated. Then in the act of proffering the quarter, it somehow got away from him, struck the pavement, and rolled into a sewer grating.

"Dang!" he exploded. "Lost my lucky quarter."

The other eyed him suspiciously, remarking, "It was *too* lucky, if you wish my opinion of the matter." His tone was tinged with vitriol.

"No one asked your daggone opinion," grumbled the homely human ape.

"No matter," rejoined the handsome man jauntily. "Let us be on our way, for I myself am famished."

"You go ahead," muttered the ape. "I kinda lost my appetite back there."

"Back where?"

"Back where my quarter rolled away from me. Losing money these days kinda takes away my yearnin' for food."

"The only thing that ever vanquishes your appetite," the other spat, "is when you are dead broke. Are you telling me that you are once again penniless?"

"I ain't sayin' any such thing!" the man-ape snarled defensively. "As a matter of fact I got a lucrative deal to go to London and brew up some new chemicals for the British war effort."

"Is that so? You had not mentioned this before."

"It's kind of hush-hush, if you want to know the truth. I leave tomorrow on a passenger boat, which docks in Southampton next week."

The dapper one regarded the homely fellow unkindly. "You must be hard up for cash if you're taking that job. What if something interesting comes up and Doc Savage needs us for an important mission?"

"Doc will have to do without me this time. The British have offered me a lot of dough."

Mention of Doc Savage would have helped in identifying the two unusual arguers. For they have been associated with the remarkable adventurer for many years now.

Doc Savage was an individual as unique as any in human history. He was renowned as the Man of Bronze, as Doc Savage was called in the dignified newspapers. Papers which were not dignified called him a man of mystery, and sometimes things less complimentary. Doc Savage did not like publicity.

Doc Savage followed the rather strange profession of helping people who were in trouble, the kind of trouble with which the law did not seem able to cope. He accepted no pay for this work, for Doc was independently wealthy and one of the most philanthropic individuals of the modern age.

About him, the bronze man had assembled a band of equally remarkable experts in their respective lines. The homely man was known professionally as Lieutenant Colonel Andrew Blodgett Mayfair, one of the world's foremost industrial chemists. His gorilla-like physique had earned him the nickname, obviously inevitable, of "Monk."

The handsome fashion plate was known in legal circles as Brigadier General Theodore Marley Brooks, more crudely referred to as "Ham," a nickname he detested but was unable to throw off permanently. Ham was probably the most seasoned attorney Harvard University had ever matriculated. Not satisfied with that distinction, he was frequently voted best-dressed man of the year for many years running, something in which he took equal pride.

Monk and Ham had quarreled famously since the beginning of their association, and as a result they were wont to play tricks upon one another. For years, Monk had been fooling Ham Brooks with an assortment of trick quarters, so cleverly constructed that even upon inspection the hairy chemist's duplicity rarely came to light.

But losing so many times to Monk's nimble finger work, the dapper barrister had decided to beat the homely Monk to the draw, with evident success.

Ham glowered at Monk and demanded, "Are you reneging upon your promise to pay our luncheon bill?"

"I ain't renegin'. I am regretting."

"Well, regret all you want after we have had our fill, for that is what we are about to do."

With that, Ham Brooks marched off to the restaurant in question, leaving Monk Mayfair to amble along in his wake, wearing an unhappy expression and furtively examining his wallet for greenbacks, which numbered a precious few.

MONK MAYFAIR'S hangdog expression was only slightly less droopy when he caught up with Ham Brooks at the entrance to the eating establishment, which was one of the swankiest at this end of town.

Monk had never eaten there before, but the sight of the place caused him to swallow hard and momentarily consider dropping his wallet down the storm drain, with the firm intention of fishing it out again later, in order to evade the doubtless lavish bill.

Only the disreputable state of the apish chemist's finances had compelled him to consider risking such a subterfuge, and the possible loss of the billfold.

Frowning hard, Monk started into the elegant eatery as Ham Brooks held the door open with his dark cane.

"Hurry it up, you hairy mistake!" urged Ham. "For the place is packed with diners."

"Hold your horses, you fashion—" Suddenly, Monk squawked, "*Oof!*"

For the apish chemist had, in his preoccupation, managed to collide with someone.

The person into whom he bumped unwittingly bounced back and almost lost her footing.

A hairy paw reached out and snagged the individual before she could topple over.

This was how Monk Mayfair found himself holding a rather delectable blonde woman. That she qualified as a woman was a matter of dispute, for she might have been no more than nineteen. Conceivably, she could have been all of twenty years of age.

The blonde morsel was not so much tall as she was willowy, but her hair was very, very blonde. It was the color of cornsilk, and rather long as well.

Dancing blue eyes locked onto the apish man and Monk was prepared to receive a scolding, accompanied by a withering look from those same brilliant blue eyes.

Instead, he became the recipient of a hurricane of feminine enthusiasm.

"Well—goodness gracious me! If Ah can believe my eyes, Ah have bumped into Mr. Monk Mayfair himself!"

Monk was hardly slow-witted, but he had been girded for a scolding. This ration of enthusiastic approval took him off guard.

He hauled his battered hat off his bullet head and said, "You got the right number, toots. I'm Monk, all right."

"Well, Ah declare! This must be my lucky day! Ah have hardly been in the big city a full day and Ah bump into my first celebrity."

Pleased, Monk beamed. He showed great white teeth that created a smile that threatened his cauliflower ears.

Seeing all this, Ham Brooks skillfully inserted himself into the conversation.

"You will have to pardon my goonish friend," said Ham smoothly. "As you can tell from casual inspection, there is no more homely specimen of manhood parading about the city. Had he not been classified 4-F, no doubt Monk would be in military fatigues on some battlefront at this precise moment. But the United States Army considered him unfit for duty."

"That's a bald-faced lie!" roared Monk. "Don't listen to that slick shyster, Miss. The only reason he's not overseas is because he's too dang old, not to mention the fact that he's the sole support of a fat wife and thirteen half-witted children."

Ham drew himself up to his full height and announced, "I have not, and never have been, married."

"Yeah? So where did the thirteen half-wits come from?"

Waving his slim cane about madly, the dapper lawyer sputtered inarticulately for a full minute, his composure entirely ruined by the false canard.

During this interval, the blonde bestowed upon Monk the most amazing smile he had ever beheld. The pearly masterpiece of dental perfection made him feel warm and tingly all over.

Monk and Ham were both two old wolves, with many conquests behind them. Their rivalry, such as it was, extended to outdoing one another with the fair sex. Whenever they encountered a suitable specimen of femininity, invariably they attempted to paint the other in satanic colors, while gathering saintly robes about themselves.

Sometimes Ham won out through his dashing good looks and cultured demeanor, but other times Monk got the upper hand, there being something about his homely face and amiable disposition that bowled over certain types of women.

This corn-fed blonde appeared to belong to the latter category.

Seeing this, Monk gave it all he had. "Please accept my apologies for bumping into you," he said, stealing a leaf from the smooth Ham.

"Think nothing of it, honey," the blonde replied enthusiastically. "In fact, Ah do declare that Ah am the one who bumped into you. Ah was so startled at the sight of you that Ah—um—momentarily lost my senses."

Recovering from his spluttering, Ham Brooks said archly, "You would not be the first woman to be shocked out of her wits by the sight of this ape's flat-nosed face."

The blonde refused to take her eyes off Monk. "On the contrary, I adore homely men."

"What—you do?" sputtered Monk.

"Honest to my grandma, Ah do. Ah used to have a favorite bulldog, and y'all remind me of him somehow."

Monk did not know how to take that remark, but then remembered that small children and babies often responded to his anthropoid features the same infectious way.

Thinking fast and moving even faster, he asked, "Were you about to dine in this joint?"

"Ah was indeed, Mr. Mayfair. Ah thought Ah would have lunch in the most swellegant place Ah could find."

"Oh, you don't want to eat here," inserted Monk hastily.

The overfriendly blonde frowned prettily. "Ah don't? Why on earth not?"

"Because," Monk said with studied sincerity, "this joint serves French food. If this is your first time in Manhattan, you'll want to eat New York style."

Ham began to object, but the woman said, "You are exactly right. Ah should eat as the natives do, now shouldn't Ah?"

"I know a place that serves the best spaghetti in Little Italy," said Monk. "I can take you there."

The blonde looked as if she was about to swoon with sheer pleasure. "Oh, would you? That would be such a delight. Ah would love to have lunch with y'all and hear all about your famous self."

Monk beamed so broadly that his head looked as if it had separated in two. Taking the blonde by the arm, he said, "Come on, then. It's only two blocks south of here."

Fuming visibly, Ham began hectoring Monk. "I thought we were going to dine here!"

Monk flung back, "You go ahead and eat that measly French cuisine, me and my new friend here are going to chow down on spaghetti and meatballs."

"But—but you don't even know her name!" called out Ham in exasperation.

"It's Davey Lee," the blonde cooed. "Ah hail from Louisiana."

Monk's grin got even wider. "Is that right? I'm from Tulsa myself."

"Ah was raised in Shreveport, so that makes us almost neighbors."

"I think I'm going to like gettin' to know you," said Monk as they disappeared around the corner.

Standing in the open doorway of the lavish restaurant, Ham Brooks seemed not to know what to do with himself. The dapper lawyer was obviously torn between following the hairy chemist and his bubbly blonde companion, or disappearing into the restaurant for his intended meal.

Instead, he raced to a nearby drugstore and popped into a telephone booth, dropping a nickel into the slot and asking for the operator.

"Connect me with Doc Savage. The number is Empire 1-7900."

# Chapter II

# DITHER

**H**IGH ON THE eighty-sixth floor of the tallest sky-scraper in midtown Manhattan, a number of telephones commenced ringing at once.

Not all of the instruments rang, technically speaking. Some did, but many others simply buzzed, and a few were silent, but indicated an incoming call by flashing a red light attached to the designated devices.

The headquarters of Doc Savage was distributed all over the eighty-sixth floor, and so it filled the greater portion of an acre. The smallest room was the reception room, which gave into a library that would have been the envy of many Ivy League universities. Beyond the library was a laboratory-workshop that was virtually unrivaled in all the war-weary world.

It was in this laboratory that a giant man of bronze was engaged in scientific work when the many telephones set up their jangling, buzzing, flashing commotion.

Doc Savage—for he was the giant bronze-skinned individual—did not hear them. He was seated before an apparatus from which ran a pair of earphones. The device was creating sounds that ranged the auditory scale, beginning with a deep beeping and progressing, or more correctly diminishing, to a succession of electrical noises that sought lower and lower registers.

These frequencies were similar to the device ear doctors use to test a patient's hearing. In this case, the tones dropped by stages to produce sounds below the auditory threshold that the human ear could normally detect.

Doc Savage was testing his hearing. He was not looking for any problems, however. His ears were fine. In fact, they were phenomenally acute, a consequence of a childhood spent in training for the work that he did now.

The work of Doc Savage was a Galahadian affair. It all began when his father, a renowned explorer and medical man, had turned him over to a seemingly inexhaustible array of scientists and other top experts to train up young Clark Savage, Jr., to become superior in all human endeavors.

All this fit him for the job of troubleshooting other people's troubles, and for no pay. This was the life's path his father had set out for him. Why remained a deep and dark mystery.

Part of this regimen was a routine of exercises Doc had practiced since very young. These honed his mind, his body and his senses to razor sharpness and were as indispensable to his life work as the ability to fire a rifle with uncanny accuracy or swim underwater for long periods without surfacing, to name just two skills at which he had become proficient.

Specialized apparatus were a part of this daily routine. There were corked vials containing exotic scents that were changed regularly. This routine enabled Doc to identify odors that might be encountered in the far corners of the world, where his life could depend upon it.

A modest device reproducing difficult-to-hear tones was another useful component of this regular routine.

The apparatus before which Doc Savage sat was a more advanced version, and much improved. With it, Doc was endeavoring to detect sounds definitely below what was normally audible to the human ear. Dogs and some other animals could hear these sounds. It was a rare man who could, however.

By intensive practice, the bronze man was training himself to detect sounds that were conventionally beyond human hearing.

So engrossed was he in these tones, Doc Savage failed to hear the ringing of the many telephones, for he sat in a sound-proof cubicle, rather like those used by radio broadcast announcers.

It was the flashing of one telephone's red light that brought him to awareness of the insistent phones, which had been ringing some two minutes now.

Whipping off his earphones, the bronze man raced to the nearest instrument, revealing that he was a giant of a fellow with an amazingly symmetrical physique. He scooped it up.

"Doc Savage speaking," he said in a vibrant voice.

"Doc! It's Ham. Something has happened to Monk."

"Go on."

"We were entering a fashionable restaurant for lunch when this blonde floozy managed to bump into him. The next I know, that hairy lump of muscles had squired her off, leaving me in the lurch."

"Who agreed to pay for lunch this time?" asked Doc.

"Monk did, but that was beside the point. There is something amiss here."

"When either of you come into contact with blondes, not to mention redheads and brunettes," said Doc Savage pointedly, "there usually is. Or soon will be."

Ham snapped, "I am *not* joking."

"Nor am I. Why do you think this particular blonde represented trouble?"

"The way she gushed over him."

"In other words, she paid you no mind."

"That is not the point," raged Ham. "I did not see how it all began, but I am highly suspicious that this peroxide Jezebel deliberately bumped into Monk in order to capture his attention."

"If you feel so strongly about it, why don't you follow them to the restaurant and invest in a little eavesdropping?"

"Monk would spot me a mile away."

"Bribe a waiter to listen in."

"That is a very good idea," replied Ham in a mollified tone. "I will get right on it."

"Contact me if you discover anything out of the ordinary," directed Doc, hanging up.

Returning to his apparatus, Doc again donned the headphones and engaged the device. Soon, the earphones were reproducing their weird beeping and the bronze man concentrated on following the tones as they sank into inaudibility.

When ten minutes had elapsed, Doc ceased the experiment and picked up a dog whistle. He blew in it. A frown touched his regular bronzed features and the metallic flakes that perpetually stirred in his golden eyes grew troubled.

Despite an hour of practice, he could not hear the dog whistle. He wondered if the act of blowing into the whistle himself might interfere with his perception of the inaudible sound.

Doc decided to have one of his men experiment with the dog whistle at the next opportunity to determine if his theory had any credence. Leaving the soundproof booth, Doc moved about the vast laboratory, checking on experiments in progress, and reflected upon Ham Brooks' frantic call. There was nothing out of the ordinary about Monk and Ham getting into disagreements over the latest morsel of femininity to cross their paths. They were a pair of wary old wolves, but yet not wise enough to forego such foolishness. A time or two they had nearly been dragged into matrimony, but somehow managed to evade the Justice of the Peace in the end.

This latest eruption was probably another false alarm. But Doc Savage decided to wait in his laboratory rather than go to lunch in case another call from Ham Brooks came.

HANGING up the drugstore telephone, Ham Brooks exited the establishment and sought out the Italian restaurant where

Monk had taken the attractive blonde calling herself Davey Lee.

It was not hard to find. Ham had only to seek out the most disreputable looking spaghetti joint in the immediate vicinity. This place was called, predictably, Tony's.

The dapper lawyer stationed himself across the street and attempted to locate Monk and the blonde girl with his sharp eyes.

He soon found them, much to his exasperated indignation. For the girl appeared to be laughing uproariously and having a grand old time. Monk's grin was so wide it looked as if a blunt-toothed shark was swimming about the checkered cloth table.

By observing, Ham was able to pick out their waiter, a reedy fellow with a pencil-thin mustache and a dark head of hair that looked as if it had been soaked in hair oil.

After observing for several minutes, the lawyer crossed the street at the corner and found his way to the back of the establishment through a convenient but rather slovenly alley.

There was a back door next to a large industrial rubbish container. Ham entered, slipping into the kitchen.

Finding a loose busboy, Ham flashed a folded five dollar bill and hissed, "This is yours, young fellow. All you have to do is ask the waiter with the pencil-thin mustache to step back here for a chat."

The busboy was having trouble seeing anything other than the fiver, but he tore his eyes away, and hurried to the front of the restaurant, departing like a sparkler.

Ham did not have to wait long. The waiter came back, eyes narrow in a curious way, and asked smoothly, "You wish to speak with me?"

"I do. I happen to be aware that a good friend of mine is dining in this place. Name is Monk, and he looks like a slovenly ape. He's recently fallen into the clutches of a flossy blonde gold digger, and I promised his wife I would keep an eye on him."

The waiter nodded solemnly. "I know the one of which you speak."

"Monk is hard to miss. What I would like you to do," said Ham, producing a ten dollar bill and holding it under the waiter's nose, "is eavesdrop on the conversation and report everything back to me."

The waiter was very impressed by the sawbuck. "Will you wait here?" he asked politely.

"I must, for I dare not lose sight of poor Monk."

"As you wish," said the waiter. "If you'd like, I will have any meal prepared for you that we serve in this establishment. No charge, of course."

Mindful of his appetite, Ham said, "Yes, thank you. A plate of ravioli would suffice."

The busboy escorted the dapper lawyer to a nook reserved for the staff to take their meals, and quietly took his order. He went away with a dollar bill and a big grin.

Ham Brooks waited, and the ravioli was soon served. The dapper lawyer had not expected much, but the smell of the stuff was very pleasant. Soon, he became engrossed in his meal.

Two hours later, the waiter came back for the fifth time to say, "Your friends are still here. They are enjoying themselves immensely."

Ham scowled and said, "Monk's wife will not be happy about this. What is the trend of the conversation?"

"The young woman has been telling your friend all about her plantation in Louisiana and has invited him to come back with her on a vacation."

"I suspected as much! She is nothing less than a gold digger. If she only knew the state of Monk's finances, she would whistle a different tune."

"Mr. Monk appears to be very interested in going to Louisiana."

"Monk always talks like that. But I happen to know that he has no time for any such frivolous trip at present."

"On the contrary," corrected the waiter. "They have just now agreed to take the morning train to Shreveport, from there to drive to the young lady's plantation."

"You don't say!" Ham blurted out. His eyes grew narrow. "Perhaps that hairy mistake is just leading her on. Monk is not going to turn down an opportunity to make some money for a vacation he doesn't need."

"From what I overheard, Mr. Monk sounded very sincere," supplied the waiter.

The *maître d'* came from the front of the restaurant and signaled to the waiter that he was needed. The waiter made excuses, was gone ten minutes, after which he returned to report, "Mr. Monk and the attractive young lady have departed, sir."

Removing his napkin from his throat, Ham snagged his elegant cane, and bolted out the back without another word.

Circling the block, he emerged onto a crosstown street in time to see the hairy chemist pouring the smiling blonde into the back of a taxicab. Monk clapped the door shut, handed the driver a bill, and waved the cab away.

His grin was so wide, the ends could have met at a point over the back of his neck. He rubbed his hairy hands together gleefully.

Sauntering up, Ham Brooks accosted the homely chemist and remarked, "So there you are! I have been searching for you."

Monk's grin half collapsed. He turned, eyeing the dapper lawyer suspiciously.

"You been followin' me, you sneaky shyster?" he growled.

"Hardly," sniffed Ham. "I have eaten and merely wished to ascertain that you had done so as well."

"Dandy of you," said Monk blandly, noticing a suspicious dab on spaghetti sauce on Ham's chin his napkin failed to sop up.

They stood staring at one another for a few seconds, after which Ham remarked casually, "So how did it go with your latest obsession?"

"She thinks I'm the niftiest thing to be found in New York City," boasted Monk.

"She has not yet been to the dog pound, I presume?"

Normally such a cutting remark brought a surly response from the hairy chemist, but Monk was so intoxicated by his blonde lunch companion that he failed to offer any riposte.

Instead, he said, "Davey and I are takin' the train back west to her stamping grounds, and she's going to show me her father's plantation. It's a sugar mill now."

"What about your sea trip to Europe?"

"Aw, I can do that another time. There's no rush. There are plenty of boats crossin' the Atlantic in the convoys."

"And a goodly supply of German raiders prepared to sink them during the crossing," chided Ham.

"All the more reason to put off that trip for a better time," said Monk.

By now, they were walking along in the direction of Doc Savage's headquarters.

"Has it occurred to you that that glossy wench may be up to no good?" inquired Ham.

Monk grinned and said, "When I bowl 'em over, they go down like tenpins."

"It might behoove you to do a little background checking on your new friend, in case this is a clever trap."

Monk scowled like a gorilla who discovered a coconut he had taken the trouble to crack open was dry as a bone.

"What kind of trap would be waitin' for me out in Louisiana? And why would anyone set one? We ain't involved in anything right now. Neither is Doc Savage. There's no trouble in the air, so there can't be any trap."

Ham reminded, "There have been times in the past when traps have been laid for us before we discovered the trouble back of them."

"Maybe. But Davey's a nice kid, and pure as the driven snow."

Ham admitted, "So she struck me, but perhaps she has drifted."

Monk said nothing to that. Abruptly, he suggested, "You go on ahead. I'm headin' back to my penthouse digs. I suddenly got a lot of packin' to do."

With that, the homely chemist went bounding off on his bandy legs, leaving Ham Brooks making disapproving shapes with his wide, mobile orator's mouth.

"Drat!" snapped Ham. "That dish-faced ape is going to end up in a pine box or worse if he keeps on chasing skirts he does not know."

Clutching his sword cane more tightly, Ham hailed a taxicab and directed the driver to take him to Doc Savage headquarters.

"Snappy!" he urged.

THE BRONZE MAN was waiting in his laboratory when the dapper lawyer arrived ten minutes later.

Barging into the laboratory set-up, Ham said excitedly, "I have discovered that that fool ape has agreed to train south to Louisiana and visit the blonde woman's plantation out there."

"What is wrong with that?" asked Doc.

"In two days Monk was supposed to ship out to Europe to do some chemical work for the British."

Doc nodded. "I remember that now. And Monk is more broke than usual this month."

"It is not like him to turn down an honest dollar, never mind a windfall," insisted Ham.

"Neither is it like Monk to forego the company of an attractive blonde when the wind blows one in his direction," reminded Doc.

Ham studied the gold head of his cane, and said slowly, "It was an ill wind that blew one in his direction this time."

Interest flickered in the bronze man's peculiar eyes. "Do you know this young woman's name?"

Ham nodded curtly. "She called herself Davey Lee."

"Describe her, please," requested Doc.

Ham did, painting a fairly colorful picture of the young woman, and at the end remarked, "Although she claimed to be from Shreveport, her accent smacked of Virginia."

"Young women raised in Virginia might easily fall heir to a Louisiana plantation, you know."

"She did not strike me as the plantation owner's daughter type. More the vapid Southern Belle variety."

"She could easily be both," said Doc Savage absently.

The bronze man had been racking chemicals in a special cabinet while the discussion took place. He became engrossed in this activity.

Impatiently, Ham asked, "What should we do about this predicament?"

"To all outward appearances," said Doc Savage, "Monk's latest passion appears to be exactly what it presents itself—a star-struck young woman in the big city who happened to meet someone she perceives as a famous celebrity."

"The whole affair smacks of trouble," insisted Ham.

"If you feel that way," suggested Doc, returning to his work, "feel free to keep an eye on Monk until your specific suspicions are confirmed, or allayed."

"Why, I intend to do just that!" snapped the dapper lawyer. "For someone has to block that infernal ape from barging into trouble, if not matrimony."

"Please keep me informed," requested Doc Savage as Ham Brooks closed the laboratory door behind him, making determined footsteps through the spacious library and on out of sight and hearing.

# Chapter III

# SMOKE FOR HAIR

**M**ONK MAYFAIR GREETED the dawn with a grin. He flung aside the silk sheets of his four-poster bed in his Wall Street penthouse, a rookery in which he had lived for more than a decade, but on whose rent he was disastrously in arrears.

The homely chemist gave no thought to his money worries, however, as he hastily showered, wolfed down a hearty breakfast, and dressed for his trip to the sunny South.

Finishing his eggs, Monk rang his secretary, who had the reputation of being the prettiest in captivity.

"I'm going out of town for a few days," he told her. "Be sure to check up on Habeas twice a day and make sure he's fed."

The secretary's voice came over the wire questioningly. "You're not taking him on this trip?"

"Not this time," said Monk. "I'm going on vacation, and that includes a vacation from Habeas."

"Yes, Mr. Mayfair," the secretary said. "I will see that all his needs are attended to."

"Thanks," said Monk, hanging up.

The hairy chemist ambled into an adjoining room, which was over-decorated, but lacked much in the way of furniture. The floor was of Italian marble, and in the center of this marble expanse was a large mud wallow in which lolled the most unseemly-looking pig imaginable.

Habeas Corpus had been named to rankle Ham Brooks, whose distaste for pork in any form was one of his notable pet peeves. Habeas was a runt specimen of the porcine family, and looked as if he borrowed his legs from a skinny dog, his long snout from an anteater, and his ears from a baby pachyderm. He should have grown up to become a full-size hog by this point in life, but the freak shoat never progressed beyond juvenile size.

That suited Monk just fine, which made Habeas handy to tote around on his various adventures. This time, however, the apish chemist decided to leave the porker behind. Sometimes, Monk employed the pig to overcome any female dislike for his homely face, but since Davey Lee seemed especially attracted to Monk exactly as he was, Habeas was unnecessary.

Also, Monk had his doubts that he could smuggle Habeas on board the train, which would be packed with servicemen traversing the country. Train tickets for civilians were in short supply, but Monk had pull. He had already solved that problem. Adding Habeas to the equation would have complicated matters and possibly jeopardized the trip.

So Monk sauntered over and patted the shoat on his bristly skull and said, "Be a good pig while I'm gone, hear?"

The runt poker grunted, and his beetling eyes grew slightly sad. Habeas was extremely intelligent, and could not help but notice his master packing the night before.

Habeas knew he wasn't going along, otherwise he would have been given a bath. He grunted disconsolately, and his dark eyes grew sad as he lowered himself back into his mud, settling in for a long sulk.

"I won't be but a few days," reassured Monk.

Something suspiciously like a dog-like whine escaped the pig's elongated snout. But he closed his eyes and pretended to go to sleep.

"Don't be that way," muttered Monk. "I'll bring you back some fresh apples."

Habeas elicited a disgruntled noise, but otherwise did not stir.

Gathering up his luggage in both hands, Monk shoved his way out the door, down the elevator and hailed a taxicab at the street corner.

"Pennsylvania Station," he told the driver as the cabbie filled his trunk with Monk's luggage.

Struggling with the baggage, the driver quipped, "Where are you goin', buddy? The moon?"

"Don't be wise," shot back Monk. "I'm just takin' a little train trip, is all."

"Well, you sure packed for the wild blue yonder."

They climbed into the cab, the driver got his machine in gear and whined off into traffic. The hack had seen better days, but with the war the driver was having to make do with an older model. The engine knocked, and the exhaust disgorged enough smoke to rival the stacks of a steamship.

The ride was not far, and since it was a Saturday morning, there was not enough traffic to be bothered about.

Monk was dropped off in front of Pennsylvania Station and begrudgingly handed the cabbie his fare and a half-dollar tip. Monk didn't mind paying the fare, but hated to part with that coin. He had been a lavish tipper in more flush days, and was not about to change. Old habits died hard with Monk Mayfair.

Lugging his baggage under his long arms, he toted them inside into the commodious granite cathedral that was Pennsylvania Station, ignoring all Red Caps. He was anxious to find his track, and meet his date.

The main concourse never failed to take his breath away. It was known for its vaulted ceiling and bustling energy. The place was packed, and the concentration of men in Army, Navy and other military uniforms attested to the preferential treatment accorded servicemen over civilians that had been the norm since Pearl Harbor.

By the time Monk made his ambling way down to the staircase leading to his track on the lower platform, he was early. He set down his baggage, and exchanged it with a porter who handed him his check stubs.

"I'll get them right on board," the porter said. "The train departs in twenty minutes."

"Oh, thanks," said Monk, reluctantly parting with a dime.

While he waited for Davey Lee, the hairy chemist took an inventory of his wallet. He did not enjoy what he discovered.

"Well, maybe I should've bummed a few bucks off that shyster," he muttered to himself. "Ham is always rollin' in dough, just like a lawyer would."

Although Ham Brooks devoted a great deal of his time to adventuring with Doc Savage in the odd quarters of the globe, he maintained a law practice and, while he was very selective about his clients, he made an annual fortune. Not so Monk Mayfair, who took on work when his bank balance kept him awake nights.

Monk swiveled his bullet-shaped head around anxiously, looking for signs of Davey Lee. He checked his watch several times, then one of the big wall clocks. According to the display board, the train was scheduled to leave at nine a.m. sharp, and as the big hands of the clocks inched inexorably closer to the digit 12, there was no sign of the flirtatious blonde.

Monk began to grow concerned. He knew the *Crescent* would depart with clock-like efficiency, with or without Davey Lee, for the railroad boasted of the train's efficient forty-hour run. As he waited, wrinkles making his glowering brows resemble corrugated sheet steel, Monk suddenly remembered a dream he had had the previous night. The attractive blonde had to catch a train. Try as he might, Monk could not recall the dream in detail, which seemed to be a condition of dreams. But he recalled that the blonde woman had acted confused and possibly lost.

Since Davey was a stranger to New York, it made perfect sense. Monk once read that dreams were a product of daily anxiety. Probably this dream was a consequence of his fear that Miss Lee would be unable to reach Pennsylvania Station in time for the train departure. New York City being the overwhelming metropolis that it was, and women having a distressing tendency to arrive late even to important assignations.

As Monk's worried eyes scanned the sea of faces around him, they fell upon a rather large mature individual with striking amber-colored eyes. The man's hair was neither white nor gray, but some vague hue in between. He had very fine but full hair, and its fineness combined with its coloring reminded Monk Mayfair of cigarette smoke in suspension.

The mature man with the smoke-colored pompadour appeared to be aping Monk Mayfair in that he was also searching the milling crowd for an expected but overdue face. His own features were weathered to a hue resembling lightly creamed coffee, which contrasted sharply with his vaporously pale hair.

From time to time, the man's gaze skated in Monk's direction and when Monk looked back, the catlike eyes veered away. Monk suddenly thought that suspicious. For he wore the kind of face that made babies laugh or cry, depending on the disposition of the infant. People did not look at his wide, homely face with indifference ever. They were either fascinated, or repelled, according to their lights.

This man with the weird vaporous hair and the searching eyes seemed to go out of his way to avoid looking directly at Monk. That was strange. In between searching for the missing Davey Lee, Monk kept one eye on the man with the smoky pompadour.

Eventually, the mature man noticed a figure in the distance that he recognized. He took off like a shot, determination on his lined face.

After that, Monk stopped paying attention to him.

This inattention proved to be short-lived.

For suddenly, the cavernous hall that was Pennsylvania Station, which had been buzzing with the chatter of passengers, the clattering arrival of trains from far distances, and the incessant tramping of feet on flooring, was pierced by a feminine scream.

Monk Mayfair had not known Davey Lee long enough to recognize her individual scream. But something about the way the cry echoed made his heart jump up in his chest, and his entire body pivot in the direction of the sound.

He saw at once that the mature man with the smoky hair appeared to have discovered the person he was waiting for. It was a woman. He took hold of her roughly. She struggled.

And in struggling, a second scream erupted from her throat.

The distance was great, and it was blocked by a constant traffic of people. Monk Mayfair's eyes popped and his jaw sagged as he recognized under a pert hat the distinctive blonde tresses of none other than Davey Lee!

"Daggone it!" howled Monk. He charged into the crowd, jostling packed people aside like a human battering ram. He tried to be gentle about it, but the scream made him fear for the worst. Pennsylvania Station in the early morning hustle and bustle was no place to commit a murder, but this was New York, where anything is possible.

"Get out of the way!" Monk yelled, shouldering between two men who had stopped to rubberneck in the direction of the screaming woman.

The hairy chemist made credible time, even with the human obstacles continually blocking him.

Unfortunately, the smoke-haired man made better time.

He could be heard to say, "You're coming with me! And no backtalk!"

"No, no, I won't!" This from Davey Lee in her recognizably syrupy but now fear-warped voice.

Monk pushed an obstructing soldier aside, weaved between two others, and managed to reach the spot where he had last seen the girl and the large man. By the time he reached that point, they were deeper in the crowd, and nowhere to be seen. Swiveling his almost neckless head around, Monk yelled out to no one in particular, "Dang it! Where the heck did they go?" Grabbing a porter at random, he practically tore off his red jacket, demanding, "Where did that gray-haired guy and the blonde gal go?"

The porter stabbed a finger in what appeared to be a random direction and said, "That away, suh."

"Did you see them go that way or are you just making it up?" demanded Monk.

"Whatever suits you. Just let go of my jacket."

Monk did and went charging into the milling crowd, flailing and floundering and calling out to the girl.

"Miss Lee! Where are you?"

"Over here!" shrilled the blonde.

Monk looked about wildly. "Where?"

"Here! *Oh!*—don't let them take me!"

"Where is here?" bellowed Monk angrily. "I can't see a dang thing!"

The answer that came started off strong and became muffled in the way that voices sound smothered when a hand compresses the person's mouth.

"Cigarette—"

Monk took that to mean a cigarette vending machine, and went in search of one.

The first one he found offered no proximity to the missing Davey Lee.

By this time the homely chemist was beside himself and went charging around like a madman, calling her name over and over again.

This uproar brought a policeman charging up, looking very red in the face.

"What's going on here?" he demanded.

Monk yelled, "A woman is being abducted! We gotta find her. Fast!"

"What woman? Where?"

Monk growled, "If I knew where she got to, I'd be right on her heels, wouldn't I now?"

"Slow down, buddy," said the cop, sticking the round end of his truncheon in the hairy chemist's barrel chest. "Let's hear your tale."

Monk Mayfair was in no mood to slow down. He knew if he didn't move fast, Davey Lee's abductors would spirit her out of the station, or possibly onto a departing train.

Growling, "I'll explain later," Monk shoved the copper aside, whereupon the bluecoat lifted his truncheon and laid it against the back of Monk's close-cropped skull with such force that the hairy chemist fell flat on his very flat face.

WHEN Monk woke up, there were three policemen standing over him, the one who had struck him down and two others who wore peculiar expressions. Behind them curious bystanders stared.

"Your identification says you're Monk Mayfair. Is that right?" asked one of the officers, who wore sergeant stripes.

"Do I look like him?" demanded Monk, sitting up and rubbing the sensitive spot at the back of his blunt skull.

"That you do," said the police sergeant. "You're one of Doc Savage's men. Mind explaining what's going on here?"

Monk struggled to his feet, knees rubbery, his senses swimming in his skull.

"I was meetin' a blonde babe, and we were goin' out west on a trip. She got here late, and some overgrown fellow with smoky gray hair wrapped her up and took her off."

"What are their names?"

"Davey Lee, and I don't know the other one," muttered Monk.

"And which one is Davey Lee?"

"That was the blonde. I don't know the guy's name."

By now Monk was steady enough on his feet to start firing questions back.

"Didn't anybody report a kidnapped blonde?"

The sergeant said, "There was a commotion that a lot of people saw and heard. A sailor accosted the two, and the big guy said he was the girl's father and he was taking her home."

Monk growled, "In a pig's eye!"

"Witnesses said this gal was quite young, the man much older. It might be true, you know."

Monk said, "He looked to be about fifty, and she was probably nineteen."

"And you're no spring chicken," inserted another cop. "If you were running off with a girl that young, maybe her father did decide to take a hand in the matter."

Monk growled, "Don't start that masher stuff with me. She was from out of town. Didn't say anything about her father bein' in New York. I say it was a kidnapping. We gotta find her!"

"Since you're with Doc Savage, and the big bronze guy has plenty of drag with the police commissioner," allowed the sergeant, "we'll put out a radio call to bring them in. In the meantime, you might as well get on your train or be on your way. This is not necessarily a police matter, given the lay of the land."

Rubbing his head in annoyance, Monk said bitterly, "Thanks a million for all your help."

To which the police sergeant returned, "In some places, you could get arrested for running off with a young woman probably half your age."

"Well, I didn't exactly get to run off with anyone, now did I?"

"Not *this* time," agreed the sergeant.

The bluecoats bustled off to find police telephone boxes, leaving behind not so much as an apology for the bloody conk on the head inflicted upon Monk Mayfair.

Bustling out of the train station, Monk found the cab stand and began asking the drivers if they had seen anything of a smoky-haired man and a blonde girl who weren't exactly friendly with one another.

One cabbie offered, "Yeah, the guy threw the gal into the back of a Blue Eagle cab and they took off."

"Any idea where?"

"None whatsoever," replied the cabbie. "It happened pretty fast."

"Did you get a good look at the guy?" asked Monk.

"Which one?"

"The big guy with the smoky gray hair."

"Of him, not so much. But I got a glimpse of the other man."

"What other man?" asked Monk, surprised.

"The gray-headed man came out with the blonde babe, and met this other man. He was on the short side, kind of wiry. His hair was that color that you can't tell is brown or red unless the sun is shining directly on it."

This was the first Monk had heard of a second man, which tended to cast doubt on the police theory that this was a father-daughter misunderstanding.

"I sorta need to find out where they went," Monk told the driver.

"You can call the cab company, but unless you've got a badge backing up your court request, you're not gonna get very far."

Monk muttered, "But he can't have got very far yet, so I think that it won't hurt to try."

Monk made a call from a pay phone, got into a heated argument, and was told where he could go, and how quickly to be about it.

The hairy chemist would have hung up on the radio dispatcher, except the dispatcher hung up on him first.

"A fine day this has turned out to be!" fumed Monk. He grabbed the next taxi in line and barked, "Doc Savage headquarters."

He did not have to give an address. Probably every cab driver from Albany to Newark and places in between knew that famous address.

The cab whirled Monk away from Pennsylvania Station, his luggage, and his improvised vacation.

"That Ham Brooks is gonna have the horse laugh on me when he hears about this!" mumbled Monk.

In the front of the machine, the cabbie asked, "Trouble?"

"Woman trouble," replied Monk.

"That's the worst kind of trouble there is," sympathized the hackman.

Monk muttered, "Normally, woman trouble is my favorite kind of trouble. But not this day, or this woman, either."

"You have my sympathy, buddy," clucked the other.

"Thanks," said Monk miserably. "But what I hanker for right now is answers."

"Those, I don't have. In fact, I'm fresh out today."

# Chapter IV

# THE HAYWIRE BLONDE

**M**ONK MAYFAIR DID not retreat to the skyscraper headquarters establishment of Doc Savage because he was uncertain what to do next. Not at all. It was a manifest fact that he had no clue, inkling, or idea of where to locate the smoky-haired man and his blonde captive, Davey Lee.

Otherwise the apish chemist would have hied off in any direction he thought fruitful. Nor did Monk lack bravery. In fact, he was a bit on the reckless side when it came to plunging into or after trouble.

The real reason Monk betook himself to the Man of Bronze was because Doc possessed many amazing gadgets and devices with which to track down quarry.

As a chemist, Monk had had a hand in perfecting some of those gimmicks, but he knew he needed the astute brain of Doc Savage in order to initiate the so-far unfruitful search.

So Monk hectored his driver to cut corners, race traffic lights, and make all speed toward the towering stone edifice out of which the bronze man operated.

"Keep your shirt on, buster!" the hackman burst out at last.

Monk reached ahead and slapped him on the top of his head and snapped, "Pay attention to your daggone driving!"

"Then stop riding me, mister!" the driver retorted.

Monk settled into the back seat, big paws clutching his knees nervously, his tiny eyes skating out the cab windows in the vain hope of spotting the large man and Davey Lee.

33

Soon, the taxi ground to a halt in front of the limestone and steel spire that was his destination.

Throwing the hackman his last few dollars, the apish chemist charged into the lobby, arrowed for the special elevator that ran directly to the eighty-sixth floor, and hit the solitary button as the doors rolled closed.

The elevator shot upward like a rocket. Monk landed on the seat of his pants, and remained that way until the lift coasted to a stop and the doors mechanically opened.

Thereupon, Monk bounced to his feet and raced down the corridor until he came to a bronze door whose modest letters proclaimed *Clark Savage, Jr.*

Barging into the reception room, Monk found it empty, then shoved into the library, calling out, "Doc! Are you home?"

No response came. Only echoes rebounding off the myriad shelves of the scientific library, which was impressive indeed.

The homely chemist crossed the enormous library, banged into the laboratory, and repeated his call.

He found the great white-enamel walled workshop deserted.

Monk's simian face fell. He took several turns around the glittering array of apparatus, test tubes and other modern wonders until he was certain that no one was present.

"What do I do now?" he muttered to himself.

The hairy chemist did not have long to wait, for not fifteen minutes later appeared a new arrival.

It was Ham Brooks, fashionable clothes askew, his face flustered, waving his elegant dark cane about like Scrooge berating Marley.

"There you are!" squawked the excited barrister.

"I'm looking for Doc, you shyster. Seen anything of him?"

"No, I have not. But I have seen plenty of other things."

"Whatcha mean?" demanded Monk.

"I followed you to Pennsylvania Station this morning," replied Ham firmly. "And there I witnessed that flossy floozie being abducted by a gray-haired man."

"You did!" blurted out Monk.

Ham nodded firmly. "I was suspicious of her all along. Now it appears that my suspicions were confirmed."

"What the heck do you mean by that?" bellowed Monk. "She was kidnapped. I saw it. Now you say you saw it. What makes her suspicious?"

"It makes the whole set-up suspicious," returned Ham tightly. "If her invitation to go south was an innocent one, why was she taken off by a person unknown?"

"You got me," mumbled Monk. Then, eyes narrowing, he said suspiciously, "Hey! How did you know about my trip in the first place?"

"You were overheard in the restaurant," Ham supplied.

Monk growled, tiny eyes shooting sparks. "You mean that you spied on me, didn't you?"

"I meant nothing of the sort," snapped the elegant attorney. The nervous way in which he twisted the head of his cane indicated otherwise.

Monk advanced upon the handsome Ham, and Ham took three quick steps backward, gave his cane a twist, and pulled out a slim blade of Damascus steel.

"Keep back! You hear me, you man-brute," Ham warned, flashing the sword cane about.

Monk balled his rusty fists, and cocked one as if he was about to launch a haymaker at the dapper lawyer's chiseled chin when suddenly a buzzer sounded and a red light began flashing consistently.

"Someone at the door," mumbled Monk.

Ham took that opportunity to turn on his heel and race across the library and into the reception room.

Monk followed hard on his heels, but moving much slower, because he was still wrestling with the tumbling events of the morning.

When the hairy chemist arrived in the reception room, Ham was seated behind the great inlaid table that served as a desk, staring down at a frosted glass panel set into the desktop. This was a television device, which displayed images of the corridor. It was fed by several cameras and by pressing different ivory and rosewood inlays on the desktop, entirely different views of the outer hallway could be obtained.

The black-and-white image in the glass was crystal clear. And when Monk saw the personage depicted, he gave out a rumbling grunt of surprise.

For the man at their door was no less than the large mature man whose thick and wonderfully coiffed hair suggested cigarette smoke.

Monk growled deeply, "Let 'im in."

HAM obliged by pressing another inlay, this one of mother-of-pearl. This actuated an electrical relay that caused the bronze portal to valve open obediently.

Monk bounded out from behind the desk and charged up to meet the unexpected visitor.

The fellow seemed momentarily taken aback by the door opening of its own accord, for he had been standing there looking downward, worrying a white Panama-style hat in his sunburned hands. The brim was curled, and the hue of the hat almost matched the white of his cotton suit, giving him the look of an old-fashioned Kentucky Colonel, but without the additional adornment of facial hair.

He had only a moment to register surprise, for Monk drove out a massive paw, seized him by the front of his white coat, entangling starched shirt and string tie, and hauled him waddling into the reception room, while Ham sealed the door automatically.

"Ah do beg your pardon?" the large man stuttered.

"You'll be begging for mercy if you don't give out with some sense," barked Monk. Before the man could reply, the hairy chemist added, "Where is Davey Lee? Don't give me any doubletalk, either. My mood is foul."

"Ah declare," said the man nervously. "Ah can explain everything. Be good enough to give me a moment to do so."

"You got thirty seconds to spit out some sense before you taste my knuckles," warned Monk.

Coming around from behind the desk, Ham Brooks strode up and said, "One moment, Monk. This man seems to have something to say. We should hear him out."

"Was this the dude who you saw makin' off with Davey Lee?" Monk demanded hotly.

"If it isn't, it's his twin brother," remarked Ham. To the man with the Panama, he said, "We would like to hear your account of the morning's events."

"Ah should be glad to do so, entirely glad," the other said in an forthright tone.

"Proceed," invited Ham.

"This is difficult to confess, but please hear me out. Ah have a daughter, a daughter whom Ah love with all my heart. Ah was forced to raise her myself, her mother having passed away at a very youthful age."

"Get down to brass tacks, will you?" demanded Monk.

"Oh yes, of course. As Ah was saying, my daughter, Davia, has had a difficult upbringing."

"Wait a minute," interrupted Ham. "Are you claiming to be the father of Davey Lee?"

"Not only claiming, but Ah am, in truth, he." Whereupon, the smoky-haired individual produced a billfold and his draft registration card and other articles of identification, and they showed him to be Mr. Raymond Lee of Shreveport, Louisiana.

"These look genuine," allowed Ham.

Monk grabbed the items from Ham, scanned them quickly and said, "He's a phony."

"What makes you say that, Monk?" demanded Ham.

"He smells like a phony, that's why!"

Ham Brooks involuntarily sniffed the air, and declared, "All I smell about him is cigarette smoke."

Given that the man's wonderfully full pompadour resembled a kind of frozen smoke, this fact was remarkable, but otherwise insignificant.

Ham invited, "Please continue with your story."

Accepting his billfold back, the man pocketed it and began worrying his Panama hat, once more turning it in incessant circles, clockwise then counterclockwise. His serious amber eyes were a little on the agate side. Hard and glassy. He had the skin and physique of a man who had been outdoors a great deal, and accustomed to exercise, if not physical labor.

"Well, you see," the man continued in an embarrassed tone of voice, "my Davia grew up to be kind of a tomboy. I sent her off to one of the best finishing schools to kind of sand the tomboy out of her—but only sawdust resulted. Davey is not what you call a hellion exactly, but she's kind of—ah—corkscrewy."

"What do you mean by that?" wondered Ham.

"Well, as much as it pains me as her father to admit this, she has a kind of a peculiar yen."

"A what?" asked Ham.

Raymond Lee looked as abashed as a Quaker who had wandered by mistake into a honky-tonk establishment. "A hankering, you might call it."

"You are not getting to your point very efficiently," Ham pointed out.

Impatiently, Monk interjected, "A hankering. For what?"

The man's eyes went to Monk Mayfair, careened away. "For homely men," he said thickly.

"What?" muttered Monk.

"You heard me right." Raymond Lee dropped his feline eyes to the floor sheepishly. "Homely men fascinate her. Ever since she got out of that finishing school, my Davia's been trying to run off with one after another of the breed. No offense to you, Mr. Mayfair. But you just happened to be someone she cottoned onto her first day in New York City."

The homely chemist's tiny eyes began to flutter, and his generous mouth slowly sagged until it was a gaping cavern full of blunt teeth.

Ham Brooks stared, his face stiff. He was watching the smoky-haired individual for signs of deceit.

"What?" repeated Monk dully.

The man nodded somberly. "The long and short of it is, the homelier the man, the more Davia is spellbound. Ah had sent her to New York on a vacation, but decided to follow just to keep a fatherly eye upon her. After the last adventure in which she took up with an oil-field roughneck, Ah kind of hoped she'd gotten that homely-fellow taste out of her mouth."

Monk muttered for a third time, "What?"

"When Ah learned from the staff of the hotel at which she was staying that Davia was running off with you, Mr. Mayfair, Ah knew Ah had to put a stop to it. So as any father would, Ah waylaid her in Pennsylvania Station. Ah guess the sight of her old father showing up unexpectedly made her go haywire. Not that there is anything new in that. Davia has been haywire most of her life."

Monk's mouth shut like a steel trap. His tiny eyes seemed to sink into his round skull, and disappointment was written all over his apish physiognomy.

"My apologies to you for the behavior of my dear daughter," Raymond Lee continued, "but you are not the first hairy-chested brute Davia's tried to sink her hooks into. Nor, Ah fear, will you be the last one."

As Monk absorbed the full weight of these words, Ham Brooks started to laugh. The mirth began as a restrained titter, turned into a giggle, and before long he threw his head back and was laughing uproariously.

"Oh, this is too rich!" he howled. "Wait until the others hear about this! Monk is the victim of a love-struck woman who is only attracted to ugly men."

"Ah would not say *ugly*, but rather ill-favored," countered Raymond Lee. "Homely, if you will. Ah believe there is a difference, after all."

Monk stared at the smoky-haired individual, then his eyes seized upon Ham Brooks convulsing in laughter, and for a moment the hairy chemist did not appear to know what to do with himself. His fingers worked into fighting fists, then opened up again several times.

Suddenly, he leaped, seized hold of Ham Brooks' elegant cane and bent it over his knee without seeming to give it any more effort than necessary. The fine Malacca wood of the barrel splintered alarmingly, and the flexible blade inside bent nearly double.

"My word!" Raymond Lee burst out, aghast.

Ham Brooks abruptly ceased laughing and retreated behind the big table of a desk, whose protection was doubtful.

Monk spun on Raymond Lee, and barked, "I don't believe you! I don't believe a word of it!"

"Ah would hardly have come here to offer such a tall tale if Ah were not who Ah claim to be," the abashed man pointed out.

Monk glared at him. "Where's Davey now?"

"After calming her down, I put her on another train."

"Which train?" demanded Ham in his best lawyerly style.

"We have kin in Virginia. I sent her to Richmond."

Monk and Ham exchanged looks, and some of the irate skepticism seemed to leak out of the hairy chemist while Ham Brooks appeared to become slightly more skeptical. Of course, that was their way. They were always assuming contrary postures toward one another. Rarely did they agree upon a subject, and if one's mind ever changed, the other party invariably switched sides in response.

"It is my firm intention to join her there by evening," resumed Raymond Lee. "Ah realize the ruckus Ah created in the train station, and assumed there might be repercussions. Hence, my appearance here, which is my pitiful attempt to explain the excitement of this morning."

Ham Brooks stated, "We will check your story out, Mr. Lee."

"Ah expect you to do so. You'll find the Lee family is of impeccable character, and above reproach."

"I imagine that I will," Ham said smoothly.

"Well, now that you have my story, Ah am obliged to take my leave and catch up with my wayward daughter in Richmond." He bowed his head in Monk's direction. "For now, please accept my sincere apologies, Mr. Mayfair. Ah do not know what Ah will do with my only daughter. She is too old to turn over my knee and administer a fatherly reprimand. Perhaps Ah will seek out a psychiatrist on her behalf. These embarrassing antics must cease; the family will never live it down otherwise. And we have long-lived reputations to uphold."

With that, Mr. Raymond Lee exited the reception room, the door opening and closing behind him, operated electrically by Ham Brooks from the desk.

AFTER the visitor had departed, Ham looked sternly at Monk and announced, "I expect you to pay for that damaged cane."

"You can have whatever is left in my wallet," said Monk hollowly.

"Well, hand it over then," demanded Ham.

The billfold went sailing across the room, landed in Ham's cupped hands, and he riffled through it, producing not a single dollar bill.

"What! Are you that broke?" asked Ham in an injured tone.

Monk's neckless head sank between his sloping shoulders, and he looked at the floor. "Broke is the least of my worries right now. I canceled my trip to England."

"Doesn't your ship sail tomorrow?"

"Yeah, but my luggage is on its way to Shreveport."

Ham eyed Monk severely and said, "Let this be a lesson to you. In the future, you should be more skeptical of women, especially of the blonde variety."

Monk backed up to a comfortable leather chair and slammed his broad body into it, looking crestfallen.

The hairy chemist looked so dejected that the dapper lawyer decided not to pursue the point. Instead, he asked, "Where is Doc Savage?"

"How would I know?" Monk said miserably. "I ain't seen him in two days."

"Nor have I since yesterday. But no matter. I am sure he will return presently."

They sat in silence for several minutes until abruptly Monk Mayfair sprang to his feet. He leveled a hirsute finger at Ham Brooks. "Say, if you witnessed that rumpus at Pennsylvania Station, why didn't you follow them?"

"Why, I did. But I lost them in Brooklyn."

Monk made curious faces and asked, "Why would they go to Brooklyn?"

"Of course," Ham said thinly, "I have no idea."

"That Raymond Lee looks like he has dough, and if he was stayin' in New York, he'd put up in the city, wouldn't he?"

Ham Brooks considered this for a moment, then said, "If his daughter is visiting Manhattan, he might be lying low in Brooklyn to avoid encountering her by accident."

"It's a big city, and if he was following her, why would he make it harder to get on her trail?"

"You have a point," Ham admitted. "Still, his story stacks up."

"Yeah," growled Monk. "Like a stack of jokers. And I ain't buyin' it. I think he kidnapped Davey, stashed her somewhere, and came by to give us the breeze."

"You mean to say that display was all an act?"

"It was," returned Monk savagely, "a polished version of the bum's rush."

Picking up the telephone, Ham snapped, "I'm going to look into his story."

"You do that little thing," growled Monk, charging for the door. "I'm gonna see if I can't pick up his trail!"

"Try not to blunder into any more trouble than usual, you magnet for the mentally impaired."

"The trouble I got in mind," Monk gritted, "is the kind I dish out, not the kind I collect from others."

The door closed behind the hairy chemist, and Ham Brooks briskly began dialing the telephone number.

# Chapter V

# GRIM GENTLEMEN WITH GUNS

**F**OR MANY YEARS now, Doc Savage had maintained a secret institution in the heavily forested wilderness of upstate New York, nestled in sheltering mountains renowned for their remoteness from habitation.

This establishment did not have an official name, but among Doc Savage and his associates, it was euphemistically called the "College." The College was perhaps the most unique educational establishment in the world. For it transformed criminals of all types into upright citizens.

During the course of his globe-girdling undertakings, Doc Savage had often collected the survivors of the criminal gangs which he smashed. Not believing in the concept of capital punishment, and knowing that prisons were incubators for further criminality, Doc erected the secret installation, where he sent crooks and murderers he captured alive.

Were it to become public knowledge, what ultimately befell these prisoners would have created a scandal of historic proportions. For first they were subjected to delicate brain operations, which wiped away all memory of their pasts, criminal and otherwise.

Once these men—and a sprinkling of women, too—were remade into human blank slates, Doc Savage's staff assigned them new names, identities, and commenced a process of re-education designed to remove all thoughts of future criminality, which was followed by any number of vocational training regimens until they were pronounced fit to be set free by the medical staff.

In the years before the war, these men were permitted to merge back into ordinary society, there to live out their lives productively in some law-abiding profession.

After the attack on Pearl Harbor, Doc Savage instituted a change in this regime of matriculation. Graduates who were able-bodied were channeled into the Armed Forces, thereby bringing whatever remnants of their old criminal skills into the mighty task of vanquishing America's enemies.

In times past, some of these men had gone to work for Doc Savage, but since the new program was instituted, the bronze man had had to make do with the rehabilitated specimens who were found unsuitable for national service by the draft board.

There was a taxi stand in front of Doc Savage's headquarters in New York, and several of the drivers, as well as the doorman, were graduates of the criminal-curing College.

Riding the speed elevator to the ground floor, Monk bolted out into the lobby and on through to the sidewalk, where he accosted one of these men.

"See anything of a gray-haired guy sportin' a smoky pompadour?"

The starter said, "Sure, Mr. Mayfair. I put him in a cab."

"One of ours?"

"Yes, sir. Harry was the driver. You remember Harry?"

Monk grinned. "Sure. Flat feet and a bum left eye."

"That's him. That's Harry. Want I should call his dispatcher?"

"No, I'll do it. I don't want his passenger to know I'm doggin' him. Thanks."

The starter all but saluted as Monk dashed back into the lobby to find a pay telephone. The man had no inkling that in years past he had been one of the most vicious bank robbers in the Midwest. A man who had been written up in the same terms as John Dillinger and Pretty Boy Floyd. Now he was content to be a cog in the vast machine that was the Doc Savage enterprise.

Closing the pay telephone door behind him, Monk called the dispatcher of the cab company and spoke rapidly.

"When Harry Miller calls in, ask him where he took his fare. I'll hold the line."

"Yes, Mr. Mayfair," said the dispatcher, who also worked for Doc Savage and had once masterminded a child kidnapping racket.

Monk fit more nickels into the slot, and began to worry. He was getting low on loose change.

Finally, the operator came on and said, "Please deposit an additional ten cents to keep this line open."

"Hold your horses!" growled Monk, snapping open the booth door and grabbing the nearest passerby. "Hey, buddy, can you spare a dime?"

The fellow started. "All I have is a quarter, and I'm afraid I cannot part with it." The man continued on, but Monk snagged him by his coat sleeve and pulled him into the wooden booth. "This is an emergency," Monk growled. "Give me that quarter, then go up to Doc Savage headquarters on the eighty-sixth floor and a dude named Ham will give you a replacement quarter on my say-so."

"Well, who the hell are you to rough me up like this?" demanded the other.

"Monk Mayfair, famous chemist, and even more famous as a Doc Savage associate. Now hand over that blasted quarter!"

The accosted man did not know what to think or do, but finally the quarter was produced. Monk dropped it into the slot, where it produced a satisfactory clink signifying acceptance by the mechanism.

Shoving the individual outside, Monk closed the door, and continued holding the line.

Finally, the dispatcher came back on the line, and reported that the fare was deposited in Brooklyn. "Here's the address."

Lacking anything with which to write it down, Monk committed it to memory, asking, "What kind of joint is it?"

"According to Harry," the dispatcher said, "it's an Old Sailors Home."

"Old Sailors Home? That doesn't sound quite right."

"That's what Harry said."

"Thanks," Monk said, slamming down the receiver and barging out.

On his way out the revolving front door, he got tangled up with the man from whom he borrowed the quarter.

"You got the coin okay?" demanded Monk.

The man grinned. "I asked for a dollar, and he gave it to me, so I made seventy-five cents on the deal."

Monk moaned, "That means I owe that shyster a whole dollar."

"Take it up with him. It's between the two of you now," returned the man, tipping his hat and taking off.

Grumbling to himself, "This has not been my finest twenty-four hours," the hairy chemist jumped into the back of a cab and said, "Take me to the Old Sailors Home in Brooklyn."

"Never heard of any such place," replied the cabbie, looking puzzled.

Monk recited the address, and the car got into gear and took off into busy Manhattan traffic.

As the taxicab wended its way through vehicular traffic, the driver became talkative.

"I have a cousin in the Navy, and another cousin in the Merchant Marines, and I never heard of any Old Sailors Home in Brooklyn, or for that matter anywhere in these parts."

Monk frowned and muttered darkly, "Well, we will soon see about that."

"In fact," said the cabbie expansively, "I got a dollar in my pocket that says there is no such place."

"I have not been doin' so hot with my money lately."

"Does that mean you won't take me up on it?"

"Take an I.O.U.?" asked Monk hopefully.

"Since you're Monk Mayfair, I guess I will."

Monk shoved a furry paw forward and they shook hands awkwardly. After that, the driver grew more intent upon reaching his destination.

THE SIGN in front of the decrepit building said in faded gold letters against a black background, OLD SAILORS HOME.

The driver muttered some choice profanity, and said, "The fare is three dollars, so you owe me two bucks."

Monk suddenly realized he did not have the two dollars. He made an effort to fish around in his pockets, but the only thing he produced were three steel war-issue pennies, at which the driver sneered.

"Say, what *is* this? Are you trying to beat the fare on top of taking me for a dollar?"

"Tell you what," suggested Monk. "Just drive back to Doc Savage headquarters and say to Ham Brooks that I borrowed three dollars off you. That way you get the full fare back. How's that?"

"Fishy, I calls it. Mighty fishy."

"Unless you want to call a cop, and let him sort it out," countered Monk, "that's the best I can offer you, pal."

The cabbie sighed. "I guess I will take it." Reaching behind to throw open the rear door, he snarled, "Now *out*, deadbeat."

It was about the noon hour, and a working day for those who still toiled on Saturdays, so the residential area was rather on the deserted side. The Old Sailors Home had once been a residence. It obviously had been rededicated to a rest home for retired seamen.

Monk considered how best to attack the situation and decided that barging up to the front door and knocking was the most direct approach, and so it was the one he favored. Monk was the direct sort.

The hairy chemist applied his rusty knuckles to the front door, which was a Kelly green whose surface was so cracked that an older mustard-hued coat of paint could be discerned behind.

Monk knocked three times, very loudly, while slipping from an underarm holster a peculiar pistol. This weapon was an intricate little gadget, with a number of knobs and horns, a compact ammunition drum set in front of the trigger, and a barrel approximately the diameter of a pencil.

This was a supermachine pistol, a product of Doc Savage's inventive genius. It fired all manner of rounds, but rarely lead slugs owing to the bronze man's admonitions against killing foes.

Despite his sometimes thick-headed directness, Monk also harbored several cautious bones in his body. If there was to be trouble, the homely chemist wanted to be prepared for it. He unlatched several safety catches, and placed one hand behind his back, concealing the powerful weapon, while the other fist made the ancient door shake in its frame.

A voice bellowed from within, "Diamond! Are you expecting callers?"

"No," a cold voice returned.

Both voices were muffled by the thick old door that had once been the color of dried mustard.

Monk applied one cauliflower ear to the panel and attempted to discern more of the conversation.

"Should I answer it?"

"How do I know?"

"Somebody make a decision!"

There followed a rough argument about the issue of whether or not to answer the door.

Listening, Monk tried to make sense of this argument. It seemed rather vociferous for such a small matter. If this was an Old Sailors Home, visitors might not be common, but neither would they normally produce an issue of admittance. While

Monk was focusing on his cauliflower ear, two grim gentlemen with guns had crept around from either side of the house, stole up behind him and pressed the hard muzzles of their weapons against his broad shoulder blades.

One man snatched the supermachine pistol out of Monk's hand.

Here, the hairy chemist was taken completely by surprise. Normally, he would have whirled and brought the heads of the two men together, but he recognized the familiar prod of hard steel against his back, having had the drop gotten on him many times in the past.

"What's doin'?" growled Monk.

"You tell us, brother."

"I'm just payin' a call on Raymond Lee. Know him?"

"No," said one.

"Who is he?" chimed in the other.

"Maybe I got the wrong address," Monk said hopefully.

"Maybe we should ask Diamond about that," said the man who did not know who Raymond Lee was.

A key was produced, the door unlocked, and Monk was herded inside. The two hard gun barrels never left his shoulder blades, and the hairy chemist knew that if either or both discharged, his shoulder blades would crack like china plates.

"It worked!" said one.

"Yeah," added the other, "he fell for our phony fracas like a ton of bricks—the dumb ape."

"Watch who you're callin' a dumb ape," yelled Monk. "I got feelings."

"You feel the gun muzzles at your back, don't you? Those are the only feelings you need to bother about right now."

The smoky-haired gentleman who had called himself Raymond Lee came bounding down the stairs from above, took one look at Monk and groaned, "This is a hell of a note." His Southern accent seemed to have escaped him.

"Who is he?" demanded one ambusher.

"Who is he!" echoed Raymond Lee. "Who do you think he is? This is the character we've been trying to get out of the way."

Monk looked baffled. "Who? Me?"

Raymond Lee charged up to Monk and looked down at him like he had found a cockroach in his kitchen.

"This is Mayfair?" asked another gunman.

"It is."

"I thought you gave him a bone to gnaw on."

Raymond Lee growled, "He must be one of those guys who wolfs down his food and comes around looking for more."

A gun barrel pushed in hard. "Is that right, Mayfair? Do you gobble your grub?"

The polish that Raymond Lee—if that was indeed his name— had displayed earlier in the morning had now been rubbed off. He looked to be a rough sort, and he talked as tough as a dock walloper. He no longer wore his Southern gentleman's whites.

"We sail in a few hours," he bit out. "We need to get him out of the way."

As if he had not heard that, Monk asked, "I gather you're not really Davey's father after all."

"Gather what you want, squat and stupid," returned the smoky-haired man. "It won't matter to you anymore. Nothing will."

"Is that the way of it?" returned Monk.

"That's how she lies," said the man, sounding like a seaman of some sort.

"What do we do with him, Diamond?" asked one of the gunmen.

"March this lump of hair down to the basement, and empty your guns into him, Weedy."

Monk said abruptly, "Let's not be hasty."

Diamond returned in a brutal voice, "We should have done it this way in the first place!"

Behind him, two voices said out of joint, "March!"

Gun muzzles urged the hairy chemist in the direction of a door that evidently led into the basement.

Monk immediately became stubborn. "I ain't goin' down there. And you can't make me."

Raymond Lee, who was evidently going by the name of Diamond, laid cold amber eyes upon Monk Mayfair and re-marked, "It's not a big bother to shoot you on the spot and carry your corpse down."

Whereupon the man who had lifted Monk Mayfair's super-machine pistol, offered, "I took this off him. It's supposed to fire trick bullets. I read that in a fancy magazine."

Diamond grabbed the pistol, examined it with curiosity, and said, "Now that you mention it, Weedy, I read the same thing in the tabloids."

Lifting the pistol, he trained the muzzle on Monk's chest, and pulled the trigger.

A great many strange things began happening all at once, altering the picture as definitely as if an earthquake, a hurricane and a stray tornado had decided to converge upon one spot.

# Chapter VI

# FLOP

SOMETHING CYCLONIC EMERGED from the basement, slamming through the door with the juggernaut force of a Sherman tank.

The thing that made such an unexpected appearance moved so rapidly that it could not be clearly tracked with the eyes, especially after it began flinging gunmen around as if they were department store mannequins.

As one of the gunmen later expressed it, "It was all metal and wide as a truck."

This was an exaggeration, of course. But such was the impact of the hurricane force that stormed the men in the room that they could be forgiven for thinking a squad of commandos had burst out of the basement.

In actual fact, it was only one man.

But that man was Doc Savage. This explained much.

The bronze giant had charged up and out of the basement, seized the man named Diamond, and flung him away, simultaneously harvesting the supermachine pistol that he had been fiddling with, and tossing it in Monk's direction.

The pistol was designed to defeat use by anyone not familiar with its intricate series of safety catches. It was unlikely the man would have gotten the weapon to discharge. The violence was purely Doc Savage's doing, hence its hurricane qualities.

Doc Savage next seized Monk by the shoulders, spun him off in the direction of Diamond, doing this so rapidly that the two gunmen who had impaled Monk's shoulder blades with their pistol muzzles did not understand what happened until a colossus of bronze was suddenly towering over them, moving like a ricocheting thunderbolt.

The gunmen reacted instinctively. They squeezed their triggers, and a pair of .38-caliber slugs struck the bronze man in the chest, driving him backward.

Meanwhile, Monk Mayfair had the supermachine pistol firmly in hand and was scrambling to his feet. He tried to lay his gunsight on one gunman, but Doc Savage's backpedaling form blocked his view.

From somewhere above came excited shouts, and other men suddenly put in an appearance, charging down the stairs from above.

This reserve crew brandished revolvers and automatics, and started looking for people to perforate.

One shot Doc Savage in the back, but his weapon was of insufficient caliber and velocity to do much more than arrest the bronze man's active progress.

Seeing this, Monk opened up with his supermachine pistol, and aligned the stitching tracers to cross the man's chest on a diagonal, causing the fellow's loud tie to flip up. The man fell backward, stumbled, and then began rolling down the stairs, completely helpless.

The amazing weapon was charged with "mercy" bullets, which were hollow shells of soft lead filled with a chemical anesthetic which acted instantly, once the mushrooming rounds broke skin.

After shrugging off a small-caliber bullet in the back, Doc Savage was suddenly moving on the gunmen again, and these two worthies fired anew.

Doc's bulletproof chainmesh undervest absorbed the dual impact. The bronze giant was staggered slightly, and threw himself off to one side, lest one of the gunmen strike his unprotected head or hands.

The smoky-haired individual who had called himself Raymond Lee and was now going by the name of Diamond took immediate charge.

First, he drew a blackjack, a nasty-looking leathery pouch of a thing, and bopped Monk Mayfair across the top of his bristle-furred skull.

Then, turning to the men charging down the steps, he roared, "Finish them off! Then let's clear out of here!"

Guns commenced barking like angry dogs, and Doc Savage ducked around the corner into a side room, simultaneously fishing into his pockets and extracting a number of objects that resembled glass marbles.

The bronze man had every intention of hurling these into the hallway, where they would shatter and release a volatile chemical mixture that would produce virtually instantaneous unconsciousness.

Before he could do so, there was a new arrival.

The front door flew open, and there stood Ham Brooks, supermachine pistol in one hand, a fresh sword cane in the other, looking ready for battle.

"What's going on here?" he demanded.

The dapper attorney was promptly shot, one bullet striking him in the belly, the other knocking his cane out of his hand, with the result that both man and cane went flying backward, tumbling down the short flight of porch steps.

"Scuttle him, too!" roared Diamond.

Doc pegged his tiny grenades at that point, and they landed out in the hallway, coming to rest on the thick carpet.

Unfortunately, the deep nap prevented them from breaking, and nothing useful happened whatsoever.

Doc Savage plunged out of the side room at that point, but was driven backward by a hail of punishing lead that chewed and chipped at the framing of the door.

More bullets punched through the plaster walls, one shattering a light fixture, the other breaking a window, causing glass to crash and jangle.

Someone brought up a shotgun, set the muzzle against the hallway wall, and blew a large hole in the plaster.

This was done at about shoulder height, which gave the determined gunmen a fresh loophole through which to insert their gun muzzles and take turns blasting away half blindly.

Exhibiting an understandable concern, Doc Savage managed to evade the first burst of bullets, and threw himself out one intact window, taking the glass and the window sash with him. He had first doffed his coat, clutching it before him to protect against glass shards so sharp they could sever an artery.

Reaching grassy ground, the bronze man rolled in tight against the granite foundation of the old dwelling for protection.

Considerable yelling came from within the house, and orders were chopped out, "Fan out! Hunt him down! Shoot him into splinters."

The desperate voice belonged to the man who went by the names of Diamond and Raymond Lee, true name unknown.

Hearing that, Doc Savage came to his feet, charged around the back of the dwelling, found the hatch that opened into the basement, flung it up. Diving in, he landed on a set of cobwebbed timber steps, and pulled the hatch shut behind him.

This was done with such speed and stealth that no one witnessed it, nor could anyone have imagined it could be accomplished so quickly.

Moving through the gloomy basement, Doc Savage went directly to the stairs that he previously mounted in order to surprise Diamond and his gang, having earlier secreted himself in the dank basement.

The bronze giant took the unpainted steps with great caution, in case anyone was stationed at the head of the staircase.

He drew from his clothing a slim black tube, which he extended telescope fashion, then manipulated in another way, fashioning a periscope of sorts.

Reaching the top of the stairs, Doc hung back, and extended the tubular periscope, peering outward to ascertain the lay of the land. The first thing he saw was Monk Mayfair lying sprawled on the floor. A reddish patch at the back of his head looked nasty.

Men were charging about, and guns were going off. The sound was of a general bedlam.

No one seemed to be concerned with Monk, so Doc took a chance, flashed out, grabbed the hairy chemist by the shoulders and pulled him down onto the basement steps.

That accomplished, Doc surreptitiously closed the door at the top, and drifted back to the basement hatch, moving quietly but with grim efficiency.

The bronze man's intention was to rescue Ham Brooks next, but the minute his head poked out of the hatchway door, lead started snapping at him, and he was forced to withdraw.

The caterwauling of a police siren could be heard, something that might have been predicted given the general conditions of combat. Quite a commotion had been produced.

This caused Diamond to execute a change in plans.

"Pile into the cars!" he ordered. "Get the hell out of here. Rendezvous at the second departure area."

There was a concerted slamming of feet down rattling porch steps, through hedges and onto the heat-cracked pavement.

Various vehicles had been parked on either side of the residential street, and evidently they all belonged to Diamond and his gang.

Listening, Doc heard a flurry of slamming car doors, and the grinding and choking of automobile engines.

Quite a number of cars roared off as the sirens grew near. Doc reemerged, swept around to the front of the Old Sailors

Home, and mounted the porch steps, discovering Ham Brooks, who was not very much worse for wear.

In the mad stampede to escape, men had trampled him rather roughly, his immaculate clothing thus picked up a number of dusty footprints, but Ham was otherwise unharmed.

As Doc Savage lifted Ham into a seated position, the elegant attorney began coughing, then complaining, for his sword cane lay in pieces, the elegant wood barrel broken, but the blade largely intact.

Ham snapped open his hands, and shook off the splintery remnants of the barrel, then climbed to his feet unsteadily.

Examining the state of his attire, he discovered a parade of footprints upon the fine fabric of his coat and trousers. His chiseled profile collapsed in horror.

"This is the worst day of my life!" he moaned.

SEEING that Ham was otherwise sound, Doc ducked into the house, opened the door leading down to the basement and pulled Monk Mayfair into the carpeted hallway, then knelt to examine his head injuries. The homely chemist had been blessed by nature with a hard skull. Possibly a sledgehammer might have dented it, but the blackjack had done nothing more than scrape off a patch of skin and smack him senseless. Doc realized with relief that he would be coming around shortly.

Doc walked out to the porch in time for two green police patrol cars with bone-white roofs to show up, sirens keening.

"Monk will be fine," he told Ham. Then he went to greet the officers.

The bronze man was known to the police, having an honorary commission and a great deal of influence with City Hall.

He gave a rapid recitation of the events that resulted in the partial demolition of the Old Sailors Home. Then, to the amazement of the officers, he gave them complete descriptions of the makes, models, and license tag numbers of the cars that had just quit the neighborhood.

The police rushed to their vehicles to call descriptions in to headquarters, then they tore off in opposite directions, seeking the fleeing machines.

Ham wandered up and asked, "Are we not going to join the chase?"

Doc Savage shook his head silently. "There may be no need. I have a good idea where those men decamped to."

Ham stared wordlessly. Despite long years of association, the bronze man's uncanny ability to deduce facts that seemed to have no antecedents baffled him.

Doc entered the dwelling, picked up the two hundred and sixty pound Monk Mayfair as if he weighed two hundred pounds less than his grown weight, and carried him down the street and around the corner to the bronze man's own waiting machine.

Ham followed with alacrity, a dozen questions on the tip of his tongue.

Doc Savage deposited Monk in the back seat where he could sleep off the lingering effects of the blackjack, then claimed the wheel while Ham inserted himself in the passenger seat.

The car—it was a nondescript black sedan—hummed into traffic. Doc Savage headed south.

Ham began asking questions, "What on earth happened here?"

Doc Savage declared, "I have been tailing a number of the individuals involved since yesterday."

"So you agreed with my suspicions?"

Doc nodded. "Certain details did not add up."

"What did you discover?"

"To begin with, the girl who called herself Davey Lee is not who she said she was."

"Then who was she?"

"That I have yet to determine," said Doc, piloting the sedan through traffic. "But after she was abducted from Pennsylvania

Station, she was taken to a certain house in a secluded neighborhood."

"How did you know that?"

"Because I witnessed the kidnapping, and followed the taxicab that spirited her away."

"Strange. I was there as well, and I did not notice you. Nor did Monk, apparently."

Doc Savage said nothing to that. Despite his great size, he was highly skilled in the art of disguise, as well as possessing the ability to lurk about unnoticed, even by those as sharp-eyed as the alert barrister.

"The girl was being held under guard, but appeared to be safe. I followed one of the captors to this Old Sailors Home which, by the way, is a fake. There is no Old Sailors Home registered in Brooklyn. Evidently, the man calling himself Diamond and his gang set it up to discourage neighborhood curiosity during their occupation."

"Peculiar thing to do," mused Ham.

"Think of it as a kind of camouflage," stated Doc. "How did you come to be here, Ham?"

"A taxi driver called headquarters, demanding to know if I was good for Monk's fare. When he told me the address, I came straight away."

"We did not acquit ourselves in our usual efficient manner," remarked Doc.

Ham said in a determined voice, "No doubt we will make up for it when we rescue the girl."

THE RESCUING of Davey Lee—or whatever her real name happened to be—did not exactly go according to plan.

Doc Savage cruised by the address, which was a modest, two-story cream clapboard home, with the traditional white picket fence. There was nothing unusual about it. Doc circled the block, driving past it twice, looking for signs of activity.

The cars which had fled the vicinity of the Old Sailors Home were not in evidence.

Doc said, "The one calling himself Diamond instructed his men to meet at a second location. It stands to reason that this would be it."

Ham wondered, "Perhaps they have not yet arrived?"

"It is possible the police ran them down, although that was not my expectation," allowed Doc.

"Why did you sic the police on them if you wanted to track the gang down yourself?"

Doc explained, "Time appeared to be of the essence, from what I have learned, and sending the police off on a wild chase was preferable to standing around answering their questions."

"I see," mused Ham, who did not exactly see at all. His high brow furrowed. Examining the remnants of his sword cane, he seemed disgusted with the trend of events thus far.

Parking around the corner from the cream-colored clapboard home, they hunkered down in their seats and Doc Savage once again brought out his handy pocket periscope and surveyed the dwelling after transforming it into a slim telescope.

Minutes passed, and the traffic moving along the street did not stop or even pause near the house under their surveillance.

"Why did you not rescue the girl if you knew she was here?" asked Ham at one point in the stakeout.

"Her role in this affair is unclear. And since the gang seems to be hiding in two separate dwellings, I thought it prudent to collect as much data as possible before making a move."

"Something big is up?"

Doc nodded. "If not big, exceedingly mysterious. I have been eavesdropping on both portions of the gang while secreting myself in their respective basements. The fragmentary talk I overheard tonight leads me to believe that they are prepared to sail on an ocean vessel in just a few hours."

"For what purpose?" asked Ham.

"The only thing I overheard was a cryptic phrase."

"Yes?"

"They were talking about something they called 'Satan's Spine.'"

"Sounds devilish," remarked Ham.

Doc Savage declined to reply to that. He continued to scrutinize the cream house. In the back seat, Monk Mayfair began snoring like a water buffalo. Ham Brooks took a silk handkerchief out of his breast pocket, and used it to squeeze Monk's nose shut, closing off the awful snoring cacophony.

"He is going to have quite the headache when he awakens," commented Ham.

After another twenty minutes dragged on by, Doc Savage opened his car door, and cautiously approached the house. Ham followed along, searching the immediate environment for any sign of lurking gunmen.

They were not challenged in any way, nor were they sniped at from the windows.

Then Doc Savage walked up to the front door, took a slim steel probe out of his vest pocket and, by jiggering it in the lock, defeated the mechanism.

The name on the mailbox was Kilroy. It meant nothing to either of them.

They entered cautiously, Ham Brooks jutting his machine pistol forward, Doc Savage ready for anything, but showing no weapon. He did not believe in them.

They made an efficient sweep of the house, but discovered no evidence.

"Dratted dead end," fumed Ham.

Doc told him, "It is not beyond the realm of possibility that Diamond and his gang might yet show up. While we are waiting, a search of the place for clues is in order."

Separating, they got to work on that.

The place had a bare minimum of furnishing, and not much in the way of personal items. They did find a bedroom that had a feminine touch to it, and Ham realized that this was where Davey Lee must have been kept in confinement.

Stripping the bed, Doc Savage discovered under the pillow a woman's purse. The material was alligator skin, and when he opened the purse, Doc found that it was virtually empty except for a piece of paper crumpled up and stuffed into a side pocket.

"Women do not normally leave their purses behind," observed Ham.

Removing the wad of paper, the bronze man unfolded it and saw that there was writing inscribed in pencil.

The note said:

> I am being taken back to Louisiana by these horrid men. I pray that you find this note, and come to rescue me, for I fear for my life. Go to the <u>northern</u> part of Louisiana and look for the Sugar Hill Plantation, east of Shreveport. <u>Start</u> now. Or all may be lost.

"Jove!" exploded Ham. "That girl is in danger. We must start out for Shreveport at once!"

"The mysterious blonde is undoubtedly in danger," returned Doc Savage, "but she has not been taken to Louisiana."

"But the note says—"

"No time to explain," rapped Doc Savage. "Even less time to waste. Come on."

# Chapter VII

## THE *NORTHERN STAR*

**W**HEN MONK MAYFAIR awoke, he did not at first feel the pain at the back of his thick skull. His small eyes snapped open, looking momentarily unfocused. Blinking, he found himself staring at an unfamiliar ceiling. He sat up, looked around.

Only then did he become aware of a throbbing at both temples. Grabbing his blunt skull, he let out a low, anguished growl like a bulldog suffering from a hangover.

In this way, Monk discovered that he had a pounding headache.

The headache was of secondary importance, however, because the homely chemist immediately recognized his surroundings as the stateroom cabin of a ship of some sort.

Rolling off his bunk, Monk found his feet, but his wobbly knees knocked together alarmingly, and he immediately sat back down.

Monk grabbed his head again and gave out another groan, and the sound would have done credit to a disturbed bull.

"Where the heck am I?" he muttered to himself.

The homely chemist tried to remember the last thing that happened to him. His thoughts went to his shoulder blades, which still ached somewhat from being prodded by cold steel gun muzzles. Monk recalled being at the mercy of the man who called himself Raymond Lee, and that he had been on the point of being taken into the basement of a phony Old Sailors Home to be executed.

The basement door had exploded outward. After that, it was as if a cyclone had entered the house....

A vivid impression of fast-moving thunderbolt resembling Doc Savage charging about the house leaped into his mind. That was about all he could remember of the wild series of events that followed.

Monk, of course, knew nothing about having been black-jacked, except his searching fingers located a moist, sticky patch at the back of his head, where his rusty hair was short and bristly, and soon discovered what appeared to be some type of bandage.

The hairy chemist added two and two and decided, "Either Doc rescued me, or them guys changed their minds and hauled me off to this place, whatever it is."

That Monk was on a ship seemed evident. Wrongdoers he had gone up against before sometimes executed wildly imaginative schemes. Just because he woke up in what appeared to be a stateroom did not make it so. For all Monk knew, this was the basement of that very same house, tricked out to look like a ship's cabin for some peculiar reason.

Finding his feet again, Monk stumbled bowlegged to the door, which proved to be locked, as well as blocked by a dark curtain. There was a porthole beside it, but the thick glass was painted over, a wartime precaution Monk knew was calculated to reduce the number of visible lights on vessels operating in war zones—which constituted the entirety of the Atlantic Ocean these days. Digging into his pocket, he produced a key ring and employed the brassy teeth of one to scrape out a peephole. Peering out, the hairy chemist saw daylight and a forest of masts and cranes that made him think he was not in any basement, but tied up at a dock somewhere.

Monk tried the door, but it refused to open.

"Locked from the outside, dang it," he mumbled to himself. "That's gotta mean I'm somebody's prisoner."

Monk began wondering what happened to Doc Savage, his erstwhile rescuer. He tried pounding on the door, just to see what would happen.

Not long after, someone unlatched it. Much to the hairy chemist's slack-jawed astonishment, Doc Savage and Ham Brooks entered.

"Doc!"

"LOWER your voice, Monk," admonished the bronze man.

Ham slipped in, carefully shut the door, as Doc Savage asked, "How is your head feeling?"

"Like a shell burst in slow-motion," complained Monk.

"You were bludgeoned," Doc informed him.

"I figured as much," said Monk. "Where the heck are we?"

"Investigating a vessel about to sail." Doc Savage produced the note that had been written by the missing Davey Lee. "The men you discovered were holding Miss Lee at another location. We went there, but they had decamped. I found this message, apparently from Miss Lee."

Monk read the message eagerly, and said, "We gotta head out to Shreveport!"

"Hold your horses," said Doc. "That note is not what it seems to be."

Monk frowned. "It reads plain as day. The girl's father said she grabbed Davey and put her on a train."

"I strongly doubt Miss Lee is on any train," said Doc. "Read the letter again, and pay particular attention to the underlined words."

Dropping his gaze, Monk read again, moving his lips, and muttered, " 'Northern' and 'start' are underlined."

"Actually," corrected Doc, "only the first four letters of the word 'start' are underlined. The stressed words actually read *Northern Star*."

"I don't get it," admitted Monk.

"Try harder," suggested Ham.

Doc Savage said calmly, "Monk, did you not think it peculiar that a young woman waylaid you with the promise of a Louisiana vacation a day before you were to ship out to England to do important war work?"

"Well, I kinda figgered it was a coincidence," said Monk, scratching his head.

"Convenient coincidence," sniffed Ham.

Doc Savage continued, "What was the name of the ship on which you planned to take passage?"

Monk's head was pounding, and he didn't feel at all well. So he had to think about that a moment.

"*Northern Star!*" he burst out. "Blazes! She's sayin' something about the *Northern Star.*"

Doc Savage nodded, "That is the name of the vessel we are presently investigating."

Ham Brooks took the note, read it with avid eyes, and his high forehead puckered.

"I am not so certain about this," he mused. "Those are perfectly normal words to have underlined under the circumstances."

Ham's inveterate habit of disagreeing with the hairy chemist may have had more than a little to do with his sudden change of heart.

"A plant," asserted Doc. "This note is a ruse to lure us to Shreveport—all of us. The initial plan was to get Monk to forego taking his sea voyage. But now that we are all involved, this Diamond fellow is attempting to shanghai us to Louisiana. But Miss Lee, having been forced to pen the decoy letter, wrote it in such a way that by underlining two words she was pointing us in the correct direction."

Monk did not appear to be convinced. For that matter, Ham Brooks maintained a skeptical air.

"Why would Miss Lee agree to lure Monk out of town and then turn on Diamond?"

Doc Savage suggested, "She may have gotten cold feet, and was prepared to reveal the truth to Monk. Realizing this, Diamond had no choice but to abduct her."

Ham frowned. "Perhaps we should split up?" he ventured. "Some of us go to Shreveport, and others to look into the question of this boat."

"Not practical," decided Doc. "The ship sails in twenty minutes."

Monk barked, "Then we'd better work fast, so we can get goin' south."

"We are not going south," said Doc Savage. "For there is nothing there to interest us. The mystery of all these shenanigans seems to center on Monk's presence on board this boat. Now that we are here, we will follow this through to its conclusion, whatever that may be."

Astonished, Monk blurted out, "Doc, do you mean that we're takin' passage on this ship?"

Doc nodded firmly. "It has all been arranged. The ship is a Merchant Marine vessel, carrying passengers as well as industrial metals destined for British industry. These are important for the war effort, and it suggests that there will be an attempt to seize the cargo."

"What the heck does that have to do with me—for that matter with Davey Lee?"

"Our investigation so far has proven conclusively that the individual called Diamond misrepresenting himself as Miss Lee's father was not, in truth, her parent. For that matter, there is no such person as Raymond Lee in that part of Louisiana. Nor is there a Davia or Davey Lee discoverable in that region. Although there are several David Lees."

Monk's jaw sagged lower. "What? You mean she's a phony?"

"At least," said Doc, "she has been operating under a name that is not her own. Her motives remain uncertain, but the fact that she was abducted from Pennsylvania Station indicates that Davey Lee is in peril. Discovering her whereabouts, and interrogating her, is of paramount importance in our investigation."

Despite his monkey-like looks, which included a forehead that appeared as if it contained no room for anything other than a spoonful of brains, Monk was not the dull-witted sort. The blow to the back of his head had addled him temporarily, but he was sharp-minded. Not as sharp as normal, but his brain began struggling with the facts at hand.

"If we ship out on this tub, who's gonna search for Davey?" he demanded.

Doc Savage said calmly, "It is not impossible that she is also on this vessel. Although that remains to be seen."

"Brothers, this is all making me dizzy."

"You came into this world in that condition," snapped Ham.

Monk looked at Ham and seemed about to offer a rude rejoinder when he noticed that Ham's sword-cane blade was exposed.

"What happened to that pig-sticker?"

"First you broke it, then Diamond and his men finished the job," fumed Ham.

"Do you reckon that Diamond is the real name of the guy claimin' to be Davey Lee's father?"

"Impossible to tell," admitted Doc. "However, I have obtained the passenger list, as well as the cargo manifest, from the captain of this vessel. It appears that a great many of the people who have booked passage on the *Northern Star* are doing so under assumed names."

This made both Monk and Ham sit up and take notice, figuratively speaking. Ham accepted the passenger list from Doc Savage, skimmed it, and then Monk grabbed it from his well-manicured hand and devoured it with eager eyes.

The list ran in part:

Bill Hatch
Lee Ward
John Anchor
Ward Wind
Joe Cannon
Homer Sail
C.C. Weed

"These names seem perfectly respectable to me," muttered Monk, unconvinced.

"They sound legitimate," agreed Ham.

"Read them again, paying particular attention to the last names," suggested Doc. "Remember that we discovered Diamond and his crowd holed up at an Old Sailors Home, which was a fabrication. Look at some of these names again. A hatch is found on the ship. So is a cannon. For that matter, an anchor. Ward Wind appears to be a twisted version of the nautical term, windward. Likewise, Lee Ward and leeward."

A light of understanding came into Ham's dark eyes and he blurted, "C.C. Weed—seaweed! These so-called passengers have taken on nautical aliases!"

"Which leads me to suspect that they are sailors, or ex-sailors."

"Something's sure up," admitted Monk. "But why don't we have the ship held in port while we investigate?"

Doc Savage said, "We have no proof of anything. According to the War Shipping Administration, it is vital that the *Northern Star* leave on time in order to rendezvous with its designated convoy. From the cryptic things I overheard the gang saying, they seem to have an interest that has nothing to do with the European destination of the ship."

"What do you mean, Doc?" asked Monk.

"Members of the Diamond gang spoke of a mysterious thing they called 'Satan's Spine.' There were other strange references. Mention of a reef. And a place or structure they called the watch tower."

"None of that makes any sense to me," muttered Monk.

"Nevertheless," stated Doc, "I have had some of our graduates bring several cases of equipment on board. We are going to sail with this vessel, surreptitiously, in the hope that we can uncover whatever mischief is developing."

Ham said, "We are sure to be recognized if any of Diamond's gang are aboard."

"Sufficient materials to disguise ourselves are packed in the equipment cases that were brought on board. We will take on other identities, lie low during the day, and do our investigating by night. The *Northern Star* is bound for Nassau in the Bahamas, from there steaming to its assigned convoy rendezvous in the Atlantic."

Monk said, "Yeah, I remember that part of it now. She's detouring to the Caribbean to pick up some British bigwigs down there. If German raiders don't happen across her first, this tub will be well protected once she links up with her convoy."

Ham shivered, thinking of German U-boats, "Nasty business, that."

Doc Savage addressed his men. "Every man will have his own cabin. We will repair to them until dusk. Monk, remain here. Stay out of sight. We will contact you when we are ready to begin patrolling the ship."

Monk looked uneasy, shifted his feet. "I still don't like this."

"Look at this way, you hairy mistake," stated Ham. "Before you met that blond vixen, you intended to sail on this very vessel. Well, now you are. Why don't you simply accept the fact?"

"Don't ride me, shyster," yelled Monk. "I've been through a lot of disappointments in the last couple of days. I ain't feelin' myself. I'm liable to rear up and unscrew your head and toss it over the rail just to teach you a lesson."

"You're just angry that I figured out Davey Lee was not what she seemed," sneered Ham.

"We'll see about that," Monk growled.

"Get some rest, Monk," advised Doc, taking his leave. Ham followed, and the door was closed.

Muttering to himself, the hairy chemist went over to the bunk, and sat down holding his head, complaining to no one present.

"Why do these things always happen to me?" was among his utterances.

Half an hour later, the deck became busy and lines were cast off. The *throb-throb-throb* of the steam turbine engines could be felt. It was broad daylight, but Monk had only an inkling of that, since the solitary porthole was blacked out. Additionally, a heavy curtain was affixed to the inside of the door. Both were calculated to mask any leakage of light when the vessel was steaming along at night, merchant ships being notorious submarine bait.

By that time, Monk was pacing the cabin in an agitated state, fretting over the fate of the missing blonde, Davey Lee.

Possibly Monk decided that he wanted no part of this voyage. Lunging out the door, he mounted the companionway steps and raced toward the gangplank—which was still in place—and attempted to disembark from the boat.

He did not get very far.

In the pell-mell commotion of busy sailors on deck, something stole up behind him and robbed the homely chemist of all consciousness. Monk did not get a glimpse of the thing that waylaid him, only that suddenly something like a powerful vise arrested his forward momentum, and both his vision and his consciousness evaporated like so much boiling water.

# Chapter VIII

# GATHERING STORM

THE CONVERTED LINER *Northern Star* departed
New York City just before noon.

After being guided out through the submarine nets by snorting and tooting tugboats, she pushed out into the open Atlantic, and turned southeast in the direction of Bermuda, en route to the Bahama Banks. The weather was clear, the wind brisk, as the ship—a three-stacker—built up a head of steam, propelled by her laboring engines.

Those who watched her passage from coastal towns would have recognized her great smokestacks and sleek lines for, under her original name, the *Northern Star* had been one of the glamorous queens among passenger ocean liners, conveying tourists to England and Europe on regular Atlantic crossings. Since war had broken out in Europe, there was no longer any tourist trade and vessels such as this one had been remade into troop and cargo ships to augment the Liberty Ships being turned out by shipyards all over the nation at an astounding rate.

Her new name was not visible on her stern and bows, for no Allied ship crossing the Atlantic in these perilous times bore hull identification. Although her profile was the same, gun stations had been added to the port and starboard rails, as well as at the stern. These steel tubs held Browning machine guns. There was another set in the bow. All were manned by Naval Armed Guards under the command of a Navy ensign, a lieutenant (j.g.).

Fore and aft, a naval gunnery crew manned an Oerlikon 20 mm. anti-aircraft autocannon. They were situated on deck, steel stop posts mounted behind them to prevent overeager gunners from shooting up the ship's superstructure in their zeal to fling hell at diving enemy warplanes.

The *Northern Star* hugged the shore, taking the ten-fathom depth course as a precaution against lurking subs, but soon pushed further out, as if to taunt any prowling enemy vessel. After only a few hours out, the skies became strange, and the atmosphere turned uneasy.

"Looks like a storm brewing," said Ham Brooks, who was visiting Doc Savage's cabin.

"Tropical storm possibly," said Doc. "This will complicate matters. We are in the season for hurricanes."

"Monk will be boiling mad when he wakes up," Ham commented. "But what you did had to be done."

"Monk can be headstrong where his heart is involved," agreed Doc Savage. "It was fortunate that I anticipated that he might disobey orders and loitered by the gangplank in order to intercept him, should he bolt."

Ham chuckled. "He probably never knew what hit him."

Doc Savage changed the subject. "I have conferred with the Captain. This ship is crewed by the Merchant Marines, naturally, along with a contingent of Naval Armed Guard. The individuals who comprise the passenger list are all displaced foreign sailors—seamen whose vessels have been confiscated by the United States for the duration of the war, and who, when given the opportunity to continue serving on board their ships, elected instead to be sent back to their home countries. Since many of them hailed from conquered countries that have since been liberated, they are sailing under assumed names, lest this vessel fall into enemy hands and they be subjected to reprisals."

"What nationalities?"

"Dutch. Danes. Norwegians. Some Free French. And a sprinkling of Poles," replied Doc.

Ham made thinking faces. "So their names are not as suspicious as they first seemed."

"No. But remember that the circumstances that brought us on board remain exceedingly suspicious. Diamond—whoever he may be—did not want Monk on board."

Ham mused, "A tabloid had reported the big ape's planned voyage. Monk denied it, of course, but the cat was out of the bag. Anyone reading that squib would suspect the truth. No doubt Diamond acted upon his suspicions."

Doc nodded. "So something underhanded is in the offing. It is our task to determine what it is and forestall it, if necessary."

Ham's eyes darkened. "What can it possibly be?"

"Recall that the gang spoke of a mysterious thing they called 'Satan's Spine,'" reminded Doc.

"Could it be a landmark?"

"If it is, I have never heard of it. North of Eleuthera in the Caribbean, there is a dangerous reef called the Devil's Backbone, so-called because its half-submerged coral heads have snagged many an unwary ship's hull. But the shoal is not on the present route of this ship."

Ham frowned. "Then it must be something else. But what?"

"There is another possibility," said Doc. "In a remote portion of the Caribbean lies a speck of sand known to mariners as Satan Cay. But insofar as I know, it possesses no feature called Satan's Spine."

"Drat. We are groping in the dark then."

"On the contrary," said Doc. "It is in the dark that we can expect to make our best progress, since all things are equally concealed in darkness, including ourselves."

Ham looked at his watch, an expensive platinum gadget. "It will be a few hours until nightfall. What shall we do in the meanwhile?"

Reaching into his pocket, Doc Savage removed a long stainless steel object. It was the dog whistle with which he had been experimenting on the previous day.

"A whistle?" muttered Ham.

"A Galton or so-called 'silent' whistle," corrected Doc. "One that emits a sound on an ultrasonic frequency only dogs and a few other animals can hear. I have been endeavoring to train my hearing to detect these higher frequencies. But I cannot manage to hear this one. I thought if someone else blew on the whistle, it might aid my efforts."

Accepting the thing from the bronze man, Ham studied it carefully, wiped it clean with a silken handkerchief and tested the gimmick.

He blew into it several times, producing no audible result other than the prolonged hissing of his breath.

Pausing, he asked Doc, "Hear anything?"

"I thought so on your last attempt. Try again."

Ham blew and blew, while Doc Savage closed his golden eyes and concentrated his entire consciousness on the sound being produced.

The dapper lawyer blew himself crimson and then purple until he gave it up.

"Did you hear anything?" panted Ham.

"Yes, but not consistently," said Doc Savage, accepting the return of the whistle. "Practice may prove useful."

"Your practice or mine?" asked Ham, looking confused.

"Mine. I am certain the whistle functioned perfectly."

Doc Savage went to a trunk that had been delivered to the cabin, and threw up the lid. From this he removed a flat case, which he opened on the modest dresser.

Ham recognized it as a remarkably complete make-up kit, one that the bronze man had developed over a number of years.

"Take a seat," Doc directed. "Let us see what we can do with your face."

"Are you going to disguise yourself now?" Ham asked Doc.

"In due course," replied the bronze man. "First, let us see what can be done with you."

Although not an old man, Ham Brooks was blessed—or cursed—with prematurely white hair. It was easier to work from that distinguishing feature rather than dyeing the locks a different color.

Digging around in the make-up case, Doc Savage removed a van Dyke mustache and beard made from similarly-hued hair. With spirit gum, the bronze man fixed these articles of adornment to Ham's patrician features. Then, using an astringent solution, he daubed the dapper attorney's face with cotton balls, which produced a puckering of lines and wrinkles appropriate for an older gentleman.

This was insufficient to fool anyone who had spent more than ten minutes in Ham's presence, so Doc added a pair of glasses with dark lenses.

Donning these, Ham regarded himself in the pocket mirror the bronze man offered.

The artificial wrinkles were still settling in, but the beginnings of the transformation had already commenced.

"Not bad," allowed Ham. "But what shall I call myself?"

"How about Brom Van Bummel?"

"It fits, but what is my nationality?"

"If you read Washington Irving, you would know that. You are Dutch."

Standing up, Ham complained, "My attire will give me away."

"Not necessarily," suggested Doc. "Merely remove your vest and watch, as well as some of the more expensive adornments."

Reluctantly, the dapper lawyer did so, lastly surrendering his damaged sword cane, which he had gripped tightly during the process of transformation.

Doc Savage regarded Ham and suggested, "Perhaps we had better weather your coat to make it look as though you are a down-at-heels refugee, and not a man of means."

Ham made a face. "This is a rather expensive outfit."

"It cannot be helped," said Doc. "But I will let you attend to those details."

The expression on the dapper attorney's face was mixed. He was justifiably proud of his attire, and his reputation as one of the best dressed men in New York, an award he earned annually as a general rule.

Noticing this, Doc asked, "Unless you would rather I rough them up for you?"

Wavering, Ham finally said, "No, I will do it," dispiritedly. Stepping into the washroom, he began to undo seams and rub his sleeves against the steel walls, endeavoring to weather the impeccable fabric. When he was finished, Ham was not so much a sorry sight as a slightly distressed item.

"Do not wear your hat," said Doc.

Ham nodded dejectedly. "I will leave it here with you, along with my cane and other items."

"Why don't you take a turn around the deck and see what you can discover?" suggested Doc. "While you are at it, look in on Monk. Make sure he's abandoned his wild ideas."

"That misbegotten baboon," said Ham harshly, "can no more abandon his wild notions than his pet pig could shed his favorite fleas." With that pronouncement, the no-longer-dapper lawyer took his leave of the stateroom cabin.

HAM went straight away to Monk's cabin, making no effort to be furtive about it. He wanted to be seen because, if his disguise did not stand up to scrutiny, it would be better to know that sooner than later.

With him, he took the key to Monk's cabin, and used it to open the door.

He found his friend sprawled on his too-narrow bunk, flat on his back, gaping mouth wide open, snoring through his flat nose like a movie cartoon character.

The apish chemist seemed dead to the world. Ham had no interest in altering that situation. Once his tiny eyes snapped open, Monk was certain to take out his wrath on the first person he spied. Ham wanted no part of that exchange, especially as he was temporarily bereft of his sword cane.

Shutting the homely chemist in his cabin, Ham began to walk the decks of the great converted liner, searching the faces he encountered.

Many were the features of Merchant Mariners, who crewed the vessel. None of these, of course, were familiar to him.

Then, walking down a companionway with suitably stiffened gait, he happened to spy a casually attired young Merchant Marine who struck Ham as faintly familiar. Puzzled but interested, Ham began following this individual.

The Merchant Mariner was going about the business of tending to the ship, and did nothing outwardly suspicious. Try as he might, Ham could not get a good look at the man, for he was following from behind.

Twice, the disguised attorney overheard other sailors casually refer to the young man as "Boats," which he knew was a common nickname for boatswain. The fellow therefore was the *Northern Star*'s bosun.

So piqued was his curiosity that Ham continued shadowing the fellow long after the light began to fail and no useful purpose would come of it.

Finally, he lost the mariner, who went below into the complicated innards of the ship where passengers could not follow.

There, Ham paused in thoughtful contemplation, searching his memory. But no matter how he cudgeled it, the lawyer could not recall to mind a name to go with that youthful face.

Thwarted, he returned to Doc Savage's cabin, knocked twice, but received no answer.

Now that darkness had arrived, the bronze man had departed. Turning on his heel, Ham went in search of his chief, wondering if he could or would recognize him, however cleverly he was disguised.

His search had an interesting result. Wandering about the after-deck, he spied a hulking Merchant Marine who fit Doc Savage's general proportions. The Marine was a Negro, as dark as they come, with a head of hair that was cropped close rather like the curly back of a buffalo. Atop this thicket perched a greasy oiler's cap.

Assuming he had discovered Doc Savage in disguise, Ham sidled up to the big black Merchant Marine and hissed, "Doc!"

The man turned toward Ham dubiously and asked, "Something I can do for you, bud?" The big black man did not sound anything like Doc Savage.

Ham studied the wide features and for a moment felt confusion course through him.

"I am sorry," he said apologetically, "You resemble a fellow I used to know."

"Well, I don't know *you*."

"In that, we are in full agreement," said Ham, retreating.

Ham walked away, and doubt immediately seized him. Doc Savage was a master of disguise, but his great size and metallic skin placed strict limits on his ability to conceal himself by the usual theatrical methods. One of his tricks was to impersonate a large Negro, which the bronze giant had done several times in the past. He was also an astounding voice mimic.

Ham realized that it was entirely within the power of Doc Savage to transform himself so much that it could fool his close associates, even to altering his vocal expression.

Turning, Ham sized up the big Negro once again. Could Doc have fooled him?

The hulking Negro discovered the genteel but disheveled passenger staring at him, and glowered back.

"Are you looking to cause me trouble?" he demanded.

"No, no," said Ham hastily. "No trouble. No trouble at all."

With that, Ham hurried away. By the time he had returned to his own cabin, the doubt crept in again. Perhaps Doc did not want attention called to himself—and that large fellow was in fact Doc Savage.

Sitting down on his bunk, Ham looked flustered and fidgeted with his hands. He was without his ever-present sword cane, and he still could not make up his mind if the big Negro was Doc Savage. Or was not.

# Chapter IX

# TRANSFORMATION

**D**OC SAVAGE WAS *not* disguised as the hulking Negro. He was, however, trailing that fellow. Doc wore the casual attire of a Merchant Marine seaman, but it was two sizes too small for him. He had darkened his bronze hair and bleached his deeply metallic skin until it was merely tanned. Whitening it was out of the question.

Exhibiting a tigerish stealth, keeping to such shadows as he could attach himself, Doc measured the big Negro. He was taller than the bronze giant by a half inch and outweighed him by perhaps fifteen pounds, but other than that, they were not far apart in general characteristics.

The man's work clothes would fit him, Doc decided.

Stepping out of the shadows, the bronze man accosted the fellow.

"Seaman, come with me."

The big black sailor looked up from what he was doing, glowered and demanded, "I don't recognize you."

"New man. Now come with me."

The Negro was not dumb. He did not recognize this crewman, and neither did Doc outrank him.

"What's up?" he asked.

Doc told him, "Bosun needs a couple of strong backs. You have one, and so do I. Let's go."

Shrugging, the mariner fell in behind Doc Savage, a perplexed but resigned expression on his beefy features.

He accompanied Doc to the latter's private cabin, which Doc unlocked and, stepping aside, waved him in.

"You go first."

Dubious of expression, the seaman ducked his head in order to clear the blackout-curtain-shielded door. The bronze man followed him in, shutting the door firmly after them.

The big man turned. "Hey! What is this?"

Doc Savage had intended to seize the fellow by his thick neck and apply expert pressure on sensitive nerves found there—a specific spot that would produce rapid unconsciousness. It was the same technique by which the bronze giant had earlier overcome Monk Mayfair, but here, the suspicions of the big black had caused him to turn about, and Doc faced a dilemma.

Having no choice in the matter, the bronze man uncorked one bone-hard fist and dropped the man with one punch.

The Negro collapsed on the floor. Doc Savage hoisted him up in his corded arms and laid the fellow out on the bunk, swiftly stripping him of his clothes and replacing them with his own. As a precaution, he injected him with an anesthetic that would keep the seaman sedated for many hours.

Going to the make-up case, Doc opened it. His eyes continually shifting to the sleeping man's features, the bronze man undertook to transform himself into a mirror image of the large fellow.

It took nearly an hour, but at last it was done. A chemical preparation darkened Doc's bronze skin. Optical eye shells did the same for his flake-gold eyes. A suitable wig was affixed to his close-cropped hair, after Doc trimmed it properly to match the man's haircut. There were other touches. Wire loops were carefully inserted to flare Doc's nostrils and he had built up his corded facial features to give them a heavy-featured cast.

The hulking Negro's own mother, conceivably, would have known the difference. But only in very good light and at close proximity. Otherwise Doc Savage was the spitting image of Seaman Jury Goines, A. B.—which was the name on the identification card the bronze man discovered in the fellow's pocket. His rating was Oiler. No doubt Goines spent much of his time below deck, in the engine room, propeller shaft alley and elsewhere, attending to lubrication-thirsty machinery.

Satisfied with his efforts, Doc locked Goines in the stateroom cabin. He would straighten out the matter with the fellow later, along with sincere apologies. But for now, this impersonation was absolutely necessary. For all Doc Savage knew, the lives of every man on this vessel were at stake. He did not know that to a certainty, but neither could he exclude the possibility. And that, for the moment, was a salve to Doc Savage's troubled conscience.

ONCE out on deck, Doc Savage moved about freely. His work uniform of open-necked cotton shirt and blue demins proved to be a little loose but this was a considerable relief after the brief period walking around in a too-tight one. The night air had a salty tang that Doc tasted in his nostrils. The wind moving across the open deck blew steadily. Not hard, but the steadiness was unnerving. Doc recognized it as the type of wind that presaged blows that could turn violent quite suddenly. The bronze man made a thorough reconnoiter of the ship and its many decks. He saluted officers where necessary, then moved briskly on, a determined look on his disguised features.

Doc was searching passing faces for any of the men he had encountered at the Old Sailors Home, should they be aboard. He assumed that they were, but assumptions were chancy propositions. He had seen no sign of any of them thus far. Worse, the bronze giant did not obtain clear glimpses of all the men, but their large-framed leader—the amber-eyed man calling himself Diamond—would be hard to miss with his rugged brown face and smoky-gray pompadour.

Doc went to the dining area, which had been converted into a ship's mess. In years gone by, he had sailed to Europe on the very same vessel, in connection with an adventure that had long ago been crowded into the back of his mind. And in those comparatively carefree days, the dining room was open during set hours, so passengers could dine at their convenience.

Now, with the ship under military rules and regulations, it was no doubt more regimented.

Entering the dining gallery, Doc saw that the formerly ostentatious tables and chairs had been replaced with long barracks-style dining tables. Men were filling these out, and others were jostling one another in the chow line.

As his dark eyes patrolled the room, the bronze man carefully scrutinized faces, seeking those with familiar lines.

He found one in an unexpected spot.

One of the ship's stewards was dishing out corned-beef hash and potatoes, and Doc's ever-watchful orbs fell upon him.

The steward was rather round of face, but not as round as Doc had remembered him. He was also older, and for the slightest pause the bronze man was not quite certain of his identity. Doc drifted into the chow line, picked up a cafeteria-style tray, grabbed a shiny crockery plate out of the stack, along with some utensils. Thus equipped, he worked his way up until he came to the steward in question.

The man's name was stenciled over his right shirt pocket. It said: TUCKER.

It was all the confirmation the bronze man needed. The steward was older and while not slim, he had lost considerable weight since the last time Doc had encountered him.

Seeing the bronze man, the steward gave Doc a broad smile and said, "How are you doing, Oiler?"

For a moment, Doc experienced a mild shock, thinking he had been recognized, but the use of the seaman's nickname erased that fear entirely.

"Doing all right," Doc said in a low voice that mimicked that of Seamen Goines to the best of his ability, which was considerable.

"Better eat this hash while it's still hot," grinned Seaman Tucker. "We are running low tonight."

"Second cook's hash is always good," said Doc, smiling back.

That was the extent of the exchange, and Doc took his tray to a table where he could survey the crew as they ate.

Despite loitering over his meal, he spied no more familiar faces. But the presence of the round-faced steward gave the bronze man an inkling of something. Dropping his dishes into an enameled metal tub and putting the empty tray atop a stack, he departed the dining room, and resumed his methodical search.

This time Doc concentrated his efforts on the faces of the Merchant Marines who crewed the *Northern Star*. They were a varied lot, with more than a few black faces, the Merchant Marine not going in for Jim Crow the way other branches of the service did.

He was not looking for Negro sailors, however.

Seeing Doc passing by, the Chief Engineer accosted him. "Seaman Goines, you are needed down in the engine room. Hop to it."

"Aye-aye, chief," said Doc.

The bronze man started in that direction, then reversed himself. He almost bumped into the Second Mate, who, seeing him seemingly at liberty, gave him yet another order.

"Have you chowed down, Oiler?"

"Yes, sir."

"Then get about your duties. Make it snappy."

By the time the third officer had ordered him to another part of the ship, the bronze man had had enough. Doc found a coil of manila rope, thrust one arm through the opening and lugged it around as if taking the line somewhere important.

Thereafter, he was left strictly alone.

Before much longer, Doc spied another familiar face. This individual was youthful, probably in his early twenties, and looked like a younger edition of Abraham Lincoln, sans the Billy goat chin whiskers.

This lank fellow was busy inspecting the canvas covers on the lifeboats, which hung from their cradles.

Doc sidled up to him, got a good look at the name on his blouse, which rather matched his recollection. Taking a chance, he walked up and asked, "Have you seen any sign of Seaman Worth?"

"Boats?" said the young man who resembled the sixteenth President of the United States. "Not in the last hour."

"Thank you," said Doc, moving on. By this simple ruse, he had ascertained that three of the four were on board. But the one he was most interested in encountering was Seaman Worth.

Given his thorough job of reconnoitering the ship's decks, Doc Savage was likely to locate Worth sooner rather than later, except that he turned a corner and almost collided with a bald fellow.

The man was not entirely bald, for there were fringes on either side of his head, but these were close shaven. In the darkness of night, he might as well have been entirely hairless. He was very muscular, and his skin was brown as a coconut shell, minus the stringy hair. He wore dark glasses.

"Excuse me," said Doc, shifting around the man.

The bald man said nothing, simply pushed forward, evidently having no wish to exchange pleasantries. He was dressed as a civilian, but one who wore the casual attire of a man who had been around boats. His shoes had gum soles, and he walked with a careful and silent tread.

Doc Savage let the man pass on, paused, and then reversed direction. He shadowed the individual to the ship's dining room, and watched him go in.

It would not do to follow him inside since he had already eaten and been recognized as Jury Goines by the steward. Second helpings were probably not frowned upon, but he did not wish to draw attention to himself.

Doc spent the next twenty minutes trying to look busy while he waited for the bald man to reemerge.

Finally, the hairless fellow stepped into view, and took a beeline back in the direction from which he had originally come.

Moving as quietly as possible, Doc shadowed him, staying far behind, until the man came to his cabin on the B deck, port side.

Pausing to take a quick look around before entering, he saw Doc Savage rolling along, the coil of rope heavy over one shoulder, and studied him momentarily before stepping inside.

Doc took note of the cabin number—Twelve-B—and passed on, deciding that he had accomplished as much as he was going to in the guise of Seaman Goines.

The bronze man went directly to Ham Brooks' cabin.

# Chapter X

# CONFUSION

**B**Y THIS TIME, Monk Mayfair had wakened.

His first act was to check the back of his head by feel. The bandage from the bludgeoning he had earlier suffered was still in place. He winced at the sharp pain touching it brought.

There was no other wound, he discovered by gingerly groping around.

Going to the washroom mirror, Monk looked himself over and discovered no bruise or lacerations. That was when he felt a soreness on his neck.

"Doc done this," he said at last. The memory of his last conscious thoughts flooded back. Monk weighed about two hundred and sixty pounds and the unseen person who had arrested his headlong flight had stopped him cold. He had not been struck upon the head, yet he had lost consciousness with almost instantaneous speed.

All that spelled Doc Savage, who apparently had robbed the homely chemist of his natural senses by pressing down on the nerve centers of his virtually non-existent neck and applying surgical pressure.

Monk spent half a minute growling into the mirror, expressing his anger, but the raw emotion soon evaporated. As much as he resented being waylaid, Doc Savage was his chief. He could not remain upset with him for long. Their association was too deep and significant.

"Aw, I'll just take it out on that shyster somehow," he told himself.

Ambling to the door, he expected it to be locked. It was not.

Since it was dark, Monk slipped out, looking both ways before exiting.

It was obviously night, and the ship well underway. Monk had already realized that from the way the cabin had lurched and sank as it rode the heaving waves of the open Atlantic.

Upon reaching the weather deck, Monk noticed the steadily blowing wind and the feel of the ocean.

"Uh-oh," he said to himself. "Storm brewin'."

It was the hairy chemist's notion to seek out Doc and Ham, but he had not progressed very far when he realized that he had no inkling of their cabin numbers. This created a quandary.

Modest brow furrowing, Monk peered about. Had he not been insensate for so long and suffering from a mild concussion before that, the apish chemist would have sooner realized that he was barging about without benefit of a disguise. Not that it was an easy thing to mask his inordinately long forearms and apish outline. Hardly. A circus tent could not conceal his gorilla-like physique.

Monk would have turned around and retreated to his cabin if it were not for his nose.

The homely chemist's nose was a mashed-down thing that might once have projected more forcefully, but it had taken repeated batterings from horny-knuckled fists over the years. It had also been broken several times and pounded flat a time or two, which added to its simian configuration.

Despite all the damage that had been done to his nostrils over an active career, Monk's sense of smell verged on the animalistic. Hesitating on the lower deck, he caught a whiff of a familiar hair oil. It was an expensive brand, one unlikely to be wafting about on the deck of a Merchant Marine ship. Monk knew it well. It was Ham Brooks' favorite hair preparation.

"He's gotta be around close somewheres," muttered Monk.

Following his dilating nostrils, Monk sniffed his way forward, and happened upon a piece of luck that started out being good, but ended up being very bad indeed.

Monk's sense of smell brought him around the corner where he discovered Ham's shoes sitting outside his cabin door.

The dapper lawyer was a creature of habit, and he was accustomed to sending out his shoes for shining when staying in hotels or traveling on ships. The habit died hard with Ham, even in these lean days of wartime shortages, sugar, butter and gas rationing.

There was no possibility of a steward coming by to collect shoes for shining and returning them in the morning. No such amenities were provided aboard the *Northern Star*. No doubt the leaving out of the shoes was an act of absentmindedness on Ham's part.

But there they were.

Bending over, Monk stooped with his entire upper body and picked up the shoes, ascertaining to a certainty that they belonged to Ham Brooks. Inset into the soles was the initial B. Peculiar place for a monogram, but it had a definite purpose. The *B* would leave a mark wherever Ham walked, provided he walked in soil, or even wet pavement. The initial made it easier to track Ham, should he ever go missing.

Monk had a momentary urge to throw the footwear overboard, as a way of getting Ham's goat. But he thought better of it. Another certain sign that Monk wasn't thinking very clearly, for he rarely passed up an opportunity to vex the dapper lawyer.

Straightening, Monk applied rusty knuckles on the steel door and knocked briskly. He rapped two short and one long, which was a signal.

Features alarmed, Ham threw open the door, looked at Monk, noticed his shoes and demanded, "What are you doing with my shoes!"

"You left them out to be shined, didn't you?"

Various expressions paraded across Ham's chiseled features, going from puzzlement to a flustered twitching, and finally settled into red-faced embarrassment.

Since he could hardly deny the lapse in judgment, Ham snapped instead, "Give me those and get in here before you are seen!"

Monk did both, and the door was clapped shut.

"Where's Doc?" asked Monk, looking around.

"I do not know," confessed Ham. "I was just about to pay him a visit, since I have not heard from him since before night-fall."

The formerly elegant attorney was still tricked out in his van Dyke facial adornment, artificial wrinkles and threadbare attire.

Monk asked, "Who are you supposed to be now?"

"Brom Van Bummel, if you must know."

"Well, you didn't fool me."

"You are not the one I am trying to fool. Besides," added Ham archly, "you were born in that low state."

"At least I ain't turned gray from guilt for havin' robbed all those widows and orphans you have sued over the years," retorted Monk.

Ham purpled. He would have whacked the homely chemist over his bullet skull with his sword cane except that the item was not at hand.

Instead, Ham said, "Come with me, you inveterate liar. Doc should have finished his work of searching the ship by now."

HAM led the way, Monk following behind, trying to stay in the shadows of stanchions and gangways. It was hopeless, like putting a full-grown gorilla in a football jersey in the hopes that he would not stand out in a crowd.

For all that, they managed to reach Doc's cabin without encountering any difficulties.

Stopping before the door, Ham rapped two short and one long, which brought no results.

"He must not be back as yet," murmured Ham.

"Risky to sneak back to your cabin," suggested Monk.

"No need. Doc gave me a spare key in the event it was needed," explained Ham, producing said key.

Opening the door, he invited Monk to enter first.

Upon stepping in, the simian chemist found the light switch, snapped it on, and saw the black man lying in the bunk.

"For crying out loud!" he burst out.

Shouldering in behind him, Ham Brooks quickly threw the door shut and laid narrowing eyes on the same figure. The dapper lawyer's mobile mouth made fish shapes as he tried to synchronize his brain with his tongue.

Walking over to the sleeping figure, Monk looked down and saw a very large Negro, who was obviously out cold.

"Who is this swabbie?" demanded Monk.

Ham found his tongue, although it proved shaky in operation.

"I believe that is Doc Savage, but I am not quite certain of it."

Turning, Monk stared at Ham questioningly.

Ham explained, "I encountered this man earlier in the evening, and mistook him for Doc Savage. But he quickly disabused me of that notion."

"So this ain't Doc?"

"Now I am not so certain," admitted Ham, fingering his white-whiskered chin. "If this is not Doc Savage, what is he doing lying in Doc's bunk?"

The two men examined the sleeping figure and Monk prodded the slumberer in the shoulder with a blunt finger. The man did not rouse. "If this is Doc Savage," said Ham, "he's out cold."

"Drugged?"

Monk inserted a hand behind the man's skull, lifted his head, examining by sight and by feel for any sign of a head injury. He found none.

Letting the fellow's head fall back, Monk said, "He hasn't been bopped, that much is sure."

Frowning, Ham opined, "He is large enough to be Doc Savage in disguise."

"Well, if he's Doc, there's only one way to find out, and that's to peel off the stuff he put on his face."

The hairy chemist made a motion to do exactly that, but Ham blocked him, saying, "That elaborate a make-up job took a great deal of time. If you ruin it, Doc will be upset with you."

"But we gotta find out if this is Doc Savage!" pointed out Monk.

While the two were poised to argue the point, there was a knock at the door, followed by a rapid rattle of departing footsteps.

Both men stared at the door as if not certain what to do.

"That's not Doc knocking," stated Ham suspiciously.

"Should we answer it?" wondered Monk.

The answer to that conundrum was not immediately obvious, and the two stared at each other, uncertain what to recommend, as much puzzled by the knocking as they were afraid to make a wrong guess, which would no doubt result in one ribbing the other mercilessly over the upcoming hours.

Finally, Monk went to the door, threw it open, and found a sack sitting outside. He hardly had to stoop to pick it up, so long were his arms, and when Monk brought it into the room, kicking the door behind him, he deposited the thing on the table.

It was an oilskin sack of the waterproof variety sailors use to carry small personal items. Normally such a container would be closed by a drawstring, but this appeared to be sealed by several turns of soft wire, making for a very tight seal.

Monk easily undid the wire and, opening the sack, reached in and withdrew a singular object.

It had the semblance of a human hand, clenched into a tight fist. However, the first and last fingers jutted upward, curled thumb holding down the center digits. The object appeared to be composed of some black substance that might have been obsidian or some similar mineral.

The thing had been fashioned so that the severed wrist served as a base. Monk examined this fist from several angles, as did Ham, but it appeared to be nothing more than an artifact hewn from mineral rock in a way that made it seem weathered and natural.

Its surface texture was very rough, and the more they studied the ebony thing, the less it seemed life-like and more like some freak rock formation that had managed to look like a human hand.

It seemed to have no other significance, so Monk set it down on the table and they returned to the problem of the sleeping Negro who might or might not be Doc Savage.

Having nothing better to do, they resumed their argument.

Frustrated because he had been twice rendered senseless and was now stranded on a Bahama-bound vessel against his will, Monk Mayfair started taking it out on Ham Brooks.

"If you hadn't poked your sharp nose into my personal business," growled Monk, "I would be on on my way to Louisiana right now."

For his part, Ham was more worried about the insensate Negro than he was Monk's mental state, which was entirely of his own doing.

"None of this would have happened had you not fallen for that blonde vixen!" reminded Ham.

The matter of the missing Davey Lee having been raised, Monk changed the argument.

"Well, that was my dang business, and your opinion don't count!" raged Monk.

"Now see here," countered Ham. "The only reason we are on this boat steaming into who-knows-what peril is because certain persons did not want you sailing on the *Northern Star*."

That undeniable fact was brought forcefully back to Monk's consciousness. It stopped the argument cold. The sheer mystery of it caused the chemist's homely features to go rubbery.

"What is this all about?" he wondered.

"Let us hope that Doc Savage is even now discovering some clue that will point us toward sensible answers," said Ham.

The force of their argument having been spent, they returned their attention to the sleeping Negro whose identity they did not yet know.

Ham began studying the man's shirt, which bore his last name, which was Grant. He tried to remember if he had noticed that name on the shirt before, but he had not.

The name meant nothing to him, one way or the other. It might very well be an alias for Doc Savage.

While they were pondering the matter, Monk abruptly sat down on a wooden chair, which immediately collapsed under his sudden weight, leaving him sitting stupidly in a pile of kindling.

"What have you done now?" demanded Ham.

"I don't know," admitted Monk. "But suddenly I felt like sittin' down."

The dapper lawyer noticed that Monk's features showed a trace of paleness.

"Let me get you a glass of water," he suggested, ducking into the washroom.

"Good idea," said Monk thickly. He passed a hairy hand over his head and commenced looking befuddled in a dull way.

But once Ham began filling the glass, the disguised attorney suddenly felt lightheaded and drank the water himself.

Without finishing the glass, he filled a second one for Monk and brought them both out.

"What took you so long?" demanded Monk belligerently.

"I suddenly felt rather lightheaded," said Ham.

"I kinda feel that way myself."

Ham noticed that Monk had not bothered to pick himself up off the floor.

In order to hand the hairy chemist the full glass of water, the pale lawyer had to bend over deeply.

While he was doing that, he suddenly decided to sit down himself.

Monk accepted the glass with both hairy hands, and both men drank greedily, emptying their drinking vessels.

Ham looked toward Monk and asked, "Do you feel better now?"

Monk shook his head woodenly, saying, "No, I don't."

"Well, neither do I," declared Ham.

Both men regarded one another with slightly dulling expressions, whereupon they seemed to melt, losing their grips on their glasses, their heads wavering and wobbling on their shoulders, until they had essentially collapsed into two human piles.

Now three men lay in the cabin, unmoving.

The strange black rock in the shape of a human fist continued to squat on a table, reflecting light, gleaming wickedly in the silence of the cabin where only the regular breathing of three insensate men disturbed the atmosphere.

# Chapter XI

# MYSTERY IN IRON

**D**OC SAVAGE WENT to Ham Brooks' cabin, knocked twice, then once, but received no response.

Employing an extra key, the bronze man let himself into the cabin, and switched on the light. The stateroom proved to be untenanted.

Exiting quietly, Doc made his way to Monk's cabin and discovered the hairy chemist was also absent. For a brief second a piece of sound escaped his lips.

This was the nature of a trilling, a sound the bronze giant made reflexively whenever he was perturbed in some way, great or small. It was an unconscious habit he had picked up in his wandering youth, somewhere in the Orient, and in recent months he had endeavored to shake the quirk for good. Doc Savage had not quite succeeded, hence the soft trilling—just a few fragments of unbroken melody that soon trailed off.

Reasoning that Monk and Ham may have gone off in search for him, Doc went next to his own cabin. The staterooms were all situated sufficiently far apart to minimize the chances that the three men might be spotted coming and going, or moving around the ship as a group. It was an excellent precaution for those reasons, and a damned inconvenience for keeping tabs on one another.

Doc went to his own cabin, and let himself in.

The light was on, and the bronze man's dark disguised eyes took in the situation at a glance.

Monk and Ham were distributed about the floor; the Negro sailor named Jury Goines still lay supine in Doc Savage's bunk.

Doc's appraising glance noted only one other oddity. On a table next to an open sack reposed a fragment of black rock that resembled a human fist with two upraised digits, the outer ones. The dark thumb curled over the folded middle fingers, holding them down in a strange salute.

The bronze man had never seen the article before.

First, he knelt and examined Monk, followed by Ham, and found them more groggy than unconscious.

"Monk! Ham!" he said, shaking them.

The two men produced sounds that were combinations of a moan and a groan. The noises they emitted were extremely weak, almost kittenish.

The only other thing the bronze man noted was that the pores of their faces stood out rather coarsely, as if they had somehow dilated.

This did not make any sense, for this was not a condition that the bronze man recognized, and he was versed in all things medical, having been educated as a physician in the finest teaching hospitals. Hence his nickname.

Doc went next to the fist sitting on the table, and picked it up.

Almost as soon as he did so, the bronze giant felt slightly strange. The sensation was curious, almost inexplicable. The clenched hand appeared to be made out of some form of volcanic rock, possibly basalt. It was difficult to say because it was extremely weathered.

Doc examined the thing. Turning it in his hand, he noted with slightly widening eyes the fact that the pores on his fine-textured skin, normally invisible, were becoming apparent.

Hastily, the bronze man set down the weird fist and backed away. Again, his eerie trilling piped up, but was quickly stifled. It possessed a peculiar timbre, as if puzzlement and worry were mingled in its melodious musical bars.

Doc noted the oilskin pouch with its loose wire fastener and reasoned that the rock fist had originally reposed within it. Advancing, the bronze man swept up the artifact, dropped it inside the sack and rewound the wire as tightly closed as possible.

After he had finished, Doc Savage took stock of himself.

A vague fatigue had stolen over his mighty frame, and Doc went into the bathroom to a draw a glass of water, which he quickly imbibed. He had not felt thirsty, only fatigued. A lifetime of daily exercise, not to mention a strenuous existence, had all but banished ordinary fatigue from the bronze man's magnificent physique. Yet weakness had stolen into his system somehow.

Putting down the empty glass, Doc returned to the cabin, and began performing manipulations on Monk and Ham in an effort to revive them. Nothing seemed to work. They continued to make utterances that were dull and slow and virtually worthless, so far as comprehension went.

Doc went next to Seaman Goines and found that his pores, which were coarser than those of the others, were also unnaturally dilated. Thinking that perhaps this was an indication of some strange dehydration, Doc pried open Goines' jaw, and examined his mouth.

The man's tongue and teeth and gums did not appear to be dry. That left out dehydration, and brought a flicker of bafflement to the bronze man's normally stoic metal features.

A check of Monk and Ham's mouths showed also that they were not dehydrated. Doc pinched flesh at the back of their hands, and released them. The skin snapped back with natural elasticity, further disproving the bronze man's dehydration hypothesis.

While Doc Savage was puzzling over the matter, there came a peremptory rap on the door.

Doc hesitated. He did not know if he had been spotted entering the cabin in the guise of Seaman Goines. Had he, Doc could not very well decline to answer the door, lest he raise an alarm. Neither could he open it to crew inspection, given the awkwardness of the two men lying on the floor, not to mention the extra seaman sprawled on the bunk.

While he was considering what to do, the knock returned, more strongly this time, and a voice barked, "Open up! I saw you go in there!"

That left Doc Savage no alternative but to answer the door.

Moving to it, he crowded up against the steel panel, and opened the panel only a crack.

"What is it?" he asked in a voice that was neither his own nor that of Jury Goines.

A serious-faced seaman whose uniform displayed the crossed anchors of a Merchant Marine boatswain's mate met the frank challenge of his gaze and demanded, "What are you doing in that cabin?"

Doc's dark eyes went to the name stenciled over the man's blue shirt pocket and he flung open the door, looked both ways to see if the sailor was alone, then hauled him in by main strength, kicking the door shut.

"HEY! What's the idea?" demanded the astonished Merchant Marine.

He struggled in Doc's two-handed grip. For a youth, he appeared sturdily strong. But his knotted muscles were no match for the metallic might of the Man of Bronze.

Doc Savage made his voice low, and said, "If you will settle down, I will be happy to explain everything, Seaman Worth."

The words were in the distinctive tone that could belong to only one man, Doc Savage.

Seaman Worth evidently recognized those tones, for he subsided and looked up at the bronze man's dark face with wondering gaze.

"You—you—what I mean is—you don't sound like Oiler Goines!"

"Goines is laying on that bunk, if you will turn your gaze in that direction," suggested Doc.

Seaman Worth obliged, and his intelligent eyes went extremely wide. He looked up at Doc Savage towering over him, and then back at Jury Goines. For a short eternity of seconds, his mouth worked without producing any words.

Removing one of his tinted eye shells to reveal the striking flake-gold of his iris, Doc said quietly, "I am Doc Savage, Donald."

Seaman Donald Worth stabbed slightly-bugging eyes all around the cabin, and his gaze fell upon Monk and Ham sprawled on the floor.

"That's Monk and Ham!" he said wondering. "What happened to them?"

"That is exactly what I've been attempting to learn," replied Doc, replacing the glass shell. "I have just discovered them in that condition."

Seaman Donald Worth seemed to have lost all energy to struggle, so Doc released him.

"Are they out cold?" he asked.

"No, they are still conscious, although extremely depleted. But I do not know why," supplied Doc.

Seaman Worth went over to Monk and Ham, and immediately asked, "Why are their pores wide open?"

Which showed how perceptive Seaman Worth was, not that the intelligent cast of his face suggested otherwise. He seemed to be a sharp lad. He would have to be to have achieved the rank of boatswain at such a young age.

Doc said, "They do not appear to have been attacked, yet they are out of action." Changing the subject, the bronze man asked, "I have already encountered Seaman Tucker and one other of your group. Is every one of your old crowd on board?"

Donald Worth nodded. "All four of us. This is our ship. We signed up for the Merchant Marines before Pearl Harbor, figuring it would enable us to be useful faster than any other way. We sort of saw what was coming."

Doc nodded as if he would have expected no less of Seaman Worth and his friends.

For the first time, Don Worth smiled broadly and said, "It has been a long time, Doc."

"A number of years," Doc agreed. "I have always wondered how you fellows were getting along."

"You know us," shrugged Worth. "We were always actively trying to better ourselves, although in different ways. We meant to stay in touch longer than we did, but that's life. Then came the war in Europe. It was not hard to see that America would have to take a stand." Suddenly, a slightly reflective look leapt into Donald's intelligent eyes and he asked, "What are you doing on this ship?"

Swiftly, Doc filled in the young man, beginning with the attempt to lure Monk Mayfair away from boarding the *North-ern Star*. He described the man known as Diamond in great detail, emphasizing his hair, burly build and feline eyes the color of amber.

Don nodded. "We are carrying passengers, but most are foreign sailors being returned to their homeland. The man you describe with this hair like cigarette smoke is not one I recall noticing."

"Nevertheless, he is on board. I spotted him earlier. But now he is bald. The smoky hair looked artificial, suggesting a wig. I do not know what his game is, nor what he intends. Only that it must be some form of mischief. Of that, there is no doubt."

Seaman Worth nodded gravely. Eyeing Monk and Ham, he asked, "Shouldn't we be trying to wake them up?"

Doc stated, "I am reluctant to inject them with any stimulant, inasmuch as I do not know what constitutes their ailment."

"But you can't just leave them there. For that matter, Oiler Goines is going to be missed before long."

"It is—or was—my intention to impersonate Seaman Goines for the next day or so."

"Risky," commented Worth.

Doc Savage ignored that cautionary remark, and returned to examining Monk and Ham.

"How about giving them water?" suggested Worth.

"The empty glasses strewn about suggest that they were drinking water when they were overcome. I am not sure water would help, but I am at a loss to explain their condition."

The bronze man went to a black bag that rather resembled a doctor's satchel, such as would be used by a physician making house calls. It was far more elaborately equipped than that, and Doc began preparing two syringes to draw blood from his men.

This took several minutes. Then Doc extracted a black tube resembling a mechanical pencil from a pocket. By telescoping its segments and outwardly manipulating its component parts, he converted it into a very simple microscope.

Doc squirted out a small quantity of serum blood on the porcelain sink top, and applied the microscope lens to both samples. He did not seem to understand what he was perceiving, but then went to a small trunk, which he opened, and which proved to be an extremely complex chemical laboratory.

Extracting items from this, Doc fell to analyzing the blood in a number of ways that were simple but comprehensive. At the end of it, he seemed slightly dumbstruck, but that might have been a combination of his ordinarily impassive features lurking beneath the disguise of Seaman Goines.

"What is it?" asked Worth, recognizing that the bronze man had arrived at some determination.

"Both blood samples are identical in one respect," Doc said. "These men are showing an extreme lack of iron in the blood."

"Well, that doesn't sound like Monk and Ham," mused Seaman Worth. "They're pretty hearty eaters, the both of them."

Taking up another syringe, Doc drew a sample of his own blood, and gave it a similar analysis.

Donald Worth observed this operation in absorbed silence.

When Doc was finished testing his own blood, he announced, "I am showing the slightest symptoms of the same condition or ailment that has overcome Monk and Ham."

"What does that mean?" asked the other.

The bronze man's steady gaze went to the oilskin pouch and he said, "When I found them, the object currently resting within that waterproof sack was sitting open on the table. After I picked it up, I began to feel strange."

"Strange in what way?" asked Seaman Worth.

"It felt as if I were losing vitality," said Doc slowly.

"What's in the bag?" asked Worth.

"Merely a rock carved into the shape of a human fist, or possibly naturally formed that way."

"Mere rock wouldn't do that, would it?"

Doc Savage looked at the hand he had used to pick up the rock artifact and saw that the coarse open pores had somewhat contracted back to their normal appearance.

Instead of answering directly, the bronze man said, "It does not make sense that anything, no matter what it is composed of, could draw the mineral iron out of a human being through his pores, but that appears to be what has happened."

Seaman Worth thought about this for a few moments then asked, "What can be done for them?"

"Can you lay hands on some iron pills or, better yet, a raw steak?" asked Doc.

"Steak is kind of hard to come by; it's reserved for officers. But I know where we can get some iron pills."

"Bring them here as quickly as possible," requested the bronze man.

"I'll be back in a flash," said Seaman Worth, slipping out the curtain-muffled door so that the bizarre sight of two identical Negros and two other men lying on the floor would not be seen by a chance passerby.

After the door banged shut, Doc Savage reflected upon the unusual circumstances that brought him back into contact with Don Worth, whom he had encountered during the course of an adventure several years back in which the young man, then a teenager—along with his three friends—had become embroiled in a bizarre criminal scheme, in which Don's father was an early victim.*

The bronze man had liked the four boys, as they were good-natured and industrious as American youth are inclined to be, and they had stayed in communication by letter. Over time, they had fallen out of regular contact.

Now it appeared that fate had thrown them together again. Examining Monk and Ham with his dark eyes, Doc Savage began to feel as if it was a very provident fate, for he may need extra help if he was to unravel the mystery of Diamond and his presence aboard the *Northern Star*.

Beginning with the question of how the uncanny fist of stone came to be in the cabin in the first place.

---

\* *The Gold Ogre.*

# Chapter XII

# REUNION

**B**OATSWAIN DONALD WORTH hurried to the ship's dispensary, and accosted a slender young Merchant Marine whose shirt pocket bore the name of DEXTER.

At sight of Worth, Seaman Dexter began talking excitedly. His eyes snapped with every syllable, all but throwing off sparks, as if electrically charged.

"What brings you here, Don?" Without waiting for reply, Seaman Dexter went on rapidly, "I've been thinking of this nifty idea all day long. When we reach Europe, what do you say we—?"

Serious-faced Donald Worth cut him off at the pass. "Don't get excited, Dex, but Doc Savage is on board."

"Doc Savage!" blurted the excitable Dexter. His full name was B. Elmer Dexter, and he was one of the quartet who had been friends with Donald Worth seemingly forever, but in actuality since they were pups.

"Quiet!" hushed Worth. "I told you not to get excited. Doc is on board with Monk and Ham. Doc is pursuing a mystery, but Monk and Ham are in trouble. They need all the iron tablets you can muster up."

"What do you mean by all? There's a ton of them in the stores. I can't take every one!"

"Well, I don't actually know how much they're going to need, but hand me a couple of bottles to start with."

B. Elmer Dexter went into a back room, rummaged around several medicine cabinets and came back with three bottles, quipping, "One for luck."

"Thanks," said Don. "Have you seen any sign of Mental?"

"You mean Seaman Byron? He's trying to shake that nickname, the same as Funny."

In more innocent days, Morris Byron had been known as "Mental" because he was a thinker and a dreamer. Funny was a ship's steward who was born Leander Tucker and who was also trying to unburden himself of his youthful predilection for juvenile humor, which naturally led to the nickname of "Funny."

"I know that," snapped Don Worth patiently. "But where is he?"

"I think he goes off duty about now."

"Go round him up. And find Funny, too."

"You mean Tuck," corrected B. Elmer Dexter.

"Just round them up and meet me at cabin Six-A," said Seaman Worth, rushing out of the ship's dispensary with all speed.

B. Elmer Dexter was not off duty as yet, but with the prospect of Doc Savage on board and, as excited as he was, he was not at all about to let a minor matter such as ship's discipline trip him up. Face eager, he charged out of the dispensary, and raced over to the dining room.

He had a little bit of luck, for on his way to hunt down Leander Tucker—whom Doc Savage had earlier recognized in the ship's mess—he happened upon Morris Byron, who was chewing the fat with Tucker.

Drifting up to them, trying to contain his excitement, Dex hissed, "Hoist anchor and follow in my wake. Both of you."

Morris Byron acquired an interested look on his rugged face. This was the individual whom Doc Savage had earlier spoken to, having recognized him from his rugged, Lincolnesque features.

"What's up?" he asked placidly.

"It's not what's up, but who's on board?"

"Who?" burst out Seamen Tucker and Byron so close together they sounded like a pair of calling owls.

"His initials are Doc Savage."

That got the attention of the two young Merchant Marines, and they followed B. Elmer Dexter out of the dining hall and into the ship's cramped corridors.

Making their way to cabin Six-A, they both barely contained their excitement.

Don Worth let the trio in, and said, "Be prepared for a shock."

It was good advice, but it didn't quite take. The three young men were too excited to hear the words so that their brains fully understood them.

When they beheld a man they recognized as Seaman Jury Goines administering to another man they also recognized as Oiler Goines—who was lying on the bunk—their jaws seemed to lose all self-control, for they dropped like marionettes whose strings had been cut.

"What in blue blazes?" blurted B. Elmer Dexter.

Don advised, "The one standing is Doc Savage. You know the other one. That's Monk and Ham lying on the floor. Doc and I just fed them more iron pills than should have been necessary."

"Why do they need so much iron all of a sudden?" wondered Morris Byron.

"Because somehow the iron in their blood got sucked out of their bloodstreams," answered Worth.

Three young Merchant Mariners chewed on that morsel for a moment and the expressions on their faces registered bafflement.

Doc Savage turned and smiled a smile that would not have fit the face of Seaman Goines even though he wore that identical visage. In revealing his teeth, he showed clearly that he was not Goines. Goines had bad teeth. The bronze man hadn't been able to do much about that except stain his front teeth, keeping his mouth closed as much as possible.

"How are you men doing?" asked Doc.

The trio beamed, for even though they had successfully joined the Merchant Marines, the last time they had encountered the bronze miracle man they had been mere boys. The acknowledgement signified that they were now seen as adults by their idol. This meant something to them. Their chests practically puffed out.

They babbled answers, and the words collided, entangling in the close air of the stateroom cabin.

Finally, Seaman Byron exclaimed, "I know it's August, but it sounds like the Fourth of July in here!"

Doc addressed them. "With Monk and Ham temporarily out of action, I have use for your eyes and ears—and perhaps more if the going gets difficult."

The trio all but saluted. Then Don Worth inserted a sober note.

"Let no one forget who is in command of this ship, or what our duties and responsibilities are."

The three men assumed serious expressions and Dex said, "Nothing says we can't do double duty."

"Exactly," said Doc Savage. "But bear in mind that I have the full cooperation of the captain of the ship."

Seaman Tucker asked, "Does he know you're tricked out to look like Seaman Goines?"

Doc Savage shook his head. "He does not, Funny."

Seaman Tucker frowned, saying, "I don't go by that name anymore. But you can call me Tuck."

"Very well then, Tuck," said Doc. "I have not apprised your skipper of my imposture. It is necessary for me to conduct a search of the passengers without anyone knowing who I am."

Morris Byron said hastily, "Our lips are sealed, Mr. Savage."

"Thank you," said Doc. "On this ship is a man of about fifty years of age who is almost entirely bald. You will also recognize him by his amber eyes. This is the individual I encountered on land under the name of Diamond. He appears to be the leader of a group of men who were up to no good."

"What do you want us to do about him?" asked Leander Tucker.

"Keep a close eye on him, all of you. But give special attention to anyone with whom he is seen associating. I suspect his gang are also on board. I do not know all of them by sight. But I have seen the passenger list and the names of many of these men sound ersatz."

"We'll get right on it," said Don Worth. "Is there anything else we can do for Monk and Ham?"

Doc shook his head. "Not at the moment. I will remain here to monitor their condition. If you men see or hear anything unusual or suspicious, tell it to me before you report to the captain."

Donald Worth hesitated. "That's highly irregular, if not out of order," he suggested. The expression on the young Merchant Marine's face wavered between a kind of worshipful devotion to Doc Savage and a grim resolve to do his sworn duty.

"Nothing significant will be withheld from your captain," promised Doc, "but the utmost secrecy is necessary until the plans of Diamond and his men are brought to light."

This made sense so Bosun Worth said, "All right. But if circumstances change, I'm afraid I will have to go straight to the Old Man."

"I would expect nothing less of you men," said Doc Savage. "But we understand one another?"

"We do," came a chorus of voices. Seaman Tucker started to salute, but B. Elmer Dexter slapped his hand down.

"Only salute officers," he snapped.

"Sorry, I just got excited, is all."

With that, the quartet left the cabin, one by one, taking their time with it so as not to draw attention if they were seen leaving a private cabin where they had no business.

ONCE outside, they dispersed and began moving about the ship, eyes hunting and straining, looking for anything unusual or out of place, paying particular attention to the few souls on board who were not wearing seaman duds.

It was a big ship, and there were plenty of crew, so many that the four young men did not know everyone by name or sight. But they knew which cabins were occupied by passengers, and so onto those decks they made their way singly, acting as if they were going about their normal routine, but in actuality watching for anyone who might be aboard as passengers.

Leander Tucker happened to come across the balding passenger whom Doc Savage had indicated, was the man known as Diamond. He was at the stern, leaning over the stern rail, thoughtfully smoking a cigarette in flagrant violation of wartime blackout restrictions. At least he had the good sense to hold the coffin nail cupped in both hands in order to conceal its glowing tip.

Tucker went to the rail, and took a stance several yards from the other man, where he pretended to be watching the moonlight on the whitecaps of the Atlantic Ocean.

From time to time, Seaman Tucker glanced at the man. He looked rangy and strong and very serious of purpose, even though he was only smoking a cigarette.

There must be something to the idea of a sixth sense, because the individual calling himself Diamond seemed to possess a pair of eyes at the back of his head that gave away the game. Suddenly, he tossed his cigarette into the heaving sea, and departed the deck, all the time eyeing Leander Tucker coldly.

Tuck waited what he thought was an appropriate interval, then started to trail Diamond. It truly was not the most adroit shadowing aboard ship. In fact, it was rather clumsy, for Tucker had in his youth formerly been on the chubby side. But through discipline and a sound diet, he had managed to shed a great many of his adipose pounds.

This was a relatively recent development and Tuck was not yet fully accustomed to his less round shipshape body, and so his feet tangled from time to time as he slipped down a companionway stair.

This alerted Diamond, who ducked around a corner, stood in place and waited in ambush.

When Seaman Tucker bustled around the same corner, he did so hesitantly poking his head around, hoping to spy Diamond several paces ahead.

Instead, the rangy fellow suddenly came up on him and demanded, "Are you following me, sailor?"

"Who—me?" blurted Leander Tucker. "No. I'm just taking my evening constitutional. I've been losing weight." He patted his stomach, which was hardly flat, but much improved from its former rotund configuration.

"If you don't find another direction in which to perambulate, tubby," warned Diamond, "I'm going to report you to your First Mate. Get me?"

The gravelly tone of the man was more than threatening. And so Seaman Tucker said, "I'm sorry, sir. You're mistaken, but let me apologize for that false impression. I will be on my way now."

"You do that," growled the other.

With that, Seaman Tucker slipped away, the amber eyes of Diamond boring into his back.

Rushing about the ship, Tuck found Bosun Worth in the middle of his own reconnoiter.

"I have good news and then I have not so very good news," he panted.

Donald Worth eyed his friend of long-standing and sighed once. "Out with it."

"I found the bald guy, Diamond. He was smoking at the after rail. I watched him for a while. Got a good look at him."

"Get to the bad news," suggested Worth.

"After he got done smoking, I followed him for a while, but when I popped around the corner, he popped back."

"Popped?" wondered Don.

"Accused me of following him, which I naturally denied. Threatened to report me to the First Mate if I didn't cut it out."

"In other words, he knows you suspect him of something?"

Tuck shook his head violently. "In other words, he's the suspicious sort. I don't know what he suspects or does not suspect. But he's a mean cuss, if you want my opinion."

"I sincerely hope," said Don Worth, "that you didn't stir up a hornet's nest before the hornets were set to fly."

Tuck's face fell. "Should we tell Doc Savage what just happened?"

"That's your job, considering that you aroused the boss hornet. I'm going to stay on watch. Let Doc know right now. Understand?"

"On my way," said Leander Tucker, and the expression on his face was that of a boy facing the prospect of being taken out to the woodshed. But Tuck was no longer a young lad. He was a grown man in the Merchant Marines. So he took himself to the woodshed on his own initiative, hoping in his pounding heart that Doc Savage remained the understanding man he once knew him to be.

# Chapter XIII

# FAST ONE

**T**HE MAN WHO was known as Diamond rushed past the door of his cabin, going directly to another cabin door instead. His dark face was grave as granite.

"Open up!" he demanded.

A muffled voice inside snapped back, "Hold your damn horses!"

"My damn horses are about to bolt in all directions," retorted Diamond hotly.

The cabin door was flung open and an annoyed face showed itself around the blackout curtain. It was a weather-beaten countenance that looked like it had seen too much of the elements. Whatever color hair he had been born with, strong sunlight had bleached it to the hue of old straw. This gave the man a sailorly look.

"What is it?" he demanded. "I had turned in for the night."

"Well, now you're being turned out. Collect your things, Cannon. We're swapping cabins."

"What for?" asked the sailorly man, alarm coming into his sleepy eyes.

"Some nosy-nosy seaman has been shadowing me. That's what's for. Now, hop to it!"

Cannon began assembling his gear, while Diamond closed the door behind him.

"But what does the sailor look like?" asked the awakened one.

"A little tub of guts who looks like he used to be a big fat tub of guts. Round face, kind of on the mama's boy side."

"What's his interest in you?"

"Damned if I know," bit out Diamond, amber eyes narrowing. "But let's not take any chances. If he was shadowing me, he probably knows my cabin number. You're going to throw him off the scent. We went to a lot of trouble to arrange things, and no one's going to get in our way."

"It doesn't make sense, someone shadowing you. No one knows who we really are."

"That's what you think. Earlier, a big black sailor seemed to be trailing me, too."

"Well, it *is* wartime. And we're supposed to be foreign sailors headin' home. The crew may not exactly trust us."

"Earlier, I spied another guy I didn't like."

Cannon was throwing items in a duffel bag, and asked, "What didn't you like about him?"

"He was a passenger, like us, but not one of our crowd. White-haired. Van Dyke beard. Looked rumpled and worn around the edges."

"So?"

"So I didn't like his looks. He seemed to be sneaking around. We can't take chances, so I left a little present at his door."

Cannon looked up. "What kind of present?"

"You might say I left the devil's horns on his doorstep."

The other's eyes flared up. "You didn't? Did you, Diamond?"

"I damn sure did, brother."

"What if the guy up and dies?"

Diamond shrugged elaborately. "So he up and dies. They wrap them in canvas, slap 'em on a plank, and slide the whole works over the rail. Burial at sea. It's done all the time. So what?"

"How are you going to get the damn thing back?"

"Don't worry. I'll get it back. It might prove *handy*." He chuckled ghoulishly at his own pun.

"What if Naval Intelligence is on to us?"

"It's not Naval Intelligence I'm worried about," Diamond said slowly. "It's Doc Savage. We stirred up a lot of attention back in the big city."

"Yeah," admitted Cannon. "The plan backfired. But we got aboard, all right, didn't we? And there's been no sign of that human gorilla, Monk."

Diamond pondered this a moment. "If Doc Savage is on board this vessel," he said slowly, "he would keep that Monk under wraps. Savage would lie low, too. He'd have crew or passengers do his dirty work for him."

"If Doc Savage is skulking about," Cannon murmured, "All bets are off."

From a pocket, Diamond removed a marlin spike, a vicious steel fang used to work knots. It gleamed in the weak cabin light. He eyed it appreciatively.

"Savage has guts, all right. And I got just the thing for a guy with guts."

Diamond made a sudden move, as if to insert the gleaming spike into a man. Pulling it back, he made the tool disappear into his pocket so fast it looked like a magician doing a vanish.

Passenger Cannon finished packing up and said, "Give me your key. Are you going to come along and grab your gear?"

"No. Turn in. I may come knocking in the middle of the night and you can hand that stuff out to me. But I want everything to settle down. We got to keep things on the quiet until we clear Nassau. Then it will be our show the rest of the way."

"But—what about the blow the crew says is comin'?"

"If it comes, brother, we'll just add it to the mix. That's all. Maybe it will help us. Could be it will hinder us. Since we can't control the weather, we're just going to have to steer into it or around it or whatever it is we can do. But we're going to do it. Understood?"

The sailor hung the bag over his shoulder and said, "Loud and clear, Diamond. See you at first light."

Diamond opened the door for the man and shut it behind him, then threw himself onto the bunk, staring at the white ceiling, his rangy brown face tight and determined.

He did not look or act like a man prepared to go to sleep, nor did he. Diamond just stared at the ceiling thinking and scheming.

# Chapter XIV

# WHISPERS

LEANDER TUCKER—FORMERLY KNOWN as "Funny"—knocked timidly on Doc Savage's cabin door. Too timidly, as it turned out, since there was no immediate response.

Setting his pudgy knuckles to rap against the steel more determinedly, he repeated the knock and finally got a reaction.

"Who is it?"

"Tuck! I mean—Seaman Tucker reporting."

Doc Savage let the young man in.

"What is wrong?" he asked.

In a violent rush, Leander Tucker blurted out his misadventure shadowing Diamond, sparing no detail. When he finished his recital, he hung his head in sorrow, as if awaiting a thorough dressing down.

Instead, Doc Savage stated quietly, "It probably could not be helped. I ran into the same man earlier and he seemed suspicious of me as well."

Letting out a sigh of relief, Tuck changed the subject hastily. "How are Monk and Ham coming along?"

Doc said slowly, "I do not know what to expect, since this condition of extreme iron deficiency is new to my experience. I expect they will have to sleep it off."

Leander looked down at Monk and Ham, who had been laid out in more comfortable positions, with pillows tucked under their heads, and asked, "Too bad we can't get them into bunks."

"We cannot move them without being seen," stated Doc. "It is altogether too crowded in here, what with Seaman Goines sleeping off a dose of sedative as well."

Tuck sighed again, and a helpless look settled over his roundish features.

"Things have gotten terribly complicated awful fast," he agreed.

Doc Savage said, "Since Diamond thinks he is being watched, perhaps amplifying that sensation will produce some kind of helpful result."

"What kind of result do you have in mind?" asked Seaman Tucker.

"While we don't want to provoke him, it would be desirable to dissuade him from any mischief, at least for the foreseeable future. Perhaps I will pay him a call."

Tuck quivered all over. "Is that wise?"

"I do not honestly know," admitted Doc Savage. "But I do know that a watched man is either going to uncoil like a spring or draw himself in more tightly, also in the fashion of a spring. Either action is better than waiting to see what he will do unprovoked. Keep an eye on everyone until my return."

"Good luck!" called Seaman Tucker as the bronze man carefully eased through the door.

Doc went directly to the cabin inhabited by the mystery man called Diamond, and loitered outside for a time. He had taken from his black satchel a physician's stethoscope, and, placing the earpieces in his ears, applied the diaphragm portion to the steel panel.

The door was thick, but he managed to detect an intermittent sound that made him think of a man snoring in his sleep.

On the theory that an individual rudely awoken from sleep will be off guard and more easily managed, Doc Savage pocketed the stethoscope and pounded on the door with great force.

"Open up!" he called loudly.

"I'm coming! I'm coming! What is it now?" the sleeper demanded as he flung open the door.

From the expression on his weathered face, he evidently expected a different caller, for when he saw the dark features of Seaman Goines, he almost jumped out of his skin.

"What do you want?" he asked, flustered. "I was sound asleep."

"Sorry," said Doc Savage in a thicker voice than his normal resonant tone. "I must have gotten the wrong cabin. You're not the party I was looking for."

The man was sleepy, and therefore caught off guard. He asked what was under the circumstances a stupid question. "Who are you looking for?"

"Bald fellow, about fifty. Know him?"

The passenger blinked several times before answering and saying, "No, no, but I think I seen him around."

"Well," said Doc in a serious tone, "if you see him around, tell him I'm looking for him."

Sleep still in his voice and eyes, the passenger asked, "What for?"

"What business is it of yours?" demanded Doc Savage.

"None, I guess. Forget I asked. Good night." And the door was slammed in Doc Savage's face.

THE BRONZE man retreated up the corridor a safe distance. He turned around. Pressing his back to a bulkhead, he waited for the door to open again.

It did. By this time Doc Savage had out his trick optical instrument which he had again rigged as a periscope, employing this to observe the man entirely unseen.

The passenger sidled down the corridor. Doc Savage followed him at a reasonable distance, pausing at each turn to use his periscope before rounding the corner.

In this fashion, he trailed the nervous man to a cabin where he knocked on the door and had a brief but heated exchange through the steel panel before he was allowed inside.

All that Doc could hear distinctly was that man identifed himself as Cannon. The bronze man recalled that a Joe Cannon was listed among the passengers. The name might or might not be an alias in this instance.

Creeping up to the door, Doc Savage applied the stethoscope bell, and heard fragments of an argument. The blacked-out porthole prevented him from being seen.

"A big black bruiser of a sailor," the nervous passenger was saying. "He pounded on my door, askin' for you."

"By name?" asked Diamond, suspicion threading his voice.

"No. He just called you the bald guy. Pegged your age at about fifty."

"Must be the same sailor I ran into a while back. But what did he want?"

"That's what I tried to get out of him. But he wasn't talkin'. Said it wasn't any of my damn business."

"Something is in the wind," Diamond said with grinding fierceness. "It isn't good. People are watching me, but no one is challenging my right to be on this overgrown scow. I think it was a mighty smart idea changing cabins."

"What are you gonna do about this?" demanded Cannon.

"Nobody knows I'm in this cabin," countered Diamond. "So I'm gonna stay here. You'll bring me my meals. But get back to your berth. I need to think about this. I wasn't planning on getting any sleep, and now I'm damn sure of it. Now get out of here!"

"Should I relay any of this to the others?"

"Tell Weedy, but only him. No sense making the others nervous. They got enough on their minds. Now get out."

Doc Savage retreated out of sight, and moved back until he could reach his own cabin.

Once inside, he told Seaman Tucker, "It looks as if whatever they're planning isn't going to come off tonight. So we have time to watch them and learn more."

"This can't be good," said Tucker.

Doc nodded soberly. "Rest assured, it is not. We are going to be running across the Atlantic to rendezvous with a convoy. These men are up to no good. The only question is: what are their intentions?"

Tuck shrugged elaborately, as if to say that he had no idea either.

Doc directed, "Find the others. Let them know what we now know. Tell them to turn in for the night. We will start fresh in the morning."

A relieved look on his rounded face, Seaman Tucker again resisted an instinct to salute the Man of Bronze, and took his departure.

He found B. Elmer Dexter first, and related everything he knew in low whispers. Then they split up to locate Don Worth and Morris Byron, confident that the rest of the night would be peaceful.

# Chapter XV

# EXPLANATIONS

THE NIGHT, AS it turned out, was anything but peaceful. The steady wind picked up, and the weather began assuming squall-like conditions. The sky had a dreary, dead look, as if it were made out of slate.

There was nothing to be done about it, of course, except to push on to the Bahamas. The *Northern Star*, displacing twenty-five thousand gross register tons, was not bothered much by line squalls, but nothing of the sort materialized, except that the night winds blew as steadily as if King Neptune himself had thrust up his great bearded head from the Atlantic heave and was expelling his powerful breath upon them, endeavoring to push the ship back toward land. Doc Savage remained in his cabin, giving his full attention to Monk and Ham, who were slow to come out of their stupor.

From time to time, the bronze man attempted to engage the two in conversation, putting to them simple questions, but receiving only mutterings and mumblings that hardly made any sense.

As a physician, Doc was interested in unusual maladies and this was one of the most exotic he had ever encountered. He watched as time passed and their facial pores shrank back to their normal circumferences. He employed a magnifying glass to monitor these changes, recording everything in a little black notebook.

Seaman Goines had remained in the bunk. Not for the first time, Doc Savage wished he could spirit him away to another berth to give his aides a more comfortable place on which to lie. He had fetched blankets from Monk and Ham's cabins to provide makeshift pallets on the floor.

When morning came, Doc was amused to discover that Ham Brooks was the first to regain his full senses. The dapper lawyer—hardly dapper now—groaned once loudly, lifted his head and shook it slowly.

"Where am I?" he murmured groggily, his van Dyke mustaches in disarray.

Doc Savage had been sitting nearby and stood up. "What do you remember, Ham?"

Without looking up, Ham took his head in his hands and murmured, "I remember Monk having some kind of spell and fetching him a glass of water. The next thing I recall was sitting down on the floor, feeling as if all the life was draining out of me."

"Describe your sensations at the time," prompted the bronze man.

Ham did his best, but it was clear that his brain was still foggy.

"Where did the fist of rock come from?" asked Doc.

Ham had to search his memory for that one. Finally, he got his thoughts organized and said, "There was a knock at the door. Monk answered it. A waterproof pouch was sitting outside the door. We opened it up, and found the stony hand."

"It was after that that you began feeling woozy, was it not?" asked Doc.

"I'm not sure. Not long after." Ham seemed to be ready to stand up and, as a first step, the befuddled lawyer looked all over, then in Doc Savage's direction.

The expression roosting on his face was almost comical. For Doc was still disguised as Seaman Goines.

"Where is Doc Savage?" he demanded, searching the room with bleary eyes.

Clambering to his feet, Ham discovered the second Seaman Goines lying on the bunk bed, and he did a memorable double take.

The dapper lawyer had a reputation for being sharp-eyed, and quick-witted, too. Despite the fogginess of his mental machinery, he seized upon the truth rather rapidly.

"You are obviously Doc Savage," he murmured.

"Not too obviously, I hope," countered Doc with a trace of wryness.

Ham discovered that Monk was still flat on his back and remarked, "You would think that misshapen man-monkey would have come out of it by now."

"His constitution is very different than yours, and for some reason he was more seriously affected."

Looking around, Ham asked, "Where is that hand of stone now?"

"In the washroom, safely sealed in its waterproof bag," explained Doc.

Ham declared, "In some strange fashion, I believe that infernal member cast some sort of spell upon us."

"Not a spell," corrected Doc. "As clearly as I can determine, the relic has the uncanny property of leaching mineral iron from the bodies of those who come under its influence."

Ham blinked. "How is that possible?"

"It should not be possible," admitted Doc. "And I may be mistaken. During your period of unusual stupor, the pores of your faces were dilated to an extreme degree. My theory is that whatever was drawn from your constitutions was pulled out through your pores."

Alarm on his face, Ham felt his features, and said, "Now that you mention it, my face feels queer. Dry and tough, like leather."

"Are you thirsty?" demanded Doc.

Ham managed to run his tongue around the inside of his mouth and made a smacking sound with his lips. Finally, he admitted, "Not unusually so."

Doc nodded. "You did not seem dehydrated, according to my examination. It is very bizarre, and I cannot account for the influence of the rock fist on your health."

Frowning, Ham murmured, "What puzzles me most is who left the infernal thing at the door?"

"Obviously someone who recognized either you or Monk, and sought to eliminate you from the picture."

Absentmindedly smoothing his hair, Ham decided, "That means Diamond and his crew may have seen through our disguises. This is not good, is it?"

"Not good at all," allowed Doc Savage. He was on one knee, again examining Monk. After a time, he decided to give the apish chemist a little encouragement to come back to his full senses.

The bronze man did this by slapping Monk sharply against one side of his head then, switching hands, slapping the other side.

Monk's head lolled slightly, and he began mumbling.

Ham asked waspishly, "If you need any help, I will be happy to assist you. Slapping that stupid ape around is one of my hobbies."

Doc said nothing to that. He did not take Ham's request very seriously. The two were always bickering, and would always pick on one another.

After a bit, Doc left off and Monk began to rouse slowly.

WHEN his eyes came open, the homely chemist stared at the ceiling and did not show much interest in his surroundings. But his voice came squeakily.

"Where the heck am I?"

Doc Savage answered, "On the floor of my cabin, where you have been recuperating."

Monk sat up slowly and painfully, looked around, saw Doc Savage disguised as a big Negro, and was not fooled for an instant.

"Nifty disguise," he said. "Did you make it up?"

Doc shook his head slowly. "No, I am pretending to be Seaman Goines, who is resting on the bunk behind you."

Without standing up, Monk swiveled his bullet head, saw Seaman Goines and grunted, "His own mother wouldn't know who was which."

Monk had some difficulty climbing to his feet, but his extraordinarily long arms helped him to lever himself until he stood his full five foot, five inches tall. Not very tall at all, when you came right down to it.

Monk's gorilla arms hung loosely at his sides and he seemed not to know what to do with his hairy hands. He just looked around the cabin and blinked slowly.

"I feel like Count Dracula had sunk his teeth into me, and hung on for a good long while," he mumbled.

"That is a very good description, if fanciful, of what actually happened," Doc told him. "Your blood has been depleted of its iron content in a remarkable manner."

Monk's tiny eyes narrowed and he said, "I'm rememberin' that black fist. It was made of rock. I think it did something to me."

"It exerted a force or power that literally pulled mineral iron from your bloodstream in such a way that your pores opened up to accommodate the escaping iron."

Monk was a chemist and he naturally understood the nature of chemistry. He exploded, "That's impossible!"

"That is my conclusion," said Doc. "There appears to be no other explanation for the bizarre phenomenon."

"So Diamond tried to kill us, huh?" muttered Monk.

"So it would seem," allowed Doc. "But there are more interesting developments to relate."

Monk and Ham regarded the bronze man, who paused in his speech.

"Among the crew are four individuals we have previously encountered. You remember Donald Worth, as well as his three friends."

Monk grunted, "Yeah, we met them over in Crescent City, back a few years when those little gold cavemen were running amok, terrorizing the place."

"They joined the Merchant Marines after war broke out in Europe. All four are stationed aboard this ship," explained Doc. "I have them out looking for signs of Diamond and his crew."

"Any luck?" inquired Ham.

Doc nodded. "I previously encountered Diamond. He was no longer wearing the smoky gray wig that resembled a cloud of cigarette smoke. The man is rather bald, and his face looks coarser without the artificial hair, but he is—or was—berthed in a certain stateroom. When I checked on him a few hours back, another man had taken his place in the cabin. Diamond has relocated in an effort to avoid detection."

"Well, that means he knows we're gunnin' for him," grunted Monk.

"A conversation I overheard tonight indicates they have no plans to pull off anything dangerous overnight," Doc continued, "so it is my intention to let them be until we can figure out their plan."

Ham asked, "Why not round them all up and interrogate them?"

"We may yet do precisely that," allowed Doc, "but without knowing which passengers belong to Diamond's crew and which do not, I do not think it is wise to stir up this particular pot until we have made an inventory of its ingredients."

This made perfect sense to Ham Brooks, who tended to be deliberate, but impulsive Monk growled, "I'm for rousting them out of their bunks and danglin' 'em over the ship's rail until they talk."

"It may come to that," stated Doc. "But the weird properties of that stony fist cause me to believe there is something unusual back of their planned operation. A substance that resembles volcanic rock, which can have the effect this stone hand appears to extert, is not a substance known to science. Discovering its origins and purpose on board the ship may be as important as learning Diamond's plans."

Ham asked, "How long until we put into port?"

"We should be passing Bermuda's latitude shortly. In another day or so, the vessel will dock at Nassau. Until then, I think we should all lay low. I will reconnoiter as Seaman Goines. If Don Worth or any of his friends should show up, let them in and take their reports. They are going to be our eyes and ears, since we are hampered by the risk of discovery."

Monk made a fierce face and thumped his chest like a bull gorilla, saying, "I ain't hampered by nothing! Turn me loose and I'll pluck arms and legs off these guys until they talk their faces blue."

"Let us see what develops when we reach port," suggested Doc Savage calmly.

It was a sound plan, except for the knock at the door. It was an imperative rapping. Doc Savage sidled up to the door and asked in a voice that was neither his nor that of Seaman Goines, "Who is it?"

"Bosun. Let me in."

Doc Savage obliged. Donald Worth stepped in, looking anxious of face. He acknowledged Monk and Ham with his troubled eyes.

"What is wrong?" asked the bronze man.

"Half the ship is hunting for Oiler Goines. Everyone noticed he wasn't in his bunk overnight. What are you going to do, Doc? They're starting to wonder if he went overboard."

Doc Savage said without enthusiasm, "Perhaps I should speak to the Captain about this."

Don Worth warned, "The Skipper is pretty hard-nosed. This won't sit well with him."

Ham Brooks inserted, "Doc Savage has impeccable naval credentials, and advises the War Shipping Administration in Washington."

"I know that. But you don't know the Old Man. The *Northern Star* is his ship and out here on the high seas, he's the law."

Doc said, "Then perhaps it is time that Seaman Goines returned to duty and attempted to make explanations."

"The Captain might throw you in the brig if your explanation isn't up to his expectations."

"I will have to chance that."

"Good luck," said Donald Worth, exiting the cabin.

# Chapter XVI

# THE DEVIL'S OWN LUCK

THE CAPTAIN OF the *Northern Star* was a rangy fellow named Carson McCullum. He was a by-the-book ship's master, but he heard out Doc Savage as he attempted to explain the absence of Seaman Goines during the preceding evening. Doc still wore Jury Goines' beefy bulldog face.

The tale Doc Savage told in the thick voice of the missing Merchant Marine oiler was embroidered in such a way as to cover the sleeping sailor once the sedative had worn off and Goines was fit to return to duty.

"I believe I had a fit or something, Cap'n," explained Doc. "I was on my way to the engine room when I felt dizzy. Found a quiet place to sit down for a spell, and the next thing I knew I was hearing my name called. So I came topside."

"You were derelict in your duty for over ten hours," Captain McCullum pointed out sternly.

"That's what they tell me," admitted Doc. "But all I know is, I keeled over and then I came to later. I still feel weak as tea water."

In the Captain's cabin where the interview was taking place, McCullum looked Seaman Goines up and down sternly, re-marking, "You look none the worse for wear."

Doc Savage said nothing. He thought it prudent not to comment.

"This ship was searched from stem to stern without result," continued the skipper. "Can you explain that?"

Doc shrugged his broad shoulders and did his best to look baffled.

Captain McCullum didn't seem to put too much thought into what he said next, or possibly he had made up his mind beforehand. Consequently, Doc Savage did not see coming what struck him with full force.

"I'm confining you to the brig for the next forty-eight hours. Consider yourself logged out. Rough rations. Report to the Master at Arms. Dismissed."

Doc Savage hesitated only the merest of seconds, and then made an instant decision. He saluted the Captain, and exited his office.

This was not a development the bronze man managed to foresee. Far from it. He had assumed he could talk his way out of the situation, and keep both himself and the real Seaman Goines from severe punishment.

Having miscalculated, Doc decided that he had no choice but to go along with the punishment. To reveal the truth even in the privacy of the Captain's office might have made matters much worse than they were, given McCullum's temperament.

So he reported to the brig, and was promptly locked in a cell by the Master at Arms. This was not a particularly new experience for him. Over the course of his remarkable and dangerous career, the bronze man had been locked in many cells all over the world. If need be, Doc could break out by one means or another. He felt confident on that score.

Doc also had every confidence that word would sweep the ship of his fate, and Don Worth or one of his fellow mariners would report the situation to Monk and Ham. So Doc settled onto the bunk to wait.

An hour along into Doc's confinement, Seaman Tucker showed up, bearing a tray piled with table scraps, three pieces of dry bread and a full glass of warm water.

The guard opened the door, and let Seaman Tucker serve the meal.

"Tough break," undertoned Tucker.

Doc nodded. Under his breath, he said, "Everyone keep a weather eye on Diamond. With any luck, I will be out of the brig around the time we leave Nassau town."

"There you go, Oiler," said Seaman Tucker, not answering directly, but indicating that he had heard every word.

The door was locked. Doc Savage looked at his meager meal and, remembering the brief period in which he had felt depleted by the fist of rock after he had handled it, wished fervently that the meal included a steak cooked rare.

As he ate the crusty bread, which was fast going stale, Doc hoped Monk and Ham would have sense enough to sedate Seaman Goines if he showed any signs of waking up.

Upon finishing the miserable meal, Doc turned in. He had not slept all night, and this unexpected confinement was at least an opportunity to refresh himself without interruption.

Before he fell into slumber, the bronze man turned the mystery of the stony hand over in his mind, but failed to construct any explanations for its peculiar properties.

Up to the point where the weird element had entered the picture, Doc had assumed that Diamond's plans had something to do with the cargo of important war metals, or possibly the convoy rendezvous. But now he wasn't so certain. The uncanny stone fist put a different complexion on the matter, and sent his mind wandering off in disquieting directions.

WHEN Leander Tucker brought the news of Doc Savage's confinement to Bosun Don Worth, the latter went rushing to the cabin where Monk and Ham guarded the real Seaman Goines.

"This is a fine development!" Ham raged when he heard the news.

"Tuck said that Doc Savage wants us all to keep operating until he's released," Worth added.

"I got me a better idea," growled Monk. "Let's all march to the Captain's office and make pretzels out of his arms and legs until he sees things our way."

Bosun Worth shook his head vigorously and said, "Doc Savage has the correct idea. If this gets out, we could *all* end up in irons. Then Diamond and his crew will have free rein."

It took some persuading, but at last Monk subsided.

Donald Worth promised, "Diamond will have to turn up for breakfast, or at least lunch, and Tuck will pass the word to us."

"Speaking of breakfast," piped up Monk, "I'm famished."

Ham said, "If you show up looking like your anthropoid self, it might have unpleasant repercussions."

Monk glowered. "Diamond suspects we're on board. What repercussions could there be?"

"Well, just the same," suggested Ham, "let me take my breakfast first. I'll let you know if the coast appears to be clear."

That made enough sense that Monk decided to do it Ham's way. Besides, someone had to guard Seaman Goines. If he were to be discovered at this juncture, it would be disastrous.

Ham and Don Worth departed, leaving Monk to his solitary duty.

Since he was bored as well as hungry, the homely chemist went to the washroom and picked up the waterproof bag containing the mysterious hand of rock.

Touching the smooth surface of the bag gave Monk the creeps. He was tempted to peer inside, but did not. The artifact had looked unsavory, as if an actual human hand had been charred and petrified, but the influence it exerted on ordinary human beings was beyond the pale.

As an industrial chemist, Monk would have loved to chip off a piece and subject it to a battery of chemical tests. He could think of no way to open the bag and break off a fragment without exposing himself to the same mysterious depleting force that had cost him a great deal of his physical strength. It was even now still coming back slowly.

Unhappily, Monk left the bag on the porcelain sink. Had he the freedom to do so, the hairy chemist would have found a way to return the grisly relic to its owners, and seen how they liked it. But Monk knew that Doc Savage would wish to study the object when he had the next opportunity to do so.

For the bronze man loved mysteries, was intrigued by the unusual, above and beyond his personal scientific curiosity. This was seldom discussed openly, but one of the driving instincts of the Man of Bronze was the pursuit of the unknown, and the discoveries which invariably followed.

Checking on Seaman Goines next, Monk observed that the large fellow was showing some signs of returning to wakefulness.

Knowing that this, too, would be inconvenient if not catastrophic, Monk rooted around in Doc Savage's equipment until he found the sedative that had been used. Charging a hypodermic needle, Monk gave the big black sailor a full dose.

The man had been breathing rather raggedly, but now his respiration settled down to that of a peaceful slumberer.

"That oughta hold him another twelve or so hours," Monk muttered to himself. "By that time, maybe we'll figure a way out of this awful mess."

Monk sat down to await Ham's return when there came a knocking at the door. The knocking was very bold and insistent.

Jumping to his feet, Monk ambled over and called through the panel, "Who is it?"

"Captain McCullum. I want to speak with Doc Savage."

"Uh—he ain't here," retorted Monk. "I think he went out for breakfast."

"I need to convey to him a message," insisted the skipper.

"Go ahead," invited Monk, perspiration popping out on his minuscule brow.

"It is a private message," said the Captain testily.

Now the sweat was pouring down Monk's brow, and his small, worried eyes shifted to Seaman Goines reposing on the bunk. To let the ship's master in would be, at best, a calamity.

Thinking fast, Monk said, "O.K., I'll come on out. I was just about to step out for some fresh air anyway."

"That will not do," returned the Captain firmly. "I do not wish to be overheard. Let me in."

"Well, just a minute," said Monk, rushing back to where Seaman Goines reposed on the bunk. The latter was a huge fellow, weighing over two hundred pounds. He was not light.

Nevertheless, Monk wrapped his brawny arms around the man's chest, shifted him over and then dragged him by the heels into the washroom where he dumped him unceremoniously into the modest shower bathtub. Wiping his brow, Monk closed the door behind him and then hurried to the cabin door.

Captain McCullum stepped in, looked around suspiciously, then turned his full attention on Monk Mayfair.

Monk tended to wear his emotions on his homely features, and this occasion was no different.

"You look like you've just seen a ghost," remarked the Captain pointedly.

"Boats don't agree with me," mumbled Monk. "I keep gettin' seasick."

That seemed to satisfy the skipper, who then launched into his own concerns.

"One of my sailors is in the brig, claiming to have been overcome by some strange sort of spell last night."

"Oh, is that right?" mumbled Monk.

"But the circumstances are suspicious. Has Doc Savage learned anything about our mysterious passengers?"

"Not a blamed thing," insisted Monk. "But he can tell you all that himself."

No sooner had the words escaped Monk's wide mouth than he regretted them. He did not want the skipper to go hunting for Doc Savage, and swiftly said so.

"On second thought," he added hastily, "why don't you give me all the dope you have and I'll take it to Doc? It might not look good if you were seen talkin' to him."

"But I understood Doc Savage would be keeping out of sight."

"Actually, Doc is wearin' a disguise, I'm not even sure what he looks like. Except of course he'd be powerful big."

Captain McCullum studied Monk, searching his simian face, not sure what to make of the apish fellow's wandering tale.

"When you see Doc Savage," he snapped, "let him know what I just told you. It may be important."

"I'll do that," promised Monk.

"Thank you," McCullum said curtly. With that, the skipper took his leave. After he had gone, Monk collapsed into his chair because his knees were shaking so much.

HE WAS not certain why he was so upset, only that between one thing and another, they were getting mighty tangled in a web of circumstances they didn't fully understand. There was no point in having the ship's master discover that Doc Savage had been exceeding his authority, which was, after all, limited. The captain of the ship is the captain of the ship, the first and last word, and the final law at sea.

"No sense gettin' our pants all clapped into the pokey," grumbled Monk as he began wishing that Doc Savage had not managed to get himself confined to the ship's brig.

Not long after, Ham Brooks returned, knocking insistently in code. Monk let him in.

The sharp-eyed lawyer noticed at once that Seaman Goines was not resting on the bunk.

"What have you done with him, you miserable miscreant?" demanded Ham.

"Stashed 'im in the tub," returned Monk.

"Why would you do that?"

"The skipper of this barge came callin'. Wanted to talk to Doc. I had to let him in. I couldn't let him see the big guy on the bunk, now could I?"

"What did McCullum want?"

"He was lookin' for Doc. He thinks the story Doc fed him about Goines havin' a spell was fishy."

"Well," mused Ham, "it *was* fishy. Considering that it was not the truth."

"I told him I would give Doc a message, hopin' he wouldn't go lookin' for him. The Captain knows of Doc skulkin' around in disguise, but he doesn't know what he looks like. And he sure doesn't know he's coolin' his heels in the brig right now."

Ham released a sigh that caused his fake mustaches to come to life. "We are making very little progress, and sinking in quicksand at the same time."

Monk nodded somberly. "Let's just hope that Diamond and his gang stay holed up in their cabins until Doc is set free. Otherwise, you and I are gonna have to handle things."

"At least we have Don Worth and the boys to fall back on. It was the devil's own luck that they happened to be stationed on the ship."

"The devil's own luck," mused Monk, "is kinda like a coiled rattlesnake."

Ham eyed Monk skeptically. "What do you mean by that?"

"What I mean," returned Monk unhappily, "is that the devil's own luck can sometimes rear up and bite you while you're congratulatin' yourself that it happened to you."

"Sometimes," admitted Ham, "you almost make sense."

"That's because the devil's own luck has nipped me a time or two in the past," muttered the hairy chemist worriedly.

# Chapter XVII

# STORM WARNING

**T**HE *NORTHERN STAR* steamed south without incident over the following day, pushing against the cyanide-blue waters of the Gulf Stream, pulling into Nassau on New Providence Island around seven in the evening. The season being mid-summer, it was still light.

Due to the air-like clarity of the sea, a characteristic of Bahamian waters, one could easily spy tropical fish in the harbor. Dolphins. Flying fish. There were a few leaden sharks, as well. The presence of the man-eaters discouraged any prolonged fish-watching.

The gangplank was lowered, but few disembarked. The skipper had already put out the word that the ship would not be long in port, and was merely taking on additional cargo, along with a few British dignitaries.

Ham Brooks watched the gangplank from the stern rail. He loitered several minutes, observing quietly, still disguised by his worn suit and white van Dyke mustache and dab of a beard. He gripped the rail because, without his sword cane, he did not know what to do with his hands. They tended to fidget without the slim stick to grip and twirl.

The absence of deck chairs—an unnecessary luxury in war time—also annoyed Ham. Also, the disguised barrister did not like the way the weather had shifted. All day and night long, the sea air had blown steadily. Now it was uncannily still.

After about a half hour, Ham decided that no one else was getting off. Noting the time, and not being fond of the quality of food being dished out by the ship's mess, he decided to disembark and take a chance on a local restaurant.

"I will be less than an hour," he told the First Mate as he stepped off.

The First Mate nodded, but said nothing.

Ham wandered around the Royal Palm dock, maintained as part of the service by one of the finest hotels in the Bahamas, taking in the sights. As he sauntered along quaint colonial streets, he noticed the ubiquitous palm trees. They hung their shaggy heads in a manner that was lifeless and a bit surreal. The customary dry rustle of palm fronds was strikingly absent, the air also having a definite quality of being charged with something or other, not promising anything good.

A visit by a hurricane, Ham recalled, was not unusual in the Bahamas in August, and the clarity and the stillness struck him as being definitely hurricane symptoms. He began to look around for a barometer as he walked down the street; presently discovering one in a jewelry store window. He wasn't surprised that several persons were standing around, looking at the barometer.

He looked himself. It was low. It was low enough to surprise him.

"That doesn't look so good," one of the observers remarked.

"No, it doesn't," Ham agreed, noticing that the speaker was a lean, mahogany-skinned individual. A native, obviously.

"I take it you live around here, so you would know what the barometer reading means," added Ham.

"Nobody can tell about hurricanes. They're as unpredictable as chickens," the man replied.

"I wonder where it is now?" mused Ham, fishing for information.

"The Miami radio station reports the thing is centered south and east of here, off the northeast tip of Cuba," the man added.

"What I wouldn't give to live on the mainland where they don't have those things. These Bahamian blows ain't fun."

"Then there *is* a hurricane?" Ham asked.

"Sure."

"I hadn't heard about it," Ham remarked.

"From the way folks are talkin'," the other remarked, turning away, "this one is a roaring monster."

Ham rushed off, continuing on his way. This was important information and he must get it to Doc Savage. But first he would eat.

The Central Bahamas Hotel had a dining room—a seafood restaurant specializing in lobster. Ham entered, was seated, and ordered two, with a baked potato and butter beans. It was not his usual dinner fare, but seafood appealed to him.

Ham noticed that preparations for a hurricane were already being taken, for workmen were carrying the light garden furniture to some place of safety, and heavy hurricane shutters were being placed on some of the windows.

The restaurant seemed to be half deserted, so he struck up a conversation with the bored waiter.

"What are the latest meteorological reports concerning the anticipated hurricane?" Ham asked casually. "Is it expected to make landfall?"

"Yes, the barometer is pretty low and there's a blow headed this way," the other man admitted. "However, it will probably be twelve hours or more before anything nasty gets this far. Can't tell, though. Hurricanes have a way of fooling a body."

The food was served with uncommon swiftness for the tropics, and Ham ate more briskly than usual. Whatever impulse to loiter he might have had was dispelled by the hammering of workmen constructing hurricane shutters on the hotel building, working with an alacrity not ordinarily seen in the Caribbean, where time seemed to pass more slowly than on the mainland.

The waiter presented Ham with his bill of fare before the dapper lawyer had quite finished shelling his lobster.

"I live in Grants Town," he explained solicitously. "I want to get home before this hurricane hits, to see that things are properly taken care of."

"I understand perfectly, my good fellow," said Ham, tendering a ten dollar bill and indicating that change would not be necessary.

When he stepped out, the palm fronds and shrubbery stood completely motionless in the unusually bright and still tropical air. The weird frozen clarity of the ominous pre-hurricane sky promised trouble.

Returning to the *Northern Star*, Ham mounted the gangplank with a crisp step that marked him as a decisive man of action.

He went immediately to Monk's cabin.

WHEN Ham Brooks entered the stateroom cabin, the homely chemist jumped up from his chair and demanded, "Where the heck have you been? I'm starvin'."

"I will have a banana sent up from the galley later," Ham snapped back. "There's a big hurricane roaring up from Cuba. We have to let Doc know."

"How big?"

Ham replied, "I just came from Nassau town and they tell me it's a monster."

Worry immediately wrinkled up Monk's simian features. "I've been in Caribbean hurricanes," he said slowly, "that make Oklahoma twisters look like those little dust devils you see scootin' by the side of country roads."

Ham nodded soberly. "It is nothing to take lightly. And it may affect whatever is due to transpire. I must get word to Donald Worth so that he can relay this message to Doc Savage. The storm is due in about twelve hours."

"We're supposed to ship out by midnight," muttered Monk, "on account of we want to make the Caribbean run by night in case of German raiders."

"For my part," declared Ham, throwing open the cabin door, "I would rather face a Nazi U-boat than a storm of this ferocity."

The disguised attorney clapped the door shut. Monk called after him, "Don't forget my grub!"

Ham went in search of Donald Worth and, failing to find him, made a beeline for the ship's dining hall.

He found Seaman Tucker cleaning up the breakfast plates, the dining hour having expired.

"I just came from shore," confided Ham, looking about to make sure he was not overheard, "and there is a hurricane coming this way that is said to rival Gargantua in size."

"I wonder if the Skipper knows?" murmured Tucker.

"Has Doc Savage been fed his dinner yet?" inquired Ham.

"No. I was going to be doing that shortly."

"Let him know that the blow is due in twelve hours."

Leander Tucker frowned. "If I know the Old Man, he's not going to put out into that kind of weather."

"Whatever he does, it is certain to throw off Diamond's plans—provided his plans are set to any sort of fixed timetable," warned Ham.

Seaman Tucker grinned. "Anything to throw a monkey wrench into whatever's cooking."

As Ham prepared to leave, he asked, "Do you have a few bananas?"

"Bananas? I can look. Why?"

"Monk asked for them specifically," said Ham with a straight face.

"You would think," remarked Tucker, "that being cooped up in that stateroom all day and night, he would want something more hearty."

Ham maintained a serious expression. His remark about a banana had not been serious. "Monk Mayfair," he said superciliously, "was raised on a diet of bananas and coconuts. Three bananas will get him through the afternoon."

Retreating into the back, Leander Tucker came back with four of the yellow-skinned fruit, and Ham took them along with him.

Not many minutes later, Seaman Tucker was carrying a tray of scraps and water down into the brig. He made a point of detouring to the section of the ship where Donald Worth would normally be found while in dock, the cargo holds.

"Do you know about the blow that's coming?" he asked.

"Well, I know that this still air is not natural. But I haven't heard the weather report."

"It's a monster," said Tucker. "Driving up from the south, set to hit in about twelve hours."

Now it was Don Worth's turn to wrestle with his frowning features.

"Good. I would imagine that the Skipper knows. The question is what is he going to do about it?"

"The real question is what will *Diamond* do about it, since it probably wasn't part of his plans," suggested Tuck.

"I will see what I can find out," promised Seaman Worth.

"And I'll inform Doc Savage."

Don Worth looked over the bread and water and asked, "It's a shame we can't slip him some decent food."

"My thought exactly, but if I'm caught doing that, I'll be bunking with him."

Don nodded somberly. "Doc is going to need all the help he can get, if anything breaks loose. That means all four of us have to be at liberty."

Seaman Tucker grinned. "This is turning into a heckuva sea voyage, isn't it?"

"The heck part," said Donald Worth heavily, "just might turn out to be sheer hell."

With that, the two friends went in opposite directions.

SEAMAN TUCKER worked his way down to the brig, and stood aside while the Master at Arms opened the cell door, which was a blank steel panel pieced by a round porthole.

"Oiler, how are you this fine afternoon?" Tucker greeted.

"Hungry," replied the bronze man in a steady tone.

"Well, I wish I had more for you than these sorry rations," said Tucker. "But it will have to do, since captain's orders is captain's orders."

Leander Tucker knew from past experience with Doc Savage that the bronze man was an expert lip reader. Turning his back to the watchful jailer, he caught Doc Savage's gaze and mouthed several fragmentary sentences.

"Big hurricane heading this way. Twelve hours away. Don't know if we sail or not."

Doc Savage caught every unspoken syllable, looked down at his tray of table scraps and stale bread left over from the morning meal and sighed heavily in a manner he expected would be consistent with Seaman Goines.

"If I had a twin brother," he said heavily, "I sure would trade places with him right about now."

When he looked up at Leander Tucker, his dark eyes held a meaningful light.

"I know what you mean," agreed Seaman Tucker, "if I had a twin brother, he'd serve every other meal. But I don't, and you don't, so what can we do about it?"

Doc Savage laughed irregularly. "Well, I guess all I can do is chow down and keep on wishing."

"I'll be back for the tray later," said Tucker to the Master at Arms as the latter locked up. He hurried topside, trying not to make it look as if he were rushing. But he was.

When Tuck reached the stateroom where Monk and Ham held forth, he knocked and was admitted surreptitiously.

"I told Doc," he said breathlessly. "He read my lips. The Master at Arms couldn't hear us. Then Doc said a strange thing. He wished that he had a twin brother to take his place."

Monk and Ham swapped glances. At first, their expressions were slightly stunned, then became clearly frightened.

"Are you thinkin' what I'm thinkin'?" Monk asked Ham.

"I fear that I am," moaned Ham, wringing his hands for lack of a sword cane to twist.

Leander Tucker was a little slow on the uptake, but he suddenly got it.

"My word! Are you two thinking what *I'm* thinking?"

Ham said slowly, "If you are thinking that Doc Savage has requested us to spirit Seaman Goines down into the brig to take his place, that is exactly what Doc Savage just requested."

"It can't be done!" blurted Tucker.

"No, it cannot," agreed Ham. "But it will be. Mark my words. When I can, I will find a way."

"Well," said Tuck, edging back toward the door in order to make his escape, "leave me the heck out of it. You two fellows may be headed for the brig, and you don't need any more company than you will have when you get there."

"Tell no one," admonished Ham.

"Not even Don?"

The lawyer hesitated. "If it becomes necessary. Use your own judgment. But for the moment, the fewer who know of this plan, the better."

"You might be right," admitted Tucker. "Don is as straight an arrow as they fly. If he learns of this, his conscience would rebel. He might even go running to the Old Man and tell the plain truth. And you can bet that Captain McCullum might just hang Doc Savage on general principles. But if you two get caught, nobody's going to be sprung."

With that, Leander Tucker thrust his head out the partially open cabin door, looked both ways twice, and slipped through, looking as guilty as all get out.

# Chapter XVIII

# DOUBLETALK

CAPTAIN McCULLUM WAS not a nervous man. Yet he had every right to be nervous, as nervous as a seasoned seaman could possibly be.

The Skipper was about to make a run across the middle of the Atlantic in a vessel so large it would be a natural target for a Nazi raider.

It had been customary since the beginning of the war, when the wolf packs came out in full force, to cross the Atlantic at the higher latitudes. Departing from Newfoundland or Nova Scotia, and thereby making the shortest possible run to the British Isles. Captain McCullum had made a few of those runs, too, invariably in convoys.

This time there would be no convoy. He could not afford to loiter until his scheduled departure hour for convoy rendezvous. He would have to go on ahead. His new orders were to cross the middle of the Atlantic alone. The days in which the enemy U-boats had free rein in the Atlantic were about done. The enemy submarines, which had taken such a horrific toll on Allied shipping, had in turn been sunk in overwhelming numbers. Some still lurked out there, in the cold depths of the ocean. But very few compared to even a year ago.

Simply because it was comparatively safer to make a solo dash across the Atlantic Ocean did not mean it was safe. Not at all. Then there was the added complication of the matter of the Doc Savage crowd being permitted on board to keep an eye on a group of foreign sailors who might not be what they seem.

If it had been up to Carson McCullum, the suspect passengers would have been thrown into the brig and clapped in irons. It was not up to him. No. Instead, he was stuck with watching over an unknown number of passengers who were suspected of having dark intentions, and the problem of Doc Savage having the run of the ship, and there was little he could say about it. It rankled him.

As he paced his bridge, looking out at the strange stillness that overlay Nassau's colonial waterfront, each silvery palm tree looking as if they were painted on glass in the pre-storm light, Captain McCullum decided that he had run out of patience.

Unlike other men, who would exceed their patience and react accordingly, McCullum made the calculated decision that he had no more patience left. His store of it had been exhausted. He was that way. Disciplined even in his emotions.

Turning to his Chief Warrant Officer, he barked, "Mr. Greer. Find Doc Savage and tell him I wish to speak with him immediately."

"Yes, Captain."

The C.W.O. started down the companionway steps. Captain McCullum called after him, "And don't come back until you relay that message."

Chief Warrant Officer Greer went directly to Doc Savage's cabin, knocked once.

Monk Mayfair's squeaky voice demanded, "Whatcha want?"

"The Captain requests Doc Savage's presence on the bridge."

"Doc ain't here."

"Where is he, then?" demanded Greer, banging on the door again. "And why don't you have the decency to open the door when you speak to me?"

The suave voice of Ham Brooks inserted itself and said, "Stand aside, Monk. Let me handle this."

The door opened a crack and Ham showed his sharp-featured face. He was no longer wearing the van Dyke beard. In fact, he was no longer the imaginary Dutchman, Brom van Bummel. Believing his disguise had been penetrated, he had darkened his hair, donned a monocle and pencil mustache, and was planning to pass himself off as one of the British dignitaries who had boarded in Nassau, Lord Ronald Hathaway by name. There was no such person.

"Actually, neither of us have seen Doc Savage since yesterday," Ham said calmly.

The Chief Warrant Officer grunted. "A man like Doc Savage would be noticed moving about the ship, even at night. Where do I find him?"

Ham hesitated, a slightly guilty look on his face.

Chief Warrant Officer Greer had had enough by that time. He shouldered his way in, nudging Ham aside. After barging in, he saw the large sheeted figure lying on the bunk. The unmoving form was covered from head to toe.

"What the hell is this?" he yelled. Before anyone could stop him, he lunged for the bunk, whipped the sheets off the sheet gear, half expecting to find a corpse.

Greer stared, stupefied, his eyes batting in his baffled confusion.

"What the hell is this?" he repeated, turning slowly toward Monk and Ham.

Monk Mayfair stood there with his blocky jaw askew, trying to form an intelligent response. Instead, he burbled something inarticulate.

Possessing more presence of mind, Ham Brooks said, "That is Doc Savage."

"It is not!" bellowed the Chief Warrant Officer. "I know Jury Goines when I see him."

Ham's composure grew grave. "No doubt you're aware that Seaman Goines was remanded to the brig two nights ago, for the infraction of dereliction of his duties."

"I am well aware of that!"

"Since he was out of action," Ham explained, "Doc Savage decided to impersonate him as a way of keeping an eye on our mysterious passengers without them suspecting his presence."

"Do you mean to tell me that is Doc Savage laying there?"

Monk Mayfair had recovered his usually nimble wits. "Yeah, that's Doc, all right. He's just asleep, is all."

Chief Warrant Officer Greer looked at the prostrate man and said, "If he was asleep, why did you have him covered up like he was about to be given sea burial?"

Monk had no answer to that, so he looked to Ham Brooks hopefully.

The dapper lawyer came through like a champion. "As it happened, Doc was overcome by the same strange dizzy spell that apparently overtook Seaman Goines. Fortunately, we found him and conveyed him back here, inasmuch as the presence of another unconscious sailor would have been difficult to explain away."

"Difficult! It's impossible. Preposterous!" thundered the officer. "How could Doc Savage sneak around the ship disguised as a man known to be in the brig without arousing the suspicions of the crew?"

"The big fellow is quite adept in the art of stealth, and shadowing people," explained Ham.

"Sure," added Monk, beaming sheepishly. "Did you get any reports Seaman Goines was on the loose last night?"

The troubled look on the officer's stern face told plainly that he had not. That look, and the way his eyes kept going to the slumbering figure, told that Chief Warrant Officer Greer had not fully bought Ham's cock-and-bull story.

Still, he was not certain, so he asked, "How long has he been out like that?"

"Since about four a.m.," said Ham, picking an hour that sounded plausible.

The officer went over to the bunk, and with intent, searching eyes, studied the recumbent figure lying there. Clear signs of respiration brought relief to his expression.

"Well, he looks just like Seaman Goines," he commented suspiciously.

"If you popped over to the brig, you'll find another man who looks exactly like Seaman Goines," remarked Ham. "That resemblance will also be remarkable."

"In that case, how will I know which one is the real one?"

"Obviously," Ham reassured him, "the one confined to the brig is the genuine article."

"Yeah," laughed Monk, "unless you think Doc Savage let himself be confined to the brig for some goofy reason."

Ham's sharp elbow drove into Monk's barrel-stave ribs in remonstrance.

Straightening, the Chief Warrant Officer turned and said darkly, "I will have to report this to the Captain, of course."

"Of course," returned Ham smoothly.

"Natch," seconded Monk.

Greer started to stride out, stopped, turned smartly in place, and stood staring at the figure on the bunk intently.

"First, I will check in at the brig."

"By all means," encouraged Ham. "Satisfy yourself on that score."

"Yeah," added Monk. "You do that very thing."

THE DOOR slammed behind the departing officer, and Ham whirled on Monk, hissing, "Did you have to put that thought into his head? The one about Doc Savage being in the brig?"

"I was just tryin' to help embroider that web of lies you were feedin' him," said Monk defensively. "It's called misdirection. It works every time."

"That's not misdirection!" exploded Ham. "That's redirection. *I* was misdirecting him."

"Well, let's just hope he's really confused right now."

"Of what use will that be when Captain McCullum shows up?"

Monk's face twisted into a number of expressions, some comic, others merely foolish. He always made faces when cogitating, and it was something that could have been filmed and shown as a short subject on a Saturday afternoon movie matinee, so amusing was it.

Finally, Monk shrugged two sloping shoulders and said, "Search me. This is the daggonedest mess I can remember bein' in for the longest time."

"Well, if this were the dead of night," mused Ham, "I would attempt to swap this man for Doc Savage and be done with it."

"Broad daylight ain't the time to pull a stunt like that. Even after dark, that would be more than tricky."

"We cannot wait until darkness. We'll just have to try to bluff our way through it."

"Ain't that what we been doin' all along?" Monk pointed out.

"I would much prefer to be making progress on this investigation," ground out Ham. "Instead, we appear to be sinking into a quagmire of our own creation."

# Chapter XIX

# COMPLICATIONS

**D**OC SAVAGE WAS pacing his cell, attempting to drain away the nervous energy that went with his confinement.

Not for the first time, the disguised bronze man was regretting his decision to acquiesce to being thrown in the brig. He did not wish to reveal his imposture, not even to the ship's captain, for a great many reasons. Not the least of which was pride.

Neither did Doc want to look foolish by having to explain how he came to fall into such a ridiculous predicament. Too, the bronze man had not really expected to be confined for a full forty-eight hours.

The fact that he had subsisted on bread and water for six meals in a row was making his stomach growl and Doc was becoming irritable as a consequence.

But there was nothing he could do except wait for Leander Tucker to convey his secret message to Monk and Ham. Oh, they acted clownish at times, but when they teamed up, the two men could pull off a miracle an hour. If anyone could spirit Seaman Goines down into the brig so Doc Savage could escape, it would be those two.

The bronze man's confidence was shaken when Chief Warrant Officer Paul Greer showed up unexpectedly.

Greer strode up to the round porthole of a window. Without saying a word, he peered through the glass pane and began studying Doc Savage in a way that the bronze man did not like at all.

Doc said nothing, shipboard regulations calling for a respectful silence.

Finally, Greer spoke. "Seaman Goines, tell me what happened the other night? What got you into this trouble?"

Doc made his voice deeper and less resonant. "Well, you see, sir, I was going about my usual business and I took a spell of some sort. When I woke up, I was in this here trouble."

"Did you smell anything beforehand?"

"No, sir, I did not."

"So you cannot account for your dereliction of duty?"

Doc shook his head heavily. "Near as I can tell, sir, I had a fit. It was out of my hands."

"Well, you're not the only one to have a fit," said Greer tightly.

"You don't say?" said Doc.

"I just came from a cabin. There was a man lying on a bunk looks like your twin brother."

Doc kept his voice unexcited. "I don't have a brother, but if I did, he's not on this boat."

"His friends told me he had taken a spell exactly like the one that overcame you."

"That makes me feel a little relieved," offered Doc, although his private feelings were exactly the opposite. He had to suppress an urge to release his pent-up emotions through his quirk of trilling.

"It does?" prompted Greer.

"Yes, sir," said Doc. "I don't feel so bad about falling down on the job if it's happened to another man."

The Chief Warrant Officer stared at Doc Savage for the longest time without speaking further.

Turning on his heel, he stormed out, warning loudly, "I will get to the bottom of this one way or the other."

The outer door slammed, and the Master at Arms looked at the man he thought was Seaman Goines and asked, "What the heck is going on?"

Doc lowered his voice. "I'm afraid to say," he hissed.

"You know something?"

Doc shook his head solemnly. "No. But I sure do suspect things. Strange things, too."

The job of guarding the brig was a boring and lonely one. The Master at Arms drifted up and said, "Tell me more, brother."

"Well, it's like this," Doc began, dropping his voice even further.

The jailer leaned in to catch every syllable in his attentive ear, the glass window inhibiting his hearing somewhat.

"In the cargo hold," whispered the bronze man, "they got a new type of poison gas. I think one canister is leaking."

"Leaking!"

"That's right," returned Doc. "The reason I got into this here fix was that I smelled something peculiar. Went out like a light. Came to, and it was almost the next day."

"You don't say!"

"Swear on my momma's apple pie," Doc asserted.

While he was talking, the bronze man removed one shoe, gave the heel a twist, and extracted from the hollow that was exposed a single glass ball no larger than a child's marble and, holding his breath, crushed the capsule.

Released from the spherical confinement was a volatile mixture that instantly vaporized. It produced a rank odor that was difficult to pin down, other than it was nasty. The odor filled the brig's tiny cell, soon seeping out of the small space through the keyhole and the narrow gap under the door, where it infiltrated the nostrils of the interested guard so rapidly that he shrank back in alarm.

"I smell it!" he exploded.

"I do, too!" Doc yelled. "Quick, get me out of here before I'm overcome!"

The Master at Arms hesitated, but he knew that he would be held responsible if his prisoner died through his negligence. So he brought out the key to the door padlock, unlocking it in haste.

"Out, Goines!" he urged. "We'll run for it."

At that point, Doc crushed the other glass ball, the one he had excavated from his other shoe heel. This time a colorless and odorless gas was produced.

Doc waited a full minute until the anesthetic gas had dissipated before he resumed normal respiration. The mixture was now harmless.

When he opened the cell door all the way, Doc stepped out and found the Master at Arms lying on the floor, peacefully asleep.

The tiny glass balls were of a type the bronze man had been using for many years and they had never failed to extricate him from situations where physical violence was either not called for, or not practical. The first had contained a vapor concocted to make a foe think he was facing poison gas. This was often enough to trick an enemy into blind retreat.

Doc hesitated briefly. Should he remove his disguise? Or keep it? There was no question that elements of the crew were looking for Doc Savage, and it was imperative that he reach his stateroom cabin in order to make a proper disposition of Seaman Goines.

It was a conundrum. Either decision entailed risks as well as advantages.

Hastily, the bronze man removed the make-up from his face and hands, the only parts of his skin that were exposed. He used some rag waste he found and did as thorough a job as possible. The nappy wig that disguised Doc's metallic hair came off, and the bronze man stuffed this into the bottom of a half-full waste basket.

Cautiously, he stepped out, and began working through the corridors. Doc managed to get several yards when the thought struck him forcibly that he was wearing a shirt that said in stenciled letters, GOINES.

Undoing the button of one short sleeve, he exposed some of the make-up that had darkened his skin. He rubbed this off on the name, obscuring it. It was an indication of the bronze man's nervousness and haste that he had overlooked that important detail until this moment.

DOC worked his way through the ship, avoiding the cabins on B Deck where Diamond and his crew were distributed, and endeavored to turn his back and hide his face whenever he came upon a roving seaman.

The bronze giant made uncanny progress until he happened upon Monk and Ham lugging an enormous steamer trunk along a cross-ship passage.

The two were struggling with it, and it did not require the astuteness of a modern Sherlock Holmes to determine what lay within the commodious receptacle.

Monk was leading, but he was walking backward, while Ham struggled to hold up his end of the trunk when Doc Savage drifted up and remarked, "I hope the trunk contains what I think it does."

"Blazes!" exploded Monk, blunt head swiveling around, small eyes popping.

"Doc!" bleated out Ham. "We got your message."

Stepping around Monk, Doc reached for the handle Ham was struggling with and said, "Let me take that."

Ham was so astonished that his foppish monocle popped out and fell to the deck. "Doc, how did you escape?"

Doc Savage told him in succinct sentences, concluding with, "When the guard wakes up, he will think he fell victim to the same spell that Seaman Goines is supposed to have experienced."

"Smart!" grinned Monk. "But maybe you better let us handle this. Everybody's lookin' for you, and the sooner you're back in your bunk, the better it will go."

Doc's expression was blank.

Ham explained, "We told the Chief Warrant Officer that the man in the bunk was actually you in disguise. You need to hold up our end of that particular fib."

"That was no fib," said Doc. "That is a whopper."

"Just so long as it goes over," murmured Ham.

Doc thought swiftly, and decided the suggestion was not only smart, but imperative.

"Good luck," he told them. Then hurried off.

Doc Savage found the going difficult from there on in. Several times he had to backtrack and duck into alcoves, and generally sneak a circuitous route back to his stateroom cabin.

During his prowling, he encountered lanky, Lincolnesque Morris Byron.

"Everybody's looking for you!" hissed Mental. "From Captain McCullum on down to us lowly Able Seamen."

Doc said, "Pretend you just found me and are escorting me to the bridge."

Mental looked stricken. "If I'm seen doing that and you don't end up on the bridge, what do you think will happen to me?"

"Play along. I am returning to my cabin. You can say that I was having trouble navigating and had to lie down again."

Mental admitted, "That makes half sense."

"It's all the sense I have at the moment," said Doc wryly. "We are in a fix, and we need to extricate ourselves."

As they walked along, they encountered various crewmen. To cover for the inexplicable spectacle, Seaman Byron said cheerfully, "Look who I found."

That aroused no particular suspicion, and so they were not stopped.

In no time at all, they reached Doc's cabin, and stepped in. It helped that the ship's crew was busy making it ready for the blow. By now word of the hurricane approaching had filtered down to the lowermost decks and everyone knew they were going to be in for a time of it, whether at anchor or out at sea.

Once inside the cabin, Doc ducked into the washroom, and quickly showered off the last elements of make-up that would betray his successful impersonation of Jury Goines.

When he stepped out, Mental Byron said conversationally, "What do we do now?"

"You will escort me to the bridge, where I will confer with Captain McCullum. Let us hope that everything else went according to plan."

Mental looked puzzled. "Everything else?"

"It," said Doc Savage, "is a very long story."

# Chapter XX

# PREDICAMENT

**E**VERYTHING DID NOT go according to plan. Far from it.

Monk and Ham succeeded in conveying the trunk all the way to the brig below decks, where they set it down beside the peacefully sleeping Master at Arms.

"Wonder if he'll end up bein' tossed in the jug for fallin' down on the job?" wondered Monk, as Ham undid the trunk latches.

"Never mind that! Help me with this."

Stooping, the hairy chemist flipped latches, flung up the lid, and excavated the still unconscious Seaman Goines, grunting with exertion. Together, they conveyed him to the plank bunk, closed the steel door and found the key with which to lock it.

Ham was the one doing the locking and he almost succeeded when an angry voice behind him bellowed, "What the bloody hell is going on here?"

Monk and Ham turned, and their faces blanched. Blood drained out of them until they looked like proverbial ghosts.

Monk made *blah blah blah* noises, his thick tongue tangling.

Ham cleared his throat and thought swiftly. But then he realized nothing he could say could possibly explain away what they had just been discovered doing.

It proved to be unnecessary, for Captain McCullum took one look at the tableau and jumped to his own conclusions. That they were the opposite of what Monk and Ham were actually trying to pull off was beside the point.

"Why are you two trying to break that man out of the brig?"

Monk and Ham swapped befuddled looks, and each one caught the other's eye, as if to say, "You explain it."

Neither man could. In fact, it was difficult to say whether the Skipper's misperception of their actions boded for good or for ill. So they kept their mouths shut and said nothing.

"I asked you a question!" roared McCullum.

Normally, Monk and Ham would have tossed the matter into Doc Savage's lap, saying that they were under orders. That excuse would not fly here. It would only implicate Doc Savage in something that he, in fact, was not attempting to do.

The only positive development was that Seamen Goines—the real one, that is—was in his proper bunk at last. And Doc Savage was at liberty. For how long was damnably difficult to guess.

Mouths sealed, faces grave, Monk and Ham simply stood there, for once paralyzed in thought, word and deed.

"Is that going to be the way of it?" demanded McCullum. "In that case, I am confining you to the brig until I get to the bottom of this situation."

"The brig is kinda full," pointed out Monk.

From behind the Captain came another voice, that of Chief Warrant Officer Greer.

"It will be no problem," he said bitterly, "to release Seamen Goines and confine him to his own bunk in order to accommodate you gentlemen."

If this were taking place on land, Monk and Ham would have rushed the officers and made a break for it, with the blind intention of untangling the knot of their implication at a later date. Inasmuch as they were on a ship, that particular out seemed impractical.

True, they were docked. And they could jump ship conceivably. But that would leave Doc Savage alone to explain this complicated stew.

Monk simply signaled his hopeless surrender by erecting his overlong hairy arms. The blunt-nailed fingers almost touched the low ceiling of the brig.

Shrugging, Ham followed suit, his handsome face dejected.

In short order, additional crew were summoned, Seaman Goines was lugged out and away, and Monk and Ham were invited into their new quarters.

The door slamming on their unhappy faces made a regal sounding *clang* like a gong that had been struck, signaling something portentous.

The unconscious Master at Arms was also lugged off, and Monk and Ham were left in ruinous solitude. They sat down on the bunk, faces long, postures utterly sunk into defeat.

"What I want to know is how Doc Savage is going to explain all this?" mused Ham.

"He's gonna have to do some tall talkin'," muttered Monk. "Especially if he hopes to spring us."

"Somehow, I do not think even Doc Savage can extricate us from this fix any time soon."

Monk sighed heavily. "That means he's gonna have all the action to himself when he finally ties into Diamond and his crew."

"No," countered Ham. "That means Doc will have to stand alone dealing with the enemy."

Monk considered that for a time, then offered, "Maybe Don Worth and his friends will pitch in."

"If everyone isn't more careful than we were," Ham groaned, "this brig is going to get terribly crowded, awfully fast."

That happy thought ringing in the air, the two men lapsed into a sullen silence.

TRAILED by his C.W.O. and a complement of sailors, Captain McCullum came bowling up the companion when Doc Savage, escorted by Seaman Morris Byron, turned a corner.

There was nearly a collision. But Doc Savage, his metallic face impassive, said, "I was just coming to see you, Captain."

McCullum glared. "We have been turning the ship upside down for you."

"It was necessary for me to operate in secrecy. Unfortunately," Doc added, "I encountered difficulties of my own."

"Let me tell you, they'll be nothing like the difficulties you're facing now."

A bad feeling surged through the bronze man's giant frame. But he let the ship's master spell it out for him.

"Your two friends were just caught red-handed, attempting to liberate Seaman Goines from the brig. Would you care to explain that, Mr. Savage?"

Doc was so shocked by the misunderstanding of Monk and Ham's actions that words momentarily failed him.

Composing himself, he decided to make a clean breast of it.

"Captain, my aides were not trying to release Goines."

Chief Warrant Officer Greer piped up and said, "Don't hand me that rotten bilge! They had a steamer trunk open, ready to receive him."

Doc said, "The trunk was used to convey Seamen Goines *to* the brig, not from it."

Captain McCullum and his C.W.O. had been looking stern, but now their expressions simply froze.

"That does not make any sense! And you know it, Savage!" barked the Skipper.

"It will once I have explained it," returned Doc levelly.

"In a pig's eye!" said McCullum. "Turn around and march! I am confining you to your quarters. The only reason you are not being tossed into the brig is due to your high standing with the government—and the fact that there is no more damn room."

"If you allow me to explain—" protested Doc.

"Seaman Byron," ordered the Captain. "Kindly escort Mr. Savage to his quarters. I will post an armed detail outside to ensure that he does not leave without permission."

Seeing that there was no arguing the point, Doc Savage acquiesced. "Very well. When you are ready to hear my account, Captain McCullum, I will be prepared to give it."

The Skipper remained unmoved. "Washington is going to hear about this, Savage. You are jeopardizing the safety of the ship, its crew and its mission. If I have my way, you'll be put off in Nassau and, it is to be hoped, incarcerated there."

Doc objected, "If you do that, the problem of your passengers will be more difficult to solve."

"I have an entire crew of Able Seamen available to me," snapped the Captain. "My men are up to any challenge presented to them. Now get out of my sight."

Reluctantly, the bronze man turned around and, escorted by Morris Byron, retreated to his cabin.

Mental undertoned, "What are you going to do now?"

"Hope for the best," replied Doc. "But I am expecting the worst."

"I can hardly see how this could get any worse."

"Between Diamond and the hurricane," replied Doc Savage, "the potential for disaster is increasing by the hour."

"And we have no idea what shape that disaster will take, do we?" murmured Mental.

"None whatsoever," said Doc Savage tightly.

# Chapter XXI

# FASCINATING RING

**T**HE INDIVIDUAL WHO was entered in the ship's register as C.C. Weed came up to Diamond's new stateroom and knocked vigorously.

The knock was timed—two raps, followed by four—so there was no need to identify himself.

The door fell open and the man stepped in.

"Big doings, chief," he said.

"Then spill it, Weedy," invited Diamond. "I could use some diversion, after being cooped up here so long."

"That blow in the air? It's no gale. Scuttlebutt is there's a big hurricane on the way."

Diamond considered this. "How big?"

"King Kong is a chimp compared to it."

A crafty gleam came into Diamond's cold amber eyes. "That could work in our favor, or against us. No way to tell. What else?"

"Doc Savage's men got into some kind of trouble. I don't know what. I'm just hearing talk among the crew. They're in the brig."

Diamond smiled in a way that looked as though he was out of practice. One side of his mouth lifted up, and it looked as if that side of his face was about to crack. The other side just sat there, inert as stone.

"Do tell."

"And the best part is Doc Savage himself has been confined to his cabin. Under armed guard. He's not going anywhere."

"Trouble is sometimes an enemy, but often a friend," Diamond said slowly. "Up till now I figured the bronze guy was hiding on board and keeping an eye on us. I was right in my figuring. Now, he can't do that anymore."

"Don't you think he tipped off the skipper to us?" pressed Weed.

"I don't figure it either way. He might have, he might not have. We will know soon enough."

"What do you mean by that?"

"With Doc Savage out of action, McCullum is going to move against us or he's not. If he doesn't, that might mean we're in the clear."

The other man looked worried. "We're pressing our luck waiting to see."

Diamond fingered a hole in his left earlobe. "We can't exactly leave the ship, now can we? You know full well we're not at liberty to do that under the terms that we are sailing."

"So we just wait, huh?"

Diamond nodded. "We wait. Get out there and rig your ears to take in all they can. Unload them for me when you have something more."

The man exited quickly, and Diamond sat down on his bunk, his hard eyes narrowing, assorted expressions traipsing across his nut-brown features. He tried to smile a few times, as if considering the possibilities of these developments, but his face appeared not to be up to the task.

Lying down, he lifted one arm and scrutinized the ring on his right hand.

The ring was simple metal, resembling a wedding ring, but it was on the wrong finger. In the cabin light, it resembled gold, but as he moved the circlet with his thumb, reddish highlights gleamed that made it seem more coppery than golden.

The man who called himself Diamond eyed the ring, which he regarded a very long time as if it possessed more significance than simply a band of some rich metal.

"Five will get you ten that Doc Savage was the big black sailor that was shadowing me," he told himself. "I half suspected it, but now I know it. One thing's for sure, that metallic meddler doesn't have a clue what it's all about."

# Chapter XXII

## DEVIL'S BROTH

**M**ORRIS "MENTAL" BYRON went searching for Don
Worth, knowing that the young boatswain would want
to know about the disposition of Doc Savage immediately.

He searched the forward deck, then went amidships, and
finally found him standing cargo watch below decks, as crates
were being distributed about the hold and made fast. This
material consisted of tungsten and platinum and other war-
related metals that were intended for English industry. There
was not a great quantity of it, the *Northern Star* possessing a
modest cargo hold for its size, but every ounce of critical war
material counted in the struggle against the Axis.

Taking Don aside, Seaman Byron whispered, "Doc Savage
has been confined to quarters, Boats."

Don Worth was trying to control his emotions. He managed
to dampen down his expression to a disappointed frown.

"This is very bad," he murmured.

"It gets worse," said Mental. "Monk and Ham got tossed
into the brig. They were caught red-handed trying to get Seaman
Goines out."

"Why would they do a crazy thing like that?" demanded
Worth.

"They didn't. They were sneaking the *real* Goines in, and
managed to shut the door just in time for the Skipper and the
Chief Warrant Officer to barge in on them. Captain McCullum
jumped to a conclusion, and landed in a misunderstanding. Doc

Savage tried to explain it all, but that only made the Skipper even madder. So he confined Doc Savage to his quarters."

"That means it's up to us to keep an eye on Diamond and his crew."

Mental nodded. "Which will be hard to do since half of them don't even come out to eat. The others take their food in to them. Some of them are claiming to be seasick."

Don Worth pondered these developments and finally said, "We better tell the others."

Mental nodded. "Maybe we can cogitate a way out of this."

"I'm not sure even four brains are enough to untangle this Gordian knot," complained Don.

Turning over the watch to a deck cadet, Boatswain Worth and Seaman Byron went straight to the mess hall. Along the way, they collected B. Elmer Dexter.

Dex listened to their account with both ears, and by the time they reached the kitchen, he was bubbling with possibilities.

"Maybe it's time to start agitating."

"There will be no agitating until we figure out what we want to result," Don said firmly. "There isn't room in the brig for all four of us, but that doesn't mean we can't be confined to quarters. We have to step carefully if we are to help Doc Savage."

In his youth, Mental Byron had been something of a philosopher, and addicted to homespun aphorisms. He uncorked one now. "Whether walking through a cow patch, or creeping toward trouble," he ruminated, "it always pays to look at your footprints before you make them."

"And how," agreed Dex.

They found Leander Tucker in the galley, washing out the big stainless steel stewpots used to make soup for the ship's crew. He was industriously scrubbing it with a steel wool pad the size of a catcher's mitt.

Seeing his approaching comrades, and the glum cast of their faces, he asked, "What's wrong now?"

"Plenty," said Don grimly.

IN THE PRIVACY of the galley, they conferred for several minutes. At the end of the recitation, Tucker whistled and said, "Throw in a hurricane, and this is the damnedest stew you ever imagined brewing."

Elmer chimed in. "Yes, a devil's broth."

"That is why we don't want to add anything volatile to the mix," insisted Don Worth. "Here is what I want you all to do. The crew doesn't know anything about Diamond and his gang. Only certain ship's officers, Doc Savage, his men, and ourselves. Keep an eye on the cabins where Diamond's men are distributed. Watch for anything out of the ordinary. Report everything to me. And if we come up with something dire, I'll take it to the Old Man. He likes me. He will listen."

"Well, that's what we were doing all along, isn't it?" asked Seaman Byron.

Don Worth nodded. "But now we're looking for any little thing, or things, that might add up to a big thing. I want something concrete to lay before Captain McCullum. Anything. Understood?"

The three nodded their heads in agreement. "We'll come up with something," assured B. Elmer. "Count on it, Don. We won't let you down."

"It's Doc Savage I don't want to let down. He's onto something. And if we can bust it open, we may be able to save the ship and its crew from—"

Every man looked at him expectantly, curiosity written on their youthful faces.

"—from whatever wicked scheme is in the offing," he finished sheepishly.

"In other words," lamented Tuck, "we know next to nothing."

"We know more than the crew, so keep your eyes open, and find something I can lay before the Skipper so we can exonerate Doc Savage."

They began to break up, leaving Leander Tucker to his pot scrubbing, when the First Mate wandered in and said, "Make ready. We're leaving port in less than an hour."

Don Worth looked momentarily flummoxed. "I thought we were remaining in port until the hurricane passes."

"We were," the other offered. "But the latest weather report says the system is stalling down near Cuba, and the Skipper wants to make a break for it now, hoping to outrun the blow."

"Risky," clucked Mental Byron. "Even a slow-moving blow can suddenly pick up steam and break loose like an enraged bull. That thing could chase us clear to who knows where."

"Captain's orders," said the officer. "Everyone to your stations."

They filed out onto deck, and went their separate ways, intent upon their immediate duties, and worried that they had just lost their best opportunity to uncover some shenanigans on the part of Diamond and his mysterious gang.

Up on deck, the air was still unnaturally still, the sweltering humidity wringing moisture out of their skins, as the last of the palleted cargo was hoisted into the hold and made fast.

Crewmen bustled about with quiet urgency, tension on their faces, speaking less often than normally. All knew that Captain McCullum was taking a long chance, and if he had miscalculated, the *Northern Star* was bound to pile into a meteorological monster of unprecedented size.

Within very short order, heavy ropes were cast off, and tugboats began pushing the mighty former liner out to the beautiful harbor that brought to mind Homer's ancient phrase, the wine-dark sea, for it was more indigo than any lighter shade of blue.

In their fragile wooden craft, native bumboat men lazily poled out of the way, clearing a channel out of the harbor.

Except for the growing humidity and the unnatural silence of the atmosphere, it was a perfect tropical day.

# Chapter XXIII

# MISSTEP

THE SETTING OF the tropical sun changed the atmosphere aboard the *Northern Star.*

The big vessel had been stealing along turquoise waters when the sinking sun first touched the sea, causing jeweled fire to spring amid the placid calm of the Caribbean.

The Bahama group consisted of an incredible number of islands and cays, and the *Northern Star* was obliged to work its ponderous way among them, for even this far along in the war, the menace of Nazi raiders had not been abolished.

The wolf packs generally operated at higher latitudes and deeper into the Atlantic, of course. But the occasional lone raider still struck at some shipping in the Caribbean and further south. By sticking to the islands as she steamed east, the *Northern Star* had less exposure, for enemy submarines did not, as a rule, dare penetrate the islands and their tricky shoal waters.

The sinking of the sun doused the bright prismatic perfection of the sea, which turned gory and then dusky and finally dark as India ink. The blazing orb dropped like a hot stone into the waters, and when the last smoldering slice slipped below the horizon, suddenly all was blackness around them.

Where they could, Don Worth and his shipmates kept watch for signs of Diamond and his crew, who appeared content to remain in their cabins. This was not so unusual. Seamen often retreated to their quarters when not on duty, or standing watch. Most commercial vessels—even the large ones—were cramped

173

and difficult to navigate. Not much went on aboard ships that seasoned sailors would consider a novelty. These men probably passed their time reading.

When mess was piped, one by one, a few filtered out.

Where before they had watched for unusual behavior, now they were alert to anything, anything at all. No matter how minor. They were handicapped by the fact that they could not be certain which passengers were included among the Diamond contingent, and which were not. There was nothing to distinguish them. Or so all believed.

It was Leander Tucker, not surprisingly, who began noticing something that the suspicious ones all had in common.

He was serving up lumpy mashed potatoes when he observed a passenger he had not noticed before wearing what looked like a wedding ring. But it was not worn on the left hand, or on the correct finger, and there was nothing unusual about the band, which appeared to be made of gold.

Seaman Tucker made a mental note of it, and a few minutes later he found himself slapping ham and eggs onto the plate of another passenger who wore a virtually identical ring on the same finger.

Tuck stared at it, and thought to himself that it looked rather reddish for gold, but did not appear to be copper.

When Seaman Byron came by for his share of grub, Leander whispered to him, "I noticed that two of the passengers are wearing these funny rings. They look like gold, but I'm not sure that they are gold. Tell the others to watch out for passengers wearing gold-looking rings on their right hands."

"Got you," returned Mental.

Wolfing down his meal, Mental Byron went in search of the others. He found Don Worth first. The latter was on the after-deck watching the dark patch that had swallowed the sun.

"Tuck spotted something," he told Worth. "Two passengers are wearing queer rings on their right hands. Might be gold.

Might not. He thinks we should keep watch for anyone wearing a similar ring."

Don Worth considered this. "Sounds like some kind of token by which each one of these gang knows the other."

"Which, if we find more of them, it would certainly be," agreed Mental. "For bands of gold might signify a band of another, older order."

"Exactly what do you mean?"

"Seafarers of the most unsavory sort also once wore gold bands. But in their pierced ears."

"Pirates, you mean," Worth mused.

"Gold hoops in the ears would be a dead giveaway," nodded Mental placidly. "On the other hand, finger rings would attract no special attention."

They went searching for passengers wandering about the ship, sporting such rings.

They had very little luck, until they encountered B. Elmer Dexter, scrubbing a deck.

Seaman Dexter listened to their recital and commented, "An enterprising individual would start knocking on cabin doors and see who answered."

Don Worth thought carefully. "This might arouse suspicions."

Seaman Byron added, "It might also be poking the proverbial hornet's nest."

"Why don't I try one door?" suggested Dexter, "and if I strike pay dirt, we can take this to the Skipper."

It sounded like a reasonable proposition, so Don Worth said, "Go ahead, Dex. But be careful."

"I will be as cautious as a butler waking up a banker for his breakfast in bed," he vowed.

B. Elmer Dexter went off to B Deck and counted off the numbers on the stateroom doors. He had already memorized some of the cabin numbers belonging to passengers suspected of belonging to the Diamond gang. So he selected one at random. Cabin Seven-B.

Giving the door a sharp rapping, he waited patiently until a voice called gruffly from within, "What is it?"

"Routine cabin inspection," announced Dexter.

"Inspection? Inspection for what?"

"A few passengers are smelling gas. We think there's a leak. Need to enter."

The passenger door swung open.

"Make it snappy," said the passenger, a heavy-faced man with a shaggy mop of sandy hair that made one think of Tarzan of the Apes. He wore smoked glasses, which concealed the color of his eyes.

B. Elmer Dexter had no inkling that this was Diamond, but he did not like the looks of him. He made a quick circuit of the cabin, sniffing with his nose, and trying not to be suspicious about where he directed his gaze.

He managed to pull off that part of the gag, not lingering long on anything, not even when he spied a diamond-studded golden hoop lying on the modest dresser that looked for all the world like a woman's oversized earring.

But when Dexter's eyes went to the reddish-gold band on the shaggy-haired passenger's right hand, and became fixated upon it, the man stiffened.

"I've sailed on ships half my life," growled the passenger suspiciously, "and I have never heard tell of a gas leak on any boat like this."

"Experimental gas cargo aboard," returned Seaman Dexter, tearing his gaze from the golden ring. "Hush-hush stuff."

Stepping before the door, blocking it, the shaggy man said casually, "You seem to fancy my ring. I noticed you keep staring at it."

"I couldn't help but notice it. Usually a wedding ring is worn on the other hand."

"This isn't a wedding ring."

"I can see that now. It's just a plain gold band."

Stepping forward, the passenger asked smoothly, "Would you like to see it up close?"

Seaman Dexter started to say yes, but thought better of it. His head was nodding up and down, but suddenly it went from side to side as he got his tongue under control.

"I don't smell any gas here," he decided, "so I had better continue on my rounds."

"I'm mighty proud of this ring," said the other, continuing to block the way out. "Stay a minute, won't you? Let me tell you how I came by it."

Seaman Dexter thought that he might as well humor the fellow, and then vacate the cabin.

"Sure."

"Ever hear of a spot called Hy-Brasil? It's a round island near the Azores, not far from a shoal called Porcupine Bank. Rabbits live there. Big black ones."

The fellow's right hand came up, fingers spread out, displaying the ring as if to allow the setting to be examined. But there was no stone or setting.

Dex bent down to examine it, and was struck by the gold's peculiar luster—if it was in fact gold.

"Fascinating, isn't it?" prompted the shaggy one.

"Very," said Seaman Dexter.

"I found this ring on Hy-Brasil. Rumor has it that it once belonged to a wizard who lived long ago. Talk is he would wear it on his finger or in his ear, according to his prevailing mood. I guess he was part pirate, or something."

Talk of wizards and pirates was getting to Dex, who was not getting anywhere in his cabin search. "Well, thank you. I had better be running along."

"Don't let me hold you up," said the passenger, suddenly turning his hand into a fist and driving it into Seaman Dexter's open face.

The punch rocked Dexter, head backward, and the force of it knocked him out.

WHEN B. Elmer Dexter woke up, he was sprawled on the bunk, and there was no sign of the cabin's occupant.

The cabin lamp was still on, but it was impossible to tell how late it was, owing to the blacked-out portholes.

Getting shakily to his feet and finding his knees wobbly, Seaman Dexter started to make his way to the cabin door. He discovered that his mouth was very dry, so he redirected his course to the washroom where he poured a drink of cold water and downed it in three gulps.

He noticed the statuette sitting on the porcelain sink.

The figurine stood about eight inches tall, and cut from some clear crystal. It was carved in the form of a regal-looking man attired in some flowing garment that reminded him of costumes worn by the ancient Greeks.

It looked like a work of art, and not a simple knickknack. When Dex reached out to examine it, the surface felt unusually cold to the touch. He had a momentary impression that it was actually cut from ice, and not crystal. The coldness of the statuette was not that of frozen matter, but something that had been refrigerated. Of course, there was no refrigerator in the small cabin. Nor was it cool enough to chill the thing. The contrary; the night was quite warm.

Turning the figurine over in his hands, Seaman Dexter wondered why it was so cold. Nothing logical came to mind, so he replaced it.

Stumbling out onto the deck, the first thing Dex noticed was a moon riding high in the sky, and the second was how hot and humid the still air was. He immediately began perspiring.

Moving through the ship, B. Elmer Dexter located Mental Byron first, and relayed what had happened.

"We were wondering where you got to," Mental remarked. "Figured you got carried away in your door knocking."

"Diamond slugged me cold," said Dex miserably.

"How do you know it was Diamond?"

"I didn't—at first," confessed Dex. "But I noticed a thing like an earring on a table. A gold hoop with a small diamond set in it."

Mental Byron lost his perpetually placid expression. His rugged features became fixed. Dexter mistook this facial paralysis for confusion.

"Don't you see?" blurted Dex. "He wears a diamond earring. What modern man does that? He's gotta be Diamond himself!"

"Like an old-time Caribbean pirate!" exploded Mental. "I knew it! He's probably double bunked with one of his crew now. But now we know that there are at least three men wearing those strange gold rings. That probably means that everyone sporting one is a Diamond gang member."

B. Elmer noticed one unfamiliar passenger loitering near the bridge. He seemed to be watching the officers coming and going as they reported to the Skipper.

"I sure hope this doesn't cause Diamond to step up the pace of his operations, whatever they are," he murmured.

"Let's see what Don has to say," Mental advised.

They tracked Donald Worth down to his bunk, and excitedly filled him in.

"I think this is something I can take to the Old Man. Come with me, Dex. Mental, keep an eye out on deck."

Don Worth had to request permission from the Chief Warrant Officer to speak with the Skipper. The urgency of his request, combined with the bloody nose of Seaman Dexter, melted all resistance.

Captain McCullum was taking his supper in his private quarters and, after hearing their knocking, gave them curt permission to enter.

Entering, Seaman Worth stood before a modest table, and said, "Pardon, Captain. There has been a serious incident. One of the crewmen was slugged by a passenger."

Captain McCullum gave B. Elmer Dexter's battered face a hard look. "Who did this to you, son?"

"I don't know the passenger's name, sir. But I was walking past Seven-B and I thought I smelled something like gas. When I knocked on the door, the occupant let me in, but I didn't smell anything. I was making excuses to leave, and he slugged me. When I came to, he was gone."

The ship's master consulted a copy of the passenger list which was cross-indexed to the cabin numbers.

"According to this, the passenger assigned to that cabin is named Joe Cannon. Describe him for me, Seaman."

"Heavy-set, hadn't had a haircut in months. I couldn't see his eyes due to dark glasses. Tough manner."

"I think," said the Skipper, laying down his fork and pushing away his tray, "I would like to pay a visit to that cabin. Follow me, men."

McCULLUM was the take-charge type. It was naval procedure to requisition an armed guard before investigating a situation such as this. But the Captain believed in the force of his personality and his ready fists—not necessarily in that order. He led the march to Seven-B personally, Bosun Worth following in his wake.

The cabin was not locked. He threw it open, and they stepped in.

The stateroom was unoccupied.

"Search it," requested the Captain.

They did so, but it appeared as if the cabin had been picked clean.

"He must have relocated himself into the cabin of a friend," suggested Don Worth, hoping that this would inspire the Skipper to begin rounding up suspicious passengers.

Instead, Captain McCullum turned to Seaman Dexter and asked, "Did you notice any belongings when you woke up, seaman?"

Dex started to shake his head, then he remembered the crystal statue in the washroom.

"I went to the washroom for a drink and saw that there was a statuette of a man in there."

Don Worth was closest to the washroom. He looked in there and said, "I don't see any statuette."

Seaman Dexter drifted over, and said, "It was right there on the sink." But when his eyes went to the porcelain top, they widened. "There it is! It's still sitting there."

Don Worth frowned in a puzzled manner. "Where? I don't see it."

Dex stabbed out an imperative finger and said, "You're looking straight at it! It's right beside the washbowl. Can't you see it?"

Don Worth took a look at the spot being indicated and then back to B. Elmer Dexter, his eyes wondering.

Witnessing this exchange, Captain McCullum shouldered in, and took a look for himself.

"What are you talking about, Boats? It's sitting there as plain as day."

Don Worth became blank of face. Stepping into the washroom, he took three steps, suddenly froze.

"What is it?" asked McCullum. "You look as if you've seen a ghost."

"The statue," he croaked out. "I see it now. But—but it wasn't there a minute ago."

"What's the matter with you, Bosun Worth?" barked the Captain. "You usually have your head on straighter than that."

Don Worth flushed. Then he stepped back to where he originally stood. Although he kept his eyes on the statue throughout, when he returned to his original stance, it was no longer visible.

Stepping aside, he invited, "Take a look at it from this angle, sir."

McCullum obliged, and the eyes in his weathered face began expressing their shock.

"It's gone!"

Seaman Dexter took his turn and agreed that, when observed from a certain angle, the crystal figurine seemed to have vanished.

"I am remembering now," he muttered, "that when I picked it up, the thing felt as if it had come out of an icebox."

Entering the washroom, Captain McCullum took up the statuette in both hands, and felt its every inch.

"Cold as ice! Even in this humidity."

Don Worth changed his mind about suggesting that the Captain round up the passengers for questioning. Instead, he said, "That does not seem to be an ordinary statue. Perhaps this is something Doc Savage can explain."

Captain McCullum was grimly silent for nearly a minute. His gray eyes narrowed, and Don Worth, who had gotten to know him very well, realized that the Skipper was suspended on the horns of a personal dilemma.

His professional pride was blocking him from accepting the suggestion at face value. But the longer he held the weird figurine, the more its eerie coldness seemed to seep into his finger bones.

Finally, McCullum was forced to put it down. He looked at his hands for a long time. They were chilled to the bone. Literally.

Immersing them in warm water took the coldness out of his fingers. Then he dried them on a towel and, using the towel, gingerly picked up the statuette.

"Let's take this thing and your story to Doc Savage," he bit out.

Following close behind the skipper, Don Worth and B. Elmer Dexter swapped satisfied grins.

# Chapter XXIV

# THE UNCANNY FIGURINE

**D**OC SAVAGE LISTENED to the accounts of Captain McCullum, Boatswain Worth and Seaman B. Elmer Dexter in an absorbed silence.

The crystal statuette was placed on a modest table, and the bronze man studied it as he listened.

After Dex recited his account of being knocked out by a long-haired passenger, Doc pulled his gaze away from the statue and asked, "What did this man look like?"

"Dark, heavyset and tough as nails. Oh, he also wore a strange looking ring. It resembled a wedding band, but it was on his right-hand middle finger, and it was golden, but kind of reddish, too. I didn't recognize the metal."

Captain McCullum interrupted, "You failed to mention that fact before."

"I didn't think it was important before. I only remembered it now because I've noticed other passengers wearing similar rings."

Don Worth's eyes went to Doc Savage's and between them the importance of that observation did not go unnoticed.

"Go on," invited Doc.

"Well, you see, when I woke up, I needed water, and I saw the statue. It felt cold to the touch But when we returned to the cabin with the Captain, it didn't seem to Don to be there. At first."

Doc asked, "What do you mean—at first?"

Worth began, "It was—"

"Let me tell it," interrupted Captain McCullum. "From where he stood, Bosun Worth declared that it was not there. Yet Seaman Dexter and I saw it clearly. Apparently, when you look at the damned thing from different angles, it disappears and then reappears."

Doc Savage's eyes went to the crystal relic, and briefly the golden flakes that forever swirled in suspension within their depths quickened.

Doc shifted on his bunk as he listened, and in that shifting, the angle of his gaze also altered. His weird trilling, sounding like a ghostly wind through the rigging of an old clipper ship, filled the stateroom, signifying that the bronze man was perturbed. It seemed to come from no definite spot in the room, but rather from everywhere.

"I no longer see it," he said, rising to his feet.

"See what I mean?" exclaimed Dex.

Doc went over to the statuette, and lifted it in both metallic hands, making the figurine seem dramatically smaller than before.

"I would be exceedingly careful with that," cautioned the Captain. "I held it for two minutes, and I had to soak my hands in warm water to get any feeling back."

Doc gripped the statuette as he examined the workmanship, then scrutinized the chiseled features of the crystalline face of the subject.

"This does not appear to be Greek," he advised.

"Looks Greek to my eyes," stated McCullum. "What makes you say otherwise?"

"There is a general resemblance to the Grecian toga, but the cut of these robes are very different and the features of this man are not Grecian."

"You sound very sure of yourself," the Skipper said dubiously.

Doc Savage replied not to that, for he was feeling the chill of the crystal as it crept into the flesh of his metallic fingers.

"The longer I hold it," he said thoughtfully, "the colder it seems to become."

"Well, that was my experience," allowed McCullum. "It feels like ice, but it's not slick like ice and, obviously, it does not melt in your hand. So what is it?"

Abruptly, Doc Savage replaced the figurine on the table, and said frankly, "I do not know."

"You don't!" blurted the Captain. "What kind of an expert are you?"

"One who is honest enough to admit that he has encountered something unknown to him," admitted Doc.

Captain McCullum cleared his throat, then said, "I understand that you are an expert in everything from modern medicine to mineralogical matters."

"That is my reputation," allowed Doc Savage. "But in this instance all I can tell you is that this object appears to be cut from some exceedingly clear crystal, but it is not behaving like ordinary crystal. Crystal would not be this cold to the touch, nor would it disappear when an observer changes position."

No one said anything for a long time.

The Captain asked, "Well, what do you make of it?"

Instead of replying directly, Doc Savage offered, "After we sailed, someone left a present outside this cabin, a sealed pouch. My aides, Monk and Ham, picked it up, and after they opened it, they were overcome. I found them in a severely weakened state."

"Why didn't you report this to me?"

"My investigation had not progressed very far," admitted Doc. "But the object that seemed to have exhibited the weakening influence is in that oilskin sack over there."

Captain McCullum went over to the bag, and picked it up.

"I would not open that were I you," warned Doc.

"I am the master of this ship," McCullum retorted bitingly, "and I will open anything I deem necessary."

Setting down the oilskin bag next to the crystal statuette, Captain McCullum undid the wire fastening, and pushed down the edges of the bag, revealing the clenched fist of black stone with its upraised fingers.

"Ugly thing," he muttered.

McCullum picked it up, found that it was cool to the touch but not cold, and a moment later seemed to weave on his feet.

Doc Savage rushed over to catch him before he toppled. Then the bronze man laid him on the bunk.

"Seal that up," directed Doc.

Don Worth rushed in to comply, and in doing so made a discovery.

"There's something else in this sack," he declared.

Reaching in, he pulled it out. It was a lump of metal. It had no particular shape, but was roundish without being a sphere. From the opposite side grew two horns, which came to sharp points. Between these sinister protrusions was cut a cleft, like the cloven hoof of popular depictions of the Devil, but reminiscent of a weird eye that was not entirely circular, but resembled a quarter moon with the horns turned upward.

The minute he seized it, Don Worth's hand began to feel strangely. A tingling overcame the fingers.

"This thing is doing something to my hand," blurted Don.

Paling, he seemed to lose his presence of mind.

Lunging in, Doc Savage took the object from him, glanced at it briefly, tossed it in the sack, dropped in the black volcanic hand, then sealed up the entire works.

The bronze man made a quick examination of Don's afflicted hand and asked, "How does it feel now?"

"Like I took hold of one of the devil's horns," admitted Don sheepishly.

"It is possible that I made an error earlier," admitted Doc.

"Error?" blurted Seaman Dexter.

Doc nodded somberly. "I failed to investigate that bag thoroughly because I was preoccupied with the weird condition of my men. The mysterious depleting influence came, not from the rocky fist, but from that weird stone."

"Why would a stone draw the life out of a man?"

"A lodestone is capable of drawing iron particles toward it. Perhaps this is some form of lodestone science never before encountered."

Doc did not mention the disquieting fact that the matching horns and inset eye suggested that the black stone had been shaped by human hands.

Don Worth had fetched a glass of water for the Captain, who drank it down, but confessed that he was not feeling any better than before, just less thirsty.

Sitting up, McCullum said, "It is high time we take action."

"It could be dangerous to act in haste," suggested Doc.

"You may have a lot of pull in Washington," growled the Captain, standing up. "But on the *Northern Star*, I am the first and last word. And we will do things my way."

Turning to Don Worth, he said, "Boats, follow me. We will round up every passenger wearing one of those gold rings, but we are going to do it quietly, one at a time, until we have them all firmly in hand."

"Yes, sir," said Bosun Worth.

Doc Savage inserted, "I am more than willing to help out."

"You are confined to quarters until I say otherwise," returned Captain McCullum sternly. "If I have need of you, I will request your assistance. But so far your counsel has proven to be deeply disappointing."

With that sharp reprimand, the Skipper took his departure, Seamen Worth and Dexter in tow.

AFTER the door slammed shut, Doc Savage walked over to the statuette and made a circuit of it, much like a wizard of old addressing a crystal ball before attempting to divine the future. In this case, the bronze man was attempting to discern what possible natural crystal could possess such weird properties as intense inner cold and shifting visibility.

The poker face that the bronze man habitually wore did not change expression very much. But to those who knew him well, there were clear signs—an apparent slowing of the perpetual agitation in his flake-gold eyes and a fixed twist to his mouth— that told of his innermost mental machinations. Doc Savage appeared baffled.

After a time, the bronze man went to the equipment trunks stored in the stateroom. Excavating one, he undid its latches in an unusual progression, opening, closing and reopening the last latch three times. This actuated a cunning magnetic lock mechanism that could not be defeated except by this specific combination. Had anyone attempted otherwise, a chemical irritant would have been expelled from concealed vents at either end, discouraging further exploration.

Lifting the lid disclosed several layers of translucent material on the order of cellophane, but much heavier. Doc lifted out the top layer, which proved to be a garment fashioned along the lines of a cape that fell to his heels.

When he stood up, the glassy garment became difficult to discern. It might have been a trick of the weak cabin lights, but that was hard to say, since only Doc Savage was a witness to the phenomenon, and he did not appear perturbed by the performance of the plastic material. The bronze man's perpetually poker face did not register any outward emotion as he examined the peculiar garment. But his unusual golden eyes seemed to sparkle quietly.

# Chapter XXV

# PHANTOM SUB

**T**HE *NORTHERN STAR* steamed through the Caribbean, threading its ponderous way through deep-water channels, avoiding the treacherous shoals and shallows that could ruin the hull of a ship even as large as the former passenger liner. She was not blacked out, except insofar as all stateroom windows were obscured. Her running lights showed plainly. Out in the open Atlantic, this would be a problem, but here in the Bahamas it was a necessity, even in wartime, to avoid collisions with inter-island sea traffic.

The night air was sweltering, due to the prevailing pre-storm conditions. Consequently, such sailors who were not on duty loitered on deck in order to take advantage of the cooling ocean breezes. A few who were not on duty slept on hammocks. Air conditioning was not a feature of a Merchant Marine vessel.

A great many of the free crew were congregated at the fan tail, where a three-man gunnery crew stood ready at a 30-caliber Browning machine gun affixed there in a great flat pan of a gun platform. It was manned by a uniformed Naval Armed Guard gunner, assisted by two Merchant Marines. They were reasonably alert, but the look on their faces was that of vague boredom.

The big anti-aircraft gun was unmanned for the moment; the risk of submarines or enemy aircraft being very low and the gunnery officer short-handed. Earlier, they had engaged in some practice firing against a kite tied to the stern rail, with the result that the kite had been shredded. During this exercise, the Browning crew had used the black smoke clouds created by the A.A. gun for their own target practice. Now, the guns were being allowed to cool off.

It was one of those moonless nights that smothered you. Another reason the perspiring crewmen sought the relief of the open deck.

The *Northern Star* plowed steadily through calm seas, and so there was little rolling. All seemed peaceful. Men smoked and the glowing coals of their cigarettes in the near dark brought to mind fireflies flicking about lazily. The rule against smoking on deck was suspended until the ship reached open water.

The mutter of conversation was low, and had the air of idle gossip. From time to time, a man ducked in and out of the radio room to learn from "Sparky" the latest war news. For some unknown reason, all shipboard radio operators are called "Sparky" or "Sparks." These tidbits were conveyed back and passed around, along with spare cigarettes.

Talk tonight was of the hurricane stalled off Cuba. It was still there, churning and growing in force and intensity in the vicinity of Navidad Banks.

"Bet she breaks south," a mariner opined to no one in particular.

"With my bum luck," grunted another, "she'll come chargin' up this way and chase us clear into the Atlantic."

"What makes you say that, sailor?"

"I've been on two other boats in this man's war, and had both of them blown out from under me. Just my luck to ship out on a third."

"Don't talk like that," the other admonished. "You'll jinx this hooker."

"I pulled plenty of convoy duty," the first sailor grumbled. "Don't believe what you read in the papers. We lose almost as many ships as we send across."

His shipmate sneered back, "Spare me that defeatist jabber. We're winning this war. Handwriting's on the wall."

"Sure, we're winnin', all right," groused the disillusioned one. "But me, my mind's on survivin'. And I've had me some mighty close shaves on account of enemy raiders."

The mention of Nazi U-boats caused both sailors to fall into a sober silence. At the height of the war, Liberty ships and converted liners similar to the *Northern Star* were being sunk at a frightful rate, with devastating casualties. Vital war material got through to England and Europe, despite the horrific destruction of vessels and crews. But losses had been alarming.

It was better now, but the wolf packs continued to prowl and Allied ships were still going down to watery graves on a regular basis.

During the strained silence, worried eyes flickered across the heaving water on either side of the ship's agitated wake. Due to the absence of moonlight, this made the churning stern waters resemble the heaving back of some reptilian monster. Nothing could be clearly seen, except such waves as rolled.

Morbid, unspoken thoughts dwelled upon stories the crew had heard of wolf packs shadowing merchant vessels, sometimes surfacing in front of their cleaving bows in order to attack. The damage wrought by a single torpedo was often devastating. Lifeboats were often chopped to pieces by submersible deck guns. Sometimes, those unfortunates were the lucky ones. For lifeboats were often set adrift in the open Atlantic longer than a man could survive.

These dark ruminations were broken by the arrival of Captain McCullum, accompanied by Chief Warrant Officer Greer and the Master at Arms, who had recovered from his brush with Doc Savage in the brig.

They were going from group to group with the Master at Arms shining a flashlight into the faces of every man congregated on deck.

"Looking for passengers," said Officer Greer. "Have you men seen any on deck?"

Muttered answers indicated a negative. Inasmuch as most Merchant Marines were casually attired in khaki or dungarees, a passenger could easily mingle with them undetected, especially in this tropical murk.

The trio moved on, looking very determined.

During their makeshift inspection, a voice lifted shrilly.

It spoke one word. And that word brought a cold dread to every heart.

*"Submarine!"*

WITH amazing synchronization, every cigarette went flying into the drink. The Chief Warrant Officer doused his flashlight. Lungs ceased working.

"I *knew* this tub was sub bait!" hissed the sailor who had been talking jinx.

At the Browning, the three-man crew sprang into action. The long barrel swiveled about, and the gunnery crew began inserting plugs into their ears in anticipation of unleashing loud bursts of lead.

Captain McCullum called out, "Point out the enemy!"

Several voices began crashing.

"There! At our stern!"

"No, it's over to starboard!"

"Are you crazy?" demanded another. "She's lying off the port quarter!"

The confused Browning crew rapidly swung their gun barrel this way and that, ready to open up on command.

Captain McCullum rushed about, endeavoring to pierce the black night with his eyes. Myriad pointing fingers only confused him.

"General quarters!" he cried out. The Master at Arms rushed to the ship's loudspeaker system to relay the order to the entire crew.

This led the crew to believe that the master had spotted the lurking raider. But his next actions belied that assumption.

McCullum lifted his flashlight and drove a beam off the stern rail, sweeping the heaving waters to port and starboard and back again, attempting to fix the reported submarine.

Try as he might, his flash ray failed to illuminate anything resembling the lean conning tower of a U-boat. That did not mean one was not lurking nearby. But the combination of moonless night and dark water made locating the enemy raider difficult.

By this time, the loitering crewmen had scattered to their battle stations. The deck settled down and the tension in the air was as thick as the atmospheric heat.

At the Captain's command, a searchlight was turned on and its broad, powerful beam swept about like a gargantuan finger.

Before long, it picked out something dark in the water. What it might be was not easily discerned. It was not a moving wave and, given the situation, the Captain had no choice but to give the command to fire.

The Browning opened up, emitting a deafening racket and a stream of tracer-laced lead. The object was quickly riddled. The water about and around it jumped and splashed. Soon, pieces floated up. Pieces of what could not be immediately identified. There was no clang of bullets striking metal. Rather, the noises were on the order of rounds punching into hard matter and unresisting water.

Finally, the Browning's ammunition box ran empty. A man swiftly and efficiently removed the empty steel box and replaced it with a fresh load.

Before the Naval Armed Guard could resume firing, Captain McCullum barked out, "Cease-fire! Cease-fire!"

The searchlight was sweeping again, then became fixed on something. It could be seen that numerous small fragments were scattered about the swells.

Chief Warrant Officer Greer spoke up. "Looks like driftwood to me."

McCullum nodded solemnly. "False alarm," he muttered. "Damn nervous Nellies."

The Skipper and his men resumed their flashlight inspection of the men on the deck, but by now many had scattered and if there were any passengers mingling with the ordinary crew, they had eluded apprehension.

Completing his circuit of the after-deck, Captain McCullum huddled with Greer and the Master at Arms, saying, "It appears that all the passengers are in their cabins. So we will commence rounding them up, cabin by cabin."

The others nodded in silent agreement. The Chief Warrant Officer said, "If we go about this the right way, we can minimize the fuss created."

"I would rather have taken some of them on the open deck," returned McCullum.

Greer had a sudden idea.

"Captain," he said, "all that shooting has no doubt roused the sleeping ones. Why don't we use that as a pretext to have them assemble for instructions in the event of enemy action?"

"That's an excellent idea, Mr. Greer," returned McCullum. "Since we are still in the dark about the exact number of men sailing with this Diamond, we can look them over for those identifying rings and pull them out of line."

That settled, they embarked upon the shipboard operation. If all went according to plan, the entire affair could be concluded in a tidy and orderly fashion.

Going from cabin to cabin, they banged on doors while the Master at Arms announced, "Assemble on deck, all passengers! Assemble on deck for instructions in the event of enemy action!"

Sleeping passengers, some clad only in their shorts, stumbled out, looking surly or confused according to their individual temperaments.

"What's the matter?"

"What the hell is going on?"

To all of these outbursts, the Master at Arms barked back, "Assemble on the stern deck for instructions from the Captain."

It proved to be a very efficient manner of clearing out the cabins.

Only Doc Savage was permitted to remain in his quarters. The bronze man naturally heard the commotion and gunfire, and had demanded of his guard an accounting of what was happening.

The guard, of course, did not know at first, but as Captain McCullum made his rounds, he took pains to inform the bronze man that a submarine sighting had proven to be a false alarm.

"What about Diamond?" Doc called through his cabin door.

"My officers are rounding all passengers up as we speak."

"Take every precaution," suggested Doc.

To which the Skipper responded tartly, "I will thank you to keep your suggestions to yourself, Savage. I know my damn business."

With that, the master of the *Northern Star* resumed his rounds.


IN SURPRISINGLY short order, the passengers were assembled on the stern deck, in the shadow of the elevated deck-gun station.

Not all of them wore surly expressions, but many of them did. Among them the man who had once called himself Raymond Lee, but now was going by the name of Diamond.

A big brown man, he stood out among the men assembled on the deck. The fellow towered from bare feet, and wore white sailor pants that were as tight to his hide as his thighs. Beneath his knit polo shirt, the power and vitality of an animal bulged; it leaned in bars of sinew across his neck as he jerked his head back to toss luxuriant sandy hair away from his insolent eyes.

His unnaturally long hair looked ridiculous in a wildman kind of way, although the fellow did radiate a physical power that was impressive.

He spoke up, demanding, "What's the meaning of this midnight drill? We ain't crewmen."

Captain McCullum ignored this question in particular, but addressed the assembly as a group.

"No doubt you men heard the gunfire a few minutes ago. I want to reassure you that it was a false alarm. One of my crew thought he spotted an enemy raider, but it proved to be merely driftwood. Since we woke you up and we are navigating British territorial waters, the opportunity seemed ripe to convey to you all your status responsibilities as civilians in the event of enemy action."

Half under his breath, Diamond asked the man standing next to him, "Weedy, what is this bilge he's handing us?"

The other undertoned, "It was me that done it."

"What do you mean?"

"I-I couldn't sleep, so I was having a smoke at the stern rail. The Captain came along with the Master at Arms. He was looking over every face. I figured he was looking for you. Or one of us. So I acted like I spotted a sub. That started the ruckus. I tried to hustle back to tell you, but it was no go. I had to hide."

Diamond said nothing, but his serious amber eyes became as hard as the substance his name implied.

The Captain continued speaking, but his words were merely a calculated distraction for the operation at hand. The Chief Warrant Officer and the Master at Arms were running their flashlights about, painting faces with hot glare and trying not to be obvious about it.

It was very dark, so the inspection team paid particular attention to hands rather than faces.

When a roving beam caused the red-gold ring on one man's finger to gleam, Diamond folded his arms truculently.

"Ape me," he hissed to Weedy.

"Eh?"

Weedy received a sharp elbow in the ribs, got the hint and folded his arms as well, covering his telltale ring.

No one was taken out of line, but it quickly became clear that the men were being tabulated and mentally segregated from one another.

"These damn rings," groaned Weedy. "They've cottoned onto them!"

"Get ready to follow my lead," Diamond grunted. "All of you men."

Weedy swallowed twice, so hard his Adam's apple bobbed like an actual apple.

During this process, Seaman B. Elmer Dexter was brought up on deck. Under instructions from the Master at Arms, Dex studied the faces of the men at parade rest before them, and quietly conferred with the skipper.

There was by now no question as to which of the men was Diamond. His long-haired sandy wig fooled no one. But none of the inspection team gave any indication of possessing that knowledge.

But once Diamond saw Seaman Dexter, whose nose he had smashed, he realized that it was now or never.

So he barked one word, *"Now!"*

Perhaps this should have been expected, but Captain Mc-Cullum and his officers had overestimated the superiority of their position. With an entire crew of nearly forty able-bodied seamen, he did not expect concerted trouble.

Nevertheless, that is what the Skipper received. In spades. Diamond had been standing near the Master at Arms. He went for the latter's sidearm.

Weedy lunged hard, just two steps behind his boss.

Between them, they bore the startled Master at Arms to the deck and, with pummeling fists and feet, made short work of him, during which altercation Diamond jumped up and showed Captain McCullum the destructive end of the .38-caliber automatic.

"Bark," drawled Diamond, "and I'll bark back. Get me?"

Captain McCullum was too surprised and shocked to speak. So Diamond did it for him.

"Let's see a show of hands."

Reluctantly, empty hands were hoisted high. Not as high as desired, so Diamond barked again, "Try washing your hands in a cloud."

Hands that hovered at shoulder and head height now strained upward like the masts of old-time clipper ships.

The gunnery crew had not missed any of this activity. They swiveled the Browning about and pointed it directly at Diamond.

Unfortunately, Captain McCullum stood between the steel barrel and the hijacker, foiling their bloody-minded intention.

In the confusion of men wearing red-gold rings shoving aside innocent passengers and seizing officers, it quickly became apparent that to unleash the annihilating power of the Browning machine gun would be to inflict severe casualties where none were desired.

Captain McCullum recognized the peril of the situation, as well as its hopelessness.

"By the rules of war," he said sternly, "I cannot surrender my ship to you."

Diamond sneered, "Keep your surrender. But we're taking your ship."

"I would like to see you do that," returned McCullum. "And survive, that is."

To that challenge, Diamond responded by placing the short muzzle of the Master at Arms' sidearm to McCullum's temple and saying, "I would say that my chances of survival are about equal to yours right about now."

The undeniable reality of that statement took a little of the wind out of the master's over-starched sails.

"What do you want me to do?" he demanded grudgingly.

"That, I'm keeping to myself until the right time. Meanwhile, you're going to take me to Doc Savage. Get me?"

"I get you perfectly clear," replied Captain McCullum flintily.

# Chapter XXVI

# CAPTAIN DIAMOND

**I**T WAS NOT fear for his personal safety—or any emotion akin to that—that impelled Captain McCullum to obey the harsh directives of Diamond.

The skipper of the *Northern Star* was a man accustomed to command. He was not accustomed to being ordered about his own ship like a mere deckhand. The cold steel of the .38-caliber automatic depressed to his right temple was a consideration, of course.

McCullum had no desire to be dealt a swift death and so ignominiously by a mere pirate—for that is what he considered Diamond to be. True, the shock of this turn of events had momentarily taken him off guard. But the seasoned skipper very quickly shook off that mental paralysis.

No, truth be told, the ship's master had every confidence in his crew. The pirates, at best, numbered less than a dozen. The crew of the *Northern Star* was quadruple that company.

Captain McCullum did not think that Diamond would make it all the way to Doc Savage's cabin unchallenged, so somewhat overconfidently he led him to the port companion leading below to B Deck.

That this was a tactical and strategic mistake was made clear halfway down the companion stairs to the lower deck, when above and behind, the stuttering snarl of the .30-caliber Browning unexpectedly erupted. It was coming from the after-deck, where the crew were congregated under the threat of imminent death.

McCullum froze. The muzzle of the automatic pressed into the hollow where his upper spine fitted into his lower skull.

Behind him, Diamond's cold voice stated, "Just thinning out the herd. We can't have a bunch of nosy sailors walking around loose."

Through clenched teeth, Captain McCullum ground out, "You damn devil!"

"Correct on both counts," laughed Diamond harshly.

Cold steel again prodded his vertebrae, forcing McCullum to continue descending the companionway stairs. Sounds followed them down. Men—or probably bodies—being hurled overboard. There were pitiful screams of wounded men, running sounds—thuds, blows, kicks and other auditory manifestations of mayhem.

Stepping onto the lower deck, Captain McCullum prepared himself to pivot and apply commando tactics in order to disarm Diamond before he could get off a snap shot.

Some tensing of muscles must have communicated itself to his captor, because Diamond swiftly lifted his automatic and brought the flat side of it down on top of the Skipper's skull.

Caught off guard, McCullum lurched for the rail, grabbed hold with both hands and managed to keep himself from falling. That was all.

"No more horseplay," growled Diamond. "Take me to Savage."

Biting back salty oaths, Captain McCullum recovered his sea legs and walked woodenly to Doc Savage's cabin.

The solitary guard stationed there had not budged, despite the commotion coming from the stern deck. His shadowed eyes were worried, but his discipline held him in check.

He soon paid for that admirably disciplined attitude.

Seeing the skipper approaching, the sailor in Navy blues snapped to attention. That proved to be his undoing.

His eyes at full attention, directed rigidly forward, the sailor did not see Diamond reach around behind the Skipper and uncork a single leaden pellet. Scientists say that the speed of a bullet travels faster than the sound of its report. If that is so, the guard never heard the shot that killed him. The slug entered his brain. In all probability he never felt the ugly thing, either.

Which was cold comfort to Captain McCullum, who had had enough.

Whirling, he threw himself on Diamond's upraised gun arm. Both hands clutched, found meat and muscle, and there ensued a scuffling struggle. It was unfortunately brief, for the Captain was still dizzy and disoriented from his head blow.

Diamond added to his misery by kicking him in the kneecap, then hooking one leg behind the damaged knee, slamming the Skipper onto the deck.

Stunned, Captain McCullum lay there, gasping. Diamond rushed to the twitching body of the dying guard, found the key to the cabin, and unlocked it with great haste.

All this time, his confederate, Weedy—who was down on the passenger manifest under the name C.C. Weed—had been trailing closely.

Weedy rushed up and said, "Don't monkey with this bronze devil. Just shoot him on sight."

"I know my business, dammit!" snarled Diamond, his askew wig slipping back off his forehead, half revealing his naturally bald pate.

The lock surrendered. Diamond stepped back, gave the door a wide berth and threw it open. The blackout curtain blocked their view of the interior.

"Savage! I've got the skipper here. This old scow is mine! Come out peaceably."

A long silence followed.

"He ain't buying it," hissed Weedy. Diamond raised his voice harshly. "One more time, Savage! I know you're in there. Come on out or I'll bust in shooting!"

The silence got longer.

Diamond and Weedy exchanged uneasy glances across the threshold of the open door. Weedy mouthed a question: "What are you going to do now?"

He did not bother to reply. Instead, Diamond threw himself into the cabin with great violence, his automatic sweeping before him, his free hand ripping down the dark blackout curtain.

He must have been nervous, because the hijacker put two slugs into the empty bunk before he got control of his trigger-finger.

There was no sign of Doc Savage in the stateroom. Diamond put a round into the small closet before opening the door, but it, too, proved empty. That left only the bathroom.

The door to that was open, and Diamond slipped up to it, breathing hard and heavy before spraying coughing lead into the opening. Punctures perforated the thin walls. Poised tiger-ishly on the threshold, Diamond craned his head around. And saw clearly no one under the small sink, nor in the tiny shower, whose waterproof curtains had been thrown back. The bathroom proved to be entirely empty.

Seeing that the small space was devoid of occupants, Diamond did not bother to enter, but instead gave the cabin a last sweep with his felinely amber eyes.

There was no other possible hiding space, so he withdrew to the deck, dark face twitching with uncontainable fury.

"You get him?" Weedy asked wonderingly.

"Not there!" Diamond gritted.

"But he was under guard! You saw the guard. Hell, you shot him in cold blood."

Diamond looked up and down the corridor, half beside himself with rage.

"One of the damn crew must've beat us here and tipped off Savage."

Weedy looked doubtful. His mouth went slack. He did not appear to be very bright. But he was no fool.

"But we came the most direct way," he pointed out. "How could anyone do that?"

"Well, someone did," Diamond returned savagely. "Unless you want to go back in there and take a second look."

Weedy looked doubtful of expression. "I'll take your word for it, Cap'n. If he was in there, he'd be full of holes by now. I know that much."

Storming back to McCullum, who was getting his breathing back under control, Diamond stood over him and barked, "Get this straight. I'm the master of this ship now. We're going to the bridge and everything that happens from here on out happens because I command it."

Captain McCullum was in no position to give argument, but neither did he show any signs of cooperation. So Diamond and Weedy grabbed hold of one arm each and yanked him to his feet, spun him around and shoved the defeated man in the direction of the bridge.

ALONG the way, they encountered sailors who ducked back ahead of snarling slugs. No one was hurt, especially after the Captain warned, "Stay back, you men. That is a direct order."

"Now you're showing some brains," encouraged Diamond.

Behind them, more gunfire erupted. It was the Browning, evidently picking off straggling crewmen.

"After this bloody night is over," Weedy said thickly, "the weather deck will need a lot of swabbing."

In short order, entirely unchallenged, the three men mounted to the bridge and Diamond transferred his wrath to the officer stationed there.

To Captain McCullum's shock and horror, Diamond immediately gunned down the Second Mate in cold blood. He sprawled around the big ship's wheel.

The Skipper had been counting shots. He decided that Diamond had emptied his magazine. Springing for the man, he got his long fingers around the pirate's throat, and began crushing the other's windpipe with his strong thumbs.

This time, Diamond was caught entirely by surprise. But it did not matter.

Seeing his leader suddenly struggling for life and oxygen, Weedy fell to smashing his fists into the skipper's face, back and sides—anywhere he could land a blow. And he landed many. His fists were like small mallets of hard bone and connecting ligaments.

The Captain was remorseless. He refused to relinquish his death grip. His features were very red, and the sweat of exertion poured down his craggy, wind-weathered face.

Ultimately, it was Diamond who preserved his own life. No doubt a red curtain had begun descending over his vision due to lack of air. In that ultimate moment, the pirate found the reserve of vitality that saved his life.

Diamond was sinking, his knees turning to water, his hands flailing. Perhaps it was sheer luck that he remembered that he had previously damaged the skipper's left knee. His broad, horny knuckles abruptly slammed out against that knee. The pain that shot through Captain McCullum's afflicted leg was too much to ignore.

With an anguished cry of pain, he let go.

That was when Weedy brained McCullum with the dropped automatic.

His features suffused with crimson, Diamond fought to fill his lungs for over a minute until he was in a position to breathe normally.

Seeing Captain McCullum sprawled on the bridge floor, Diamond began kicking in the ribs on one side of the skipper's chest and then repeated the process on the other. The violence of his kicking dislodged the sandy wig atop his head, leaving him once again completely bald.

Weedy said nothing. He had seen his leader fly into such rages before. Nothing could be done or said until Diamond's wrath was spent.

When Diamond was finished, he went to the ship's great wheel, took hold of it firmly, and said to no one in particular, "I am the master of this vessel now."

# Chapter XXVII

# VIOLENT APPARITION

**B**OATSWAIN DONALD WORTH had not followed Captain McCullum and B. Elmer Dexter to the stern immediately after his difficult conference with Doc Savage.

That had been the skipper's intention upon leaving the bronze man. In the master's grim determination to round up Diamond and his crew, he had planned to storm every passenger cabin until the job was done.

It was Don Worth's quiet suggestion that there was a better way.

"Excuse me, Cap'n," Worth had said. "But if you start dragging passengers out of their cabins in the middle of the night, they are sure to raise a fuss and arouse the others. You could have a riot on your hands."

McCullum considered this carefully. He was not a man to take advice readily, but he had come to know Don Worth well and understood that the young man was very level-headed, as well as an excellent Merchant Mariner.

Knowing that he had his ear, Seaman Worth added quickly, "Some of these men may be prowling the ship and not in their berths. Perhaps we should start with them."

The Captain nodded. "Sound thinking, Boats. Go keep an eye on B Deck while I organize a search party for any flotsam and jetsam belonging to that man, Diamond."

With that, they had gone their separate ways and Don Worth, understanding that serious trouble was brewing, rushed below decks to collect his other shipmates.

Leander Tucker and Mental Byron should have been asleep, their watches over. But they were not. Excitement was keeping them up. So they were easily rousted from their bunks and led back to B Deck.

There they loitered, waiting and watchful, while the Captain took his Chief Warrant Officer and the Master of Arms on a tour of the boat, seeking unsavory types.

The ruckus created by the misadventure with the imaginary pigboat had keyed up their nerves substantially. Shouts from the stern told the story of the false alarm, so Don and his shipmates remained in place.

When Captain McCullum decided to use the ruse of a drill, Don shooed the others away, ordering the pair to station themselves out of sight, and watched as the passengers were rudely awakened and then driven from their cabins to the stern rail.

Silently, he counted the number of gold rings and totaled up ten of the unusual bands.

As the passengers filed up, Chief Warrant Officer Greer said to Seaman Worth, "Remain here and be prepared to round up any strays, Bosun."

"Yes, sir," replied the boatswain. He managed to keep the disappointment off his face because he wanted to see how the operation played out. As events quickly unfolded, it was well that he had not.

The second burst of gunfire was not as startling as the first. The subsequent cries and sounds of pain, distress and mortal injury were a different matter.

Don had his orders, but this was different. His eagerness to race to the stern was counterbalanced by clearheaded thinking. A man rushing into a storm of biting lead had very little chance to accomplish anything useful.

Therefore, Don retreated and, pursing his lips, emitted musical sounds very much like those of a whippoorwill. It was a call he and his friends had used back in their youth at a summer camp called Camp Indian-Laughs-and-Laughs. Even in adulthood, it was their secret signal to one another.

Don Worth continued emitting calls mimicking the whippoorwill, which wintered in the Bahamas, so it might not sound suspicious to the uneducated.

Very soon, similar musical warblings came floating back on the sultry night air.

Triangulating from the sounds, the three shipmates found one another and huddled in the shadow of the Number Two lifeboat hanging on its cradle.

"What's going on?" demanded Seaman Tucker.

"I don't know," admitted Don breathlessly. "But it sounds like a massacre."

"And here we are without any guns," groaned Morris Byron.

"There are guns in Monk's cabin," Don related quickly. "Supermachine pistols. If we can get hold of those, we might accomplish something."

Another burst of the .30-caliber Browning machine gun set them to jumping half out of their skins.

At that point, a whippoorwill call sounded nearby. They answered it.

A furtive shadow that proved to be B. Elmer Dexter, his khaki work clothes spattered with blood, stumbled up, panting like a pony. His features were white with shock.

"What's happening up there?" Don demanded.

Dex struggled with his words, terror having tangled up his tongue.

"Diamond got the drop on the Skipper," he groaned. "There's been a massacre."

"Captain McCullum?" Don breathed.

"A prisoner. We gotta do something before he takes over the entire ship!"

Without further discussion, they pounded in the direction of the stateroom in question.

They managed to reach it without incident, but the cabin door proved to be locked.

Since it was an emergency, Leander Tucker found a fire extinguisher and smashed the porthole, clearing it of jagged fangs of glass, after which B. Elmer Dexter, being the skinny one, crawled in, rooted around and handed out a pair of the compact supermachine pistols.

When Dex emerged through the door, his arms were full of the flat ammunition drums that resembled canisters of eight millimeter movie film.

"Enough to commence operations!" exclaimed Don Worth, inserting an ammunition drum before the trigger guard, and seeking the safety latch.

There proved to be several of these, and he managed to disengage two of them. But when he pressed the trigger experimentally, there was no discharge of rounds.

Morris Byron was having similar luck, and when they realized they could not make the intricate pistols perform, the quartet exchanged stricken glances.

Don Worth sighed. "It figures that Doc Savage would design these things so no one but he and his men could fire them."

"So what do we do?" blurted Tuck.

A glint of steel came into Don Worth's clear eyes. "Maybe we can run a bluff on them."

"Well, it's worth a try," said Dex without a great deal of enthusiasm.

They all felt the same pang. They knew what a withering thing a .30-caliber Browning machine gun in operation could be. But they did not hesitate. Bosun Worth leading, they pounded up the companionway stairs and raced for the stern.

There they saw a sight they could never erase from their minds.

The stern deck was awash with crimson and fragments of entrails and other signs that told them that bodies had been dragged through the vital fluid and thrown over the rail. Some of these bodies still lay there, hideously disfigured.

There had been a bloodbath, right enough.

Manning the Browning were a trio of men whom they recognized as members of Diamond's crew, owing to the unfamiliarity of their faces and the fact that red-gold rings were visible on the hands of two of them.

Don Worth crept up to them, got their attention and said, "Hands up, all of you!"

The crew manning the Browning showed that it was not an unfamiliar weapon. Without hesitating, they pivoted the vicious machine gun, dropping the long muzzle, bringing it to bear on the new arrivals.

The supermachine pistol firmly in hand, Don Worth froze. To the others coming up behind him, it appeared as if he were mentally prepared to stand up to the Browning. In truth, a strange paralysis gripped him, for he knew that he could not return fire, much less initiate battle, with the machine pistol mechanism locked up.

Undaunted, B. Elmer stepped out from behind Don's shadow and shouted, "You're outnumbered!"

The short spiky snout of his supermachine pistol seemed to back up his words.

There was only the briefest of hesitation as the man behind the Browning finished lining up his weapon. It did not last long.

His face tightening, the gunner started to trigger his weapon.

A STRANGE thing happened next. Several strange things, to be perfectly clear.

The gunner suddenly jumped to one side. It happened so fast that he became a blur of motion. He seemed to desert his position, falling off the elevated gun station in his hurry, but the way he went sliding on his stomach along the blood-soaked stern deck suggested that he had been thrown forcibly.

What had hurled him bodily from the station was not visible. That was the queer thing. It was very queer. The gunner's initial action gave the impression that he had jumped back of his own volition. It was only the way the man went sliding along helplessly that changed the minds of the transfixed witnesses.

The man who stood ready to replace the ammunition box once it had exhausted its load of death and destruction went flying next. He landed on his face, and did not slide very far. Nor did he get up again.

The third gunner had been a loose-jawed observer to this sudden and inexplicable mayhem. He got his wits together and lunged for the Browning gun trips.

Something struck him on the chin with such force that one side of the jaw mandible literally unhinged while several teeth flew out of his mouth in a spray of blood.

He folded up like an unstrung puppet, and did not move after falling, except for a muscular twitching that soon subsided.

Seamen Worth, Byron, Dexter and Tucker gaped at this sudden change in fortunes, not understanding any of it at all.

Something that could not be seen began dismantling the Browning with great force. A box of ammunition flew off the thing, described a half circle in the air and suddenly flung itself overboard. A splash came back, proving that the phenomenon was no trick of their stunned imaginations.

Other pieces of the Browning mechanism began to come off until the weapon was entirely disabled. The barrel fell away, made a loud clank in dropping to the floor of the steel tub of a gun position.

Nothing visible was performing these operations. Nothing at all. In the evening murk, the four shipmates thought they spied a vague shadow moving, but every time they focused on it, the elusive thing did not seem to be there.

They blinked, rubbed their eyes, stared some more. Still they could not see anything solid.

When the Browning finally settled down, two vaguely yellow eyes turned their gaze upon them. The orbs floated over six feet above the deck and were disembodied.

"Shades of Davy Jones!" gulped out Seaman Tucker.

The hairs began standing up at the back of their necks and the two men holding supermachine pistols let the weapons sag, as if they had forgotten they were holding them.

As the quartet searched the stern with wide orbs, staring and staring, the sound of approaching footsteps smote their ears. To their credit, the four shipmates did not retreat. They did not seem to know what to do with themselves. They were, in a word, awestruck.

Then a disembodied voice filled their ears with somber words.

"I was too late to save any of the crew." The voice was charged with a deep regret. But they recognized it.

Don Worth blurted, "Doc Savage!"

"Yes," said the bronze man who could not be seen.

A faint rustling accompanied the shifting of the shadows before their eyes and the supermachine pistols were plucked out of the hands of the two sailors wielding them.

The weapons floated in midair, no one holding them.

The yellow eyes scrutinized them for a few moments. The weapons were evidently being manipulated, clickings being heard.

Don and B. Elmer found the supermachine pistols being pressed back into their hands and the voice of Doc Savage instructing, "These weapons will function now. Take them to Monk and Ham in the brig. Release them. Tell them that

Diamond and his crew are trying to take over the ship. Organize whatever resistance you can."

"Right," rapped Don. "But what about you?"

"If you can stop at my cabin on the way, take from an open trunk two translucent garments you will find there. Bring them to Monk and Ham. When they don them, they will be as difficult to see as I am."

Leander Tucker beamed. "I get it now. You're wearing some kind of invisibility gimmick."

"There is no time to lose," admonished the bronze man. "Captain McCullum is Diamond's prisoner."

Don Worth lost no time getting into motion. They hurried forward.

In the smothering tropical darkness, the two yellow eyes watched them go, then disappeared in a brittle rustling of plastic fabric as Doc moved stealthily and almost entirely invisibly to another part of the ship.

No eye could track his movements, nor could he be heard, for Doc Savage was as silent as a scudding cloud. But the bronze man was heading in the direction of the bridge.

# Chapter XXVIII

# SPRUNG

STUFFED INTO THE ship's cramped brig, Monk Mayfair and Ham Brooks spent the first hour quarreling vigorously. It was to be expected. That was their nature.

But the close confines and the dreary position in which they had found themselves soon suppressed their spirits.

Monk noticed a shadow created by light coming in through the round glass window in the door and remarked, "Reminds me of a hangnoose."

"Cut out that morbid thinking," snapped Ham. "We are not subject to court-martial. It will be just a matter of time before Doc Savage convinces Captain McCullum to release us."

Monk growled, "Can't come soon enough for me."

There was only one bunk, and they would have matched for it, except that all change had been removed from their pockets before they were locked in. Their belts and shoelaces were likewise confiscated.

Ham's high-strung nature prevented him from sleeping in such austere circumstances, so he gave very little argument when Monk claimed the bunk.

Soon, the homely chemist was snoring in his peculiar fashion, sounding like a combination of an angry goose and an equally annoyed bumblebee having at it.

Ham, his nerves already frayed, inserted fingers into his ears for relief. But nothing seemed to shut out the awful snoring. So the dapper lawyer, after removing the fake mustache that was his sole remaining gesture at passing as a fictitious British diplomat named Lord Ronald Hathaway, resigned himself to squatting on the floor and awaiting developments, if not the dawn.

Inasmuch as the brig was secreted deep in the innards of the great ship, only monotonous engine sounds penetrated. So it was that Monk and Ham were entirely ignorant of the initial commotion at the stern and the horrible events that transpired afterward.

It was deep into the night when the nervous rattle of the key reached Ham's alert ears.

The startled attorney jumped to his feet and stuck his face into the round window. He was mildly astonished to see Don Worth and his friends brandishing supermachine pistols and endeavoring to unlock the door.

They managed to do this, and the steel door was thrown open.

By this time, Ham had roused Monk, and the hairy chemist was rolling out of his bunk, sleepily dry-washing his unlovely features, blinking tiny eyes and muttering, "What's up?"

"We are being sprung," explained Ham.

This woke up Monk completely. Jumping to his feet, he all but pushed the dapper barrister out of the way in his desire to leave the cramped confines.

"Doc sent us!" Donald Worth said breathlessly. "He said to give you these."

One of the translucent garments was thrust into Monk's hairy paws. Grabbing up the thing, he looked at it, blinked stupidly for a moment, then grinned his widest.

"This is one of those special capes we took off those guys over in Romania last year," he said.[*]

Stepping out, Ham accepted the other garment, which was equipped with an enveloping hood of similar material.

---

[*]  *Death Had Yellow Eyes.*

Swiftly, the two men donned the unusual capes, adding gloves which they removed from the pockets, and very quickly they became shifting shadows that were difficult to see. More amazingly, their eyes seemed to turn a yellowish color, for their orbs were the only things that could be seen of them. The hoods of the things came equipped with twin screens that enabled them to see out after a fashion, and which created the yellow orb effect.

"Is this a breakout?" demanded Monk.

"It's bigger than that," said Mental Byron breathlessly.

Don inserted, "Diamond and his crew are trying to take over the ship. There's been a massacre. A lot of dead. Doc Savage saved us. He wants you fellows to get to work. We have to take the ship back."

Ham demanded, "Where is the captain?"

B. Elmer blurted out, "A prisoner, maybe dead by now."

"Don't say that!" snapped Don Worth.

Monk and Ham took their supermachine pistols, which seemed to float in the air as if they were suddenly weightless. Only their intricate weapons and the hazy yellow eyes could be seen of them, although from time to time portions of the cloaking garments shifted in the light, permitting a vague visibility.

It was an eerie phenomenon to which the four shipmates struggled to adjust.

"Let's go," said Monk, baring his teeth fiercely. "We're gonna mop up on Diamond and his gang the way the infantry took the Normandy beaches."

Together, they flooded out of the brig area, Monk and Ham taking the lead.

As seen from behind, moving from zones of light into shadowy corners, Don Worth and his fellow sailors had difficulty following. Only the floating machine pistols were visible, and these not always clearly so.

"They remind me of the crystal statuette that played tricks on the eyes," hissed Morris Byron.

Don Worth nodded and, reaching out, pressed the other's forearm for silence. For they were walking into who knew what definite peril.

It was not long before they encountered trouble.

A single pirate was walking along, toting one of those submachine guns that had been rushed to production during the early days of the war. It was popularly known as a "grease gun," for it resembled one. When turned into operation, it could fill a man so full of holes that he could not shoot back in the short interval between being struck with mortal lead and dying.

The man happened to turn a passage corner, evidently on the hunt for stray crewmen, when his eyes fell upon Don Worth and his friends.

Thanks to the capes' weirdly shifting invisibility, he failed to immediately notice the two floating supermachine pistols.

So it was that the Diamond henchman trained his thin-snouted machine pistol on the four Merchant Mariners, not realizing that Monk and Ham had already gotten the drop on him.

Ham fired first. A burst of mercy bullets stitched across the man's chest, dropping him almost instantly. The fellow had no chance to squeeze his trigger.

Don rushed up to claim the fallen grease gun. Removing the sticklike thirty-round magazine, he examined it in the fitful light. "Only half of the rounds left."

B. Elmer said grimly, "I would hate to think where the other half are right now."

"Buck up," encouraged Don. "We have work to do."

"With any luck, we can collect a few more of these babies," grinned Monk.

They moved on, grim and silent. Somewhere, the ship's clock struck two bells.

# Chapter XXIX

# BRIDGE STAND-OFF

**D**OC SAVAGE WAS not challenged as he worked his way through the weather deck of the *Northern Star* toward the navigating bridge.

He was not being particularly prescient when he determined to go there. The bronze man had no way of knowing that Diamond would seek the bridge, but it was a reasonable assumption. Since it was the nerve center of the great ship, seizing control of the bridge would logically be of paramount importance. If it was possible to do so, Doc desired to beat Diamond to the command center.

But getting to the bridge was not so easy as all that.

The miraculous cape the bronze man wore permitted him the luxury of not being seen, but that did not mean he could not be felt, nor could he pass through obstacles in his path, as if he were intangible. He was hardly that. Doc Savage was also rather large of frame, and vessels like the *Northern Star* tended to be cramped, even in their upper decks.

Thus it was that Doc had to work his way through and around numerous obstacles, keeping close to the lifeboats suspended in their cradles, hugging the great ventilator funnels, and more than once nearly collided with an anxious crew member who was struggling to figure out what was going on.

Once, traversing a cross-ship passage, Doc found a Naval Armed Guard going in the wrong direction toward trouble.

Without hesitation, the bronze man seized him by the shoulders, spun him around and sent him stumbling back.

"Danger in that direction, sailor," he warned. "Find other crewmen. Gather weapons. Prepare to fight to take back the ship."

"What the hell is going on? Is this a damned mutiny?"

"Piracy."

Only then did the Navy man notice that he was talking to thin air.

"Where are you? I can't see anything in this blasted darkness."

"Get moving!" barked Doc, giving the man another encouraging shove.

The sailor took the hint. He disappeared below.

Doc Savage moved on. Had there been time, he would have stopped by his cabin and gathered up all the gadgets he could. He carried a few on his person, but more would be preferable. There was just no time. He had to reach the bridge.

The bronze man did so without further incident, which was a tribute to his stealth and skill. By this time, the pirates had redistributed themselves about the ship and were in the act of rounding up or locking in every crewman that they could find. They were very efficient in this, for Doc stumbled across no more members of the *Northern Star* crew.

It was beginning to look as if Diamond's gang was well along in their violent seizing of the gray steamship. Coming upon the radio shack, the bronze man discovered the set in ruins. Someone had taken a hammer to the equipment, disabling it beyond repair. No doubt this had been accomplished before any S.O.S. could be sent. There was no sign of the radioman, other than a spattering of blood indicating that a battle had taken place.

Doc found his way to the bridge, slipped up the stairs and found the door locked.

Hunkering down, he produced his periscope gadget, and lifted it in order to gain a view of the bridge interior. The bronze man was not greatly surprised to discover Diamond standing at the wheel, his nervous confederate by his side.

There was no sign of anyone else, which was very alarming. Manipulating the periscope carefully so as not to draw attention to it, Doc spied Captain McCullum lying in a corner of the bridge, as if flung there. The skipper was bloody and disheveled and looked very much like a broken rag doll that had been cast aside.

Doc studied him for several minutes before he discerned outward signs of respiration in his chest, proving that McCullum was still alive.

Collapsing the folding periscope, Doc considered his options. They were few in number, none of them very satisfactory.

It might be possible to jimmy the bridge door, but chances of discovery were significant. Breaking the door down would probably draw a bullet before it could be accomplished, although the bronze man flexed his knuckles a long time while he considered the odds.

Waiting for reinforcements made the most sense, but the essential problem remained. Reaching the door without being shot at, or worse, risking that Captain McCullum would again be used as a human shield.

After considerable reflection, Doc Savage decided to take an unorthodox approach.

Standing up, he knocked on the door.

This was not so foolhardy as might be imagined. The bronze man's superb reflexes would allow him to drop down out of sight ahead of any seeking bullet before it could find him. True, some of the other risks remained. The bronze man was reluctant to simply retreat.

So he knocked, simultaneously throwing off his plastic hood, which revealed his metallic features and his uncanny golden eyes.

The heads of Diamond and Weedy turned, and their faces collapsed in a kind of incredulous consternation. For all they could see was Doc Savage's disembodied head, floating in midair.

The incredible sight held the pair spellbound long enough for the bronze giant to replace the hood before they could get a bead on him. As a further precaution against flying lead, he stepped well to one side.

From the point of view of Diamond and Weedy, Doc's head vanished as if a hungry fragment of the night loomed up and swallowed it whole, leaving only two disembodied yellow orbs that did not look exactly like human eyes. This was a trick of the suit. No matter who wore them, their eyes showed yellow through the screened eye-holes.

"This is Doc Savage!"

Diamond could be heard barking, "Go see what he wants!"

Weedy hesitated. "I ain't lettin' him in! Are you crazy?"

Diamond lifted his voice and said, "Speak your mind!"

"You can't get away with this!" As soon as the words left his lips, Doc Savage realized how absurd they must sound. Diamond had control of the ship. And his men had unfettered range over all decks. It could not be denied that he was succeeding in his plans, whatever they were.

Diamond flung back, "I *am* getting away with it. Now beat it, or the skipper gets it. Get me?"

"What do you want, Diamond? If that is your name."

"I have what I want. This ship."

"Think you can hold it?" Doc challenged. "Think again."

"You don't scare me, Savage," sneered Diamond. "I'm a guy who got plenty from his ancestors. Maybe you heard of some of them. François l'Olonnois, Captain John Avery, Henry Morgan, Bartholomew Roberts and Edward Teach."

Doc Savage had heard of all of them. The last named was better known as Blackbeard, who had once all but ruled these same Caribbean waters. They numbered among the bloodiest buccaneers in history, and there was no possible way that

Diamond was related to all of them, even if he might conceivably be kin to some of those rogues. But the boast told the bronze man one thing. Diamond was not an enemy agent. He fancied himself a 20th Century corsair. And he had a definite objective.

"I know those names, but have never heard of you before this," Doc called out.

"I'm well on my way to remedying that," Diamond barked back. "Now you listen. There's no need for us to tangle any further. You and your bully boys climb into a lifeboat and take off. Hear me? Just go, and we will have no more trouble. After that, what I'm doing is my business. You can save your skins— or my men will have your hides. Your choice."

It was an impossible situation and Doc Savage did not answer it directly.

Instead, he said loudly, "You will be hearing from us."

Without waiting for a response, Doc faded down the stairs and melted into the gloom of the vessel superstructure. No bullets sought him. It would have been futile to expend lead on his fleeting form.

The bronze man moved about the ship and got lucky only once. He came up on one of Diamond's gang, who had discovered a seaman at liberty.

The mariner proved to be the Negro oiler, Jury Goines. The big fellow looked vaguely dazed. No doubt Goines was still shrugging off the effects of the anesthetic Doc introduced into his system days before.

Seaman Goines had his great hands lifted over his head in abject surrender. The expression on his face held no surrender, however. And the look in his dark eyes held a crafty gleam that said that if the pirate who had the drop on him got too close to those great hands, they were going to sweep down and do damage.

The gang member caught that glint, understood its significance and made a snap decision.

He decided to shoot.

COMING up from behind, Doc Savage recognized the peril of the situation. His gloved hands, entirely invisible, swept up and came together. The bronze giant made the great clapping motion with both hands, capturing the man's head between them.

The force of Doc's palms striking the man's ears all but ruptured his drums, and before the Diamond henchman could find the trigger with his finger, he dropped his gun and commenced thrashing, head feeling as if it was caught in a vise.

Doc Savage flung the man to one side with such force that the latter's skull rebounded off the bulkhead, and the corsair was immediately laid low.

Observing all this, Seaman Goines looked about, failed to comprehend what he had just witnessed, and various expressions crawled over his dark features.

Doc Savage spoke up. "Seaman Goines."

Goines blinked, seeing nothing. "Yes, sir?" he responded.

"The ship has been captured by pirates. Find a place to hide and await rescue."

"Rescue? What about fighting back?"

"Later. The captain is a prisoner. Many of the crew are dead. Those who remain are unarmed. Conceal yourself and wait for word to liberate the ship."

The big Negro didn't like what he had heard, but the common sense aspect of it was undeniable.

"How come I can't see you?" he muttered uneasily.

Doc Savage did not reply. He simply passed into another section of the ship, a softly rustling fragment of shadow.

Moving through the lower decks, the bronze man used all his senses, paying particular attention to what his nose told him. Years of special training had sharpened his olfactory nerves to the point that he could recognize individuals in absolute darkness by their personal scent alone.

Both Monk and Ham were addicted to expensive colognes they were convinced appealed to the opposite sex. When Doc Savage caught a whiff of the mingling of both of those scents, he glided in that general direction.

Before long, he found Monk and Ham, leading Don Worth and his companions through twisting corridors that smelled of oil and grease.

They were only recognizable because their supermachine pistols floated before them. The pair displayed two sets of yellow eyes that were not natural.

Hastily, the bronze man undid the hood portion of the electrical cape, revealing his bronzed features and active flake-gold eyes.

"Doc!" Monk and Ham cried in unison.

Monk grinned from ear to ear. "Whoeee! Now we can go to town on these dang buccaneers."

Doc Savage shook his head firmly. "Diamond has control of the ship. And Captain McCullum is his prisoner. No doubt most of the crew are in similar straits."

Expression ferocious, Monk growled, "So we take the blasted ship back!"

"No. Diamond has offered a deal. If we leave in a lifeboat, he will spare the skipper."

Ham looked doubtful. "Can we believe that cutthroat?"

"Ordinarily, I would not. But for the moment Diamond has the upper hand. If we play along, we might be able to turn the tables on him."

"From a lifeboat in the middle of the Bahamas?" Ham countered.

Doc said earnestly, "Diamond does not know about Don Worth and his friends here. I have also encountered Seaman Goines and instructed him to secrete himself until rescue comes. Altogether, that makes eight of us, with possibly an equal number of the Diamond gang surviving."

"Not much of a plan," muttered Monk.

"Have either of you a better one?" demanded Doc.

Monk made a fighting gesture with his machine pistol, indicating he simply wanted to charge about, unleashing violent hell and mowing down all opposition. Ham Brooks looked more thoughtful.

In the end, they had nothing much to offer. The situation aboard the *Northern Star* was beyond bleak. Conceivably, they might lurk about the ship indefinitely, a trio of virtually invisible men, picking off the enemy at will. But they could not conceal the fact that Diamond's gang were being whittled down during such a dangerous operation. Such losses, when Diamond became aware of them, would doubtless provoke him to murder the captain.

There also remained the mystery of Diamond's objectives. This was wartime, and discovering the pirate's plan might be of greater importance than regaining the ship in the short run.

So it was settled.

TURNING to Seaman Worth and his friends, Doc said, "Conceal yourselves. Await developments." He handed Don Worth a small steel object.

The young boatswain accepted it, regarding the object curiously.

"A whistle?"

The bronze man nodded. "A so-called silent whistle. Let's hear how well you blow it."

Placing the stainless steel tube in his mouth, Don began blowing. No discernible sound emerged, however.

But as Don continued his efforts, excited lights came into Doc Savage's flake-gold eyes.

"You have just the right touch for this," the bronze man told Don.

Don blinked, startled. "You can hear it?"

"Clearly. Apparently, the manner in which the whistle is blown makes a difference in the pitch. In the future, use the whistle exactly as you just did. No one will be able to hear it except me. If Diamond reaches his objective, or stops the ship anywhere, blow the silent whistle as many times as practical. Pass it among yourselves, and keep blowing until you receive a signal from me."

A light of understanding dawned in the young men's eyes.

"Can you imitate a whippoorwill?" Don asked Doc.

In response, the bronze man's throat pulsed, producing an excellent imitation of that nightjar's lonesome call.

Don brightened. "Perfect! That's the agreed-upon signal, then."

The matter settled, Doc Savage drew on the hood that caused his head to all but vanish from view. Moving quickly and softly, the bronze man led his men to the upper deck.

They picked a lifeboat sufficiently far from the bridge as not to invite a sniping bullet. The canvas cover came off swiftly. Working the thing out until it was dangling over the water, they climbed aboard and lowered themselves by the manila rope falls.

Once in the brine, they detached the lifting rings and pushed off. The bronze man waited until they were a fair distance behind the steaming ship, which was running with its masthead, stern and sidelights illuminated. Then he produced a flare pistol from the lifeboat's meager emergency stores.

Firing this into the air produced a ghostly brilliance that sputtered and soon fizzled. Doc awaited developments.

A response was not long in coming.

A shadowy form appeared at the stern rail, lifted a rifle of some type, and squeezed off a single shot that proved to be a clean miss. More slugs came, carefully spaced apart. The bullets skipped along the waves, sounding like flutes. None struck anything.

Taking a supermachine pistol from Ham's hand, the bronze man latched it into single-shot position, sighted carefully, and fired twice.

The result was immediate. The sniper was driven backward, his rifle falling overboard. No more attempts were undertaken to snipe at the lifeboat, and in the absence of moonlight, they were soon lost from view.

Sitting in the sweltering darkness, Monk Mayfair wondered, "I don't suppose that was a lead slug you uncorked?"

Doc shook his head. "Mercy bullet."

"A mercy bullet was too good for that low-down buccaneer."

No one disputed that, despite Doc Savage's long-held policy of not taking human life if it could be avoided, not even in wartime.

# Chapter XXX
# ADRIFT

**THE PLAN OF** Doc Savage seemed wildly impractical on the face of it.

Permitting himself and his men to be set adrift among the sprawling chain of sandy cays and coral islands that comprised the Bahama group, without an outboard motor, or any means of propulsion, not even an oar, made no sense with the *Northern Star* steaming in the direction of the open Atlantic, her ultimate destination unknown.

The trio sat on the plank benches of the lifeboat, essentially marooned at sea. Perched at the stern sheets, Monk and Ham looked crestfallen. Doc Savage was characteristically stoic of feature.

For several hours, they continued to wear their weird capes that defeated the eye. These garments had not been perfected by Doc Savage, but he had come into possession of them as the result of an escapade in which they had figured largely. The bronze man had brought them along in the event they would be useful. Despite their transparent appearance, the garments were not as effective as they appeared. Worn in broad daylight, they were rather useless. In lesser light, one could navigate without detection, but could at times be dimly perceived. The bronze man had not brought them into play in the early portions of the voyage for that reason. The narrow passages and cramped crew spaces of the refitted former passenger liner made it virtually impossible to operate undetected for very long.

But under cover of darkness, especially the moonless variety, they were nearly perfect camouflage. Doubtless the hooded capes had helped to preserve their lives this eventful evening.

Doc Savage was saying, "The crystal statuette of which I spoke seemed to possess properties reminiscent of these garments."

More so than Ham, Monk the chemist understood the underlying theory which gave the translucent garments their uncanny properties. But he was having trouble with Doc's assertion. "I don't see how any crystalline gimcrack could operate the way these cape gimmicks do," he grunted.

The homely chemist then went on to elucidate the underlying properties, going into great detail, and explaining why the figurine of crystal could not duplicate the effect of invisibility. His recitation was complicated, but it involved billions of minute crystals being imbedded in the translucent fibers which comprised the plastic cloak. These crystals were specially treated with a sulphide mixture, which possessed the peculiar property of storing light energy and releasing it later.

"There ain't nothing like that set-up in rock crystal you mine out of the ground," he concluded.

Listening patiently, Doc said, "The statuette appears to possess the unique property of what I will call super-refractivity."

Ham, who had appeared somewhat puzzled heretofore, now looked utterly baffled.

"I fail to understand," he mused.

"Seen from different angles," explained Doc, "the figurine was either clearly visible or wholly invisible. There existed no intermediate stage. But it is very different from the capes, which can be discerned in certain conditions of light."

"I wonder where the object originated?" murmured Ham.

Doc replied, "I strongly suspect that the statuette may have something to do with Diamond's objective. The lodestone that appears to leach chemical iron from the bloodstream in such an uncanny manner also figures into the mystery."

"It beats me all to hell and gone," mumbled Monk. "Diamond sure has hold of a fancy bag of tricks for a low-down dirty pirate."

"He may be a common corsair," admitted Doc Savage, "but there is nothing commonplace about his manner of operating. He is very clever and, and more importantly, supremely ruthless."

"I'll tell a man!" growled Monk. "He must'a wiped out a third of the *Northern Star*'s crew."

"And he will pay for it," promised Doc Savage with a low vehemence.

They were silent after that, contemplating the carnage that they had failed to forestall. It weighed heavily on them all.

Hours passed in which they drifted, and the oppressive heat made wearing the translucent garments unbearable. When they felt it was safe to do so, they doffed and folded them, feeling relief immediately.

Monk removed most of his outer clothing and took a dip in the water in order to cool off. A grim gray passing shark motivated him to clamber back aboard.

"Glad I didn't bring Habeas along on this cruise," he admitted.

Ham said nothing to that. He was too discouraged to comment. He still lacked his sword cane, which was as dear to him as his right arm.

"Wonder where we are," muttered Monk, looking around in the impenetrable murk.

Doc Savage surprised both Monk and Ham by stating calmly, "Based upon the last position of the *Northern Star*, the period of time during which we drifted, and prevailing ocean currents at this time of year, I would judge that we are approaching the passageway between Big Queer Cay and Little Queer Cay, the former a true island and the latter a mere hump of sand and coral. We will raise Big Queer Cay to our port in another hour or so. Both are uninhabited."

Since there was no help there, Monk and Ham's spirits were not lifted.

Doc unearthed the flare pistol he had previously discharged, broke it open and loaded the clumsy thing. Pointing it straight up into the night, he squeezed the trigger.

The weapon coughed violently, released a hissing star shell, which exploded over their heads with a magnesium intensity that illuminated the boat, but not much else. It was discouraging, that black emptiness through which they sailed.

There was nothing to do but sit and sulk, and occasionally glance back to study the phosphorescence swirling in the lifeboat's wake like a myriad of sparks poured out of a silent rocket.

ANOTHER dull interval passed. Doc Savage seemed unconcerned by their predicament. He was ever thus. The bronze man appeared to have a plan, but even when he failed to formulate one, his foresightedness and preparedness often won the day.

Here, it seemed, luck played a role. Before long, a marine motor came chugging in their direction, and Monk and Ham began calling out.

In the darkness, the pilot shouted back, "Was that you fellows who fired off those flares?"

"It was," called back Doc Savage. "We have been cast adrift."

The schooner chugged alongside. It was a Chesapeake Bay bugeye, only thirty-six feet long at the waterline, a picturesque little sailing vessel with two raking masts and a clipper bow. The boat was sixty years old, as sound as the day they drifted her bottom of five great logs together with Swedish iron, and a honey of a hooker. She could make four points into the wind, with the centerboard up, in three feet of water. The shallow draft made her a sweet hooker for cruising the shoals of the Bahama cays.

The trio climbed aboard the boat, whose stern bore the name, *Albatross*.

Doc Savage identified himself, which impressed the owner of the schooner, a nut-brown individual of advanced years who looked like a professional beachcomber, if there is such a creature.

"We would appreciate the loan of your boat," he said. "Urgent war business." He produced his Naval credentials, which were examined by flashlight.

The amiable fellow proved agreeable after the fashion of one who dwelled among these scattered cays of the Caribbean. No doubt he was a "conch"—one of the white natives of the Bahamas, so-called due to their their diet of sea snails such as conch. "You fellows can drop me off on one of the islands and be about your official business. I'm a little too old to get into a shooting war." He chuckled in a funny sort of way. "Besides, I went tropical back during the last big fracas."

"Will Big Queer Cay suffice?" asked Doc.

"That will do," assured the other. "Hurricane coming, you know."

"Good. Big Queer is in the general direction we are heading."

"Where are you boys bound?"

"Satan Cay," replied Doc.

Monk and Ham swapped semi-astonished glances.

"I missed that turn in the trail," remarked Ham.

"Me, too, come to think of it," added Monk, scratching his bristled head.

Doc Savage waited until the motorboat man had stepped off at a decrepit old landing stage at one end of Big Queer Cay, a green streak of an island boasting moderate proportions, a handful of clustered coconut palms that stuck up like dark clenched fists, and a cream beach. Casting off, the bronze man steered out past the markers to open water, powered only by the muttering engine. All sails remained reefed. Their white wings would stand out should there be moonlight.

Only then did Doc Savage commence his explanation.

"You will recall that Diamond was overheard speaking of a spot he called Satan's Spine."

Monk snapped his fingers. "That's right. I clean forgot!"

"The *Northern Star* was headed on a dead reckoning course for Satan Cay, and it stands to reason that Satan's Spine would be associated with that island."

"That's a bit of a reach," suggested Ham. "Given the profusion of islands in this part of the Caribbean Sea."

Doc nodded in agreement. "But it is the best lead that we have, and we are going to follow it."

There was no argument on that score. They now had possession of a capable boat, a pair of supermachine pistols and the marvelous plastic garments that conferred the power of invisibility under appropriate conditions. It might not have seemed sufficient to take on a large ship equipped with a skeleton crew of buccaneers. But the bronze man and his aides had overcome greater odds in the past, and they were bound and determined to bring Diamond and his gang of cutthroats to justice before everything was concluded.

# Chapter XXXI

# AGROUND

**THERE WAS ONE** thing that could be said of the food freezer in the kitchen galley of the *Northern Star*. It was pleasantly cold, especially when compared to the tropical heat outside its frigid interior.

There was also plenty of food, even if it was for the most part uncooked and therefore unappetizing.

Boatswain Donald Worth, along with Seamen B. Elmer Dexter, Leander Tucker and Morris Byron sat on the stainless steel floor, in total darkness, considering the situation.

Tuck remarked, "Come breakfast time, they're going to open this food locker for grub."

Donald Worth said reasonably, "That's a ways off. Right now, we're safe here."

Seaman Dexter had found a tomato and was methodically eating it in the dark, at one point spitting out the leafy stem he had by accident discovered with his teeth.

Morris Byron had been sitting with his back to a wall, but the chill was getting to his bony spine, so he shifted about trying to find a comfortable spot. There was none to be had. But the alternative was to be at risk of capture by Diamond's bloodthirsty crew.

Seaman Tucker asked, "Don, that dog whistle Doc Savage gave you. The sound of it couldn't possibly penetrate this icebox, could it?"

"No, it could not," admitted Don. "But until something breaks, that is nothing to worry about."

Dex finished his tomato, including a small green leaf off the stem, which he had inadvertently consumed in the absence of illumination.

"I wonder where Oiler Goines got to?" he ruminated. "Doc Savage wanted us to tie up with him, but wherever he hid himself, he did a very good job."

There was no point in speculating about the whereabouts of the missing Goines, so no one wasted breath on the subject.

Instead, they sat in contemplation, listening to the *throb-throb-throb* of the steam turbine engines. Although the converted liner was only about a decade old, its engines were obsolete by the standards of today. But it had been cheap and easy to refit for military purposes, and the rapidity with which cargo ships were being sunk in the Atlantic necessitated efficiency of production.

The engines pushed the *Northern Star* along at a meager fourteen knots. At that speed, she would not clear the Bahamas until well into the following day.

What transpired next caught all four shivering shipmates entirely by surprise.

The engines slowed, abruptly going into reverse. The ship shuddered its entire length, then she ground to an unexpected halt. The throbbing engines went ominously silent.

"We've stopped!" blurted out Tuck.

"Quiet!" admonished Don Worth.

Ears tingling, they listened with all of their might. Next came a grinding groan, and the entire ship shuddered. This was immediately followed by an interval of silence.

"We're aground!" exclaimed Dex.

Not a great deal of noise made its way into the cold-storage locker, but before long a commotion they associated with the lowering of the great steel anchor confirmed what they had started to suspect, but deeply doubted.

"They dropped the hook!" Leander Tucker blurted.

Mental Byron added, "Looks like Diamond has reached his destination already."

This came as a great surprise to the four Merchant Mariners. All along, their imaginations had painted dark pictures of Diamond and his murderous henchmen planning something nefarious to happen deep in the Atlantic Ocean regions. They did not know what. Perhaps the pirates had planned a rendezvous with a Nazi raider. Or possibly they were determined to take the ship to South America, where German sympathizers could be found in certain nations, and offload the cargo of war metals into a friendly port.

In truth, they had nothing but rank speculation to go on. But now the *Northern Star* had ground to a halt—presumably still within the Bahama group of more than seven hundred islands.

It was difficult to tell from the intermittent noises exactly what was transpiring. The ship had presumably run aground, but instead of backing off—which would be the usual procedure—the anchor had been lowered. The ship was now fast. Where, was a deep, dark question. It loomed ominously in their minds.

Their thoughts went to the rumors going back to the beginning of the war of secret submarine bases the enemy was reported to maintain in the Caribbean. At that time, wartime censorship prevented any concrete facts from reaching the press, so it was not known if such bases actually existed. Scuttlebutt was that some had been found and secretly demolished.

Morris Byron asked of no one in particular, "Do we wait, or do we sneak out and see what's what?"

Don Worth gave that great consideration.

"This looks like an opportunity to make good use of the silent whistle Doc Savage gave me," he said at last.

B. Elmer Dexter had custody of their single weapon, a half-empty submachine gun. He handed it over, saying, "You'll be needing this."

Don refused it, saying, "You fellows will need it more than me. In case you're discovered, you can hold them off. It will just get in my way."

There ensued a brief argument about the inadvisability of going out on the deck unharmed. Bosun Worth won by virtue of a silent but firm stubbornness.

Going to the food locker door, he pushed it open and slipped out, visible only briefly in the dim light beyond.

Moving through the darkened galley, Worth found the door leading to a maze of corridors. Eyes wide open, he looked both ways and slipped out as silently as he could step.

There was one advantage to his nocturnal perambulations. Diamond was shorthanded and could not possibly have men stationed everywhere. Up a companion Don Worth drifted.

Moving with great caution, he picked his way through coils of rope and other shipboard litter, hunkering down where necessary, peering around bulkhead corners before drifting on.

He was on the starboard side of the vessel, and even in the darkness, he could see that the starboard Brownings were unmanned. Creeping along, he reached the ladder that led up into the flat steel platform where one of the machine guns rested, its long barrels pointing upward at rest, like twin insect antenna.

Crouched in that shelter, Don began blowing the whistle. The original plan was for the four of them to take turns, thus keeping the tiny device in continuous operation. But that plan was not practical now.

So Bosun Worth blew hard, rested, blew some more as he experimented with the silent whistle, searching for the exact pitch Doc Savage had requested. He himself could not hear it, of course, so he had to trust that it was emitting a sound Doc claimed he could hear.

Nearly an hour passed, but there came no answering call of a whippoorwill. Discouragement began to roost in Donald Worth's courageous heart. Mustering up his resolve, he resumed blowing experimentally, endeavoring to vary the silent sounds into longer and shorter blasts.

The boatswain was prepared to do this all night, if necessary. Before long, the fact that it might be necessary to do so became apparent. The ship's clock struck three bells.

Donald Worth's only consolation was that no matter how hard he blew the small instrument, the Diamond crew would never suspect that the signal was being sent out over open water. As a means of signaling, it was superior to radio, which could be overheard by nearby receivers.

If only Doc Savage would respond….

# Chapter XXXII

# MIDNIGHT SEARCH

**T**HE HUNT FOR the *Northern Star* was no easy one.

Had it been daylight—or even moonlight—Doc Savage would have been able to spy the hijacked ship from many miles away, owing to the flat openness of the Caribbean Sea.

But in this midnight murk, nothing was visible, not the low-lying coral cays, not even the more substantial islands with their bone-white beaches and shivering palm crowns.

It was impossible to ascertain whether Diamond had doused the running lights of the *Northern Star*, or if the drab gray vessel was now beyond the range of their vision.

Doc Savage piloted the borrowed schooner *Albatross* eastward; he kept his golden eyes fixed on the impossible darkness that lay before him. Since there was the ever-present danger of scraping over submerged reefs and shoals, he had the centerboard up.

The hump of an island designated Satan Cay lay somewhere ahead. Owing to overcast skies, Doc was forced to navigate by dead reckoning, but his keen sense of direction, combined with the familiarity of these islands, meant that his rough heading was undoubtedly true.

The bronze man had been born near an island in this group. He knew its cays and channels well. If necessary, he could locate any spot within hundreds of miles, without resorting to a marine chart.

Satan Cay had been fully explored, therefore Doc was virtually certain that there were no associated spots going by the
name of Satan's Spine. The coincidence of the names and the
direction in which the *Northern Star* had been bound were all
that he had to go on.

If Diamond and his men were taking the *Northern Star* out
into the deep Atlantic, it would be impossible to follow them
very far in the shoal-draft sailboat. Doc Savage reasoned that
if his search proved fruitless, he might locate a radio transmit-
ter on Satan Cay and fetch official help. Owing to wartime
restrictions, there was no such apparatus on the bugeye.

Doc Savage was not prepared to do that as yet.

From time to time, Doc cut the engine to the motorboat and
allowed the boat to coast along under its own hissing momentum. This served two purposes. One, it conserved precious fuel.
Two, it permitted a silence in which he could listen intently.

This second reason was by far the most compelling. For if
the bronze man was correct in his surmise, the destination of
Diamond was not far from the spot.

The absence of any sound beyond tropical breezes became a
focal point of frustration for Doc Savage. It was impossible for
him to tell if the silence meant that he was unable to hear the
silent dog whistle, or if in fact it was not in operation.

There was no telling which. So Doc engaged the motor
clutch, which sent the craft lunging ahead, bumping and squirming over the slow-moving waves.

Sitting in the cockpit back of the big wheel where Doc stood,
Monk and Ham were uncharacteristically silent. The events of
the overtaking of the *Northern Star* had been bloody and awful,
and had sobered their spirits demonstrably.

The perpetually quarreling pair were in no mood to crack
jokes, or snipe at one another. So they were silent. Other than
a murmured remark that he wished he had salvaged his sword
cane, Ham Brooks had nothing to say. For his part, Monk was

massaging his hairy paws, as if aching to apply his furry knuckles to a piratical jaw.

There was no mistaking that those were the chemist's intentions. Once they caught up with the *Northern Star*, Monk was
going to wreak assorted havoc. He was infamous for that.

Another hour along, Doc Savage throttled down, and the
*Albatross* was again gliding along in the inky night, ocean breezes
once more filling their ears.

Even that mild murmur was becoming irritating. Doc wished
for a break in the flow, thinking that complete silence would
enable him to catch the high-pitched silent whistle if and when
it blew. It was unrealistic to expect Mother Nature to settle
down, especially with a hurricane churning miles to the south
of them.

The tropical disturbance was another consideration. He had
no way of knowing if and when it was on the move. But Doc
felt confident it would head their way. This was no wild guess
on the bronze man's part. All captains plying the Caribbean
keep in their offices a book recording the tracks of past hurricanes. Doc Savage knew this volume well. His memory told
him that the gale which had gathered force off Cuba would
most likely track in this direction, if prior hurricane behavior
held true. They were in no position to withstand the blow, should
the hurricane come howling their way.

The bronze man was reaching for the throttle when he caught
a high-pitched sound. Swiveling his head, he attempted to zero
in on it. It came again, more strongly this time.

No mistaking it. It was the dog whistle he had entrusted to
Donald Worth!

Closing his eyes, the bronze man attempted to fix the direction, but this proved tricky. He listened intently until he felt he
got a reasonable fix.

Reengaging the engine, the bronze giant sent the *Albatross*
forging ahead, foaming at both ends as it charged in that direction.

In the stern, Monk and Ham sat up, suddenly alert. They looked at one another, and a glimmer of eagerness leapt into their eyes. But they said nothing.

Doc Savage sent the muttering motor propelling the bugeye schooner three nautical miles and abruptly cut the engine again. As the boat sank into a glide, his ears were at work again.

This time the dog whistle was blasting intermittently. The sound possessed a new, more urgent characteristic. Doc Savage listened a long time before he started up the motor.

As the sudden acceleration pushed Monk and Ham back in their seats, Doc Savage said, "The *Northern Star* has run aground. Diamond has dropped anchor. It appears that he has reached his objective."

Monk muttered, "Are you psychic now?"

Doc Savage shook his head firmly. "No. Don Worth is signaling with the silent whistle, employing Morse code. He is very skilled at code, it appears."

Monk and Ham scooped up their supermachine pistols and checked them over. The light in their eyes was one of impending battle.

Ham wanted to know, "Where did the *Northern Star* drop anchor?"

"That is unknown," admitted Doc Savage. "But we are not far from Satan Cay. Which suggests Satan's Spine—whatever that may be."

# Chapter XXXIII

# HAND IN THE WATER

UNDER PINCHED THROTTLE, Doc Savage piloted the sailboat *Albatross* as far along as he dared.

It was an unnerving journey, given the irredeemable darkness surrounding them. These waters could be frighteningly shallow where they lay close to the coral reefs and cays. There was no telling what they could run into, given the absence of navigational range lights, and the unnerving lack of moonlight to guide them.

Of greater concern was the fact that the stranded *Northern Star* stood within close range of their position, so it was unnervingly possible to run smack into it. And the sound of their noisy engine was bound to carry far.

Doc Savage was again forced to cut the motor. Once more, the bugeye settled in the swells, easing into a smooth glide. The bronze man kept the schooner on course by holding the steering wheel firmly in hand.

The sound of the silent whistle continued intermittently. There came no new information relative to the *Northern Star's* situation. Gamely, Don Worth continued blowing, having no definite reason to believe that his signals were being received.

Very soon the *Albatross* was wallowing. They were adrift. Her forty-foot high masts began rocking in the gentle heave.

Monk and Ham scrounged up a pair of boathooks from the storage locker and they dipped these in the water at the stern, found the bottom, and pushed hard. It was an awkward procedure, and it took a while for them to get organized, working in unison.

But in this clumsy fashion, the boat began to inch forward.

Doc Savage tightened down the screw that made the wheel fast, and climbed out onto the bow, the better to con the way ahead. He had a flashlight in hand, one of a spring-generator type he habitually carried. But he dared not bring its strong beam into play just yet.

As the schooner crept along, her hull suddenly scraped something, producing an ugly noise.

Monk and Ham froze, clutching their paddles. In these shallow waters lurked "blackheads"—half submerged coral knobs lying close to the surface. By daylight, a seasoned sailor might spy them by the suds created by wave action around these vicious fangs, but in darkness they were triply treacherous.

Kneeling on the bow, Doc Savage cupped the lens of his flashlight in one bronze fist and turned it on. The fist became a glowing coal that shed soft illumination that would not be seen very far away.

Leaning over the bow, he attempted to inspect the water, seeking the object the boat had encountered. Knowing that myriad reefs studded these waters, Doc expected that they had bumped into one of the coral horns that can rip out the keel of an unwary vessel.

Instead, the bronze man discovered something reaching out of the water that brought the strange trilling filtering from his lips. It had a surprised quality.

"What is it?" hissed Ham.

"See for yourself," suggested Doc.

Peering over the port side, the dapper lawyer took a look. His eyes began blinking rapidly.

"Is that a—human hand?"

"No," replied the bronze man. "It appears to be similar to the stony hand that was planted outside your cabin, the artifact we thought so deadly."

"What the heck is it doin' here?" Monk exploded.

Doc Savage told him, "It appears to be thrusting up from the water."

Monk stared. The thing was black as coal. He saw that its stiff fingers were splayed out, joints curled, as if clawing or reaching for something.

Ham murmured, "It looks like the hand of a drowning sailor."

REMOVING his shoes, Doc slipped overboard, and discovered that the bugeye was lying in very shallow water. About a fathom—six feet. The ground under his feet did not have the feel of coral, but suggested some other hard substance. Feeling about with one hand, Doc took hold of the stone hand's immersed wrist, and found that it was projecting from the sea bottom beneath. What was more, it was fixed to the underlying substance in such a way that it could not be easily removed.

Examining the bow of the hull with one metallic hand, he discovered no significant damage. Only a rough scraped patch. The weird obstruction had not penetrated the wood.

Climbing back aboard, the bronze man took one boathook from Ham and used it to push away from the unsettling obstacle.

Then, with Monk at the other hook, they returned to propelling the craft forward with as much silence as practical.

Not much headway was gained by this, but it was progress. Progress toward the unknown. The sight of the uncanny hand sticking out from the water had plucked at their fraying nerves. It had the disquieting aspect of an omen.

It was not long before they encountered another one. A quick inspection showed it was a similar member, and they pushed away from it and continued sculling.

Using his big body as a shield, Doc risked sending the thin beam of his flashlight off the stern. It illuminated other frozen hands reaching out of the water, black as ebony. There were more than a score of them arrayed haphazardly.

"What in blazes!" mumbled Monk.

Doc Savage explained, "There appears to be a reef directly beneath us. It is not a coral reef such as are common in this area."

"Then what is it composed of?" wondered Ham.

"I would venture to say that it is hardened lava," stated Doc Savage.

"What about the hands?" asked Monk.

"Hardened lava, as well. In some weird fashion affixed to the reef below."

Ham frowned in the darkness. "How is that possible?"

"On the face of it, it appears impossible," admitted the bronze man. "Hardened lava might produce unusual outcroppings, of course, but not in the shape of human hands. A human agency somehow created this unlikely series of obstacles."

"For what possible purpose?" asked Ham, knowing full well that no one present possessed a good answer.

Since no one did, his query went unanswered.

Doc and Monk poled onward, while Ham held the wheel. When the sound of the silent dog whistle became very loud in Doc Savage's astonishingly acute ears, he began emitting the call of a whippoorwill.

At once, the silent whistle fell truly silent. Its high, thin keening no longer impinged upon Doc Savage aural organs.

"The *Northern Star* is very near now," warned Doc. "We dare not approach too closely lest we be spotted by Diamond's crew."

Doc Savage quietly distributed the translucent cape-like garments that conferred a practical form of invisibility upon the wearer.

Monk and Ham threw theirs on, and Doc followed suit. By stages, the schooner seemed to empty itself of her crew. For a minute, they stood about, only their disembodied heads showing.

The bronze man handed each man a lozenge-shaped tablet and said, "Swallow these. You know what they are."

Monk felt of his and grinned, "Oxygen pills."

These were the invention of Doc Savage which, when swallowed, allowed a man to swim underwater without resorting to ordinary respiration. This dosage was good for some thirty minutes.

"The water is exceedingly shallow," warned Doc. "But it should be possible to wade in, and perhaps swim unseen for short periods of time. Just remember that these garments are too heavy for underwater travel."

That was understood. The things had not been tested in the water, but their weight and cumbersome construction was such that all of them knew that swimming would be impractical except for short distances. They were not airtight, and so would surely become waterlogged before a swimmer got very far. If the wearer did not quickly divest himself of his suit, drowning would likely result.

Lastly, they drew on their hoods, erasing almost all visible signs of their presence.

Climbing down the stern ladder, they entered the water, three rustling phantoms. They found the rugged lava bed beneath their feet, and began wading along. They did not need the garments to render them invisible; the moonless night satisfied that requirement. But once they reached the *Northern Star* and managed to get on board—if that proved to be possible—the capes would be invaluable.

And so they waded, Monk and Ham gripping their super-machine pistols, the giant figure of Doc Savage leading the way.

In the weird darkness, they were three sets of disembodied yellow eyes bouncing along as they sought their objective.

# Chapter XXXIV

# ABANDONED SHIP

**B**OATSWAIN DONALD WORTH wore a wristwatch with radium hands and numerals. Their faint green glow was the only way he could tell that it was eight bells—four in the morning. Or night, if one reckoned time that way.

The coming sunrise felt as if it were an eternity away. Whether that was to the good or to the worse preyed on his worried mind.

Don Worth knew that Doc Savage was approaching. The cover of darkness would no doubt aid the bronze man and his two friends in stealing up on the *Northern Star* undetected. Exactly what three men could accomplish against the odds that were stacked against them, remained to be seen.

But Doc Savage was famous the world over as a miracle worker. If anyone could initiate a chain of events that could retake the converted liner, it would be the accomplished bronze man.

Don Worth had seen Doc Savage in action long ago. He made a mental bet with himself that Doc would attempt a stealthy storming of the grounded liner under cover of darkness. As makeshift plans went, it made the most sense.

But if the bronze man did not arrive before the dawn, that plan was bound to be spoiled by the imminent tropical sun.

Concern etching his handsome features, Worth crouched in the gun station, confident at least that he would not be spotted there. Everything else seemed up in the air, which was exactly how his nervous stomach felt. Detached from his body and floating somewhere above him like a jittery balloon.

Twenty minutes crawled past and nothing seemed to stir except that the tropical air quieted down, restarted, and then died again. The air had a peculiar thick quality that made his boatswain's uniform stick to his skin.

Don began wondering about that hurricane. He had never experienced a tropical blow, but he had read plenty about them. The intermittent stillness of the air felt vaguely threatening, like some leviathan creature stirring to life, taking experimental breaths before opening monstrous orbs.

From time to time, one of Diamond's henchmen made a circuit of the upper deck, but since there was nothing to look at, it was all the pirate could do to avoid bumping into bulkheads and stanchions. He had a flashlight, but used it rarely.

A little further along in the night, the ship's skeleton crew began to stir.

Donald Worth dared not lift his head too far above the rim of the circular gun station, so mostly he used his ears.

Men were coming up companionways and murmuring to one another.

Don listened carefully. There was a commotion of feet. Many feet. Too many feet to be just Diamond's minions. The commotion moved aft.

The group seemed to be gathering at the stern.

Abruptly, a gruff voice began barking.

"Listen, you men! We brought you all up here to put you to work. This old scow is cocked up on a reef, and we need your help freeing her."

It was the voice of Diamond. Don was certain of it.

"But before we fall to that task," the pirate leader continued, "there's something else that needs to be done. You're all going to be the work gang."

Disgruntled muttering followed. The ship's crew did not like that idea. Diamond continued haranguing them.

"We're all going over the side. Don't worry. The water is not even up to your knees. I'll march you along this reef. And when we get where we're going, your new skipper will tell you what we need you to do. That's me. Captain Diamond. There will be no slacking and no shirking of duty. Anyone caught breaking away will be shot on the spot. If you mutiny, we will just shoot you all and come back for more. We need strong backs. So leave your brains on the ship. Or I will splatter them out across the ocean," he concluded bitingly.

Some backtalk, vague threats, a lot of grumbling, ensued.

Someone lifted a grease gun into the air and fired off a nerve-jarring burst. This quieted the crew down considerably. No more grousing was heard.

Knotted man ropes of the kind reserved for emergency evacuations at sea were dropped overboard and the crew were obliged to climb down them. Cargo nets would have been more efficient, but this way the Merchant Mariners were forced to descend in small groups and were thus more easily controlled by the Diamond force, some of whom went first.

Flashlights and strong searchlights were brought into play. This brought out the grisly fragmentary remains of the earlier massacre, which had not been policed. It made an impression on such crewmen as had the stomach to stare.

Taking a dangerous chance, Don Worth stuck his eyes above the gun emplacement rim and watched the proceedings.

Cowed crewmen were going over the side, clambering down rope lines, splashing about below. When everyone concerned had reached the water, they started moving as a group. Technically, there were two groups. In the lead marched the bedraggled and dejected crew of the *Northern Star*. Striding behind and around them, but not in front, prodded Diamond and his piratical gang.

Don quickly counted heads. His eyes grew wide.

Unless he was very much mistaken, Diamond and his entire crew were marching away from the *Northern Star*.

It seemed unbelievable. This was the dead of night, the re-maining Merchant Marine crew were thought to be locked in their quarters, so perhaps the pirates felt that it was safe to do so.

Of course, Seaman Worth was uncertain as to the exact number of Diamond's complement. There might be one or two left, standing watch. It seemed prudent that there were.

Don waited fifteen minutes, his ears very alert, sharp eyes flicking constantly to the luminous dial of his wristwatch. No one seemed to stir on the *Northern Star*.

Deciding it was worth the risk, he slid down from the gun station, and worked his way around deck, keeping to the star-board side inasmuch as the crew had dropped over the port side, in order to minimize his chances of being spotted.

Don went directly to the galley. Throwing open the freezer locker, he proclaimed, "Follow me! I'll explain on the way."

Seamen Tucker, Dexter and Byron jumped to their feet and tumbled out breathlessly.

"We have to move fast!" Don urged. "Diamond and his men have taken part of the crew off the ship. We have to collect the ones left behind and organize a counterattack."

"Why would he do that?" wondered Seaman Tucker.

"Diamond told the crew we were piled up on a reef, and it seems that way to me, but he's taking them for a long walk somewhere."

Silence followed as they rattled out of the galley.

"Do you—do you suppose they're just going to shoot them?" blurted B. Elmer Dexter.

"I don't know," confessed Don. "But we have to act fast. Doc Savage is on his way."

That lifted their spirits, but did not detract from the urgency of the situation.

They went first to the engine room and discovered that it was empty. With the ship stopped dead, there was no need for an engine gang.

They next filtered into the forecastle, where the crew had presumably been locked in their berths.

Someone had welded one of the doors shut. A thorough job had been done. It could not be opened without cutting tools.

Don banged on the door and called in, "Anyone in there?"

A chorus of voices answered, many cursed in the salty way of sailors.

It was a relief to hear the cacophony, but difficult to make any sense of it.

"How many are you in there?" demanded Don.

"More than a dozen," a voice called back, so muffled it could be barely distinguished.

"Much more than a dozen?"

"No, not much more, damn it."

Don added that number to the complement that had gone for a walk in the water-immersed reef and his heart sank. It sounded as if the original crew had been cut in half. That meant about twenty souls remained.

Raising his voice, he called through the steel door, "You've been welded in here. Sit tight. It's going to take some time to free you."

A din of angry voices combined into a dull profane roar that could not be understood.

Reluctantly, Don left them to their complaining.

"Split up," he told the others. "See if you can find the Skipper or anyone else."

DON WORTH found Captain McCullum soon enough. He was in the logical place—his private cabin. The skipper lay on his bunk, his features looking as if he had stepped out of the prizefighting ring. One eye was closed, his lip smashed up and his nose would never be the same shape.

But Carson McCullum was conscious. He lifted his head at sight of his trusted boatswain, and let out a kind of agonized groan.

"Steady, Cap'n," reassured Don. "Let me take a look at you."

The Captain had been handcuffed to his bunk, and it didn't take long to determine that several of his ribs had been stove in. Speaking was difficult, but he managed a few words.

"Where is the ship?" he croaked.

"Up on a reef. Diamond and his men have taken some of the crew off. Doc Savage was cast adrift. But I signaled him, and he may be on his way back."

McCullum groaned again, and it was difficult to tell whether it was a moan of relief or disappointment.

Looking about for something to break the handcuffs proved to be a waste of time, so Seaman Worth said, "I'll be back for you with the cutting tool."

The Skipper nodded and his head fell back on his pillow as if it had been a major exertion to keep it raised.

Rushing down to the innards of the vessel, Don next bumped into Leander Tucker, who had collected Seaman Goines from somewhere.

"Where did you find him?" Don demanded.

"In the brig. But let him tell it."

JURY GOINES rapped out a rapid explanation. "I had powerful trouble trying to find a place to hide, then I thought of the brig. I locked myself in there, figuring what was the worst that could happen? After a while, one of the pirates pressed his nose to the cell-door window, looked in, saw me sitting there and figured he might as well just let me be. So there I sat until Funny found me."

"I've been trying to shake that nickname," Seaman Tucker inserted seriously. "Call me Tuck."

"We need every hand we can get," Don told Goines. "Here's the way it shakes down. A pirate named Diamond and his crew have taken off part of the crew. We are on a reef. The other part of the crew have been hot-welded into their accommodations. Getting them out is going to be a job."

"I have handled an acetylene torch in my time," volunteered Goines.

"Good. That's going to be our first duty."

Seaman Goines led them to the place where such equipment was stored, and on their way they encountered B. Elmer Dexter and Morris Byron. Both sailors look dejected.

"We didn't find anybody else," Mental reported glumly.

Don nodded. "Well, let's see if we can free the crew."

When they reached the storage locker, it appeared to be cleaned out. There was no acetylene torch.

They stood there for a few minutes. Then Donald Worth had an idea.

"If he heard my signal, Doc Savage may return at any minute. Maybe we can get a message to him."

Mental Byron said quickly, "The Aldis lamp!"

"Exactly."

They charged up onto deck, turned on the semaphore signal blinker stationed near the bow, and Don Worth pointed in the opposite direction of where Diamond was taking the crew on the general but sound theory that it was less likely to be seen since Doc Savage would be coming from more or less the opposite direction.

Don manipulated the Aldis lamp's steel shutters, batting out a rapid message.

Huddled around it, the others peered out to the impenetrable darkness. They were silent. And when Don was finished, they remained that way.

The mournful call of a whippoorwill soon followed.

"That means he saw it!" Don exulted.

Jury Goines peered around in the inky night. "I heard plenty about this Doc Savage," he ruminated. "Hope he's all he's cracked up to be."

"Don't worry, he is," proclaimed Leander Tucker confidently.

While they were waiting, a sharp report carried through the tropical night. Followed by another.

They listened for more shots, but none came.

"I am afraid," Donald Worth said, "that someone just got shot."

"It's too much to hope that it might have been a pirate, I guess," chimed in Seaman Goines.

"Their turn will come," promised Bosun Worth.

# Chapter XXXV

# OMINOUS ATMOSPHERE

**D**OC SAVAGE DID not break his stride when the first stuttering flashes of the signal blinker interrupted the undivided blackness that was the Caribbean night.

He studied the semaphore message, reading it as easily as he would the moving electric headlines that paraded around the New York Times Building.

Monk and Ham also knew semaphore code. They understood its import.

"Blazes!" exploded the hairy chemist. "It sounds like Diamond has organized a kill party for the crew."

Doc Savage said, "That remains to be seen. But there is no time to be lost."

Picking up his pace, the bronze giant swiftly put Monk and Ham behind him. They sloshed along in his wake.

It was difficult going. The warm water was up to their knees, the footing unsure. Lava rock was cutting into the soles of their shoes. Here and there, a thin bubble that had hardened untold years ago, broke under their feet—making an unsettling crunching sound.

From time to time, they almost tripped over one of the upraised hands that was so much like the clutching members of drowning sailors who had petrified in death.

It was an unnerving trek, made possible only because Doc Savage gripped his flashlight in one big fist, which showed an eerie reddish glow that was filtered by the meat of his hand.

His rather large finger bones showed grayly, as if in an X-ray machine.

Doc Savage knew that he would need to reach the stranded vessel before he could pick up the trail of Diamond and his prisoners. So he headed directly for the spot where the semaphore blinker flashed.

Soon, the *Northern Star* loomed ahead like a great wall of gray-painted steel. The vessel canted slightly, proving that she had been reefed badly.

Reaching her first, Doc worked his way around toward the cocked bow and discovered the knotted man ropes that had been lowered for disembarking.

Seizing one line with both massive hands, he went up hand over hand, as if climbing a simple ladder. Monk soon followed, showing fabulous upper body strength combined with a monkey-like agility in the way his preposterously long arms worked, but Ham Brooks struggled, in all falling back twice before achieving any progress.

In turn, Doc, Monk and Ham topped the rail, doffing their plastic hoods, which permitted their heads to be seen. They were soon met by Don Worth and his fellow sailors. Seaman Jury Goines was a dark tower in the vague light.

"So you're the afraid-of-nothing Doc Savage," grunted Goines, apparently unimpressed by the weird sight of the bronze giant, who appeared to be nothing more than a floating head.

"Watch your loose talk, sailor," growled Monk.

"I ain't afraid of you, either. I grew up in Chicago—in Bronzeville."

Monk and Goines glowered at one another to no particular purpose, all but sticking out their chests and baring their teeth. Monk had removed his garment and was now fully visible.

Doc and Donald Worth conferred quickly.

"We heard a shot," explained Don. "We think something bad must have happened."

Doc nodded grimly. "At present, the important thing is to hold the ship. Monk and Ham will assist you in that. I will go after Diamond."

"Alone!" several voices chorused at once.

"Trailing Diamond's gang must be done carefully so as not to incite a shooting affray," explained Doc. "There has already been one massacre. We cannot afford additional bloodshed."

It made sense, and they did not wish to imperil more crewmen.

"Can you find a way to release the remaining crew?" asked Doc.

"Not unless we locate that missing acetylene torch."

"Do your best," encouraged Doc. He drew back on his plastic hood. Suddenly, he stood there, nothing more than two vague patches of yellow floating where his eyes should be.

Seaman Goines regarded this performance with new respect coming into his dark eyes.

"You are one mighty tall bag of tricks, aren't you?" he said at last.

No reply came. The bronze man had already departed. Soundless as a cloud, he went down one of the heavy cargo ropes.

They searched for him with their eyes, but of course little was to be seen in the oppressive tropical darkness other than his shadow, which itself was a fitfully intangible patch.

There was some brief splashing as Doc's feet landed in the water. When he moved on, even that noise dwindled to nothing.

Donald Worth looked at his watch.

"Let's hope he makes good time," he murmured. "Dawn is less than two hours off."

Sniffing the air like a hound dog, Monk remarked, "The way this salt air makes me feel, that dang hurricane ain't too far away, either."

To which Ham Brooks said acidly, "You would bring that up, you miserable ape!"

"Miserable or not," Monk retorted, "if we get hit, there's no tellin' what will happen to this tub and everybody around it."

Donald Worth reminded, "We have work to do, and we better be about it."

# Chapter XXXVI

# FORCED MARCH

THE PIRATE—HE WAS nothing more nor less than that—who styled himself Diamond was pleased with his progress. Almost to their destination and they only had to shoot one sailor, a Naval Armed Guard ensign who had made a lunge for a grease gun that had gotten within convenient reach.

Diamond had had his eye on the man, and could see what was coming. So when the Navy officer made his move, Diamond had already picked out a spot in the center of the man's back where he drove a single bullet, snapping the brave but foolhardy fellow's spine.

The ensign had arched his back as the bullet turned him half around. He was not a big man, but he managed to stagger briefly before falling on his face in the shallows.

Diamond called a halt, and made everybody watch the air bubbles rising from the man's submerged mouth and nostrils until the last tiny bubble broke the surface and silence followed. Unnecessarily—other than to impress the others with his cruelty—Diamond kept the man's head under water with one hard shoe.

"Let no one else make any such foolhardy move," he called out. "This is a work party, nothing more. Now march!"

The procession resumed, waterlogged shoes sloshing, but there were no more attempts to escape.

The crew of the *Northern Star* trudged on as would men who had been condemned to death. They knew that they were on some type of submerged reef, but the play of flashlights showed nothing but open water in all directions. The oppressive tropical heat did not help their mental states.

So they marched, wooden of face and limbs.

Someone remarked rather ghoulishly, "A bullet in the back is better than a torpedo amidships, I guess."

No one bothered to agree or disagree.

After considerable marching, the ground sloped upward and eventually they were on dry land.

Flashlights showed that the spit on which they found themselves was an ugly expanse of hardened lava. Some of the sailors knew the Bahamas and understood that this was not a charted formation.

A seaman took a guess. "Earthquake must've lifted this up from below. I never seen anything like this."

"You guessed right," growled one of Diamond's men. "A seaquake flung it up."

They commenced climbing a low hill that made them think they were ascending a volcanic cone of the shallow variety. The Caribbean Sea has more than a few of these dormant features.

Pointing flashlights showed only the convolutions of the rise of land. What their destination might be, it was impossible to say. The night continued to be black as pitch.

"Hell must look something like this," a Merchant Mariner commented, trying to avoid sharp projections that resembled shark fins made of glassy obsidian.

"Enough talk!" barked out Diamond. "Come to a halt, every one of you lubbers."

A surly voice in the darkness objected, "We ain't landlubbers!"

Diamond let that pass. He began issuing orders to his men, and out of their pockets came a profusion of cloth scraps.

"We don't want you boys to see the next stage of this operation. So we're issuing blindfolds. Tie them fast and no backtalk."

"What do we need blindfolds for?" asserted a sailor. "We can hardly see a thing."

"Morning's coming along. Now clam up!"

The blindfolds were issued. These amounted to rags. Reluctantly, the crew of the *Northern Star* began tying them in place, and after this was done, the blindfolds were inspected by Diamond's gang.

"They're on tight," reported Weedy.

"All right then," Diamond said loudly. "Resume marching. Gun muzzles at your backs will guide anybody who wanders off of the straight and true."

"They're going to execute us for sure," muttered a man.

"Sure looks like that way. The damn yellow cowards."

"Who are you calling a coward?" one of the Diamond gang snapped. "This ain't what it seems, but if you want it that way, I'll pick out a bullet I can scratch your name on first."

The complainer subsided and the marching continued.

Slowly, the crewmen trudged uphill, stumbling a little, losing their footing, showing no rush to get to their destination, which many assumed was oblivion.

Finally, Diamond called for a halt, announcing, "This is it."

He was immediately misinterpreted. A man gasped. A few bit out sailorly oaths. One attempted to run then, thinking a bullet was coming his way. He was tripped and someone sat on him to hold him down.

Diamond growled, "I told you men that this is not a kill party. Now listen up. We're going to enter a place. Get that? Once we're all inside, the blindfolds come off and you will receive instructions as to what to do next. Follow those instructions to the letter, or you will receive bullets. But not in the back. We will just blow your stupid brains out on the spot. Get me?"

No one said a word. The mariners were resigned to their fate or duty or whatever the vicious buccaneer band had in store for them.

# Chapter XXXVII

# DEVILISH REEF

EVEN IN THE smothering darkness, trailing the Diamond contingent through the tropical night was not difficult for a man such as Doc Savage.

For one thing, the group made a continual splashing with their feet. The heat and humidity also wrung the sweat from their bodies, leaving a salty-smelling trail that the bronze man's sensitive nostrils could follow with ease.

Doc did not use his flashlight in stalking them. He dared not. Although he was enveloped in the translucent garment that reduced him to nothing more than two floating yellowish eye spots, the bronze man knew that worried men moving in the darkness frequently glanced behind them.

If they spotted his eyes, they would not necessarily attribute much significance to them. And because he was following them by sound and smell, not by sight, Doc often walked with his eyes closed. It made no difference. His biggest concern was in not losing his footing on the irregular lava rock beneath his feet.

In time, the bronze man came to the submerged body of the Navy ensign who had been shot down in cold blood.

Treading carefully, Doc had discovered the inert form when one foot encountered an unpleasant obstruction. Kneeling, he felt of the body, discovered the spinal wound, and recognized that the man was beyond hope.

Standing up, the bronze giant resumed his methodical trek.

Doc Savage had no inkling of where Diamond was leading him. The distance was no greater than half a mile, and with each step it seemed less and less likely that an execution had been planned.

The extent of the field of hardened lava perplexed the big bronze man, who had committed to memory all marine charts pertaining to the Bahama group. No such formation was known to him.

This meant that the formation was of recent origin and most likely created by an upthrust of the earth's crust. Doc searched his memory for reports of seaquakes in this area. There had been several over the last few months, none considered significant, for they had merely shaken the surrounding islands.

More and more, the bronze man became convinced that this was the objective Diamond had called Satan's Spine. It apparently lay due east of Satan Cay, but was not attached to it. The significance of the name escaped him, but Doc recalled that Satan Cay was originally called Santo Cayo, a Spanish name meaning Holy Isle. Over the centuries, English-speaking sailors had turned the name into a more pronounceable, if sinister, one.

Coming to the spot where the ground lifted, after which his steady stride carried him out of the water, Doc suspected that Diamond's ultimate objective lay close by.

He paused once, turned his back, thumbed on his flashlight, capping it in his great fist. Through this coppery glow he was able to discern numerous wet footprints that had slogged over this spot. They told the bronze giant that he was traveling in the correct direction.

Dousing the torch, Doc turned about and continued on.

Doc Savage was not unaware of the change in the atmosphere, nor the periods of stillness that brought to mind the stalled hurricane many miles to the south. But even if the blow was on the move, it was not yet at hand. There would be time enough to concern himself with that issue later.

Walking along, Doc encountered obstacles which, by bending and feeling about, revealed themselves to be more of the rocky hands that had somehow formed in the lava bed, perhaps as far back as prehistoric times, if his knowledge of Caribbean geology was to be trusted.

How it was possible for molten lava to be so configured was frankly beyond him. But it was the least of his worries at the moment.

After much walking, Doc realized that the sounds of men moving through the night, along with the stink of human sweat, no longer impinged upon his senses.

He stopped, turned in place—eyes, ears and nose alert. The wind was blowing again. It was possible that it was carrying these impressions away from him. But the more he listened and sniffed of the air, the less likely that seemed.

Doc began reconnoitering the raised hump of hardened lava, seeking a solution to the mystery. He trod carefully, knowing that a wrong move could cause him to inadvertently break off a chunk of brittle black rock, betraying his position by the noise created.

Yet after circling the area twice, the bronze man could discover no sight, smell or sound of his quarry. He had to seal his lips to prevent his trilling sound from issuing forth. That was a mark of how puzzled he was.

Doc Savage had not climbed to the summit. In fact, he could not perceive it in the darkness. The possibility that this was a volcanic cone had instilled a reasonable caution in him. He did not want to blindly blunder into an open crater—even a long-dormant one.

Staring up at the inky spot where he assumed the summit would be, Doc attempted to pierce the frustrating blackness. Something seemed to loom up there, but it might have been a trick of his imagination.

When he gazed in that direction, an ominous feeling came over him. It was a sensation difficult to describe, but it carried with it a suggestion of ancient evil.

Shaking off the superstitious thought, Doc produced his flashlight and resumed mounting the low hill, prepared at any moment to turn on the flash ray and take his chances.

Whatever loomed up there, it should explain the mystery of what had become of Diamond and his cohorts. It was a mystery Doc Savage very much intended to solve.

# Chapter XXXVIII

# DARK DESCENT

THE CREWMEN OF the *Northern Star* did not know where they were.

Blindfolded, they had been led up the stony prominence and into something that felt as though it must be a natural enclosure.

The absence of moving air combined with a briny odor that was close and stank of indefinable sea smells gave them the idea that they had entered a former sea cave.

There was no other explanation for the change in their surroundings, nor for the weird way the voices of Diamond and his cutthroat crew seemed to change and echo hollowly the further along they progressed.

Having been led up a prominence, they were now descending. The path was circular. That much they could tell.

One of the crewmen, evidently a fellow subject to claustrophobia, began talking nervously. He did not speak to anyone in particular; he simply fell to babbling.

"What is this awful place? Are we going into a cave? I don't like this. I don't like this one little bit!"

One of the cutthroats' voices roared out, "You don't have to like it! Just keep movin'."

"This joint smells like old Davy Jones' Locker," the claustrophobic one muttered.

This was an unfortunate reference, for it caused the other blindfolded men to conjure up dark thoughts about where they were being led.

"Do they have caves in the Bahamas?" one murmured.

Another responded tightly, "I reckon they have caves anywhere you might go, except in the desert, maybe."

"Shut up!" Diamond bellowed. "You men have work to do. Keep your mind on your feet. Don't bump into anything."

The casual reference to work triggered imaginations. One of the sailors had mined coal in West Virginia prior to joining the Merchant Marines.

"I think this might be a mining works," he murmured.

"What's that?" demanded one of Diamond's men.

"I said, 'Walking along in the dark is making me lose my mind,'" the man fibbed.

"You'll lose more than that, if you don't keep your mind on the detail."

"Yeah," added another harshly, "you could lose your brain, too. It might just get shot out from between your ears."

Everyone fell silent upon hearing that threat. They pressed on. They were still meandering downward, but there were no steps. They did not understand that.

Many minutes passed as they went down what they began to imagine was a crude circular ramp.

A sailor, his nerves on edge, afraid of imminent death, but even more fearful of the blackness of the unknown, broke.

"This is surely Hell!" he screeched. "He's taking us down into the bowels of Hell itself!"

With that, the agitated sailor bolted.

Since he did not know where he was and could not see through his blindfold, his bolting had a haphazard, frantic quality to it. It also had its tragic side.

The man ran smack into an obstruction, rebounded with a bloody nose, and landed on the seat of his denim pants.

This commotion caused the others to halt in their tracks and start milling about, their ears trying to make out the sounds of what was transpiring around them, unseen.

There were no words. Just a single gunshot. And the man who had been concerned about descending into a literal Hell ceased his complaining.

Another thick silence followed.

The voice of Diamond, cold and cutting, came again.

"Listen well, you men. We are in a chamber formed by a pocket of hot gas probably hundreds of thousands of years ago. We're here to do a job, and then we're going to get out of here. Follow orders and you'll be breathing salt air soon enough. Get me?"

No one responded, for few believed they would ever see the light of day again. An oppressiveness of spirit enveloped their thoughts and clutched at their pounding hearts. But they were helpless. They had no choice but to obey.

Once more they were jostled and knocked into single file again, and so they resumed their downward trudging, a great unease creeping into their nervous systems the deeper they descended in the unknown well into the earth.

# Chapter XXXIX

# THE MOANING THING

**I**N THE UNRELIEVED darkness of night, a series of sounds reached Doc Savage's sensitive ears.

They were high-pitched, squeaky, and reminded of mice fleeing a tabby cat. But the sounds did not come from the ground around him, rather from high over his head—in the direction of the oppressive looming thing the bronze man sensed but could not see clearly.

Doc was still attired in the enveloping cape that defeated human sight. The plastic hood covered his ears sufficiently so that, at first, he was not positive what had produced the intermittent noises overhead.

They continued, and were accompanied by more subtle sounds, which Doc studied in his mind.

It was not long before he concluded that these noises signified flapping bats in flight. The question looming in the bronze giant's mind was this: Were the bats emerging from the thing bulking ahead of him, or were they fleeing it?

Bats, the bronze man knew, roosted high in trees, barns, attics and similar tall structures. Caves also were an attraction, but Doc had never heard of any species of bat that occupied dormant volcanic cones.

This led to a natural conclusion that the thing he was facing and which would soon be illuminated by the rising tropical sun, was not a volcanic structure, but something else. Possibly something man-made. But he could not conceive what it might be.

For this forbidding reef, which he had concluded was the mysterious Satan's Spine, had been thrust up from the ocean floor comparatively recently. As such, it should not possess as a natural feature any structure that would attract nesting bats.

Although it was tempting to do so, Doc dared not bring his flashlight into play. The hand torch came with an extra bulb which could produce infra-red light, but in order for that to be useful, he needed special filter goggles, which were not on his person. In recent months, the bronze man had retired many of the gadgets he formerly used with great relish. Perhaps this was a consequence of the sobering effect of the World War that had engulfed the planet, or possibly it was a growing maturity of mind that was a consequence of having been called upon by the War Department to undertake various secret missions on behalf of the Allies. Consequently, Doc had been attempting to rely less and less on his customary bag of tricks. His work sometimes took him behind enemy lines, in disguise, and the telltale gadgets could cause him to be stood up against a brick wall reserved for catching such bullets as failed to lodge in the bodies of shot spies.

The bronze man thought with some irony that the invisibility producing cloak he now wore was possibly one of the most outlandish gadgets he had ever employed. So perhaps his precautions were all for naught.

As Doc listened to the squeaky wheeling of unseen bats overhead, he concluded that they were in fact fleeing a rookery, wherever it might be. More and more high-pitched noises followed, and the air was filled with frantic flying things.

Taking great care, Doc lifted the hood attachment of his cape to allow his nose to take in fresh air unobstructed. He was not so much interested in the fresh air as he was in the scents carried along with it.

Odors of men, which had been fresh before, were less distinct now. This suggested to the bronze man's scientifically trained brain that the sailors of the *Northern Star* had been marched by Diamond and his gang into an enclosure of some kind. Whether natural or man-made was impossible to tell. But it was puzzling to imagine what sort of structure might exist on a reef that had been submerged until recent times.

Taking great care to move without making any sound, and occasionally encountering objects thrusting up from the hard rock beneath his feet, Doc worked his way to the summit, and along the way stopped to feel the weird obstructions.

They were outgrowths or extensions of the hardened lava bed beneath, but they were not evidently natural formations. Every one of them was in the shape of a human hand, his exploring fingers determined. Doc could not see them, of course, but the picture they painted in his imagination suggested the clutching hands of drowning sailors that had somehow crystallized in death.

Some of these hands were many times larger than life-sized. So any association with actual human hands appeared to be far-fetched. That is, unless in ancient times, there existed a race of men vastly larger than present-day humans. Doc doubted this explanation.

Doc Savage put all such fanciful thoughts aside. Treading cautiously, the squealing of the overhead bats covering any intermittent rustling of his plastic cape, the bronze man continued up the rough slope until he encountered something in the form of a great obstruction.

It had the feel of a curved wall. Doc removed one plastic glove, and felt of it.

Among his many mastered disciplines was that of geology, but the substance of this curved surface did not feel familiar. Doc felt along this, moving cautiously, and managed to work his way around it, coming at last to the spot where he believed that he had begun his explorations.

Whatever this thing was, it was very large, apparently tall, and built along the lines of a grain silo or tower. If there was an entrance to it, the bronze man could not locate it by touch.

Failing to comprehend the nature of the structure, Doc Savage backed away several paces, and stood listening. No sounds associated with human activity came to his ears. Nor any smells.

It was plain that Diamond, his gang and their prisoners, had somehow entered the imposing structure. This was the only explanation for the absence of human odors that had inexplicably vanished.

Doc considered bringing his flashlight into play, but for all he knew, the building had windows or loopholes and he might be observed from within. Even semi-visible, he did not want to draw sniping fire. There was little cover here. Only rocks, some quite sizable.

So the bronze man withdrew and awaited the dawn.

As he lurked unseen, the ocean breeze picked up, and a new sound began to lift above the thin cries of agitated bats.

IT WAS a low moaning. Doc listened to it very carefully. Knowing that there was a tropical storm in the general vicinity, he had initially wondered if this was the first wailing of hurricane winds.

Although the moving air suggested an approaching storm, the moaning was not the wind. Rather, the wind was producing the moaning in some way.

As Doc listened, the sound took on an unsettling quality. A chorus of ghosts lamenting the loss of their corporeal existence might produce such a dirge. But the images that ran through the bronze man's mind were of cartoon ghosts moaning, and he did not believe in manifestations of the supernatural, anyway.

The wind continued to pick up, and the moaning changed its tune. With a growing alarm, Doc began to suspect that the distant hurricane was moving in this general direction and was somehow producing this weird noise.

For the moaning grew and grew and became a low whining, and the low whining ascended on the musical scale until it swelled into a steady, insistent and extremely terrible wailing sound.

The relentless noises soon began to get under his skin, and preyed upon his ordinarily iron nerves. No matter how strong the mind of a man might be, there is something about persistent, unsettling noises that could get to one. The way the wailing went on and on—combined with the terrible darkness and all the unknowns that were surrounding Doc Savage—began steadily to work at his steely self-possession.

It would not be so bad if the wind died down here and there, causing the incessant caterwauling to pause. But there were no pauses, just the insistent noise of a creature with endless capacity for vocal expression that never once stopped to take a breath. The thing that wailed did so relentlessly and with greater and greater volume.

While Doc Savage stood watch, the tropical sun crept above the horizon line, igniting searing patches on the ocean. As it did so, the solar rays threw into sharp relief the great harrowingly loud thing before him.

By some quirk of fate—or perhaps design of man—the solar orb rose directly behind the great howling structure. While Doc watched, it painted the structure as a great black silhouette.

No details could be discerned. Nothing of its substance could be made out. The suggestion that this was a man-made tower began to resolve before the bronze man's watchful eyes.

Soon, the blazing sun struck fire against a pair of outthrust curved longhorns on either side of the thing's tapering top. They reminded Doc of the small horned stone that contained the debilitating power to draw the mineral iron out of a man. But that was not the most unsettling thing.

As the sun rose behind the wailing form, a solitary eye began to burn high in the towering summit. In the beginning, it was a tiny point of hot light. As the sun mounted, the burning eye grew in scope and intensity until Doc Savage felt as if he was being scrutinized by a great horned cyclops whose gaze was mustering up sufficient wrath to burn him to hot ashes on the very spot where he stood.

The eye was cut into the form of a crude quarter moon, its horns pointing upward. Exactly like the small black stone of evil influence.

Without warning, the interminable whining died. The air became eerily still. Then, a new sound impinged upon the bronze man's hearing. It was coming, not from the ominous tower, but in the direction of the *Northern Star*.

# Chapter XL

# SINISTER SHAPE SURFACING

**T**HEY FINALLY FOUND the missing acetylene torch in a storage locker upon which some humorist had etched a familiar cartoon, along with the words "Kilroy Was Here!" Or rather, Seaman Jury Goines found it.

As one of the ship's oilers, Goines knew more about the nooks and crannies of the *Northern Star* than anyone other than her skipper, who incidentally had been released from his bunk after Monk Mayfair had taken a hacksaw to his handcuffs.

Captain McCullum was in no condition to move around much, but he insisted upon being helped to the bridge, where he took his customary position at the wheel. He used the ship's interphone system to stay in communication with the others.

Boatswain Don Worth, along with Seamen B. Elmer Dexter, Morris Byron and Leander Tucker, brought forth the acetylene tank, but it was Monk Mayfair who took charge of it, lugging the cumbersome thing down to the crew quarters in the forecastle, carrying it across one sloping shoulder as if it was a sack of laundry.

Dropping the heavy tank before the steel door, the homely chemist donned protective goggles, fired up the torch and began his cutting.

"O.K., this is going to take a while," he called through the steel door.

"When the stink gets too much," Jury Goines put in, "I'll spell you."

"Gotcha," grunted the hairy chemist, who understood better than any the clouds of noxious chemicals that would soon fill the cramped passageway, principally oxidized metals and poisonous carbon monoxide.

On the other side, the trapped crew backed away from the door and rocked impatiently in their hammocks.

Tropical night still reigned, but dawn was imminent.

While Monk worked, Donald Worth conferred with his shipmates, Jury Goines looming a safe distance away like a worried tower.

"When first light comes," said Worth, "our top order of business will be to see if the ship can be gotten off the reef."

Dex opined, "The stern is in a good three fathoms of water, and the bow doesn't seem to be canted up very much. There's a fair chance that just by reversing engines, we can back her off the reef."

Donald Worth nodded. "We don't dare do that until Doc Savage rescues the other part of the crew."

"Well—if he does," lamented Tuck.

Morris Byron commented firmly, "Doc Savage will come through, all right; that's what makes him Doc Savage."

There was no argument on that point. But neither was the rescue of the *Northern Star* crew a foregone conclusion. They all knew that. The situation on the weird black reef was dire and desperate.

Jury Goines spoke up at that point. "I volunteer to go over the side and check out the condition of the screws."

Bosun Worth nodded and said, "Better check with the skipper before you do. I'm sure he'll think it's a smart idea, though."

With that, Goines took his departure.

The quartet remained below deck in the event that Diamond and his gang should return unexpectedly. They were armed with whatever they could scrounge up—which wasn't very much, the cutthroats having taken what weapons they could.

Ham Brooks had been working his way through the cargo holds, seeking any sailors who had been locked away in an odd corner, or gone into hiding undiscovered.

"I have found no stray sailors," he told Don Worth upon his return. "But there are plenty of bodies. Navy men all. Diamond did not take prisoners when he came upon them."

Don winced at the grim news. "That means the survivors are all trapped in the crew quarters. Monk will have them out before daybreak."

"If that ape doesn't singe off his fingers in the process," said Ham acidly.

Leander Tucker laughed shortly. "You two are a caution! Always have been, always will be."

HAVING nothing more to do, they made their way to the upper deck, slipped cautiously toward the bridge, climbed up to join the ship's master.

Despite his numerous injuries, Captain McCullum was standing at the wheel—leaning into it, actually, relying on the thing for support—and employing a pair of field binoculars, endeavoring to see through the thick tropical darkness surrounding the ship.

Saluting, Seaman Worth reported, "No stray sailors discovered in any spot, sir."

"Thank you, Bosun," replied the Captain in a voice that ached with repressed pain. "I can't see anything in this blasted ink."

"It will be dawn soon enough," advised Worth. "In case Diamond and his men can see this far, it might be advisable to go below."

Captain McCullum was silent in a fierce way. At length, he said tightly, "The *Northern Star* is my ship, and this is my bridge. I will not be chased off it by a common corsair."

Seaman Worth said nothing, but Ham Brooks spoke up.

"Captain McCullum, the enemy have rifles and we would make excellent targets in broad daylight. Also, we need to give Doc Savage time to work."

McCullum ruminated in the darkness, but said nothing. It was clear to all that here was a very stubborn skipper. Good advice might be recognized as such, but if it went against his nautical grain, he was loathe to take it.

There was also the matter that McCullum would have to explain how his vessel had been commandeered in wartime and run up on a reef by a band of ragtag pirates.

And so they waited in the darkness. From time to time, Captain McCullum lifted his field glasses to his eyes, accomplishing exactly nothing.

It was a tough wait, and first light seemed as if it would never arrive.

Well before the glimmering solar rays began creeping along the ink-black sea, a noise disturbed the waters to the stern.

Even shut up in the Captain's bridge, the disturbance reached their ears. There, they had been listening for any sound, any indication of activity on the black reef which they could barely make out.

"What was that?" muttered B. Elmer Dexter uncertainly.

"Quiet!" snapped the Captain.

All fell silent. The sounds continued. Rushing, watery noises, as of a sea disturbance.

Ham Brooks, who had adventured all over the globe in the company of Doc Savage, murmured, "That sounds like—"

"A submarine surfacing," hissed McCullum.

They had been facing forward, in the direction of the evil-looking reef called Satan's Spine. Abruptly, they turned around and attempted to discern the source of the unpleasant noises all sailors dread.

These were not so much splashings as they suggested a violent churning, along with an accompanying noise reminiscent of a small waterfall cascading.

Captain McCullum turned and said, "Bosun Worth, muster your men and man the stern deck gun. Prepare to deal with possible enemy submersible. Mr. Brooks, apprise Mr. Mayfair of the situation."

Saluting sharply, Worth said, "Aye-aye, Cap'n. Come on, men. Shake a leg."

WHILE Ham sought Monk below deck, Donald Worth and his three companions pounded down the stairs, and raced aft, taking control of the Oerlikon anti-aircraft gun mounted on the stern deck.

Swiftly, they had the deck gun turned around and ready to open fire. Mental Byron served as the loader. The others stood ready to catch the hot shells as they came rattling out of the mechanism, asbestos gloves on their hands.

In the darkness, they could not see the raider, but the ugly noises of a submersible coming to the surface were unmistakable.

They understood that should the submarine unleash a torpedo at the stern, they would be the first to die. But without a direct order from Captain McCullum, they could not open fire. And so they waited, silent and intense, their eyes open wide, but no light showed them anything.

The minutes crept past like dying snakes crawling to their graves. The humidity of the night brought perspiration beads popping out on their exposed skins. It was not a very pleasant feeling.

Came the first red rays of dawn. As natural light filtered out, they searched the graying waters with their eyes.

At first, the submarine showed as a dead-looking hulk lying out there less than one nautical mile, its sharp nose pointed in their direction. That meant it was in a position to unleash its deadly tin fish directly at their stern.

In the crawling gray light, they could not make out details. It was just a great dark shape lying ominously nearby. Nationality unknown.

As they waited for additional sunlight, Seaman Worth suddenly remembered the silent dog whistle in his pocket.

Taking it out, he gave a long blast that no one could hear. The young bosun followed this signal with three shorter blasts of varying lengths. Followed by three additional ones.

The two blasts of three notes spelled out a simple message. The only question was: Would Doc Savage hear them?

# Chapter XLI

# MYSTERY ON SATAN'S SPINE

**D**OC SAVAGE WAS considering the advisability of climbing the ominous horned tower when the first long blast of the silent dog whistle struck his hearing.

The bronze man habitually carried a silken line at the end of which was affixed a folding steel grappling hook small enough to fit in a pocket. If he could snag the hook on the burning quarter-moon orifice high in the tower, it was possible to climb the line, thereby gaining access to the tower's interior.

But the long blast stayed him.

Listening, Doc made out the series of three shorter whistles. They were in Morse code, and signified the same letter repeated three times. S.S.S., which was the wartime equivalent of the international distress call, S.O.S.

There followed another S, after a pause, but this second series spelled out an entirely different message. S-U-B.

*Submarine!*

Now Doc Savage found himself teetering on the horns of a dilemma. Go forward and brave the tower, seeking Diamond and his prisoners, or to return to the *Northern Star* and investigate the sighting of an unknown submersible.

His decision was not long in coming.

Stepping up to the tower, Doc drove a hand into his clothing, and removed the folding grappling hook and line. Uncoiling the line, he gave the small but strong steel grapnel an expert toss.

The pronged device sailed into the aperture that burned like the baleful orb of a cyclops, snagged something. Doc pulled the line taut.

Taking hold of the line with his great corded hands, the bronze giant began his ascent. He was helped by the fact that the rough surface of the tower created friction on the soles of his shoes, so he could use his feet as well.

In short order, Doc scrambled up, reached the aperture and pulled himself in.

The chamber in which the bronze man found himself was clearly fashioned by the hand of man, although how long ago was impossible to gauge. The meager amount of bat droppings and other detritus within showed that it had not been a rookery for very long—a few months possibly. This further suggested that the tower had been underwater until recently.

He was reminded of a watch tower or lighthouse, for at the other end of the circular space there was a small quarter-moon-shaped hole, through which was coming the intense rays of the rising sun.

Doc examined the circular room. The chamber was dark and glassy, as if faced by a substance resembling highly polished obsidian. It was not possible, he believed, for obsidian to be manipulated in such a way as to create a continuous curved surface such as this appeared to be. Yet when his sensitive fingers touched the black material, it was entirely slick and seamless.

Doc Savage's exotic trilling seeped out, low and suffused with amazement. He stifled it at once.

Behind him came another long blast of the silent dog whistle.

Turning, the bronze giant removed his telescopic tube, and used it to search the waters. He quickly spied the sharp gray profile of the *Northern Star* in the growing light.

The submarine, lying behind it, was not so easily resolved. The bronze man had to move about, angling his telescope, until he spotted the conning tower.

No markings were discernible, nor was there sufficient light to make out anything but the vaguest of outlines. The identity of the undersea boat was impossible to establish.

This caused the bronze man some acute concern. But there was nothing he could do about the submersible at the moment. He was in the act of removing his plastic cape and attached hood, for it was no longer of immediate use. Bundling this under one arm, Doc made a circuit of the tower room, attempting to establish its purpose.

IN THE CENTER of the chamber lay a shallow stone bowl of some sort. Doc studied this carefully. It bore streaky scorch marks, and appeared to be an urn large enough to hold a human being if they curled up. Its purpose was difficult to determine.

Perhaps it had been used for ceremonial practices, and the bronze man had to shake off the ugly thought that human victims may have been sacrificed in this blackened cup in some unpleasant manner.

Studying the curved obsidian walls, Doc's agile brain suddenly grasped the purpose of the thing. With a fire burning in the central portion of the chamber faced with black obsidian glass, the entire interior would magnify and reflect any illumination, making the cut-out quarter-moon eye at either side of the ominous tower burn brightly by night. It was a lighthouse, older than recorded history!

Even now, filled with the hot rays of the rising sun, it was becoming intolerably hot.

But there was no time to contemplate this further. Back on the *Northern Star*, Bosun Donald Worth was continuously blowing the silent whistle with increasing urgency.

Abruptly, the eerie sound broke off.

There came a report that was like uncorked thunder.

A pause followed. Then the silent dog whistle resumed its keening call. Doc listened raptly, attempting to decipher its meaning.

That Doc Savage understood what he heard soon became evident.

Returning to the grapple and line, which still trailed to the ground, the bronze man slipped down the thin cord, which was knotted every so many feet to provide better purchase. He threw the plastic garment ahead of him to save time.

When his feet slapped the hard ground, Doc Savage turned and flipped the cord several times, dislodging the hook. He gathered the entire arrangement together and, picking up his plastic cape, the bronze giant began an intent search of the immediate surroundings, seeking another way into the tower, for it had been evident that the chamber above could not be reached except by climbing through the cyclops-orb aperture.

# Chapter XLII

# PORTAL

DOC SAVAGE WAS seldom baffled. But he was baffled now.

Scouting the circumference of the weird horned tower, the bronze man searched its surface for hidden catches or seams or other means of ingress.

Three times he explored the cylindrical structure. It appeared to be formed out of the same igneous rock that comprised the forbidding black finger that was Satan's Spine. Basalt. The substance out of which the weird hands of stone had been inexplicably cast.

This tower had that same dark, weathered complexion. Studying it in the bleeding morning light, the bronze giant perceived the unsettling suggestion that the tower was, much like the clutching human hands arrayed all about, an outgrowth of the reef of hardened lava, and inextricable from it. How humans could have wrought such a miracle from what had once been molten magma seemed inexplicable.

The wind picked up again, and with it came a return of the unsettling sounds produced by air moving through the cyclops-orbed cavity high overhead.

The low-key whining of the satanic tower was getting on his nerves. Self-control was one of Doc Savage's most reliable attributes. He rarely lost his temper, and this iron composure was usually reflected in his perpetual poker face. This was a consequence of his unusual childhood, during which the bronze man

286

had been raised to master all human knowledge. It had begun with self-mastery, the suppression of inconvenient emotions and the discipline of always being in control of oneself and one's responses to outside factors.

But the unceasing howling seemed to penetrate his very soul, unseating his nearly perfect composure. Sometimes it was a mournful moaning, at other points an anguished wailing of wind.

After the third turn around the tower, the bronze man came to a reluctant conclusion. The only way in and out of the tower was through the high aperture which now radiated captured sunlight in a way that was nearly incandescent.

This could only mean that Diamond had taken the sailors of the *Northern Star* not into the upper tower as Doc had assumed, but down into the earth by another opening. There was no escaping this conclusion, but it had taken three circuits of the base before it had dawned on the bronze giant that there existed no other explanation for their complete disappearance from the flat plain of solidified black lava, which in the morning light resembled a hideous tail emerging from the spit of bone-white sand called Satan Cay.

Stepping away from the tower, the bronze man fell to searching the ground. It was wet in many places, and there were no signs of wet footprints due to this moisture. Naturally no grass grew here. There were no plants to be trampled and show sign of human feet. The surface of the moon must look something like this, the bronze man reflected.

There were only some upthrust extrusions of brittle-looking rock along with the weird clutching hands that reached up from the reef. Kneeling, Doc examined one and saw to his mild astonishment that it was a continuation of the lava that had hardened unknown centuries ago. Like the obsidian lining of the tower chamber, the means by which this had been wrought escaped the bronze man.

What purpose these hands could possibly serve was also unfathomable.

Reconnoitering the immediate vicinity of the burning-eyed tower, Doc discovered a hand in which the thumb had been broken off. The fractured digit lay nearby, suggesting the break had been recent and caused by a human being or something equally solid colliding with it.

This gave Doc something to go on and he circled about, concentrating on this general area.

Flake-gold eyes searching the ground, Doc sought any disturbance in the natural formation that comprised the basalt reef. He was mentally examining the equipment in his pockets to see if he carried anything that might be of use in his search. All human activity left traces, whether fingerprint impressions or residue of the oils secreted from a man's hands. Not long ago, the bronze man had often worn into battle a vest of many pockets, some of which would be loaded with atomizers containing chemicals that would bring out such traces. But he no longer wore that vest.

As it turned out, Doc Savage did not need any gadget to find what he sought.

HE SOON came upon a section of rock that was unnaturally square and flat on top. It was as if human hands had worked the stone, but when Doc Savage examined it, there was no sign of any such tool work. Like the clutching petrified hands, the stone appeared to have been made smooth by some unknown process that had been applied to the magma while it was still molten.

Had the bronze man not noticed this weird quality, he would still have paused in his reconnoiter. Upon the flat surface was etched a symbol, a cartoon image. That of a man whose head was peering up above the horizontal line representing a wall. The fingers of both hands and his long drooping nose hung below the line.

Below this, etched crudely, apparently by a sharp rock or tool, was the legend, "KILROY WAS HERE."

Recalling that name had been on the door of the Brooklyn house where he and his men had discovered the note from the missing Davey Lee that had set them on the trail that had ended here, the bronze man hunkered down and felt his way all around the flat stone buttress. He was seeking a catch or spring or counterweight. But he found none.

Patches of moisture glistened on top of the flat surface, and the more Doc studied them, the more they appeared to be marks of many men leaving overlapping wet footprints, none of them distinct.

Evidently, several men had recently stood upon this flat surface.

Doc Savage stepped onto the shelf, and waited. He weighed well over two hundred pounds, and that weight seemed to be sufficient to actuate a mechanism. For the shelf sank over an inch, very slowly, with no accompanying sound of mechanism.

Doc wondered if this flat stone were some form of crude elevator, operated by weights and counterweights. But the sinking sensation was brief.

The bronze man looked around to see what he had accomplished.

He should not have been surprised but in fact was quite startled to see that a portal had opened in the front of the weird tower—a door where he had been certain no door had existed, because no seams seemed to show. Yet the open portal was now there.

Moving to the tower, Doc examined the revealed entrance. There was no sign of any door, only the opening. It appeared as if a section of the curved tower wall had sunk into the earth.

Doc entered. Once he did so, his suspicions were confirmed when the curved wall behind him began rising to fill the rectangular aperture. A grinding noise accompanied this ponderous phenomenon.

Thumbing on his pocket flashlight, Doc examined the space in which he was now trapped. The interior was smoother than the exterior wall, but that had been acted upon by unknown generations of wind and water action, eroding it somewhat.

The cylindrical chamber appeared to be empty, but the far side of the tower slipped down into the earth in a fashion resembling a hewn ramp. The workmanship showed smoothness and skill.

Striding over to the ramp, Doc carefully directed his flashlight downward and saw that it disappeared in a circular fashion rather like the circular steps of a lighthouse. It followed the circumference of the tower's base, curving flush to the continuous outer wall so that the ramp disappeared from view into darkness no matter how he angled his flash ray.

Listening, the bronze man detected sounds, but they were far below. Too distant to make them out. It was clear that human activity produced those noises. This could only mean Diamond and his gang of bloody-handed cutthroats.

Dousing his flashlight, Doc drew over his giant form the plastic cape and hood that produced virtual invisibility. Determinedly, he went down the ramp, taking care to feel his way by running his hand along the exterior wall. The ramp appeared to be enclosed, but he could not be certain, without turning on his flashlight, that it would not at some point open up over a central well. The depth at which the sounds below rose up suggested that this corkscrew ramp led very far into the earth. It would not do to fall in.

Doc Savage began to form the theory that this well was a vertical lava tube, a natural phenomenon which had been reshaped by man into a passage into the bowels of Satan's Spine. For what purpose was unknown, but would soon reveal itself, he imagined.

A strange thrill of anticipation began rising in his chest, like a queer hummingbird taking wing inside him.

# Chapter XLIII

# THE UNEASY MEN

**D**OWN THEY DESCENDED. Down what felt like a ramp that corkscrewed, although it was also reminiscent of the winding steel staircases found on large ships throughout the world. In this case, of course, there were no steps, and the ramp was broader and as smooth as asphalt.

Walking deeper into the innards of the earth made the blindfolded Merchant Marines increasingly uneasy. But the deeper they went, the less they were inclined to speak. Men marching to the gallows are similarly silent.

Finally, the rough voice of Diamond barked out, "Basement floor. All out."

As an attempt at humor, it fell flat. Not even Diamond's hardboiled cohorts chuckled.

Once they reached level ground, the sense of claustrophobia actually increased. Air down here was still and deposited a peculiar taste on their tongues. It was also chilly in a clammy way.

Steel rifle muzzles prodded the fumbling sailors into a corner pocket of the chamber in which they imagined themselves to be. That they were deep underground was undeniable. There was no escaping this knowledge. As measured by maritime men, the prisoners suspected that they had descended many fathoms. It made their mouths dry up and their tongues feel like sponges left out in the sun.

It was there that they discovered they had been lied to. Or at least, some of them had.

"Keep your blindfolds on for a minute," commanded Diamond. "Some of you will have yours removed. After you do, don't say a word. Loose lips sink ships, like the Navy posters say. Yap, and we will blow your backbones apart."

Two men were taken aside, their blindfolds rudely shucked off. They looked around, and their blinking eyes went wide. They had difficulty understanding what they beheld. Soft gasps escaped their lips.

The place in which they found themselves was a sort of dome. The ground under their feet was flat and level. Walls were unnaturally smooth, jet black, dull as coal and therefore probably formed of basalt.

The ceiling of the subterranean dome reared about fifteen feet at its apex, directly above their heads. That made the two nervous mariners feel as if they were a mile below the surface of the reef. Of course, that was not so. But their imaginations made them feel like coal miners—ever mindful of the possibility of a cave-in.

Diamond stood there, his naturally bald head glowing moistly in the glow of various flashlights. His amber eyes were as cruel as a tomcat's. In one earlobe danced a red-gold hoop to which was affixed a glittering diamond.

"You see that opening over there?" Diamond directed. "Walk in there and grab everything and anything you can lay your hands on."

Their searching eyes veered in the direction the pirate pointed.

There stood an opening in the smooth wall. Not a door, but an aperture.

It was round, as high as a very tall man and as broad as four men standing abreast.

The disquieting thing about this opening was that in its upper portion, matching horns had been cut, making the shape of the entry resemble a quarter moon turned on its curved back so that its devil horns pointed ceilingward.

Beyond lay a great space, choked with shadows. Neither man could pierce the gloom with their eyes. But the air coming from the dark space beyond was cold. Unnaturally cold.

The two sailors hesitated. One asked, "Why do you need us to go in there?"

"Is it dangerous?" blurted the other.

"Just do it!" roared Diamond.

Hesitatingly, the two sailors stepped forward while Diamond's men directed their flashlight beams into the shadow-clotted space beyond. A short tunnel connected the two rooms.

The men could not see clearly until they passed into the adjoining chamber.

When they did so, their exclamations of astonishment were not mild.

"It's freezing in here!" one complained.

"This cold ain't normal," the other squawked. "It's like an ice box!"

"Don't hang around gawking!" Diamond exploded. "Just grab armfuls of loot and back out of there."

The men did their best. There came a commotion and clatter that their blindfolded shipmates heard distinctly. Abruptly, one of the searching sailors stumbled, fell over, emptying his arms of the objects he had collected.

The other sailor demanded, "Tom, what happened to you?"

Silence followed. That man also toppled.

The silence that followed was unsettling in the extreme.

Two more blindfolds were whipped off, and selected sailors were pushed roughly in the direction of the chamber door.

"Get in there and yank them out right now!" Diamond ordered.

The two Merchant Marines did not hesitate. These were fellow mariners in peril. They plunged in. Taking hold of their friends, they began dragging them back, until they, too, seemed to lose all strength and collapsed on the floor.

"This ain't workin' out so hot," a pirate growled. It was the rogue named Joe Cannon.

"It's got to work," Diamond insisted. "We practically moved a mountain to get this far. Get me two more men!"

Again, blindfolds were roughly removed and sailors were kicked and prodded into the connecting chamber. They were not told what to do. They did not need any instruction. They just plunged in, groped around, and laid hold of one of the collapsed sailors.

They did pretty well, managing to haul out a single individual, and laid him spread-eagled on the stony floor of the domed chamber. Returning for more, they dragged another stricken shipmate into the light.

After they had done this, the two men lay down as if exhausted. Their breathing was ragged, their eyes glassy and strange.

"What—what's in there?" one gulped. "I feel like I got all the life sucked out of me."

Diamond did not bother to answer. He said, snapping his fingers, "I got me an idea. One man goes in, throws out what he can, and we catch it. When he collapses, someone goes in and drags him out. Send in another man, and repeat the operation. If these guys hold out, we can clean the place out in no time."

No sailor, blindfolded or not, cared for that suggestion. As a plan, it seemed half-sound. But as a task, it was terrifying. The two men still trapped in the adjoining chamber had ceased to make any sounds.

FOR a few minutes the Diamond gang stood around, playing their flashlights on the faces of their captives. Some carried kerosene-fed hurricane lanterns. These smoked faintly, and the smell of the kerosene started to become unpleasant in the close air. Coughing commenced, and appeared to be catching. Others joined in. The vocal ruckus began to sound like dogs barking.

"Douse those hurricane lamps!" ordered Diamond. "We'll relight them when we have to. The smoke is getting to everyone. We can't have any more problems than we've already signed on for."

The glass chimneys were lifted and the wicks blown out efficiently.

The shifting illumination in the chamber became dimmer, only broken by flashlights here and there. This contributed to the spectral atmosphere. The way the light struck up against the face of the men arrayed about created the unpleasant aspect that Hollywood lighting technicians call "horror lighting."

In this weird semi-gloom, no one saw or heard a silent figure descend the ramp that wound down from the tower many fathoms above their heads.

There was not much to see in any case. Just a pair of pale, yellowish eyes floating downward, like an ethereal occupant of a tomb returning to his earthly rest.

# Chapter XLIV

# TENSE SITUATION

THE CREW OF the unknown submarine showed that they were well-trained and coldly efficient in their duties.

The deck gun was brought up, made ready, and a warning shot was fired three points off the port stern of the foundering liner, *Northern Star*.

At the ship's stern anti-aircraft gun, Don Worth keyed the vessel's intercommunicator, and informed Captain McCullum, "Sir, the submarine has fired a warning shot. Orders?"

*"Can you make her out?"*

The submarine was still commencing to rise, and gradually the submersible hull began showing its true color, which was an oyster gray. It was insufficient to identify the U-boat. Virtually all warring submarines are similarly painted.

"No, Cap'n," Don reported.

*"Return fire a warning shot,"* instructed McCullum.

Donald Worth pressed firm thumbs into the trips and made the air sizzle over the submarine deck-gun crew's capped heads. The startled sailors ducked, making it even harder to discern their nationality.

Leander Tucker and Mental Byron caught the blistering shell casings and gingerly heaved them over the rail, there being no luxury of tossing them into waiting receptacles designed for that purpose.

Tensely, Bosun Worth and the others waited for a response, whatever it might be.

When they did turn, they glanced back in the direction of the bow, where the sun crawling out of the ocean painted the weird reef called Satan's Spine in true-light colors.

It was not exactly Technicolor. The reef was a long hellish finger of blackness. It was no coral reef, such as had been created by countless sea organisms dying and petrifying. This was lava that had hardened into black basalt long ago. Nothing grew there. No salt water mangroves. Not even a solitary palm tree. All was barren. It resembled an ancient seam of dirty coal thrown up by the ocean.

The rising sun threw a squat black tower into sharp relief.

B. Elmer Dexter squinted at it.

"That—that thing looks like it has horns!" he gasped.

Don Worth stole a quick glance, just enough to make out the foreboding shape. He frowned. "That must be why it's called Satan's Spine."

"But what is it?" wondered Leander Tucker.

As a group, they had no idea and no time to fret over this new development. The submarine deck crew was getting themselves organized again.

Into the talker, Seaman Worth informed the skipper, "They are getting ready to fire another shot. It may not be a warning shot this time."

*"Stand ready,"* said the Captain hoarsely.

The wind was freshening, picking up steadily, but all thoughts of the approaching hurricane were far from their minds. If they could not stand off this unknown submarine, the tropical tempest would be the least of their worries.

From the direction of the unworldly tower came a sound— steady, unnerving, and increasing in volume and intensity. It was an unearthly and unnerving moaning, as if some great monster dwelling in the vaults of the earth were awakening in complaint.

"I don't like the sound of that," muttered Morris Byron.

To which Tucker replied, "I'll take that awful noise over the cough of an enemy deck gun."

"You don't know that it's an enemy sub yet," cautioned Don.

"Well, we don't know that it's not, do we?" Tuck retorted.

The question quickly evaporated from their mental processes when sharp-eyed Mental Byron noticed something in the chop that lay between the stern of the *Northern Star* and the blade-like snout of the submarine.

He stared. His eyes grew stark. His jaw sagged slightly.

Stabbing out an excited finger, he exploded, "Look! There's someone swimming toward the sub."

All stared hard, and saw that the man in the water wore one of the pale blue shirts that were common among the Merchant Marine crew of the *Northern Star*. He was arrowing toward the submarine, making fair time, swimming with powerful overhand strokes.

At this distance, it would not have been possible to make out who the foolhardy sailor was, except that he had rolled up his sleeves, exposing his muscular arms. The dark color of those arms as well as the woolly texture of his hair proclaimed his identity undeniably.

"JURY GOINES!" burst out Dex. "We forgot that he was in the water checking on the condition of the screws."

Tuck blinked rapidly. "But what's he trying to do?"

Don Worth leapt to a sensible conclusion and voiced it. "Oiler Goines looks like he's trying to reach the deck crew to warn them off."

"If they're Nazis," muttered Dex, "they're not gonna take well to the intrusion."

"Yeah," added Tuck. "They're liable to turn that pop gun on him."

Seaman Goines seemed unconcerned about the prospect. He swam with all his muscular might, cleaving through the water, approaching the bottom of the submarine that lay in the water like a great tomahawk blade pointed at them.

Behind the *Northern Star*, the moaning of the horned tower grew in volume, turning into a weird wailing as if something terrible impended. So intent were they upon the prospect of the submarine deck gun opening up on their position, the four sailors failed to appreciate the true significance of the rising sound.

They looked at one another and saw the ocean breeze was disturbing their hair, and then they knew.

"It's the hurricane!" Morris Byron exclaimed. "It's bearing down on us! Somehow it's creating the sounds coming from that strange tower."

This was not good news by any measure, but it had an interesting and unexpected side effect.

The awesome wailing—and awesome was as good a word to describe it as any—had captured the attention of the submarine deck crew. They were staring and pointing in the direction of the black tower that was now fully silhouetted by the rising sun, making its solitary quarter-moon eye blaze.

There could be no question but the awful keening was coming from that source. It was eerie and unnerving, and while their attention was fixed upon it, Jury Goines managed to reach the submarine and clambered up the side.

"They will spot him any minute now!" Leander Tucker exclaimed.

Turning to Mental Byron, Donald Worth rapped, "Take over this gun. I'm going to try to distract them with the Aldis lamp."

He rushed back to the blinker, turned it on, and began flashing out a brisk semaphore message, hoping to capture their attention and give Oiler Goines time to accomplish whatever it was he intended to do.

The message was the international signal A.A., repeated several times. It spelled a simple question known to all mariners: *Who are you?*

All around them, the air seemed to turn in a violent swirling as if the entire world was being churned. Gale force winds were agitating the surrounding seas, making the spume and spray splash onto deck, depositing a quivering froth that suggested the unpleasant residue of boiling soup bones.

The end of the world, Donald Worth grimly reflected, will probably look and sound something like this....

# Chapter XLV

# DEEP

**IN THE GLOW** of many flashlights, a Merchant Marine sailor was prodded and shoved through the quarter-moon portel cut out of the wall of black basalt that was marked by a pair of jutting curved horns in outline.

All of those who had eyes to see with watched him disappear into the ominous aperture. Those who were still blindfolded could only listen. Those blindfolded sailors were listening very intently.

But neither they, nor the Diamond crew, had any inkling of the new arrival, for he made no sound, nor did any trace of his arrival show.

Diamond was barking roughly, "Grab whatever you can! Sing out when you have a handful!"

The hapless sailor disappeared within, and there came the nervous sounds of him rattling about. This commotion did not last very long.

Finally, the sailor called back, "I got hold of something!" His voice shook as if his teeth were chattering from the unnatural cold.

"Hang on to it!" Diamond ordered. "Two of you go in and get him. Make it fast!"

Two mariners charged in, fumbled about, and soon dragged the unwilling sailor back into the light.

The man was half gone. His face was slack, and he looked as if he had lost some of his ruddy seagoing complexion. It was hard to tell if the fellow was conscious, for his eyes were rolled up in his head until the bloodshot whites showed, and he did not move after they laid him out on the floor. His teeth finally ceased chattering after a while.

Despite this, the fellow clutched a bundle in his arms.

Flashlight beams jumped onto this bundle and disclosed a reddish-gold gleam that brought exclamations of awe from the cutthroat crew who followed Diamond.

Diamond himself leapt upon the man, took hold of one of the gleaming objects, then lifted it high for all to see.

"This alone," he said with hearty satisfaction, "is probably worth a million bucks easy."

The avid gleam that came into the eyes of the pirate crew had probably long ago flamed in the greedy orbs of Blackbeard, Barbarossa, and others of that piratical ilk.

Another corsair stooped to lift up a second red-gold bar. For that was what it was—an ingot of some rich metal, suggesting pure gold, but its ruddy color was not that of the valuable yellow metal.

"There's a lot more where that came from," boasted Diamond. "And we are going to haul it all out if it takes until the damn war is over."

A VOICE spoke up. "Mind telling us what this place is?"

None of the *Northern Star* crew recognized the voice, but that did not bother them. They assumed that it was a member of the pirate crew who had not been informed of all the details of their dangerous quest.

His chest puffed out with a mixture of manly pride and avaricious accomplishment, Diamond unloaded just enough information to hold them all spellbound.

"A sea quake hoisted this damn reef up from the bottom. I was living down here, ducking the draft, living the life of a beachcomber. One day, I came across the spot and poked around some. I found the tower that is directly above us and almost ran away. But I knew it was something ancient. That made it something important. So I screwed up my courage and nosed around."

"And hit the almighty jackpot!" grinned Weedy.

Diamond cracked a crooked smile. "You said it! The jackpot of *all* jackpots. But I almost perished in the process. I found a way in here, explored to this depth, and managed to get out with one of these ingots. And a few other things. I got it and I got out, but I lost consciousness trying to climb the ramp to the surface. When I came to, I knew I couldn't do it all alone. So I got back to the states and began putting together my crew."

"And what a crew!" laughed Weedy.

Another man boasted, "Ex-rum runners, stevedores, dock wallopers, deserters and washed-up sailors."

"In other words, wharf rats," a mariner spat out distastefully.

"But they got the job done," said Diamond with satisfaction. "And now we're going to collect our pensions and live on easy street for the rest of our lives. Don't think we won't."

Again, he lifted the red-gold ingot over his head, and the reflection in his amber orbs was feral. It might have been noticed that the brassy light in his eyes and the gleam of the red-gold ingot were similar in hue.

"Yeah, I combed the waterfront docks and wharves from here to Miami, looking for likely men," Diamond continued. "When I had picked my crew, I had part of the ingot melted down and made rings for every man jack of them. Rings to remind them of what we were after."

"Swag," said one pirate.

"Booty!" crowed another, evidently taking the part of a buccaneer to heart.

"After that," continued the head pirate, "we had to figure out a way to commandeer a ship to get us here. In war time that was not easy. But one of my boys knew of a gang of foreign sailors who were being sent back to their home countries on a ship passing through the Caribbean. We got them tight, and did away with them, dumping their bodies in the ocean, along with the bloody knives used to do the job. So we took their places, and waited until we got close enough to Satan's Spine to make our move."

A corsair clucked, "It would have gone off much smoother if a famous Doc Savage aide named Monk Mayfair had not booked passage on the *Northern Star*. That meant getting him shanghaied elsewhere."

"Yeah," muttered another Diamond henchman. "That part could have gone a hell of a lot smoother."

A blindfolded Merchant Marine wondered aloud, "Is Doc Savage mixed up in this mess?"

"Not anymore," the cutthroat shot back. "He's out of the picture. Adrift somewhere."

Snapping out of his trance of greed, Diamond turned to his men and ordered, "Send in another sailor. We ain't got all night."

Another mariner was selected, his blindfold removed and he was propelled through the aperture, only to disappear into the frigid gloom.

The suddenness with which he had been picked had unnerved the man. As soon as he got inside, he floundered about, tripped over something and fell. In his blind panic, he began yelling for help.

"We'll help you, all right," snorted Diamond. "Just grab hold of something. If we drag you out empty-handed, it's a bullet in the brain for you. Don't think we won't do it."

The man careened about in the dark, and finally said, "I got two things!"

Two Merchant Marines were sent in, stumbled around some, finally laid hands on their shipmate. They dragged the panicky fellow back as rapidly as human muscles could perform the task.

When the first sailor was brought into the light, there was an immediate panic.

For he was clutching something that looked like a black basalt stone, except that it was marked by an cloven eye and a pair of jutting curving devil horns. Its resemblance to the iron-depleting stone discovered by Doc Savage back on the *Northern Star* was striking.

Seeing this, the pirates scrambled to get away from the man clutching the dark object. Evidently, they understood its significance.

"Somebody get rid of that damned thing!" Diamond rapped out.

No one made an immediate move. Flashlights darted about, stabbing into frightened eyes, making them blink and stagger.

In the momentary confusion, something that could not be seen floated through the underground chamber, stooped invisibly, and pitched the object back into the adjoining vault.

That the space beyond the tipped-quarter-moon aperture was a vault seemed undeniable. Making no apparent sound, Doc Savage strode into the next chamber.

Not a man had suspected the bronze giant's presence, nor did anyone hear or see his passing, for he was entirely invisible. Moreover, far above their heads, an eerie sound began to make itself heard.

Penetrating far below for the first time, the sound had a quality of moaning but altered frequently, dropping to a dismal doglike whine then rising into an unnerving keening.

Hearing this, one of the pirates remarked nervously, "Sounds like a gale building."

"Must be that hurricane that was coming our way," muttered Diamond. "Hell, it can't touch us way down here. We'll keep working 'til it passes. Let's get this work gang organized. We've just begun to skim the cream."

# Chapter XLVI

# TEMPEST

A SCRAGGLY PALM frond sailed by. Followed by another. There were no palms on the sandy spot called Satan Cay, never mind on the barren reef dubbed Satan's Spine. The fronds had no doubt been swept from the Queer Cays, or some other island. A fierce wind was bringing them in the direction of the aground merchantman, *Northern Star*.

At the signal blinker, Boatswain Donald Worth was furiously flashing at the unknown submarine to the ship's stern.

A.A., he flashed. A.A., over and over.

Abruptly, something smashed into the blinker's face, shattering the glass, producing long hissing sparks of blue electricity. Sizzling, the blinker went dead.

Seaman Dexter shouted, "Who shot at us?"

"Not the submarine!" Tucker called out. "She ain't fired yet!"

That much was true. The wind was whipping at the gunnery crew on the wallowing submarine. Sailors were clutching at their flying caps while struggling to keep their footing on the wet deck. They were having a tough time of it, for the submersible was rocking hard.

All the while, Seaman Goines was climbing vigorously up their port side. The big oiler had not yet been noticed in the churning chop.

Don Worth stepped back, examined the front of the signal blinker, and spotted the problem. An ancient bone-gray husk of a coconut, about half the size of a cannonball, was lodged in the steel shutters. The building wind had plucked it from somewhere and thrown it with impressive force against the lamp.

It was a regrettable coincidence for two reasons. One, Donald Worth needed the blinker to ascertain the identity of the mystery submarine. Two, the unfortunate arrival of the coconut almost initiated hostilities.

It was not yet clear that hostilities were called for. That was the worrisome part.

Don rushed back to the anti-aircraft gun, and regained control of it. His clean-cut features were tense, for the young boatswain knew that the next few seconds would tell the tale.

To add to their sense of impending danger, the tower at the far end of Satan's Spine continued to emit the most unearthly wailing. That was what it was—a wailing. It was as if the very earth herself was crying out in some indescribable agony.

Loose objects were being thrown about the afterdeck. The sky was filled with debris carried along by the mounting hurricane. Palm fronds choked the air like frightened green birds. Dirt, sand and other airborne grit got into their eyes.

A great white loose thing went flapping by, looking like a seagull being tossed about. But it was no seagull. This was the mainsail of the schooner, *Albatross*, ripped free of its mast and contorting in flight.

Squeezing their eyelids shut, the four fast friends turned their faces away from the punishing storm, and while they were struggling, the anti-aircraft gun got away from them. The wind pushed it, knocking the barrel to port.

Struggling, Don Worth muscled it back into firing position.

In the increasingly dirty air, the gunnery crew of the submersible mistook that sudden shift for a hostile act. They were on the point of firing when a great dark form finished clambering up the side of the submarine and appeared in their midst, unobserved and undetected.

Unstoppable as well. For Jury Goines took hold of a man and pitched him bodily into the churning sea. The hapless one was not immediately missed. So the big black sailor grabbed another and gave him the same rough treatment.

From the aft deck of the *Northern Star*, in the blustery hurricane, this activity could not be clearly seen. To the eyes of the four young Merchant Mariners, it looked as if the deck crew of the submarine were hastily abandoning ship in the face of the increasing gale.

One by one, the gun crew were deposited in the drink until only Seaman Goines stood behind the deck gun. Moving quickly, he removed the ammunition box and tossed it over the side.

Then, flashing a huge semaphore-like grin, he gave the four young men the V for victory sign.

That grin of triumph proved to be short-lived. For the force of the blow was increasing by the second.

A sudden surge almost precipitated Jury Goines into the same waters into which he had consigned his unsuspecting opponents. He was forced to take hold of the deck gun with both hands to keep from going over the slippery side.

From the deck of the *Northern Star*, Donald Worth and his shipmates shouted for the big oiler to seek shelter. There was no shelter. Not unless he dived down the hatch of the submarine and delivered himself into the hands of its unknown crew.

From the changing expressions on Seaman Goines' broad face, it was evident that the realization of grave peril came swiftly. He looked about wildly, recognized his predicament, and took a long chance.

Jumping forward off the prow of the submarine, he dived into the water and began doing a strenuous breaststroke in the direction of the *Northern Star*.

Battling the swells no doubt seemed like the least risky thing to be done. But Oiler Goines had not fully realized the power of the storm that was turning their surroundings upside down.

They shouted to him to turn back and hang onto the lee side of the submersible. But the noise of the storm, combined with the wailing of the uncanny tower, drowned out their frantic voices.

Jury Goines did not hear a word. Very quickly however, it did not matter. It was better that he had not.

For the hard wind was pushing the submarine inexorably along. It was that strong.

Mental Byron was the first to notice this phenomenon. The others were too busy grabbing hold of anything solid to keep from being blown off the back deck.

"The wind is pushing that sub to starboard!" Mental bellowed.

"What?" demanded Don, who could not hear over the roar.

"I said, That sub is being pushed around by the storm!"

His screeching words were lost in the cacophony. For the very same elemental forces started urging the *Northern Star* higher and higher onto the reef.

This did not happen all at once, but the grinding of the hull plates, along with the tortured sound of the submerged screw being mangled as it was forced onto the weird black formation told the four sailors of their own peril.

"We're goners!" Leander Tucker screeched.

"Keep your head!" Don Worth called out.


SUDDENLY, it seemed as if the entire world was coming apart. The screaming wind was plugging their ears, blocking all sound. Sand and grit came into their eyes, noses and mouths as the *Northern Star* was pushed inexorably onto the horrible black spit of basalt.

There was no place safe to flee. Airborne articles were smashing into the bridge, shattering the glass. To remain on deck was to dare the hurricane to pluck them off its open surface and fling them about.

To go below was very tempting, but the way the liner was being pushed onto land meant that it could—and very well would—simply tip over. With catastrophic consequences to all aboard.

B. Elmer Dexter gave voice to the harsh reality they faced. "O.K., boys, brace yourselves. This is it!"

Unexpectedly, a storm surge—a virtual wall of water—seemingly came out of nowhere, and dashed itself onto the stern, flooding the afterdeck irresistibly.

Helpless, the paralyzed quartet were carried over the side.

The wind-driven water swept the length of Satan's Spine, completely immersing it. This flood dashed itself against the basalt tower that wailed and wailed and wailed like a stricken thing realizing that its doom was upon it.

The force of the water was tremendous. The forbidding black tower could not withstand it. It broke, crumbling as if made of dried mud.

Vile grayish-green water carried the remains out to sea. And in the hole that had been its base, additional seawater poured down as if into a great natural sink.

The endless wailing simply ceased. But it would not have mattered. The sound would have been smothered by the deafening roar that overwhelmed the Caribbean Sea anyway. For the hurricane had arrived at full strength, obliterating all in its path, an almighty fury against which nothing natural or man-made could stand.

# Chapter XLVII

# MUTINY

A HOT ARGUMENT broke out over which captive sailor would dare the gloomy treasure chamber next.

Despite the threat of guns and the difficulty of their position so far below Satan's Spine, none of the *Northern Star* crew was eager to brave the dark enclosure beyond the basalt-walled central chamber.

This stubbornness caused Diamond the pirate to become red-faced with fury.

"No shirking of duty! I will shoot any slackers!"

"We ain't your crew!" retorted a mariner bitterly. "And we're sick and tired of being pushed around by the grubby likes of you!"

By flash-ray light, Diamond swung on the speaker, the gold hoop in his left ear jumping about.

"Just for that backtalk, you're going in next."

"Like hell I am!" snapped the sailor.

Diamond lifted his automatic and pointed it squarely at the sailor's unprotected chest.

"Take your turn," he growled, "or take a bullet where it will hurt the most."

The sailor seemed to waver. There was a hard gleam in his eye. A gleam of defiance. Enemy soldiers around the globe knew that light. It was a distinctly American brand of defiance.

Diamond was not accustomed to being challenged. Carefully, his finger constricted on the trigger of the automatic.

Before he could fire, another sailor stepped in front of the defiant one.

"You want to plug my mate," he snarled, "you'll have to shoot through me."

"I don't countenance mutiny!" Diamond barked.

"We ain't your damned crew," several men chorused at once. They had had enough. Bloodshed seemed inevitable. The seaman standing in front of the threatened sailor stuck out his chest and gave every indication of a willingness to block the bullet meant for his shipmate.

During this tense drama, no one suspected that the giant form of Doc Savage had slipped unawares into the empty chamber beyond. For he was untraceable to the ordinary eye.

So when a reddish-gold ingot of unknown metal came sailing out of the dark aperture to strike the automatic in Diamond's hard fist, all who were not blindfolded were stupefied.

Diamond not the least of them. The ingot was very heavy; it did damage. The shock to his finger bones caused Diamond to let out a yell of baffled rage. The gun fell.

Turning, his amber eyes sought the horned aperture.

"Who the hell is in there? You come out now—this instant!"

No one replied, nor did anyone emerge. There was a small rattling noise, however.

Wildly, Diamond searched the group of captives with his eyes, counting fast. He knew the number of his men, as well as that of his prisoners. All were accounted for.

His eyes grew slightly narrower, like those of an alley cat's.

"Everybody point their guns into that hole," he growled. "When I say shoot, you shoot. Get me?"

Numerous cold steel muzzles swiveled in the direction of the ominous portal.

"Whoever you are," Diamond demanded, "you have less than five seconds to step out into the light. If not, you will be riddled by every gun under my command."

A silence followed.

Next, another object came sailing out.

One gunman, understandably nervous, fired wildly at it. Miracle of miracles, his slug struck the thing, causing it to carom off one curved basalt wall, to land in their midst.

They looked down. And to their horror, they discovered that the object was the very thing that they believed had been thrown back in—the iron-leaching double-horned stone that had previously overcame three Merchant Marines.

Almost immediately, they began feeling its effects.

THERE was a mad scramble to grab hold of the dangerous artifact, but the first man to touch it collapsed at once. So did the second.

Men were already feeling weak, and their senses started to swim.

Amber eyes narrowing with sharp comprehension, Diamond snapped out an order.

"Retreat! Get topside! We'll come back when we figure something out!"

This had a pronounced effect on all the assembled mariners, seamen and corsairs alike.

A condition of general pandemonium resulted. Blindfolded sailors yanked off their vision-hampering rags, while the panicked pirates stumbled for the bottom of the ramp.

Inevitably, there were violent collisions and, amid the rout, Merchant Marine fists commenced colliding with pirate jaws. There was not much shooting. Two wild slugs found lodgment in various portions of fast-dodging anatomy. One Merchant Marine had a chunk of his shoulder shot off. A pirate who happened to get in the way of a stray round was struck in the hipbone and turned around twice before he landed flat on his back. His screaming made it sound like a mortal wound, which it wasn't.

In this confusion, it was difficult to execute an orderly retreat. Several knots of men entangled with one another. More knuckles struck, a gun went off, but the barrel was being shoved upward, so the slug struck the ceiling dome and only brought down brittle chips of basalt.

Men were stumbling, falling, sinking to the floor, unable to mount the ramp.

No one escaped, for the inexorable force coming from the sinister-looking stone could not be resisted by mere mortals.

Out of the horned doorway emerged Doc Savage, still virtually invisible, only a pair of pale yellow floating eyes marking the spot where he stood.

Stepping over to the horned rock he had pitched out, the bronze giant stooped, and heaved the thing back into the dark chamber. Apparently, the force exerted had no effect upon him, a condition no doubt explained by the plastic suit that enveloped his great form, blocking him both from the unnatural influence that had overcome all others, as well as from their sight.

Silently, invisibly, Doc Savage moved among the Diamond followers, taking their weapons, removing ammunition magazines and, for good measure, jacking loose any rounds remaining in chambers.

Above his head, the wailing and whining produced by the hurricane winds against the tower filled the chamber like an approaching freight train, blowing its mournful whistle.

A terrible cracking like a cannonade of thunder pierced the incessant roar. Then, suddenly and ominously, the roaring stopped dead.

A weird moaning replaced it. This sounded like the effect produced by blowing into a conch shell, only magnified a thousand times. It was the sound produced by the tempest against the exposed base of the suddenly shattered tower, But only Doc Savage realized this initially.

When the first rill of water arrived, it was like a liquid snake slipping down the circular ramp. Not very large, it forked like a serpent. Two tendrils crept about like the tentacles of a questing octopus, but the pseudopod of water swiftly expanded.

Above his head Doc Savage heard a new sound that reminded him of a rushing, angry waterfall. In that sickening moment, the bronze giant understood that all of the stricken men who were trapped here below ground were about to drown like shipboard rats, himself included.

# Chapter XLVIII

# FURY

**M**ONK MAYFAIR DID his best to ignore the howling wind as he worked the sealed door in the forecastle of the *Northern Star*. Behind that door, elements of the Merchant Marine crew were calling out for him to hurry.

It was tough work, cutting them free. It took time.

"Keep your shirts on!" growled Monk. "This ain't easy!"

The homely chemist was on his second trick at the stubborn door, Ham Brooks having done his share in the absence of Jury Goines until the searing heat and dangerous vapors having forced him to halt and seek breathable air—which was in short supply below decks.

Stationed at the passageway behind him, keeping his dark eyes averted from the acetylene glare, Ham guarded the approach, armed with only his supermachine pistol. Neither man knew what was going on topside, or for that matter on the forbidding finger of reef called Satan's Spine. But they did know and understand that if Diamond and his crew were to return, they were in a tough spot.

Safety goggles reflecting the hot blue torch flame, the homely chemist worked as fast as he dared, but it was necessary to pause and retreat in order to gulp down fresh air. The passageway was choked with a chemical stink that, combined with the intense heat, made breathing difficult.

Above them, the increasing roar of the wind made the entire ship rattle and sound as if they were caught in the eye of the hurricane.

There was no such luck, of course. This was just the outer skirts of the monster. The calm eye was no doubt far away.

Sounding anxious, Ham called over to Monk, "The hurricane is upon us!"

"I got two ears, don't I?" snapped Monk.

Ham fell silent. It was sheer nervousness that had caused him to state the obvious. The dapper attorney knew what they were in for once the fury of the gale matched the caterwauling of the wind.

Monk suddenly snapped off his cutting torch and flung away his goggles.

"That did it!" he exulted.

Grabbing up a crowbar that he had leaned against the bulkhead, Monk used it to pry open the hot, smoking door. Molten metal dripped onto the floor.

"Watch out for hot foots!" Monk warned.

Sailors poured out, coughing and batting acrid fumes out of their eyes, spoiling for a fight.

"Where are those damn pirates?" one demanded fiercely.

"Yeah," seconded another, "we got scores to settle with them. Blood scores."

Monk told them, "They all piled off the ship, but we can go hunting for 'em."

That idea was greeted with great and unbounded joy, as eager mariners scattered in every direction to seek out any available weapon.

This enthusiasm proved to be short-lived, for the ship gave a great shudder. Then came a grinding of hull plates that made all aboard fear that the *Northern Star* was being twisted by something so stupendously large that the old liner was but a toy in its immense grip.

"The ship is coming apart!" howled a man.

"The hurricane has arrived," Ham told them. "Do not go topside! You are certain to be swept overboard."

Not everyone heard that, and those who did were too filled with fury to give heed.

Three sailors pounded up the companionway and blundered into the teeth of the wind. Two lucky sailors stopped dead, as if hitting an invisible wall, while the third was literally plucked off his feet and hurled over the port rail. His scream of surprise so impressed the others that they retreated to below decks, visibly chastened.

Even Monk Mayfair, normally fearless in the face of danger, suddenly developed a large measure of caution.

The newly liberated sailors stayed below decks as the ship began to grind and groan and move under the force of a raw power that had nothing to do with its engines and screws.

Faced with this elemental fury, the more seasoned mariners dropped to their knees and started to pray.

# Chapter XLIX

## SATAN SLEW SEVEN

**DOC SAVAGE MOVED** among the stricken sailors of the *Northern Star*. His speed was astonishing, combining as it did a fierce haste along with the precision of fixed intention.

As water began pouring down the ramp in pulsing waves, the bronze giant took up two sailors, one under each arm, and pulled them back into the connecting tunnel leading to the gloomy chamber beyond.

He made several trips, and each time Doc deposited two men, he inserted a simple lozenge into their mouths, massaging their throats so that they swallowed. The men were not unconscious, but they were very weak and many coughed as the pills worked themselves down their windpipes.

Doc's supply of these pills was limited. But he managed to provide for all of the *Northern Star* crew, as well as a handful of confused pirates.

Once he was done with this, the floor of the combined chambers was awash with a dirty mixture of brine and stunned sea life. Purple jellyfish and coral octopus predominated. The fishy stew was soon up to his ankles, and began lifting even higher.

By now, the entire ramp was a gigantic conduit for the sweeping floodwaters. This fast-moving torrent had a quality of the inexorable about it. Mixed in were chunks of broken basalt and obsidian, which confirmed what Doc Savage had

319

suspected. That the horned tower above had been broken asunder by the irresistible force of Mother Nature.

This was not rainwater carried by the storm, Doc knew, but ocean water. A storm surge had arrived. No doubt Satan's Spine was entirely underwater now.

Grimly, Doc Savage dragged the remaining pirates to the walls and set them upright in the hope—vain he knew—that the water would not fill the entire chamber. But that hope was soon dashed by a roaring cascade.

Waves of rushing brine continued swirling down the ramp, crashing when they reached bottom, the water level mounting and mounting until it crept to his knees. The men to whom he had fed the pills were quickly submerged, and even in their weakened state, they were floundering frantically.

The lack of air did not seem to affect them. Astounded expressions overtook their faces as they realized this. Naturally, being under water they held their breaths, awaiting the inevitable. But it did not come. Their lungs did not strain for air.

For the pills that Doc had provided them contained a concentrated chemical mixture which introduced oxygen into their bloodstreams. They were in no danger of drowning. No immediate danger, that is. For each pill was good for twenty to thirty minutes, depending upon a man's physical exertions.

That might or might not be a sufficient interval to carry them to the surface, but there was yet time to worry about that later.

Doc was trying to keep the undosed pirates' heads above water, but the water would not be denied. The filthy stuff mounted and mounted and there were too many pirates to attempt to save.

Doc Savage did his best, for even though these men were callous killers, and this was wartime, the bronze giant was loathe to abandon them to their fates.

Weakened by the uncanny influence that drained the iron from their bodies, and lacking their ordinary muscular strength, the unprotected corsairs succumbed with little resistance. Seven perished that way.

DOC SAVAGE turned his attention to the remaining survivors.

They were discovering that they were at risk of drowning. Even with the chemical from the pills suffusing their systems, this was still a possibility. For, if they took seawater into their lungs, nothing could save them.

Shucking off his plastic hood, the bronze giant quickly revealed himself to the foundering sailors. He began grabbing them, hauling their heads above the surging waterline so they could hear his words.

"This chamber is about to be flooded to its roof line," he rapped out. "But there is no danger of drowning. Each of you has been given a chemical pill that permits your bodies to survive without recourse to natural respiration. Simply hold your breath, do not breathe or take in water. This will feel very strange, but it can be done. You all know who I am. You can trust me."

This was easier said than done, of course. Doc Savage was forced to take two sailors in hand, when, in their panic, they ingested seawater with disastrous results. Vigorous lifeguard artificial respiration techniques applied by the bronze giant soon cleared their lungs.

As Doc had suspected, the entire chamber quickly filled. Abandoned flashlights, which were not waterproof, went out. Darkness clamped down.

The bronze man brought forth his own spring-generator flashlight, which was waterproof. This produced a narrow beam, which he quickly widened by manipulating a ring over the lens.

By this time, the floodwaters had ceased cascading down and they were simply immersed in unsavory brine.

Pointing the light upward, Doc Savage signaled for the survivors to swim up the spiral, which was settling down now that all the water permitted had collected in the chambers. Doc gave several men hard shoves upward, keeping the light trained so that they could find their way. After the last of them had departed, he kicked backward through the strange doorway that suggested a satanic quarter moon.

Shining the light around, the bronze man found that the chamber was in the nature of a treasure house. Stacked everywhere were statuary and ingots of the strange reddish-gold metal that he did not recognize.

His flake-gold eyes became very animated as he swept the light around, taking in all details. There were other objects, some gigantic. An idol constructed of the weird super-refracting crystal, as tall as a two-story house, possessing a single orb in the center of its forehead on either side of which jutted up-curved horns that brought to mind the now-shattered black tower. In the questing flash ray, portions of the statue slipped in and out of visibility. Doc Savage could not discern its features, but they smacked of the bestial.

It was from this hideous thing that the uncanny wave of coldness emanated. As Doc attempted to glean a clear picture of its imposing lines, he could make out a rime of ice congealing around it. That was how cold the thing was. Very soon, the bronze man realized with a start, the entire chamber would be encased in solid ice....

Time was short and with great regret, Doc Savage retreated, started swimming upward through the corkscrew ramp that was now a water passageway, using his great bronze arms to shove aside the staring-eyed corpses of the drowned impeding his progress.

The things he had beheld, however, filled him with a kind of wonder.

# Chapter L

# THE DROWNED ONE

THE CIRCULAR SWIM up the ancient lava tube that had been shaped into a winding ramp was not without its challenges, Doc Savage discovered.

Had it been simply vertical, the bronze man could have kicked upward in a straight line, counting on his natural buoyancy to carry him to the surface. But the ramp formed a continuous corkscrew, forcing Doc into the curving walls, from which he rebounded painfully a time or two.

At those points, he used his hands to feel along, pushing away from its gritty surface in order to resume his dizzying ascent. It was uncomfortable going. The only light was hazy, despite the fact that it was daylight above.

Finally, the bronze giant approached what amounted to a flooded cellar hole, which was all that remained of the great horned tower of basalt that had been carried away by the fierce storm.

Doc had expected the entrance to be choked with swimmers. But he found none. No dangling or kicking feet, and the bronze man began to fear for the safety of the survivors he had propelled ahead of him.

The fury of the storm lashed the water's surface to a frenzy, so Doc arrested his ascent by finding a fresh fracture in the ramp wall, and holding himself anchored there. Looking up, he saw nothing but a churning froth of spume and seawater. Waves were running high and as pale as seashells. Even through the insulation of the waters around him, the deep continual moaning of the wind could definitely be heard.

Doc Savage held his breath pent within him. Long practice in the use of the miraculous oxygen lozenges enabled him to resist the perfectly natural urge to inhale, which would have been fatal.

Doc understood that he could not remain submerged a great deal longer. And yet to surface would put him at the mercy of the screaming winds, which were powerful enough to carry him aloft, much like a land tornado flings trees and automobiles about like toys.

Finally, knowing that he had only minutes of concentrated oxygen reserve left, Doc took the chance.

When his metallic face broke the surface, he felt a driving horizontal rain slamming into the back of his head. This was no accident. The bronze man had calculated the likely direction of the winds, and turned his face away from them.

Immediately, the howling smote his eardrums. Opening his eyes accomplished absolutely nothing. Wind, pelting rain, particles of what felt like needles but were probably sand, swirled all about him.

It looked and felt like a force 11 blow, according to the Beaufort Wind scale. Perhaps it was. That would mean the winds were blowing at some sixty knots. No place to be at their mercy.

Taking in a lungful of air, Doc plunged back down.

What he had experienced gave him little hope for the men who had gone before him—the *Northern Star* crew and their erstwhile pirate captors.

In one pocket, Doc carried a simple emergency gas mask, consisting of a cellophane hood, which sealed at the neck with an elastic band sewn into it. Removing this, he got the transparent sack over his head, wondering why he had not thought of this before.

Emerging once more, Doc was forced to hold the hood in place with one hand, but the flimsy device worked. It kept wind and airborne detritus out of his eyes. Now he could see around him after a fashion.

Not that the bronze man could make out very much. The world was a maelstrom of screaming wind and white water, and even with the cellophane hood he dared not face into the teeth of the gale. Although it was tropical morning, the hurricane seemed to have sucked much of the sunlight out of the vicinity. All was a gloomy gray chaos.

SEARCHING with his eyes, Doc could not make out the *Northern Star*—or much of anything else. A jumble of tumbled stone loomed nearby, giving the bronze man a sense of where he treaded water.

Several rocks did not look recognizable. Rather, it seemed as if the hurricane had pushed scattered large stones into a mass.

Men were clinging to this agglomeration of rock like frightened barnacles.

Seeing that the stony group afforded the only shelter in the immediate vicinity, Doc Savage struck out in that direction.

Had he been attempting to swim in the face of the hurricane, no amount of muscular strength would have permitted the bronze giant to reach his goal. Doc was helped by the fact that the wind was pushing at the back of his head.

Very quickly, he reached the tumble of stone, and, groping about, found a handhold by which to anchor himself.

Investigation revealed that this had been a popular idea among the sailors and corsairs alike. Doc counted six men without hardly trying. No doubt that very same phenomenon had happened to the luckless men clutching the cluster of basalt rocks. The hurricane had pushed them to temporary safety.

One individual was hugging a low outcropping, while swearing inarticulately in sobbing bursts. This fellow was one of the pirates, specifically the one dubbed Weedy. He seemed half out of his mind.

There was nothing that could be done for him, for Weedy was convulsed in an utter panic. Doc looked to the others.

And so it was that his flake-gold eyes met and locked with the amber orbs of the kingfish corsair himself.

Diamond possessed more than a measure of courage to go with his feline strength. He was holding on rather tightly, and holding up equally well.

When he saw Doc Savage, a kind of tigerish rage came into those amber eyes. A snarl warped his lean-cheeked features. Reaching into his flapping clothes, he dug out his marlin spike—the smooth steel fang of a thing sailors employ to work their complicated maritime knots.

Grabbing this in one fist, Diamond attempted to work his way toward the bronze man, the object of his wrath.

Instead of retreating, Doc Savage advanced to meet the man's approach. The two soon came within striking distance of one another.

Diamond wasted no time. He attempted a fast feint designed to insert the marlin spike into Doc Savage's abdomen. Doc slapped the spike-wielding fist aside, producing a great deal of pain and wringing a vulgar curse from the head pirate's lips. This was the hand that the bronze man had earlier injured when he knocked an automatic from the man's fist with a thrown ingot of metal.

Undeterred, Diamond tried again, holding onto the rock with one hand and this time going for Doc Savage's jugular vein.

Doc was not so gentle this time. One bronze hand, looking as if it was made of living metal, snapped out and snagged the knotty forearm back of the wrist.

The bronze giant gave a twist, which brought a shocked expression to Diamond's hard lean features. The marlin spike slipped out of fingers that seemed to have lost all of their iron.

As Diamond watched in horror, Doc Savage applied finger pressure that was like that of a vise. The skin at the tips of the pirate's fingers swelled, puffed up, and split, unable to withstand the crushing grip. Drops of blood popped up and were swept away by the wind.

Now Diamond's eyes sprang wide, his cruel mouth growing slack and shapeless. Previously, he had suspected the extent of Doc Savage's muscular strength. But the undeniable power of the bronze giant's metallic thews left him speechless and astonished. All fight fled from him.

Doc Savage finished the job by shifting his grip and finding the long bones that comprised the man's forearms—the ulnar and the radius—applying sudden, sharp pressure. The distinct crack of two bones surrendering could not be heard above the horrific howling. But both men felt the bones break.

That left Diamond with only one good hand with which to maintain his precarious position. Thoughts of his inevitable defeat worked his strained features into grim lines, and amber eyes slitted like those of a surly tomcat. The pirate made a decision then. He knew that he had been soundly defeated, and evidently had no further use for his own life.

"Damn you, Savage!" he raged. "Damn you to hell!"

Letting go of the great stone, Diamond kicked off with both feet and let the wind and the churning surf carry him away.

Doc Savage made a sudden swipe to arrest his escape. He managed to snag a bit of shirtsleeve. But the cloth tore, and the corsair was borne off into the howling bone-white eternity that was the all-engulfing hurricane.

Recognizing the futility of attempting to rescue the man, Doc Savage concentrated on holding onto his own stony perch with all of his considerable might.

The wind continued to cascade around him, roaring and whining and making other unearthly sounds, as if wailing demons had been let loose upon the world.

# Chapter LI

# WATER ESCAPE

THE HURRICANE HOWLING went on for an eternity of minutes.

The fury of the thing was beyond belief. Doc Savage could feel the stone to which he clung grinding and moving. In a lifetime of adventuring around the globe, the bronze giant had seen many strange spectacles. Tropical storms were not a new experience for him. He had witnessed the aftermath of the great Labor Day hurricane that had swept the Florida Keys, twisting railroad ties into fantastic shapes, and pushing a tugboat over four miles inland. Flimsy houses had been obliterated by the storm surge and men and women drowned by the score, helpless before the elemental onslaught.

Doc Savage realized that he could not cling to the stone for much longer, despite his nearly inhuman physical strength. To enter the water was out of the question. The bronze man could not remain submerged for very long without oxygen pills to sustain him, and even with only his head out of the water, he would have been at the mercy of the tossing surge, carried off in who knew what direction.

With that grim understanding in mind, he prepared himself to inevitably perish.

A remarkable thing, however, then transpired. The power of the driving wind pushed one stone into another, and these were soon knocking against a third, larger outcropping.

This towering rock stood higher than the others, and all together the knocking and grinding rocks formed a kind of rough windbreak.

Alone of the frantic survivors clinging to the stones, Doc Savage recognized what was transpiring. His position was such that if he let go, the bronze man might be plucked away by the awesome tempest. But if he could creep around, Doc could jam himself into the crevice between stones, which had formed a makeshift shelter against the relentless power of the storm.

Creeping around was out of the question. To attempt to move would have meant certain death.

Doc Savage still had his folding grappling hook and line. Groping into a shirt pocket for this contrivance, he got it loose. He did not pull it completely free, because the bronze man could not chance releasing the anchoring stone to which he clung.

Instead, Doc ducked down and took the grapnel in his strong teeth and, using his agile tongue, managed to open up one of the folding steel tines.

During an upbringing that was strenuous, and often bizarre, Doc had been trained to extricate himself from various dangerous situations. He learned to tie knots with his bare toes, and untie them, too. Similar exercises involving tongue and teeth were also practiced until he could do astounding things with parts of his body ordinarily not considered powerful.

Doc worked the grappling hook around his mouth until he got a second tine opened. It was difficult, cumbersome work, but he succeeded in not dropping the precious tool.

He elected not risk opening the third hook; two would have to suffice.

Doc then craned his head around, trying to get the hook into the wind.

This maneuver was not easy, but there was no safe way to take the hook in hand and throw it. Not without releasing his handholds, which were all that kept him from being yanked into the tempest.

When Doc maneuvered the grapnel in the correct position for what he had in mind, the bronze man gave his head a sideways toss and released the device in his teeth.

The wind carried the frail thing away, as Doc knew it would. But it also carried the trailing, rapidly uncoiling silken line attached to it.

Here is where deft reflexes came into play. As the loop of line uncoiled, Doc snapped out with his teeth, and clamped on the whipping line.

There would be no opportunity for a second chance, nor was it necessary. His very life at stake, Doc Savage succeeded in one desperate bite.

Under other circumstances, the picture would have been absurd, ridiculous, even comical. The gale was pulling at the hook as if it were a small kite straining against the wind, the quivering silk line stretched straight as a reed. The thing was anchored to Doc's mouth, which was all that kept it from blowing away into the wailing eternity of sound and wind and agitated surf.

Doc then shook his head back-and-forth like a mastiff, trying to pluck the hook out of the teeth of the wind, but not accomplishing very much.

Finally, by dint of strenuous effort, he worked the thing around, maneuvering it until, abruptly, it fell out of the storm.

Where the grappling hook had come down was impossible to say with certainty, but Doc Savage was confident that it landed among the grinding boulders.

No man can accomplish two tasks simultaneously with equal ability, nor was Doc Savage so superhuman, despite his great fund of skills. All the effort he put into manipulating the grapnel and line had taken his attention off his iron grip. His fingers were starting to loosen, and that, combined with the whipping water, was inexorably defeating his herculean efforts to hold on.

ABRUPTLY, Doc was forced to let go. Knowing that one hand would not be sufficient to stay anchored, he released the other simultaneously.

The spray-soaked line still in his teeth, the bronze man recognized the risk. There was an excellent chance that the grappling hook had found solid anchorage. Once the line went taut, the force of the hurricane propelling him out to sea could tear his teeth out of his mouth.

Doc's mighty arm swept up, found the line, and clamped hard. Simultaneously, he opened his mouth.

The sensation of being carried off was a wrenching one, and for a fragment of a second Doc was certain that he was lost. There was no time to think beyond that awful realization.

Then his metallic fists were sliding down a slippery line, clutching at the small knots and finger loops that were affixed along its length for emergencies so dire that his tremendous physical strength was insufficient.

Now the bronze giant found himself to be a human kite in the air, clothes flapping and flopping like some kind of animated flag. He was literally buoyant in the air, entirely at the mercy of the storm.

But not without resources. Twisting and turning against the line, Doc kicked and squirmed, until he presented a smaller profile against the gale force winds.

Suddenly, the punishing wind no longer had him and he fell, splashing in the water, but still being dragged along by the wailing weather.

Gripping the thin line for dear life, Doc Savage pulled strenuously, hauling himself along until he reached the bundle of grinding rock, finding sufficient shelter that he could crawl in between two great basalt stones and wedge himself into the miserably cold cup he discovered there.

Here, he found several men who had thrown themselves in, their eyes completely shut, wet hands clapped over their ears to keep out the terrible noise.

There was nothing for Doc Savage to do but hunker down and do the same, knowing that the storm in its terrible immensity might yet rage another hour or longer before finally subsiding.

# Chapter LII

# ORICHALCUM

**W**HEN CALM RETURNED, it was in stages.

The horrible unending howling began to abate, slowly dying off like the whining of lost dogs. The wind likewise dropped off by degrees.

Despite this gradual transition, when at last peace came, it seemed somehow abrupt. Even the quality of daylight improved.

Doc Savage stood up, soaked to the skin, his clothing plastered against his great frame. He still wore the cellophane hood, which he had replaced after finding shelter. It had been necessary to lift it from time to time, to let in fresh air.

Looking about, Doc studied the huddled sailors and erstwhile pirates. One of the latter had died where he cowered. The look on his pale face was one of abject horror. Had fright killed him? Had he suffered a heart attack or similar medical calamity? After a brief examination, even Doc Savage could not say for certain.

Making the rounds of the survivors, the bronze giant met with a genuine surprise.

For among the shivering men was the familiar face of Leander Tucker. The young man was considerably shaken by his experience and looked it. The paleness of his roundish features rivaled that of a freshly-laundered sheet.

"Tuck," said Doc, shaking him gently.

Seaman Tucker nevertheless jumped, and stood up abruptly. His hair was plastered to his round skull like a wet mop.

"Doc!" he blurted out. "You're alive, too?"

"Where are your other friends?" asked the bronze man.

Tucker told a rapid tale of standing off the mysterious sub-marine only to be swept overboard by the roaring hurricane.

"W-we all went overboard," he said miserably. "I found myself in the drink, and I was pushed and pushed and pushed along like a helpless hunk of jetsam until I struck a big stone. After that, I held on for dear life."

Doc asked gently, "You did not see the others after that?"

Tuck shook his head, and it was difficult to tell if the moisture leaking out of his squeezed-shut eyes was from his soaking, or the product of emotional distress.

"Likely they drowned," said Doc softly.

"I have been thinking that very thought," admitted Tuck. "Oh, what will I tell their folks?"

Neither man said anything for a long time.

Doc Savage looked up, climbed the highest hump of stone, and surveyed his surroundings.

The sea was still roiled, although it was calming down. Debris lay on the swells in all directions. Palm fronds, ragged bark and other detritus choked the waters.

A seagull sailed into view, cocking its narrow head about, and made a dive for some morsel floating on the water.

The long black finger of Satan's Spine was beginning to show through the surf, gleaming like wet obsidian.

The converted liner *Northern Star* could also be descried, and Doc Savage was more than taken aback upon discovering that he was looking down her great smokestacks. For the liner had been knocked over and was lying on her port side. Here and there, hull plates had popped. One smokestack had broken loose and lay detached and flattened.

Of the mysterious submarine, there was no sign.

Grimly, Doc Savage jumped down into the rock-sheltered pit where the storm-chastened men were gathering their thoughts and their battered self-possession. Their eyes were unnaturally round, as if they were still grappling with the realization that they had cheated death.

"We survived…" one man said dazedly.

"It is not yet over," Doc Savage told them. "This is merely a temporary respite. There is no telling how large the eye of the hurricane is, but if we do not find better shelter, we are going to be in for considerable pounding once the eye passes beyond this area."

No one needed to have that explained to him twice.

THE MEN hastened to clamber up, and began trudging toward the *Northern Star*, there being no other shelter within sight.

Glancing west, Doc looked toward Satan Cay, and realized that it had been virtually leveled—not that there was much to it other than a great deal of beach sand and a few solitary scrub plants.

They reached the *Northern Star* just as men were squirming out of her deck hatches and companionways, awkwardly seeking a way to climb down the upended deck, which was lying at right angles to the submerged foot of the forbidding black reef.

Predictably, Monk Mayfair, with his long arms and tremendous upper torso strength, managed to climb down a flung manila painter. He landed on his bowed legs with a splash.

When he saw Doc Savage leading the survivors, the hairy chemist broke out into a great simian grin. Lifting one ridiculously long arm, he waved vigorously and called out, "Doc! You made it."

Others tumbled down behind him, and the survivors of the now derelict *Northern Star* began congregating and swapping tall tales of their horrific experiences. Soon, they were vying for bragging rights to declare which element of the crew had had the worst of it.

It turned out that the ship's hull had preserved the lives of everyone who had remained on board. Captain McCullum,

who had been trapped on the toppled bridge, had to be extri-
cated, for he was in no condition to climb down under his own
power. This was accomplished with various ropes, a Jacob's
ladder, and a great deal of American ingenuity.

They congregated by the overturned bow, whose anchor chain
had been snapped. There was no sign of the anchor.

The Skipper had some choice words for the condition of his
vessel, and the general situation. All of it was salty, and none
of it was printable. But after Captain McCullum managed to
unburden himself of his ire, he was in better fettle.

Turning to Doc Savage, he demanded, "Where is that twice-
damned pirate?"

"Swept out to sea," replied Doc. "Whatever his true name
was, Diamond could not possibly have survived."

Hearing this, one of the defeated pirate survivors offered,
"His real name was Jack Morgan, if you want to know the truth.
Jack Diamant Morgan, to be exact. He claimed to be a descen-
dant of Sir Henry Morgan, the famous buccaneer of the Spanish
Main."

Doc Savage nodded. "So he boasted, although Diamond
included many other privateers among his supposed ancestry."

"Jack had big ideas," the other admitted. "Called himself
Diamond after his middle name and took to wearing a diamond
earring like the old-time freebooters. But look what it earned
him. Davy Jones' cold company."

Captain McCullum strode up to the confessing corsair, and
despite his injuries, managed to knock the man flat with one
roundhouse blow.

"What was this hijacking all about?" he demanded of the
man.

The rogue in question had managed to hit the back of his
head against solid basalt and was out cold. The frustrated skipper
went tearing about the survivors, seeking another pirate, and
soon caught one.

This one was not so talkative, but soon unburdened himself. He had sailed under the name of Bill Hatch, but admitted that his real name was Roland Rowe, a former U.S. Navy petty officer third class who had been cashiered for drunkenness.

"Well, it's like this, there was a seaquake last winter, and this damn reef was pushed to the surface, along with that watchtower or lighthouse of a thing with horns. Diamond found it, got inside, and barely escaped with his life. The stuff he found inside was worth a fortune."

"What stuff?" demanded Monk.

The brigand lifted his right hand, displaying a reddish-gold band. "This stuff, for starters."

Ham Brooks walked up and took the ring off the man's finger, examining it carefully.

"This is not gold," he sniffed.

"This is *better* than gold," the pirate insisted.

"It must be an exceedingly rare metal to count as more valuable than gold," insisted Ham.

"Let me see that, Ham," requested Doc Savage.

The bronze man accepted the reddish band, and examined it closely. His musical but tuneless trilling seeped out as he turned the band around in his metallic fingers.

"What is it?" muttered the skipper.

"Orichalcum," said Doc.

FROM the expressions on the men's faces, no one seemed to know what that was. So the bronze man told them.

"In ancient times," explained Doc, "the Greeks and other such people spoke of a rare metal by that name. Some historians claimed it was an alloy of gold and copper, others of gold and brass or perhaps bronze. There is also the possibility that orichalcum was an entirely different metal not known to the modern world, whose mines were long ago exhausted. No examples were previously believed to have survived. This trove seems to be an exception."

Monk Mayfair snapped his blunt fingers. As a chemist, he understood metallurgy.

"I remember readin' about that stuff!" he boasted. "The Greeks claimed it had been a valuable metal back in the days of Atlantis."

"Atlantis!" breathed Ham. Understanding dawned in the dapper lawyer's dark eyes. "If I remember my study of Plato, he asserted that the legendary temple of Poseidon in Atlantis had walls of orichalcum, which was second only to gold in rarity and value."

"There is no such place!" snapped the Skipper.

"The contrary," corrected Doc Savage. "In recent years, my men and I have discovered fragmentary survivals of the sunken continent in these very waters. Once it was a great underwater pyramid housing a vault containing many now-lost scientific secrets, from which I was able to concoct the pills we use to subsist underwater without needing to respire. On other occasions, we found only empty ruins, and other things of which I will not speak." *

Seaman Tucker looked down at his soaking feet standing on the coal-black reef and asked, "Are we standing on a piece of Atlantis?"

"Probably an outpost of the mainland," said Doc. "I would not be at all surprised if the hundreds of islands that constitute the Bahamas chain are not remnants of the sunken continent. That watch tower operated as a practical solar lighthouse, much like the ancient Pharos of Alexandria in Egypt, but also served to protect the cellar chambers that are now flooded by the storm surge. The horns protruding from the tower's summit, along with its cyclops eye, no doubt meant much the same in that era as it does now—keep away. The stone hands built into the reef itself conceivably symbolized the fate of any mariner who brought his vessel too close to Satan's Spine. Death by drowning."

---

\* See *Mystery Under the Sea, The Red Terrors, The Secret of the Su, Phantom Lagoon.*

The talkative pirate continued, "It was a storehouse for the red gold, as well as other stuff, including crystal statues that tricked your eyes, and dangerous things like the horned rocks that sucked the juice out of a man. Diamond thought that this was a combination treasure trove and storehouse for weapons. Either that or the life-draining stones were meant to protect the rare ingots from pirates like me. Too bad," he mused. "If we succeeded in pulling out all that ruddy gold, we would be set up for life."

Ham scolded, "And now you are bound for Leavenworth Prison."

The pirate did not seem too distressed by that. He said frankly, "After what I just went through, I'm grateful to be alive."

That comment caused Seaman Tucker to say, "I wish I could say the same for my friends."

"What do you mean?" asked Ham.

"We all got swept out over the rail," said Tuck dejectedly. "It looks like I'm the only one who survived."

While this unpleasant thought was sinking in, there was a commotion several rods away, and all heads turned in time to see the conning tower of the missing submarine breach the still-disturbed sea, spilling cascades of sea water.

"Well, maybe I spoke too soon," muttered Seaman Tucker dispiritedly.

# Chapter LIII

# LOST LIGAN

**T**HE SUBMARINE COMMANDER introduced himself as Captain Fritz Zammer.

That was only one jolt in the succession of shocks that followed the surprise appearance of the submersible.

When the undersea boat finished surfacing, the forward hatch was undogged and the sub's skipper emerged, along with a contingent of armed sailors.

By that time Doc Savage had already recognized the vessel as a United States Navy submarine. This, of course, had been a tremendous relief to all concerned.

Captain Zammer hailed from Pennsylvania Dutch country, hence his Germanic name. But he was a loyal American, through and through.

The submariner went through a rapid explanation of his presence in this remote arm of the Caribbean Sea.

"I am not in these waters by accident. My mission was to shadow the *Northern Star* as she made her way to her convoy rendezvous. You see, my boat is equipped with a new-type of magnetic torpedo, and we were hoping that a lone merchant ship might catch the attention of a prowling Nazi U-boat. I'm sorry to inform you, Captain McCullum, that you were the bait in the elaborate trap. My job was to sink any enemy submarine before they could torpedo your vessel. When your radioman failed to check in with Naval H.Q. on the prearranged schedule, I was instructed to seek you out."

Captain McCullum said brusquely, "We fell victim to pirates."

Captain Zammer cocked a quizzical eyebrow as if to ask, "In this day and age?" But the sorry condition of the *Northern Star* stayed his intended remark. The great liner was now nothing more than marine salvage.

McCullum said slowly, "I thought there was something fishy about my cargo and the sea route I was instructed to follow. It was all odds and ends. War metals. Foreign sailors. Other bric-a-brac."

The sub skipper said, "The reason your boat wasn't crammed with U.S. troops assigned to support the invasion of Europe is that the brass in Washington didn't want to lose them if I failed to sink any sea wolf who happened upon your solitary wake."

"In short," McCullum said bitterly, "we were classified as expendable."

"Fortunes of war, Captain," returned Zammer.

Doc Savage inserted, "We have less than an hour to find shelter before the hurricane eye passes through and the wall of wind and water returns."

Captain Zammer surveyed the bedraggled survivors and said, "Accommodations will be tight, but my vessel is all that is immediately available. We had best get to climbing aboard and securing hatches."

The men were assembled, and escorted on board. Distributing themselves around the cramped innards of the submarine, they received another jolt.

Seaman Jury Goines numbered among the survivors. He looked as though he had been plucked off a desert isle. One of the souvenirs of his experience was a black eye that was purplish in spots.

"I got picked up out of the drink," he said simply. "Swabbies were kind of rough about it, on account of the way I manhandled their gunnery crew. I think the only reason I was saved was that they were already rescuing their own boys, and it would look bad if they didn't grab me, too."

No doubt there was more to the big oiler's story, but when Seaman Tucker worked his way aft to find a place to sit down and sulk, he instead let out a weird howl, followed by a yelp of a question.

*"Am I seeing ghosts?"*

Doc Savage rushed to the sound of the commotion in time to behold Seamen Donald Worth, B. Elmer Dexter and Mental Morris hopping up and down and embracing Leander Tucker, who was doing his own hopping around while simultaneously attempting to embrace the others.

"We were sure you drowned!" Don Worth was saying.

"And I thought you three were finished!" Tuck returned joyously.

Doc Savage was not one for smiling, but his mouth was doing some pleasant warping as he watched the happy reunion jig.

All hands were not happy, of course, aboard the submarine, for as Captain McCullum moved among his remaining crew, counting heads, he realized that he had lost the greater portion of his ship's complement, in addition to the *Northern Star* herself. He was morose. It showed on his craggy features.

But there was no time for such unpleasant thoughts, for the submarine was hastily being rigged to submerge again. Hatches were dogged, sailors manned their crash stations, and Captain Zammer gave the order to submerge. There followed a tumult of ugly noises as the hull tanks were violently flushed of compressed air and the sub floor plates dropped under their feet like an unstable elevator.

The undersea boat was swallowed by the ocean. It settled to the bottom, coming to rest in only thirteen fathoms of water. Tensely, everyone waited.

At the periscope, Captain Zammer was searching the horizon, and finally said, "Here she comes."

A wall of water seemed to slam against the submarine's hull, for it gave a jolt, and swayed alarmingly in several directions, at times seemingly at once.

For more than two hours, the submarine was at the mercy of the churning waves, but other than accumulating bumps and bruises from being knocked about, the crew and extra passengers came through it quite nicely.

WHEN it was safe to surface again, a hatch was popped and those at liberty to do so clambered onto the deck, where fresh air was greedily inhaled. The greasy atmosphere of a sub's confines had a way of clogging up a man's airways.

Doc Savage's small party, which included Monk Mayfair and Ham Brooks and their four friends, investigated the length of Satan's Spine.

There was not much to see, except a small coral octopus, which was crawling along in search of food. It had assumed the coal-seam color of its immediate surroundings, giving it a devil aspect appropriate to Satan's Spine.

They came to what amounted to a jagged cellar hole at the far end where the watchtower had once loomed so ominously, a survival of an ancient, forgotten race of men. The broken hole was choked with water and debris. Doc Savage studied this quite a bit before pronouncing the vertical lava tube which had been fashioned into a corkscrew ramp as hopelessly sealed.

Monk was saying, "Maybe we can come back with diving suits and root around in there."

Doc Savage shook his head. "Too dangerous. The air hoses that would be necessary to keep a diver supplied with oxygen would too easily become entangled or completely severed negotiating the curving ramp. Also, the waters in the treasure room were turning to ice when I last saw it, as a result of a weird crystal idol that was extreme cold. I suspect that the ice will be permanent."

Monk was stubborn, or perhaps avarice motivated his next words.

"It would be a shame to let all that rare gold go to waste," he muttered. "If it *is* gold."

Ham Brooks said sharply, "You just want to get your greedy hands on that stuff for yourself."

"Heck," grunted Monk, "I went through enough hell to earn my fair share of it. Didn't I? What's stoppin' us? It's legal salvage, ain't it?"

Ham Brooks, who had studied maritime law, corrected the irate chemist.

"The legal term is ligan—which means salvageable goods to be found at the sea bottom. I imagine that this submerged treasure house qualifies."

Doc Savage was saying, "No doubt there are some amazing things to be found in the waters below. Including the secret of turning molten magma into useful forms such as ramps and towers. But we know from past experience that the Atlantean people, whoever they were, were of a very high intellectual order, and mastered sciences which are still undiscovered in the 20th Century."

That thought was long sinking into their brains. In silence, they contemplated the strange twists of fate that had cast Satan's Spine into the ocean when Atlantis foundered and sank beneath the waves, only to throw it up again many centuries later, to be discovered by a wicked modern-day freebooter, and all the deadly consequences that followed.

His face slack at the thought of the unsalvageable gold, Monk Mayfair grunted, "Well, I guess we're headed back to New York City, after all."

Doc Savage told him, "If you still want to go to England for that chemical job, there are plenty of Liberty ships and other vessels crossing the Atlantic every week."

Monk turned his empty trouser pockets inside out and said, "Yeah. Guess I had better catch the next boat." A funny expression crossed his homely features. Snapping his forefinger and thumb together, he produced a pop of a report.

"I just thought of something!" he shouted.

"What is that?" asked Ham seriously.

"We never did find out what happened to that Davey Lee gal. Maybe I should look her up."

Doc Savage said, "By now she is safe in her actual home in Richmond, Virginia."

Monk looked flabbergasted. "How do you know that?"

"Before we left New York, I had my cousin Patricia undertake a search for Davey Lee. Pat found her safe and sound in a woman's hotel, drugged but unharmed, and put her on a train heading south, where she should stay out of mischief. She was an aspiring actress who fell in with bad company, nothing more. Her only role was to keep Monk off the *Northern Star*, lest he gum up Diamond's plans."

Ham remarked, "Instead, his efforts backfired by bringing Doc Savage into the matter. After all his plans and precautions to sail unsuspected, Diamond's own fears did him in."

Monk looked intrigued. "Richmond, did you say?"

Doc eyed him seriously.

"I thought you were going to seek out the next boat bound for London?" reminded the bronze man.

"What's the rush?" grinned Monk. "You said boats are leavin' every week. I can catch one the same as another."

Ham scowled. "It's that girl you want to catch, not any boat."

"I'm hopin' to catch both, but one at a time," said Monk, smacking his lips. "Say, do you think Davey Lee would go to London with me? I could use an assistant over there."

"You are forgetting," reminded Ham, "that all her batting-of-the-eye fascination with your homeliness was merely an act Miss Lee put on because she was paid to do so."

The apish chemist pondered that a moment and remarked, "I always find that the longer a gal takes to get to know me, the more I grow on her."

"And I have always insisted that you are a walking wart," snapped Ham. "So, perhaps you will grow on her, but not in the way you think."

Monk's grin grew broader. "Just so long as I get somethin' out of this misadventure, I won't worry about it none."

One matter remained to be resolved. That was the ordeal Jury Goines had undergone at the hands of Doc Savage.

Before they left Satan's Spine for the final time, the bronze giant took Seaman Goines aside and quietly explained how he had been waylaid and knocked out, with the result that the innocent oiler had been logged and consigned to the ship's brig for actions perpetrated by Doc Savage.

"I will explain everything to your skipper so that your good record is cleared up," finished Doc.

Jury Goines took it well. No flicker of anger touched his beefy features.

"Normally, I would slug any man who done that to me," he said slowly.

"I would not blame you if you felt that way," Doc Savage said sincerely.

"Only one thing stopping me."

"And that is?"

"You spent two days in the brig," Goines pointed out. His rather yellow teeth flashed. "I'd say you already got your come-uppance without me having to add my knuckles to the situation."

Doc Savage was forced to admit that this was true. The two big men shook hands solemnly. That settled, they went to lay the matter before Captain McCullum, who did not listen to Doc's account with quite the patience of Jury Goines. Nor did he display a similar equanimity.

"If this pigboat were my vessel," he ground out, "I would have you consigned to the brig, Savage."

"Submarines do not have brigs," Doc Savage pointed out.

"Perhaps there is a utility closet that will serve as a substitute," McCullum returned tightly as he turned on his heel to bring the serious infraction of naval law before Captain Zammer.

Jury Goines regarded Doc Savage with a mixture of sympathy and pity.

"Was I you," he deadpanned, "I would consider swimming home."

"Captain Zammer would not dare imprison me," Doc said flatly.

"No, but once we dock, do you want to bet McCullum won't have a Navy Shore Patrol gang waiting to put you in irons?"

At that, Seaman Goines could no longer contain himself. He burst out laughing.

"Care to trade places again?" asked Doc.

# About the Author
## LESTER DENT

**A** **S A BOY** living on farms and ranches in Oklahoma, Wyoming and Missouri, Lester Dent dreamed of the sea. Like many youth of his era, his fantasies centered around living the life of a swashbuckling pirate.

Young Lester did not grow up to be a buccaneer, but he did become an adventurer in his own way, at different periods owning his own private plane and schooner.

In the latter, a vintage Chesapeake Bay "bugeye" schooner, the *Albatross,* he sailed up and down the east coast, wintering in Florida, and combing the Caribbean cays for pirate gold. If he couldn't become a corsair, Dent thought, at least he could grab off some of their treasure.

Lester never found any treasure, but he did discover gold— and immortality—in writing the Doc Savage novels for Street & Smith. Several were written on the open deck of the *Albatross* during the mid-1930s.

Early in his sailing career, Lester learned that his boat had gone missing in the Chesapeake Bay. He drove to the last reported spot, only to learn that the captain he had hired to ferry the *Albatross* south to Florida had turned pirate.

After the craft was recovered and the culprit apprehended, Lester never allowed anyone else to pilot his "treasure-hunt" schooner.

Once, the *Albatross* got caught in a hurricane.

"The wind came straight off Florida," Dent recalled. "It had palm trees, bungalows, divorcees, everything in it! For two days, it blew about 250 an hour. Then it settled back to a mere 125. Duck? Of course I wanted to duck. I was never so ready to swap a yacht for a submarine in my life."

Arriving in Miami, Lester reported, "Old Whe-e-e-e himself paid a visit. The marks he left are all about. Of the weather cover we put on *Albatross* last spring, frizzled rags remained. Stanchions were torn loose. Topmast deadeye lacings—six strands of half-inch tarred hemp—were broken like old grocery string.

"Three score of yards from where we lie awaiting drydock, a crane is taking out of the water a thing that looks like it might have been a house. Palms are stripped to a frond or two. Co-coanuts are scarce. Near *Albatross* lies a big yacht which sank and has just been raised. On shore nearby, a smaller victim lies with holes gaping in her hull through which men can crawl."

The *Albatross* was in drydock when the great Labor Day hurricane of 1935 swept across the Florida Keys. The schooner survived with minor damage. But many lost their lives. Visiting Florida in the aftermath, Lester saw railroad ties twisted into knots, and a boat shoved completely inland. This fury so impressed him that he wrote a memorable *Black Mask* story about the power of tropical hurricanes, and periodically dropped one such storm into a Doc Savage novel.

*The Secret of Satan's Spine* is in that grand Dentian tradition.

# About the Author
# WILL MURRAY

**W**ILL MURRAY HAS had the good fortune to live most of his life by the Atlantic Ocean, and although he has been out in numerous boats, he prefers to keep his two feet planted firmly on land—when he is not planted behind his computer turning out numerous novels, short stories and articles.

*The Secret of Satan's Spine* is Will Murray's 18th Doc Savage novel, and his 16th posthumous collaboration with the late great Lester Dent. Overall, Murray has written more than 60 novels, as well as dozens of short stories and novelettes. The characters he has been privileged to bring to life include, but are not limited to, Doc Savage, The Shadow, The Avenger, The Spider, Sherlock Holmes, The Green Hornet, Superman, Batman, Wonder Woman, Spider-Man, The Hulk, Ant-Man, Iron Man, The Punisher, The Phantom, Nick Fury, Mack Bolan, Remo Williams, Tarzan of the Apes, Cthulhu, Sky Captain, Honey West and Squirrel Girl, which he co-created with legendary Marvel Comics artist Steve Ditko.

That's a virtual parade of some of the greatest popular culture characters created over the last century. Of them all, Murray still holds the Man of Bronze in the highest esteem. And he remains in awe of the fact that he is permitted to work with

Lester Dent's original concepts and manuscripts, which seem inexhaustible.

As of this writing, Will Murray is brainstorming future Wild Adventures of Doc Savage, with *Glare of the Gorgon, Mr. Calamity* and *Six Scarlet Scorpions* high on his list of planned projects.

# About the Artist

# JOE DeVITO

JOE DeVITO WAS born on March 16, 1957, in New York City. He graduated with honors from Parsons School of Design in 1981 and continued his study of oil painting at the city's famed Art Students League.

Over the years, DeVito has painted many of the most recognizable Pop Culture and Pulp icons, including King Kong, Tarzan, Doc Savage, Superman, Batman, Wonder Woman, Spider-Man, *Mad* magazine's Alfred E. Neuman and various characters from World of Warcraft. Throughout, his illustrations have had an accent toward dinosaurs, Action Adventure, SF and Fantasy. He has illustrated hundreds of book and magazine covers, painted several notable posters and numerous trading cards for the major comic book and gaming houses, and created concept and character designs for the film and television industries.

In 3D, DeVito sculpted the official 100th Anniversary statue of *Tarzan of the Apes* for the Edgar Rice Burroughs Estate, The Cooper Kong for the Merian C. Cooper Estate, Superman, Wonder Woman and Batman for Chronicle Books' Masterpiece Editions, and several other notable Pop and Pulp characters, including a Doc Savage statue executed for Graphitti Designs, based on DeVito's own cover to Will Murray's *Python Isle*. Additional sculpting work ranges from scientifically accurate dinosaurs, a multitude of collectibles for the Bradford Exchange in a variety of genres, to larger-than-life statues and the award trophy for the influential art annual *SPECTRUM.*

An avid writer, Joe is the creator of *Skull Island* and *The Primordials.* He is also the co-author (with Brad Strickland) of two novels, which DeVito illustrated as well. The first, *KONG: King of Skull Island* (DH Press), was published in 2004. The second book, *Merian C. Cooper's KING KONG,* was published by St. Martin's Griffin, in 2005. He has also contributed many essays and articles to such collected works as *Kong Unbound: The Cultural Impact, Pop Mythos, and Scientific Plausibility of a Cinematic Legend* and "Do Androids-Artists Paint In Oils When They Dream?" in *Pixel or Paint: The Digital Divide-In Illustration Art.*

Of his *Secret of Satan's Spine* painting, Joe notes:

> "One of the best aspects Will Murray and I have had in writing and creating art for *The Wild Adventures* series has been conversing with the people who have commissioned the covers. So unexpected at first, it has now become an enjoyable part of the ritual. What made our experience with Victor De Long, who commissioned this cover, all the more pleasurable (particularly from my end) was that Victor had a clear idea of the kind of image he wanted—it had to feel *hot!* Better still, he was very easy to work with and open to going with what I came up with. Every artist will tell you that when he starts out with an image in his head, he rarely comes close to creating something as good as what he had imagined. So it stands to reason that it is much harder to match for someone else the vision they have in their mind. Especially since a preconceived image can be tough to erase. Since I can't read minds (yet), I was happy that Victor was very receptive to my concepts, color roughs, and the final cover painting.
>
> "Consciously or unconsciously, every artist strives for the effect of making their illustrations look natural. That is to create an image that tells the story without showing all the work that is required. We try to make like a duck: On the surface appear to be gliding gracefully and effortlessly across the wa-

ter, but underneath never let on that you are paddling like crazy. Sometimes, the simpler the image the harder it can be, because with less visual distraction otherwise minor defects can become glaring. Pulling off that illusion requires what I like to call 'the skillful use of opposites.' That is, hard against soft edges, light against dark, big against small, etc. At the end of the day, I hope I fulfilled Victor's desire that the painting look *hot!*"

www.jdevito.com
www.kongskullisland.com
FB: Joe DeVito-DeVito Artworks

# About the Patron

# VICTOR DE LONG

**I**T ALL STARTED with that copy of *The Lost Oasis* I "borrowed" from my cousin forty years ago. (He still hasn't asked for it back, so in my library it sits, along with just about every other version of *The Lost Oasis*, foreign and domestic, ever printed). The cover alone was enough to grab me—a striking bronze figure enshrouded by mist, kneeling to fire a machine gun at a horde of vampire bats. The story had everything a kid raised on comic book heroes and Saturday morning cartoons could want. A mystery ship. A ghost zeppelin. White slavery and blood diamonds. A lost oasis! Vampire bats and carnivorous plants. Exotic villains undone by their own nefarious plot. I was hooked immediately. My next Doc was *The Man of Bronze*. Exotic assassins with blood red fingertips. Treachery in the jungles of Central America. Mayan gold. More exotic villains undone by their own nefarious plot. By that point I was beyond saving.

The more Bantam Docs I read, the more I wanted to know, and for a kid in a small town in pre-Internet days, information was hard to come by. I devoured Philip José Farmer's *Doc Savage: His Apocalyptic Life*, constantly renewing our library's only copy. The good folks at Bantam Books eventually tired of my exhaustive letters (in pencil on notebook paper) peppering them with questions about Doc minutia and sicced me on Will Murray, who while very gently declining my request for photocopies of those pulps that hadn't been reprinted yet by Bantam, patiently answered every question in every letter I ever sent him.

Fast-forwarding forty years, my Bantam set is long complete. I've got ⅔ of the pulps and most of the cool ephemera from the pulp era (that rubber stamp still eludes me!) and Joe DeVito's stunning cover to this volume will join Bob Larkin's cover to *The Shape of Terror* on my office wall. All the cool stuff and forty years of reading Doc hasn't dampened my enthusiasm for the stories at all, and to be a part, albeit a small one, of the creative process of designing this cover was frustratingly awesome. Awesome because, well… duh—I got to be involved in picking Doc's pose and some of the design elements, like the feeling of blistering heat coming off that amazing yellow background. And the bats, my throwback to the book that started it all for me. That part was *COOL!* But, frustrating because my civilian friends, the non-Doc readers, just didn't get what I was so damn excited about, so bragging to them about this project was mostly met with politely feigned excitement for me. My lovely wife Bibi apparently figures it keeps me out of trouble, and that there are worse obsessions I could be spending my money on. But, there is hope. My 7 year old son, Lukas, is used to the piles of Doc books around the house and knows that Doc is "a good guy." So with luck, he'll end up hooked as well and I'll have done my part in making the next generation of Doc Savage fans.

*Victor De Long is an attorney in the Pacific Northwest, representing injured workers. He chairs his local downtown association and has served on a number of other local committees. In addition to Doc Savage and pulp-related items, he collects original comic book and strip art and vintage Disneyland memorabilia.*

# The Martian Legion: In Quest of Xonthron

- *An Epic Adventure Novel in the Grandest ERB Tradition!*
- *The Finest ERB Collectible Ever Produced!*

**Written in spirit by Edgar Rice Burroughs with an assist from Jake Saunders.**

- A quarter million words of high adventure! Like getting four ERB novels in one!
- Tarzan, John Carter, The Shadow, and Doc Savage battle the Holy Therns!
- First 100 copies signed by Saunders, Grindberg, Hoffman, Mullins, DeVito, Cabarga, and Cochran.
- Featuring 24 full color painting and illustrations, plus 106 spot illustrations by Tom Grindberg, Michael C. Hoffman, and Craig Mullins, including….
- Leather bound, full color, 11-1/4-in. x 12-1/4-in. x 1-1/2in., 423 pages.

## Now available at <u>TheMartianLegion.com</u>!

# THE ARGOSY LIBRARY™

**SERIES 1 INCLUDES:**

* DENT * KETCHUM * KLINE *
* MacISAAC * ROSCOE *
* ROUSSEAU *
* SELTZER *
* TUTTLE *
* WIRT *
WORTS

THE BEST FICTION
FROM THE FRANK
A. MUNSEY LINE

## GENIUS JONES
BY THE CO-CREATOR OF DOC SAVAGE
### LESTER DENT

## WHEN TIGERS ARE HUNTING
THE COMPLETE ADVENTURES OF CORDIE,
SOLDIER OF FORTUNE, VOLUME 1
### W. WIRT

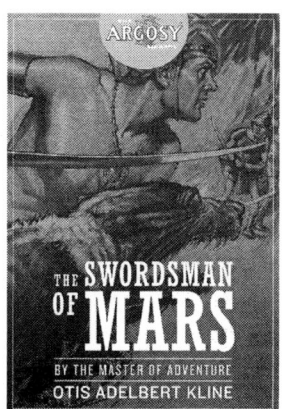

## THE SWORDSMAN OF MARS
BY THE MASTER OF ADVENTURE
### OTIS ADELBERT KLINE

## THE SHERLOCK OF SAGELAND
THE COMPLETE TALES OF
SHERIFF HENRY, VOLUME 1
### W.C. TUTTLE

## GONE NORTH
BY ARGOSY READERS' FAVORITE
### CHARLES ALDEN SELTZER

## THE MASKED MASTER MIND
BY THE AUTHOR OF PETER THE BRAZEN
### GEORGE F. WORTS

## BALATA
BY THE AUTHOR OF THE RAMBLER
### FRED MacISAAC

## BRET-WALDA
BY ARGOSY READERS' FAVORITE
### PHILIP KETCHUM

## DRAFT OF ETERNITY
BY THE CREATOR OF JIM ANTHONY
### VICTOR ROUSSEAU

## FOUR CORNERS
VOLUME 1 • BY ARGOSY LEGEND
### THEODORE ROSCOE

SERIES 1 • AVAILABLE NOW

# WORDSLINGERS

## AN EPITAPH FOR THE WESTERN

☞ **WILL MURRAY** ☜

Will Murray's Wordslingers is not only the first in-depth history of the Western pulps, it's one of the best and most important books on the pulps ever written, perfectly capturing the era, the magazines, and the writers, editors, and agents who helped fill their pages. Pulp fans will be fascinated by the rich background provided by hundreds of quotes from the people involved in producing the Western pulps, while writers will benefit from the discussions of characterization and storytelling that prove to be both universal and timeless.

*—James Reasoner*

**$29.95 softcover**
**$39.95 hardcover**
**$8.99 ebook**

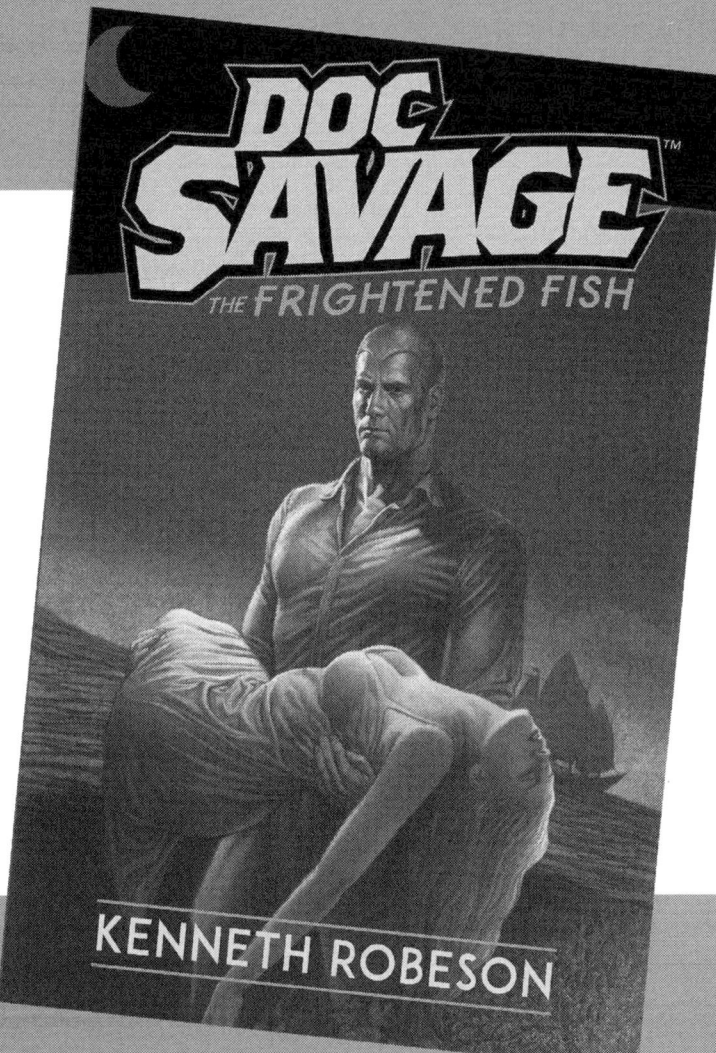

Printed in Great Britain
by Amazon